Praise for *The Reckoning at Gossamer Pond*

"Atmospheric and suspenseful, *The Reckoning at Gossamer Pond* is Jaime Jo Wright's newest masterpiece. She's an automatic buy for me, and I love her work. Highly recommended!"

—Colleen Coble, author of *The View from Rainshadow Bay* and the Rock Harbor series

"Brilliantly atmospheric and underscored by a harrowing romance, *The Reckoning at Gossamer Pond* pairs danger with redemption and features not only two heroines of great agency—separated by time though linked by grace—but one of the most compelling, unlikely and memorable heroes I have met in an age. Equal parts thrilling and beautiful, *The Reckoning at Gossamer Pond* is a treatise on faith—lost and found—and the Power greater than any human evil coursing through a century."

—Rachel McMillan, author of *Murder at the Flamingo*

"Wright's newest offering is intoxicating and wonderfully authentic. The pages of this book are delightfully shadowed with mystery that will keep readers poring over the story, but what makes it memorable is the powerful light that burst through every darkened corner in this novel—*hope*."

—Joanna Davidson Politano, author of *Lady Jane Disappears*

"*The Reckoning at Gossamer Pond* is true to Jaime Jo Wright's unique style and voice. Multilayered characters who intrigue the reader and a story the threads of which are unpredictable and well woven together make this a must-read for anyone who enjoys suspense."

—Sarah Varland, author of *Mountain Refuge*

"Warning! Read *The Reckoning at Gossamer Pond* at your own risk. Wright grabbed my attention from the first page and never let up. With characters who practically leap off the page and a story line that sizzles with tension, this novel is much more than a follow-up to her brilliant first novel. Go now to your local bookstore and buy this book. You'll thank me."

—Kathleen Y'Barbo, author of *Pirate Bride*

D0207904

Praise for *The House on Foster Hill*

"Jaime Jo Wright's *The House on Foster Hill* blends the past and present in a gripping mystery that explores faith and the sins of ancestors. . . . Deep emotional struggles are the backbone of the novel and make the corresponding mystery even more engaging. With sharp dialogue and plenty of scares, this is a gripping tale that never loses sight of the light at the end of the tunnel."

—*Foreword Reviews*

"Headed by two strong female protagonists, Wright's debut is a lushly detailed time-slip novel that transitions seamlessly between past and present, leading to the revelation of some surprising family secrets that someone would kill to protect. Readers who enjoy Colleen Coble and Dani Pettrey will be intrigued by this suspenseful mystery."

—*Library Journal*

"Jaime Jo Wright is an amazing storyteller who had me on the edge of my seat, turning pages and reading as fast as I could to get to the end of the book! *The House on Foster Hill* is a masterfully told story with layers and layers of mystery and intrigue, with a little romance thrown in for good measure. The adventure takes the reader back and forth through time, weaving the content like a tapestry—revealing a little bit more of the design with each chapter until the story is complete. I'll be excited to read more from this author."

—Tracie Peterson, author of the GOLDEN GATE SECRETS series

"A mystery from over a hundred years ago intertwines with one from the present in this spellbinding tale by Jaime Jo Wright. Rich characterization and intricate plotting combine to make this novel unputdownable. This one will fly off the shelves as readers discover the very talented Wright. Highly recommended!"

—Colleen Coble, author of *The View from Rainshadow Bay*

"Riveting! With its dual story line connected by a single house and the women it touched, Jaime Jo Wright delivers double the suspense, double the romance, and double the reasons to keep turning the pages far into the night. An outstanding novel from an author to watch."

—Jocelyn Green, author of *The Mark of the King*

The

RECKONING

at

GOSSAMER

POND

The RECKONING *at* GOSSAMER POND

JAIME JO WRIGHT

BETHANYHOUSE
a division of Baker Publishing Group
Minneapolis, Minnesota

© 2018 by Jaime Jo Wright

Published by Bethany House Publishers
11400 Hampshire Avenue South
Bloomington, Minnesota 55438
www.bethanyhouse.com

Bethany House Publishers is a division of
Baker Publishing Group, Grand Rapids, Michigan

Printed in the United States of America

ISBN 978-0-7642-3029-5 (trade paper)
ISBN 978-0-7642-3203-9 (cloth)

Library of Congress Cataloging-in-Publication Control Number: 2017964317

Scripture quotations are from the King James Version of the Bible.

This is a work of fiction. Names, characters, incidents, and dialogues are products of the author's imagination and are not to be construed as real. Any resemblance to actual events or persons, living or dead, is entirely coincidental.

Cover design by Jennifer Parker

Author is represented by Books & Such Literary Agency.

18 19 20 21 22 23 24   7 6 5 4 3 2 1

To Mom
It's not every mother who would let her daughter
trade in house chores for book reading,
cooking lessons for conjuring up ways to kidnap people,
mowing the lawn in exchange for pretending
to escape imminent death,
and piano lessons for escapades with Nancy Drew,
Trixie Belden, and Anne Shirley.

Who's the smart one in the family, I ask?
You.
All my love.

Thy soul shall find itself alone
'Mid dark thoughts of the gray tombstone—
Not one, of all the crowd, to pry
Into thine hour of secrecy.

Be silent in that solitude,
Which is not loneliness—for then
The spirits of the dead who stood
In life before thee are again. . . .

Edgar Allan Poe, "Spirits of the Dead"

CHAPTER 1

Libby Sheffield

L ibby Sheffield had never stopped to wonder what she would take specific note of if she ever stumbled upon a dead body. Still, she hadn't expected to pause in consideration of the black, patent leather shoes, the finely cut wool trousers, or the shirtsleeves cuffed at the man's wrists with cuff links boasting a scrolled G for Greenwood, his last name. Taking note of a corpse's clothing was certainly not important, but maybe it was merely a distraction to deter her from letting loose the longest scream she'd ever let scrape from her throat. The man's feet dangled in the air, any thrashing having long since ceased. His face . . . Libby looked away. His face wasn't one she ever wished to see again, though it was more likely than not permanently grafted into her vault of memories.

Movement beside her ripped Libby from her subconscious attempt to manage the repulsive shock that rendered her limbs stiff and her mouth open in horror.

Calvin shuffled forward, his shoes clomping on the wide beam

9

floors of the Greenwood carriage house. He snatched the wooden stool that had been kicked out from beneath the man. Calvin struggled to right it, pushing up against the man's unbending legs as if positioning his feet on the top would somehow encourage the body to breathe again.

"Calvin . . ." Libby's attempt to put a stop to her friend's efforts halted as she gagged. She clapped her hand over her mouth and spun on her heel, staring out at the morning light that stretched across the Greenwood driveway. The shaft of sunlight seemed to lead a path straight to the carriage house doors where it collided with a darkness that could only be described as evil. The open carriage doors had been what beckoned her inside to begin with, rather than knocking on the house's front door across the drive.

"It's not working, Lollie." Calvin sounded out of breath as he called her by his nickname for her. His desperate tone made Libby summon old remnants of gumption she had long kept dormant.

Libby turned and skimmed the face of Deacon Harrison Greenwood in all his strangled condition, the rope hoisted over a rafter beam and cutting into his neck. She shuddered and fixed her eyes on Calvin, who still hugged the dead man's legs.

"It's too late." Her words echoed through the wooden structure. "Calvin, let him go."

The boy—rather, the man—Libby had long called her best friend gave her a lengthy, searching stare. The kind he so often did when assessing how serious she was, the truth behind her statement, and how to decipher her intent. Libby despised how the town of Gossamer Grove had labeled Calvin as a simpleton. He was more empathetic and intuitive than other adults who were considered "functional." She cursed Calvin's critics many a time in the secret places of her mind. But now she grieved that Calvin could not process the difference between a man fighting for his life and a man whose face was gray and swollen in suffocated death.

"Calvin!" Libby's voice was sharp but not stern. Panic made her hands tremble, and it welled inside her until her own throat tightened, as if asphyxiating by sheer empathy for the very stiff, very dead Deacon Greenwood.

"We need to get help." Libby pointed toward the house just across the circular drive, its yellow siding cheery in the dawn.

"But you said he's dead." Calvin had released the deacon and now frowned at her.

"Yes, but . . ." Libby couldn't help but wave her hands, flustered. It wasn't supposed to have actually happened! The obituary in her pocket—the one foretelling Deacon Greenwood's death like some horrid omen—she'd thought it must have been a prank. "Please, Calvin." She started for the Greenwood house, knowing he would follow. He always did.

She was at the doorstep far sooner than she was prepared. It was seven-thirty in the morning and not a time for callers—certainly not for this type of call.

Her chest rose and fell, the soft gray silk of her morning dress ruffling as the breeze picked up and brushed her body with a late spring chill.

"Are you gonna knock, Lollie?"

She licked her lips and swallowed, almost imagining constraints around her throat.

Before she could stop him, Calvin's knuckles rapped on the door.

What could she say when the door was answered?

Good morning, Mrs. Greenwood. I received a strange missive this dawn when I arrived at the paper. An obituary for your husband. I thought perhaps it was a hoax, but I'm afraid to tell you he is most definitely hanging from the rafters in your carriage house.

That wouldn't do.

Libby tried to reconstruct her verbiage.

Mrs. Greenwood, I'm so terribly sorry to tell you this, but your husband isn't well. He's—

"Dead!" Libby half shouted as the door opened, and the questioning raised brow of Elijah Greenwood, Deacon Greenwood's son, greeted her.

11

"Libby Sheffield, what in the name of all that's holy—?" Elijah stepped out and closed the door firmly behind him, as if to spare his family from her horrible communication skills and the utter impropriety of her early morning call.

Elijah's questioning stare bounced between Libby and Calvin. He would be used to seeing them together, for Calvin was often her shadow. He would also be used to her inability to compose coherent thoughts when under duress, and even worse, anytime he was present. It didn't serve her well now. This was not a moment to be consumed by the overwhelming emotions she combatted anytime Elijah was within two feet of her.

Calvin shifted from foot to foot, tongue-tied, as usual, in the presence of the enigmatically serious visage of Elijah Greenwood.

Libby cast her friend a desperate look, but Calvin had taken to wringing his hands and humming under his breath.

She lifted her eyes to meet Elijah's. His brows had risen in annoyance, and he tilted his head as he crossed his arms over his chest—his marvelously broad chest that Libby had oft-imagined hiding herself against.

"Libby, this isn't amusing. Why are you here at the break of dawn?"

Libby stared into Elijah's brooding eyes. How was she to tell him that his father was in the carriage house, dead? History was a horrid repeat offender. She was always the storm to Elijah's serenity. She had been since she and Calvin were fifteen, and Elijah the noncompliant participant to her worst and darkest memory of all.

She shook her head. A hapless attempt to steady her thoughts and nerves.

"There was an obituary, and when I read it, I thought it best . . . my father hasn't been to the newspaper office this morning, so I had to open it, and I—most people don't submit obituaries before they die—maybe some do. No. No, I don't think one would, would you? Submit an obituary before you died?"

"Libby!" Elijah's bark brought her stumbling babble to a swift halt.

Libby widened her eyes and reached for Calvin. Someone to ground her, to make her think sensibly. But all she could see in her mind's eye was the lifeless face of Deacon Greenwood.

Elijah shook his head, his arms still crossed, his expression one of austerity. "I'm not amused. Slow down, gather your wits, and tell me what on God's green earth has landed you on our doorstep before I've even had my breakfast."

Libby swallowed hard, fished in her pocket, and rammed the obituary against Elijah's chest. That was a mistake. The heat from his body warmed through the paper and reached her gloveless palm. Libby dropped her hand, the paper fluttering toward the ground. Elijah snatched it from the air.

Calvin stepped closer to her, and Libby looped her arm around his. Elijah skimmed the words on the page, his countenance shifting from confused to outright fury. He balled the paper in his palm.

"Is this a joke?" he demanded.

Libby sputtered, "That's what I believed." Tears clogged her throat. "That's why I came so early, to check on your father, but—" She pointed toward the carriage house.

Elijah studied her face, then followed the direction of her pointing finger, and his face paled. His arm swung out, shoving her and Calvin aside. He took the stairs in a leap and sprinted across the yard. Every footstep he took was in cadence with the pounding of Libby's heart. A pounding she could hear in her ears, mocking the grim silence of the body that hung just yards away. A life snuffed out while the world slept, immune to the wickedness of death that haunted the grounds of Gossamer Grove.

CHAPTER 2

Annalise Forsythe

GOSSAMER GROVE, WISCONSIN
PRESENT DAY

If life could be a mathematical sum, Annalise would maybe understand her own story. But as it was, she could consider the past and segment her life into chaotic, misplaced chapters that ended up like a writer's manuscript dropped into a jumble on the floor—without page numbers to put it back into order.

Annalise removed her black-framed glasses and tossed them onto her desk. Her very organized desk. She looked across it at the police-uniformed frame of Brent Drury and his straight shoulders as he lowered himself onto a chair. He had grown a bit paunchy around the middle since their days in high school when he was captain of the football team alongside . . .

It didn't matter. Annalise took a deep breath, inhaling the strong scent of coffee that wafted from the shop just outside her office door. But her breath was shaky, and it didn't fill her lungs as she'd intended. Life had just handed her another confusing punch in the gut. One would think she'd be used to it by now. Apparently not.

"I don't understand." Crud, if her voice wasn't shaking too. Eugene Hayes was dead.

Dead.

Annalise shouldn't care. She had no reason to, except . . . "What do you mean, he had a picture of me in his hand?"

She'd never even met the recluse, because he was, after all, a *recluse*.

Brent's mouth was set in a tight line. Annalise could tell he was disassociating himself from her to remain factual.

"Just that. He was dead with a picture of you in his hand," Brent affirmed. "And, the old man was a hoarder. I mean, it's going to take a *hazmat* crew to clean up the place. But he had a desk with pictures of you on it." He reached into his uniform coat and pulled out his cellphone. Thumbing through the apps, he turned his phone to Annalise. "Take a look."

Annalise took the phone and stared in dumbfounded fascination. The run-down trailer aside, it was the meticulously lined up series of old, candid photographs of her that made her stomach clench. Her dance recital as a ten-year-old, her school picture when she was fourteen, with those awful braces clamped onto her teeth—was the man some kind of creeper?

Annalise stretched the photo larger with her thumb and index finger. She tensed. A quick glance at Brent told her he was studying her reaction.

Maybe not a creeper so much as a stalker!

She stared at the picture she'd zoomed in on and then half tossed the phone back at Brent. The photograph, taken when she was a senior in high school, had edges that were bent and worn. Annalise was about twenty pounds lighter at the time. Her expression looked vibrant—unlike now when her smile was pasted on like a plastic Barbie doll's. Like it had been most days since she was eighteen. When she became an adult for reasons other than the legal age.

"Did you know Mr. Hayes?" Brent asked, taking his phone back.

"Sure. Not personally, but everyone in Gossamer Grove knows of Eugene Hayes. Especially after Tyler's not-so-nice article in the paper about the old man owing back taxes and the town giving him eviction notices." Annalise hid her hands under the desk. They were shaking. She clasped her fingers together.

"But, why would he have pictures of you, Annalise?"

"How would I know?" Her voice pitched an octave higher, and Annalise focused on bringing it back down in tone. The sounds of coffee shop patrons—*her* patrons—filtered through her office door, along with the frothing sound from the steamer. She could use a straight-up espresso right about now.

"I know you're upset, but I have to show you something else." Brent directed his attention back to his phone.

No, not a picture of the body.

"Here." Brent turned the phone so that Annalise could see. She expelled a carefully controlled breath of relief at a sheaf of papers.

"What are they?"

"Old documents. All from Gossamer Grove. All from the turn of the century."

Annalise gave Brent a blank look. "So?"

She eyed the phone again as Brent swiped to the next photo. A picture of a yellowed pamphlet with huge black-inked letters, announcing *Corbin Bros. Come to Faith Revival Meeting*, and a 1907 obituary for a Harrison Greenwood.

Irony had a sharp and cutting edge. It went all metaphorically Jack the Ripper on her time and time again, and it hadn't failed this time. If she could pay money to forget the Greenwood name, Annalise would mortgage her entire life.

She raised her eyes to Brent's and chose—very specifically chose—to ignore the obituary and the fact it was next to her photograph. Over a hundred years separated them. Chalk it up to awful coincidence.

"Okay, so what does this mean? I don't get"—she waved her hand toward his phone—"any of this." Especially how Eugene

16

Hayes came to possess a picture of eighteen-year-old her, taken at a campfire at Garrett Greenwood's the night—

"You have no idea how a picture of you, an obituary, and the old revival meetings might be related?"

"Related? Hardly. They aren't related." Annalise bit back her incredulous defense. She lowered her voice. "Listen, I don't know why he had those photos of me, and I don't want to even consider why my pictures were next to an obituary of a Gossamer Grove Greenwood!"

Greenwood. The name hung over her like a demon shadow. The black ghostly kind that dodged and dipped and mocked her just when she thought she had moved on. Annalise couldn't afford to have anyone, even a hermit, digging into her past. She'd worked so hard to create a new life for herself, to be a person the town could trust, to become a benefactress who would take measures to look after people like Eugene Hayes instead of letting them become lost in a town that didn't care. It was also why she kept most people at arm's length. She was sociable and friendly, even politically inclined, but she didn't let people in.

Well, not most people.

Annalise met Brent's eyes. He knew. He would never tell, but he knew. And it was the *knowing* she was most afraid of. Those secrets never went away.

CHAPTER 3

Libby

Obituaries were the final diary page of life lived, whether pleasant or tragic, full or barren. It was an account of a rather interesting life, or worse, a dramatic end. But never were they printed *before* the person died. Until now.

Libby fell into the chair behind her father's desk at his newspaper. Her entire body trembled. The pandemonium of the morning was wrought with grief, and she knew she'd never, *never* forget the keening wail from Mrs. Greenwood's lips when Elijah broke the news to his mother. Libby would never forget the way Elijah looked at her, as if she were the one who had visited doom on his father. But, she'd not hung the man! No. The authorities had come at the beckoning call from the Greenwoods' telephone—they were rich enough to have one—and the police determined quickly that Deacon Greenwood had taken his own life.

In the chaos of Deacon Greenwood being cut from his noose and laid in the back of the coroner's wagon, to the clucking of Dr. Penchan's tongue as he offered a consoling handshake to Elijah, Libby had seen Elijah watching her. Her and Calvin. She could read his thoughts in his eyes. She was to blame. As she always had been before.

Now Libby leaned forward and grappled for a piece of paper, positioning it in the typewriter in front of her and scrolling it through the feeder. She snatched her father's horrid notes, attempting to bring some semblance of calm into her trembling hands and body. News. A story. Anything but the horridness of the morning.

The Corbin brothers' revival service has brought another round of baptisms. Eight souls were delivered and received a watery covering at the Gossamer Pond baptism service last night. Following the event, Jedidiah Corbin led the attendees in a rousing sermon with such impassioned verbiage, it resulted in several of the husbands hurrying their wives home. Errant boys lit cannon crackers, and a small fire at the edge of the pond was fast put out by quick-thinking folk.

Libby ceased her nervous typing. The *clack-clack* of the keys grated on every raw nerve that was well awakened by death's striking hand. Now this? The past week, little tidbits of news about the Corbin brothers had made their way into the paper, and the energy surrounding their revivalist meetings fell between inspiring conversion and inspiring violence.

She yanked the paper from the typewriter, the machine protesting its release of the page as if to argue.

"Yes, well, I want to go back to yesterday too!" Libby muttered at the typewriter. Yesterday, when all she had to do was hide from her memories, avoid her father and his newspaper partner, and pretend her mother wasn't piously requesting Libby attend the missionary tea tomorrow afternoon.

Libby leaned her elbows on the desk, drawing in deep, calming breaths. The police were sure to come and question her over the morning's events. She couldn't even find comfort now in boring town news. The Corbin brothers just had to keep stirring the pot, and that boded no good for anyone. Trouble was running rampant in Gossamer Grove. The town, cloaked in the image of quaint Midwestern charm and embraced with whispers of grace and charity, had been awakened to darker things. All that Gossamer Grove had seemed to be floated away like a cobweb on a breeze.

Libby squelched a yelp as her father slapped down another one of his handwritten articles on the desk. The pencil she was fiddling with flew through the air and clattered onto the floor. All the sounds of the newspaper returned to her, jolting her from her thoughts. The pulleys from the pressroom *whoosh*ed with last-minute copies, and through the large windows on either side of the office door, Libby caught a glimpse of a newsboy running down the hall, hoisting a bag of morning news over his shoulder.

"Deacon Greenwood is dead," her father, Mitch Sheffield, announced. "They found him early this morning hanging from the rafters in their carriage house."

She hadn't the ability to look shocked. She was numb now. What her father thought of as fresh news, to Libby, was already well over two hours old. She sucked in a breath, but she knew better than to interrupt her father, who had declared at her birth that he wouldn't bear the endearment of "Father" or "Papa," but instead taught her to refer to him by his first name.

Mitch waved his hand in the air. "He kicked a stool out from beneath himself. God knows there must be easier ways to take one's life!"

A sharp intake of breath from Paul Darrow, Mitch's newspaper partner, brought Mitch's exclamation to a halt. Paul was frozen in the doorway of the office, his small stature magnified by his sour expression. Black sleeves ballooned around his forearms and over his elbows, covering his white shirt to avoid ink transfer. Wispy hair waved on the top of the man's balding head.

"You will not print that." The words hissed between his teeth. He jammed his spectacles up the bridge of his nose with his index finger.

Libby was cold, down to the tips of her toes. There was so much more than either Paul or Mitch understood.

"Well, I—" she began.

"I will print the news," Mitch interrupted and rose to full height, which dwarfed Paul and made him look a bit like a puffed-up rooster trying to hide his scrawny frame.

Paul dared a step into the office. The office that had once been his before Mitch bailed him out of financial ruin and took over sixty percent of the paper. Paul really had no say anymore, although he liked to think he did.

"It's disrespectful to Deacon Greenwood's name and his family. We must handle this with deference to their grief and the church's affections." Paul's argument had trivial effect.

"We print news, Darrow!" Mitch pointed to his pile of handwritten notes in front of Libby. "Whether that's Deacon Greenwood's death or the Corbin brothers shouting hellfire and damnation at the people from their pulpit. Gossamer Grove is festering with news, and you want to print a report on the Martha Washington Ladies' Society spring fundraiser?"

"I never said—" Paul's bluster was interrupted by an equally affronted Mitch.

"Please, may I—" Libby tried again.

Mitch cut her off with a blustering wave of his hand, completely silencing her.

"The Corbins already have the town splitting in half. Eight more baptisms last night. Either it's authentic religion or fear of being condemned. Deacon Greenwood probably thought better of it and decided it would be easier to face God himself than the Corbin brothers."

"That's disgraceful! You're stirring up trouble like you always do. Dissension." Paul glowered. "This paper was never meant to publish slander."

"Hah!" Mitch sniffed.

Libby drew in a shuddering breath. If she didn't announce that she'd been the one to discover Deacon Greenwood, then she would have—well, never mind. She wasn't allowed to express *what* she would have to pay, but she'd pay it nonetheless.

"There was an obituary delivered this morning." Her interjection received an exasperated look from her father. Obituaries weren't notable news in his definition.

Mitch waved her off again, choosing instead to lambaste his partner who, for all sakes and purposes, was more of an enemy. "Did you hear about the Presbyterian church? Their windows were broken last night by a band of boys, after which they threw in a skunk for good measure."

Paul's mouth tightened into a straight line. "I will repeat myself for your hardheaded idiocy. The *Daily Democrat* was never meant to print melodramatic gossip."

Mitch laughed and tugged the lapels of his jacket. "It's not gossip when it's the truth."

Paul's eyes narrowed, and he sniffed. "You feed off others' hardships."

"Regardless," Mitch said, his tone indicating he meant to bring a conclusion to the erratic argument, "I do believe the town will notice when the deacon doesn't show up for closing prayers at the upcoming tent meeting Friday night. Whatever his reasons, he's dead."

"Fine," Paul snapped. "But you mustn't print the gory details."

Mitch curled his lip, sarcasm dripping from his words. "I'll leave out the part of him being *stiff as a board*." He shoved past Paul, but paused in the doorway and speared Libby with a well-placed look that stated he was both her employer and her father.

Most days, she hated that equation.

"Libby, see that those articles are edited and transcribed so they go to press immediately. *Word for word*."

She gave a short nod, and Mitch charged from the room.

Heavens. What a tragic mess today was. Made more horrid by the fact that every time she blinked, Libby saw Deacon Greenwood's dead face.

"Excuse me." She cleared her throat. "Paul?"

"Yes?" He spun his attention toward her. The man practically pecked her eyes out with his glare.

Libby stared at him. He was a daunting crank of a man.

"What is it, Miss Sheffield?"

Yes. All right. Libby summoned courage. Paul wasn't Elijah, nor was he doomed to die by premature obituary. She mustered her wits and launched herself into the conversation. "There was an obituary left here this morning. I'm not certain when it was slipped into the mail slot, but when I arrived here at six-thirty, I almost stepped on the envelope."

"Fine." Paul waved his hand in dismissal. "It's too late to print in today's paper. We'll set it for press tonight."

"No, but that's just it!" Curse these men who wouldn't let her finish a cohesive thought. Libby pushed against the desk, rising so her dress floated around her ankles and her height gave her a bit of advantage over the shorter newspaperman. "The obituary was for Deacon Greenwood."

Paul paused, as if unsure how to calculate the information and reach a conclusion.

Libby hurried on. "I just saw Deacon Greenwood last evening, at dinner at the Fairfield Boardinghouse. He was very much alive." She had Paul's full attention now. "I determined it had to be a wicked joke. I wanted to make sure of Deacon Greenwood's welfare, so I left the paper after I found the obit this morning. Calvin was outside and he accompanied me."

Paul's eyebrow raised and he sagged against the doorjamb. Libby could see he was reaching the correct deduction.

"Are you telling me it was *you* who discovered Deacon Green-wood?"

Libby nodded, the vision flooding her memory like a nightmare.

Paul rammed his spectacles up his nose and took a step forward. "*You* found him?" he repeated, as if she'd been bumbling in conversation again and confused him.

"Yes." Libby detested the watery tone to her voice, but she couldn't help it. She'd stood there while they cut him down too. Watched as Elijah had delivered a swift, grief-stricken kick against the wooden stool his father had once stood on, shattering it against the wall.

"Why didn't you tell us?" Paul wasn't empathetic, but more offended that she'd for some reason kept so mum while the two men sparred and wouldn't let her get a word in edgewise.

Libby cleared her throat. "This morning was dreadful. I never truly expected to find him dead. But the obituary . . ." She waited, hoping Paul would put two and two together. When he looked back at her as if waiting, she plunged ahead. "I arrived at the paper at six-thirty this morning."

"You already stated that," Paul snapped.

Libby nodded. "I was reading Deacon Greenwood's obituary *before* I discovered him dead. Before *anyone* discovered him dead."

They stared at each other. Color leaked from Paul's face, and he shook his head. "There has to be an explanation. Perhaps the deacon left it himself."

"But why?" Libby raised a brow.

"Those intent on taking their own life—" Paul paused and cleared his throat—"often leave a . . . note."

Libby nodded. She'd heard of that before, although most didn't speak of such things. There were so many emotions in the taking of one's life. Judgment, sorrow, a lack of closure . . . so many questions. But no. No. This wasn't a note of farewell or an explanation from one intent on leaving this world.

"It was an obituary," Libby insisted. "I gave it to Elijah, and I'm not entirely sure what happened to it."

But she'd memorized it. Word for word, it was burned into her mind. It was what words did to Libby. They tattooed themselves in her brain.

"Harrison Frederick Greenwood," she recited for Paul. "Born March tenth, 1853, passed away this the seventh of May, 1907. No more shall his secrets wound. No more shall his secrets shame.

24

"Thy soul shall find itself alone
"'Mid dark thoughts of the gray tombstone—
"Not one, of all the crowd, to pry
"Into thine hour of secrecy."

A fateful sensation filled the room, like one might feel while passing through a cemetery at midnight. *Thy soul shall find itself alone*. That moment, right before death came, when a soul was truly suspended.

"That last bit is Poe. Edgar Allan Poe." Paul squeezed the bridge of his nose. "The darkest form of funeral verse."

"What do I do?" Libby whispered. Poe. She'd read the morbid poet before, but in the horrors of the morning, she'd yet to credit him with some of the obituary's words.

"Nothing." Paul's voice dropped to a whisper, hissed between clenched teeth. His eyes drove into hers with authority. "You do absolutely nothing. The obituary doesn't exist anymore unless Elijah Greenwood has secured it himself. It does no one any good to revisit it."

"But," Libby argued, "if it was written and delivered here prior to Deacon Greenwood being discovered, doesn't it stand to reason that perhaps the deacon's death was—" Good gracious. She was going to say it aloud. "That his death was premeditated?"

"You've no evidence of that." Paul stared at her, and she couldn't read the expression in his eyes. "Let the medical examination speak for the truth of what happened. As for this obituary? Do nothing." Paul raised a finger as if he were going to say more, but instead he spun on his heel and strode from the room, slamming the door behind him.

Libby stared after him. The day was barely in its infancy and yet Gossamer Grove was exploding into turmoil. Now she must add secrecy to the trouble? What if the police inquired—and they would—why she was at the Greenwood home in the wee hours of the morning with Calvin? She couldn't very well *lie*. Well, she could try, but if she could barely spit out the truth coherently, how could she deceive with finesse? No, she'd have to tell them about the obituary. Of course, they would want to see it, and she didn't have it anymore. So then, Libby knew before it even happened, the authorities would wave her away as they often did. The daughter of the sensation-seeking newspaperman. She would be Mitch's pawn to create a story where there really wasn't one. The truth, they would determine—unless Dr. Penchan found evidence to the contrary—was simple: Deacon Harrison Greenwood was a disturbed man whose secrets drove him to dark results.

Libby crossed her arms on the desk as she sank onto the chair. She laid her forehead on her arms and drew in a trembling breath. *"Tell no one,"* Paul said. It wouldn't matter. Even if she told the truth, no one would believe her. Besides, she was good at keeping secrets. She had kept them for years. It's what people in Gossamer Grove did.

CHAPTER 4

Annalise

The image of Eugene Hayes's body lying cold in his trailer was vivid in Annalise's mind. Her imagination sometimes worked overtime, and while it often resulted in great ideas, it could also put her in places she preferred not to go. Sights, sounds, feelings—all of it paraded through her conscious mind with a vividness that rivaled a full-color dream. It was better to push it all away until she could mentally process and categorize it later.

Annalise steamed the milk for a customer's latte, the froth growing. Once finished, she pulled the stainless-steel pitcher from the steamer and poured the milk into the paper cup. The dairy swirled with the espresso. She hated pitying anyone, even the homeless. It seemed disrespectful. But, Eugene Hayes wasn't homeless, although he was apparently one step above it. The man probably had to drink Folgers, or worse, instant coffee.

She blinked several times to refocus on the latte. She needed to stop obsessing over the dead man, yet she couldn't forget the picture Brent had shown her. Or rather, the picture of a picture. A photograph of a Polaroid taken of Eugene Hayes. His wrinkled face, a bandanna around his head, Willie Nelson style, gray hair spiking out in random directions on his head, and skinny, bare arms with sagging tattoos. He looked like a gaunt version of a biker, or a Vietnam vet, or maybe both.

"Here you go." She handed the latte to the guest.

He gave her his credit card and mumbled with a smile, "Double charge me."

Annalise grinned, trying to shake herself out of her muddied thoughts and into the present.

"You got it. Thank you so much!"

She added an extra charge to the card and took comfort that word was spreading fast in Gossamer Grove. Her plan to raise awareness for the food pantry adjacent to the coffee shop and hopefully, sooner rather than later, open a shelter, was growing in popularity. When she'd started the pantry a few years before, there'd been suspicion and even a reticence from the public to patronize her coffee shop, where the majority of the profits went to support the pantry. Maybe now the community liked it because it was an uncomplicated way to help the needy without getting their hands dirty. But, Annalise preferred to think—hope, really—that it was because Gossamer Grove had people who genuinely cared.

Two palms rested gently on the rustic cherrywood counter. Annalise edged out of the way of her hired barista, who took the next customer. She recognized the hands, the strawberry-red nail polish, and the waft of sugary-sweet raspberry perfume.

"Hello, love." The understanding voice of her closest friend, Christen, flooded her precarious peace with a bit of relief in the mixing bowl of the morning. Christen had a way of picking up people like someone adopted a stray puppy.

"Have you heard, then?" Christen's green eyes were concerned. The normal smile missing behind her glasses.

Annalise bit her tongue. Brent had told her not to talk about Eugene Hayes to anyone. But he had to know his own wife, Annalise's best—*only*—friend, would be the first person she wanted to confide in. Still, Annalise followed rules—especially ones laid down by the police—so the no-talkee rule would be inclusive of Christen too. This was going to be difficult.

"Annalise?" Christen craned her neck, trying to recapture Annalise's attention.

Annalise twisted around, turning her back to her friend. She needed coffee.

Yes. Make the coffee. Alllll the coffee.

Annalise made herself busy tamping grounds into the espresso pod.

"You're overthinking it, I can see that already." Christen's intuitive words ricocheted off Annalise's back.

Good grief. Did Christen actually *know* about Eugene Hayes? Annalise hooked the espresso into the machine and turned the switch.

"I'm not leaving until you talk to me." Christen's voice held just the right mix of sternness and care.

Fine. Annalise faced her friend as espresso drained into her mug. She heaved a huge sigh, which earned her an extra understanding scrunch of Christen's nose. Empathy. It was Christen's strong point.

Christen brushed blond bangs from over her right eye. Her assessment of Annalise was like standing in front of an X-ray machine that read thoughts. Annalise winced. Brent *had* to know that Christen's ability to draw her out of her introverted self was akin to a hypnotherapist. Minus the hypnosis. She was that good.

"Well?" Christen blinked, her ridiculously long eyelashes brushing the lenses in her cobalt-blue frames.

"I can't say anything."

Remain mum. Mumsie's the word.

Annalise retrieved her espresso, and instead of proceeding to steam milk and make herself a latte, she sucked down the double shot, letting it burn its scalding path down her throat.

Choking, Annalise snatched a dish towel and wiped a renegade dribble from her chin.

"Wow." Christen eyed her. "You really *are* upset. What are you going to do?"

"There's nothing *to* do." Annalise shrugged, tossing the dirty dish towel into a cloth basket beneath the counter.

"Ooooookay." Christen pursed her lips, and her expression told Annalise she was not going to get away with a simple dismissal.

"Look," Annalise tried again. Although, she could feel herself caving as Christen perused her with her probing gaze. "It wasn't my fault the man died, and I don't know why he had pictures of me all over his desk." She choked and stopped. She needed to zip it.

"What *are* you talking about?" Christen drew back, a perplexed raising of the eyebrows to complete her bewildered look.

They stared at each other. Annalise had that growing realization they were talking about two completely different things.

"What are *you* talking about?" Today was a day from the Twilight Zone if ever there was one.

Christen tilted her head and widened her eyes. "Garrett? Garrett Greenwood?"

A dull thud in the pit of Annalise's stomach told her it was more than the hastily downed espresso that was going to give her heartburn.

"What about him?" Annalise eyed Christen cautiously.

"Garrett Greenwood moved back to Gossamer Grove." Christen's look of disbelief told Annalise she probably should have known this already. Somehow.

The churning in her stomach worsened.

Christen cleared her throat. "You know, Doug Larson put in a bid to the town for the property you just petitioned the board for. Well, apparently, Doug is using Garrett as his ace up his sleeve. He hired Garrett to design and endorse a climbing gym and zip-line course."

Annalise sagged against the counter. Of course. The town would far prefer Doug Larson's proposed wilderness center and resort over her proposed homeless shelter. But Garrett? That was a no-brainer win for Larson right there.

Annalise motioned for Christen to follow, and she rounded the counter and moved into her office. She sagged against her desk as Christen flopped into one of the chairs. She stared up at Annalise.

"I'm sorry." Christen screwed up her face into an empathetic grimace.

Annalise crossed her arms over her chest. Jaded. She was becoming more and more jaded as she grew older. Growing bitter wasn't something she'd ever considered for herself. It wasn't attractive, nor was it conducive to health and happiness. Worst of all, it made Annalise more and more like her mother, whom she'd separated from years ago for that very reason. Bitterness poisoned even the sweetest cup and turned it rancid.

Still, she couldn't lie and say it was all right. It was far from all right. Garrett Greenwood was a professional rock climber. Bringing him back to Gossamer Grove to design and endorse a wilderness center was akin to bringing George Clooney to town to endorse a home movie. Annalise saw her dreams of championing the town's impoverished winging its way out the window and over the trees where Garrett would be constructing a zip line. Being waterboarded would leave her with more breath than she had now. The doors of fate had opened and dumped all the what-goes-around-comes-arounds on top of her head in the same day.

"Hey?" Christen's concerned voice filled the office. "There's still hope, you know. Nicole might be the mayor, but she's not stupid. She'll look at all sides, even if Garrett has a vested interest in it and he's her brother."

Annalise gave a weak nod. But really, it was more than that. So much more. It was Garrett. It'd always been Garrett.

"There's one more thing." Christen reached out and patted the chair next to her. "You'll probably want to sit down for this."

Annalise stared at her, then spun and sank into the chair. "This can't be good." Steady. Deep breaths.

"Well, it's not the worst thing, I guess." Christen scrunched her face, her glasses hitting her eyebrows. "If you can get past the wilderness center and appreciate the muscles, your new neighbor Garrett will definitely be the best-looking garden ornament outside your house this summer."

Christen was trying to be funny, but she didn't know. Only Brent did, and Annalise's parents whose lifestyle of the rich and retired in Scottsdale, Arizona, kept them blessedly out of Annalise's life. But this?

The sick sensation Annalise was already fighting coiled her stomach into an even tighter, more assertive knot. "*My* next-door neighbor?"

The image of the For Sale sign in the yard of the modest house next door to her historical Victorian two-story flooded her mind.

Please, God, please. One break in life, that's all she was asking. Just one.

But the expression on Christen's face made it all nightmarishly clear: God had no intention of letting Annalise catch a break. It was penance, really. Now she would have to pay it in full . . . with interest.

———〰️———

Everything in her life was planned meticulously. Maybe not the little details—she wasn't OCD, or maybe she was?—but for certain, the major events. Creating this entire homeless shelter proposal, for example, came after a successful term in office by Nicole Greenwood, but with a sad lack of concern toward the underprivileged in Gossamer Grove. They needed a voice, although Nicole was more preoccupied with tourism in the quaint vintage town that had been ranked as one of the top ten best littlest places to visit. *The Biggest-Hearted Small Town in the Midwest.*

So Annalise did what she did best. She mapped it out. The needs, the budget, the property—unused by the town—and the business sense and attention to detail it took to launch such a project. Opening their eyes to a bigger picture than just their happy little homes was an important initiative.

But she hadn't mapped out this.

The red door stared back at her with two rectangular glass windowpanes for eyes. Garrett was never supposed to come home. It'd been twelve years, and he'd kept far away from Gossamer Grove. Until now. No contingency plan for his reappearance had been made.

Rapping the brass door knocker against its base, Annalise waited.

Her stomach was a puddle of nerves, and if she didn't have one made of steel, she'd be retching in the bushes right now.

A muffled "Door's open" greeted her ears. A familiar voice, mature but with the same casual tone.

Annalise drew in a deep breath and blew it out, lifting stray copper hairs from her forehead. They fell over her eyes, and she brushed them back. The doorknob turned as she twisted it. It really didn't matter how long she tried to plan for this; their first face-to-face meeting since high school wasn't something she could plan for.

She was greeted with the full-on view of two muscled legs in ratty khaki shorts and a tapered bare back inked with a shoulder tattoo of Chinese symbols that stretched around and down to his corded right bicep. Garrett's body descended as he lowered it from a pull-up, his hands gripping a hang board mounted over a doorframe. It was a molded rectangular creation, designed to be like crags of a rock. Garrett was hanging on by the tips of his fingers and pulling his entire body weight up until his chin hit the bottom.

Good Father in Heaven, hallowed be thy name. Thy kingdom come . . . please!

Yep. She couldn't have planned for this. The full view of the very fit and shirtless Garrett Greenwood was not on her list of imagined potential scenarios. Scorn, yes. A slammed door in her face, most likely. A lazy grin, perhaps. But this?

He lowered his body again and spoke over his shoulder. "Yeah?" And back up he went.

"Garrett?"

The man released his hold, and his feet thudded onto the carpeted floor. He wiped his hands together as he turned, lifting his mahogany eyes. Now he was looking at her. Really looking at her. It was disconcerting, horrendous, and altogether the most awful thing she'd experienced in years. Annalise's throat tightened. Raw anger mixed with betrayal, which couldn't be healed with an "I'm sorry."

"Q." The old moniker slipped from his lips as easily as when they were young. Q. Annalise Quintessa. The very pretentious name her parents had given her when she was born. Evidence of their own quest to position themselves in the upper echelons of the Gossamer Grove community. Garrett always found it humorous and had dubbed her "Q" for her middle name just to irritate her. It had worked. It should have been her first warning sign.

"Hi." The word was very inadequate for this moment.

Garrett snatched a T-shirt from the floor and shrugged into it, probably more to give himself something to do to fill the tense pause.

"You said you wouldn't come back." Annalise went for it. She wasn't going to tiptoe around stupid pleasantries that were so fake a mannequin could see through them.

Garrett's lip pulled up in disbelief. "You're gonna go there already?"

"Yes. I am."

"K then." He didn't bother to tug down the navy-blue T-shirt emblazoned with a climbing logo. The right side rode up on his hip while the left slouched over his pocket. "It's been twelve years."

"You said you wouldn't come back," she repeated. God help her, it was the only thing that came to mind. She was drowning in the brown bottomless chasms that were his eyes, and not in a good way. It was that same magnetic field that had sucked her in as a young girl. She hated it. She had prayed it would have dissipated over a decade's worth of distance.

"Gossamer Grove is my home too, you know." Garrett ran his fingers through his shaggy brown hair. He marched across the room into the kitchen. Annalise heard the faucet turn on and water filling a glass. She allowed herself the right to enter and follow him.

"And you're here to work with Doug Larson on the land I've been trying to get the town to relinquish. Pulling strings because your sister is the mayor?" Annalise entered the kitchen and watched him gulp down the water.

"Wow." He planted the glass firmly on the counter, his eyes narrowing. "That's low, even for you."

"Even for me? You don't even know me." Annalise's words

came out a hoarse whisper. "You never *did* know me." She knew she sounded snippy. Mean even. Like a bitter old maid set out to pasture. Whatever that meant. But if only people could see inside her, they would see the pain, the unhealed wounds. They would understand. But no one had dared to do that, not even Garrett.

He interlocked his fingers behind his head, his elbows sticking out. "It's been years, Q, let it go."

"Fine." The man really had no idea, no clue what she'd suffered, did he? "It must be nice to gallivant all over Europe while I had to stay here in Gossamer Grove and . . . 'let it go.'"

His hands dropped to his side. Garrett took a step forward. "Hey—"

"Never mind. I just came by to tell you we're neighbors, in case you didn't already know."

Garrett didn't say anything. He had to know she still lived in her childhood home.

"Well, we are," Annalise affirmed.

"Okay?" Garrett's tone registered the unspoken question of *So?*

Annalise backed away and turned toward the front door. She stopped and looked over her shoulder, once again locking eyes with the man who, as a boy, had more than broken her heart. He'd broken *her.*

"So stay away from me. Please." The wobble in her voice betrayed the tender thread of emotion hiding behind her bravado. She could tell Garrett noticed, but he didn't even blink.

"Not a problem."

Not *his* problem. She should have been, though. She should have been.

Annalise closed the door softly behind her. Wishing Garrett Greenwood away wasn't going to do a thing. Not when her bedroom window was opposite his, and not when their history together built an invisible bridge between the windowpanes.

Chapter 5

Libby

Libby stood against the yellow-striped papered walls in the Greenwood parlor. The scent of flowers suffocated her as bouquets sat on every end table, shelf, and flat surface. A mirror on the opposite wall was also covered in black crepe to comply with the customary superstition that the deceased's spirit might be trapped in the looking glass for eternity. The piano was closed to forbid music or revelry. Gauzy crepe draped the south corner of the room. Nestled in its swooping embrace was the casket of Deacon Harrison Greenwood.

They'd arrived earlier than other invited guests. A special message in their funeral invitation had been penned by Deacon Greenwood's widow to Libby's mother, head of the Martha Washington Ladies' Society, and therefore a logical first choice for support—regardless of emotional intimacy or friendship.

Standing sentinel over his dead father was Elijah. His lean body encased in a black suit, his dark brown hair tamed with some sort of fancy pomade, and his eyes steeled with emotional fortitude.

Libby's mother moved toward the casket, her black dress brushing across the Oriental wool carpet, but Libby didn't follow. Black. Mourning. It was all so dark. No wonder people avoided talk of death, and cemeteries, and *Memento Mori*, the photographs taken after the loved one had passed. It was morbid and unsettling.

Glancing at the ornate mantel clock, Libby noted it had been stopped as was customary, and in this case it was halted at the *approximate* time of Deacon Greenwood's death. Libby blinked away the image of the stilled clock hands. The time she'd discovered Deacon Greenwood was hardly the exact time he'd passed.

She wrapped her arms around herself, squelching a shudder. Doctor Penchan had concluded death by asphyxiation brought on by Deacon Greenwood's own hand. The police had questioned her, digging for answers as to why she'd been at the Greenwood home so early in the morning with Calvin. A puddle of nervous anxiety, Libby had done exactly what Paul instructed her not to do. She'd told the police everything.

"Do you have the obituary?" they asked her.

"No," she'd answered. Elijah did.

The undisguised look of disgust hurt more than she wished to admit. They believed it a ploy. A story. One of the officers even said as much.

"Why were you at the Greenwood home?" They insisted on a more plausible answer, one that didn't reek of Mitch Sheffield's attempt to monopolize on a dead man's escape from the earth.

"I told you," she said.

"It wouldn't have anything to do with your infatuation with Elijah Greenwood, would it?"

Libby had sealed her lips in that moment. She couldn't help it if the town knew she'd danced in Elijah's shadow since she was young. Rumors long abounded that Libby Sheffield had put off matrimony in hopes Elijah would take notice—more than he already had. Even Elijah knew this. But Elijah also knew *why* Libby had such devotion. Neither of them would ever explain.

The police wrote off her presence, and nothing was mentioned of the obituary again. Everything pointed toward a desperate man making an escape from the world.

How did one pay respects to the family of a man who'd taken his own life? Especially when you were the only one in the room who believed, in fact, that he'd been murdered instead? Libby's gaze darted around the room, the voices murmuring behind gloved hands positioned over mouths to discreetly converse becoming distant echoes. She blinked. The room spun, like being on a carousel. Slow, methodical, her eyes skimming the faces. What if Deacon Greenwood's killer stood here, posing as a grieving friend while reveling in the deacon's potential condemnation to Hell?

Libby blinked furiously, a strong buzzing whirring in her ears, her heart colliding with her rib cage with a force far too great for her to remain standing for long. A deep breath, inhaling through her nose and letting out through her mouth. Her own gloved hand clutched her throat, willing herself to remain upright.

She focused on her mother, who was embracing Mrs. Greenwood. Their hold was stiff and formal, that of two acquaintances who respected the hierarchy of their small town, and even appearances. What a sad waste. In a moment such as this, a grieving widow needed a dear friend, not one who led the church's women's club.

"Libby."

His dark tone jolted Libby from her attempt to avoid a dead faint. Never mind that. She was struggling to breathe now for other reasons altogether. Libby met Elijah's somber eyes.

"Come" was all he said. He took her gloved hand and held it between his even as he led her to stand over his dead father. Libby restrained herself from pulling away, from making a scene. Elijah hadn't released her hand, and she was very aware of the warmth that emanated from his grasp. She reminded herself once again it was not a hand held out of affection but a grip that insinuated much more.

Libby focused on Deacon Greenwood as was proper, though

38

she didn't miss the close proximity of Elijah's chest to her shoulder. The older man looked made of wax, and after a few days his body was already beginning to sink into itself. Flowers bordered his casket to mask the odor of death and finality.

"I'm so sorry." The platitude came from her heart, but it carried the same molded sound of everyone else's sympathy.

"Are you?" Elijah muttered as he surveyed his father's face, the gray hair combed away from his strong forehead, and the straight nose Libby recalled wrinkling when he smiled.

"Of course!" Libby cast Elijah a wary sideways glance. He had to know *she* didn't kill his father or write that morbid, plagiarized obituary. Nor did she have the strength to haul the dead weight of a body by rope over rafters some feet over her head.

"Yes. You're sorry." Resignation seeped into Elijah's voice. "You're always . . . *sorry*."

And she was. She always had been. Libby fixated on the dead man. Being alone, reading, hiding away from anything dysfunctional was her pastime of choice. Calvin was her only friend. Now she had been thrust into Deacon Greenwood's death with a force that was entirely unwelcome.

"I cannot believe my father would—" Elijah swallowed hard, his sentence left unfinished. "But the obituary you entrusted me with? I cannot fathom the implications of . . ." His words trailed away, as if reminding himself she was not his personal confidante. She never had been.

Words filtered from Elijah's mouth, and Libby leaned toward him to hear them.

"'Thrilling to think, poor child of sin! It was the dead that groaned within.'"

"Pardon?" Libby's voice notched upward a pitch.

Elijah started, and their eyes met, locking in a mutual bewilderment. Her, for horror that Elijah whispered Poe with the finesse of a devoted reader, and he for the apparent shock that he'd spoken aloud.

Libby said nothing but watched as Elijah's eyes darkened, only to sense that old familiar pang as the haunted hollowness returned to them.

"My father—he'd written it on a piece of paper. They found it beneath his feet, kicked under the straw. But it was written in his hand. It was his signature that sealed it."

Libby couldn't tear her eyes from Elijah's. Searching, aching to understand the conundrum that was the mysteriously sad and morose person she'd known since childhood. Known him in a comradery of silence. Known him as her hero and the man who would never love her, *could* never love her until she told the truth— *her* truth.

By whoever's hand Deacon Greenwood had died, his last and final penned words sucked the breath from Libby. The shared knowing in Elijah's eyes was neither accusation nor empathy. It was resigned. They both knew. Oh, how they knew! Sin had a wicked way of creeping into one's soul and tainting its edges with the inevitable groan that one carried with them, with their secrets, into the grave.

CHAPTER 6

Annalise

S leep was mocking her. Annalise stared at the ceiling from her bed, the moonlight setting off the old Victorian bedroom with a deep blue glow. She had been used to living alone in her childhood home for years now, ever since her parents sold it to her and moved south. But now? Annalise shot a look at the darker corners of the room. Of course, there was no one there, but she couldn't shake the image of an old man, bandanna wrapped around his forehead, crouching in the corner. He stared at her, narrowed eyes, wrinkled skin, flipping a photograph of her between his fingers. Back and forth, back and forth.

"Aaah!" Annalise sat up and grappled for the chain on the old-fashioned lamp by her bed. Light flooded the room. The imagined vision of Eugene Hayes dissipated.

Annalise took a deep breath and leaned back against her pillows. She reached for her cellphone. Anything to distract herself. Pulling up Facebook, she scrolled through her newsfeed filled with pointless memes, random status updates, and pictures of family and friends. She had to get this uneasy feeling under control. Eugene Hayes was dead. The photographs were a mystery to the police force and probably wouldn't ever be fully explained. It was over before it had begun, and yet . . .

Annalise looked over at her window. Laying down her phone, she flipped back the covers and padded across the wood floor. Her hand grasped the filmy curtains and pushed them aside. She looked down at the house next door, at the window staring up at her.

Garrett's window.

It was dark, as was the rest of the house. Which made sense since it was the early hours of morning yet.

There was so much coincidence. Garrett coming home right after Eugene Hayes died in possession of *that* picture. The one taken at the Greenwood home when she was eighteen. How had the old man ever gotten ahold of it? Of any of them, really? But the fact that he had an obituary of a Greenwood from years past unnerved her. He'd made some sort of connection between her and them. He must have.

Movement snagged Annalise's attention. She squinted, trying to make out the shadows, the light from her bedroom glowing behind her not helping. They didn't get much wildlife in town, but on occasion she'd seen a white-tailed deer wandering through her yard as if lost. The dark form moved behind an evergreen bush at the corner of Garrett's house. Poor deer. It must be as lost as she felt right now. Dislocated and wishing to return to normal.

A cold fear coiled in her stomach. Annalise frowned, leaning closer to the window. That wasn't a deer. She leapt backward, grabbing at the cord and tugging so the window shade slammed down onto the sill, blocking her room from the outside. The window sheers were pointless against it, and the moonlight no longer inviting. It was ominous. Revealing the form of the man crouching outside, staring up at her. Staring into her room.

He was probably one of the many homeless—the ones she was trying to help at the food pantry. The reason she was vying for the property at the edge of town to build a shelter. So they didn't have to wander.

Annalise sprinted to her bed and took a flying leap onto it, making sure her feet were nowhere close enough for any imaginary man hiding under her bed to grab them. She curled her knees to her chest.

An old man dead, one who possessed a series of photographs of her. Now a man outside of her window, watching her.

Maybe helping these people wasn't such a great idea after all. Not if her privacy would be invaded, not if they were going to develop some inexplicable obsession with her, and definitely not if she was going to spend sleepless nights in a lighted room praying away some unknown bogeyman.

CHAPTER 7

In the daylight, the idea of a man crouching outside her window seemed as preposterous as the idea of Eugene Hayes crouching in the corner of her bedroom. Yet, Annalise couldn't shake that she had seen someone.

This was all going to her head. Emotions, fears, memories? They were the fodder for imagination and illogic. Annalise sniffed, tucked an escaped strand of coppery hair back into her hair tie, and blinked rapidly as if by doing so she could clear not only her vision but also her mind.

She allowed herself a moment to skim the morning crowd that perched at tables, along the barn-door bar, and in the cozy lounge area with stuffed couches and chairs. The double doors that led into the attached food pantry were shut, locked for the morning. The volunteers would open it at ten o'clock. Thank the Lord for the members of the local Lutheran church who had taken the pantry under their charitable wing. It would have been madness to run the coffee shop and the pantry simultaneously. But, Annalise took a sip of her wimpy caffé misto, she would have done it. Her soul resonated with those who wandered into the pantry for assistance. She may never have been in need or want of material things, but sometimes the hollowness reflected in the eyes of those in need had less to do with a warm blanket and more to do with abandonment. Rejection. Condemnation.

God help her, she needed to quit with this introspection! Annalise gulped down the rest of the coffee and performed an overhand toss of the cup into the wastebasket a few yards away.

"Lebron James got nothin' on you!" One of the college-aged baristas clapped a high five with the palm she instinctively held up.

Annalise moved her hand from the high five and finished with a short wave at Mrs. Duncan, the head of the Silver Saints Knitting Club that met in the shop every Tuesday morning. She attempted to breathe in normalcy, but her breath hitched as her eyes alighted on the far corner table.

Her curse was muttered under her breath. The Lebron-James-touting barista shot her a surprised glance. She stifled a low chuckle.

Yes. Yes, you all, I can sin and swear with the best of them.

Her eyes collided with Garrett's across the room. His muscular body draped over his chair turned backward toward the round table. His arms rested across the back of the chair, and his face was expressionless when he spotted her. The trendy blonde next to him followed his stare. Her eyes, made smoky with effortless eye-shadow application, drilled into Annalise's.

Annalise realized she was going to need to sit down tonight and plan for these types of moments. Garrett was back in town, whether she approved or not, and being blindsided every time she saw him wasn't going to benefit anyone.

Summoning courage, she decided not to duck into her office like a coward, but rather to face her fear and greet them both. It wasn't fair she had to feel ostracized by the generational offspring of one of Gossamer Grove's founding families. It also wasn't fair that Nicole's chin-length, edgy haircut was so stinking attractive that it made Annalise feel old-fashioned and far too much of a librarian with her twisted ballet bun and chunky glasses.

Nicole offered a smile as Annalise neared them. It didn't reach her eyes, but then it wasn't cold either. It was . . . *impartial*. That was the word.

"Annalise." Nicole tipped her head.

"Hi." There. That was a special kind of greeting. Annalise inwardly smacked herself. It wasn't Nicole who made her tongue-tied. It was Garrett. Whose slouch hadn't even bothered to straighten, or tense, or look the slightest bit stressed.

Nicole glanced between them. "I take it you're aware Garrett's home."

"Oh, very." Annalise nodded, offering a tight-lipped smile that didn't try to disguise the underlying snark.

"I'm leaving you alone," he shrugged. As if his whole thirty-one years of maturity was diminished to a schoolboy's challenge. His dark eyes flashed.

Nicole eased from her chair, her lithe frame clad in blue jeans and a flowing tan cardigan that brushed her hips. The red hue of her filmy blouse matched the tone of her lips. She offered Annalise a smile even as she extended her hand to cup Annalise's shoulder. It was friendship for show, like almost everything else in Gossamer Grove. Nicole leaned in.

"We both know that Garrett being home may lend itself toward resurfaced hard feelings. But the past is the past, Annalise. For both of our sakes, we have critical issues to focus on, whether we agree on them or not. Many decisions are to be made, and we both have our affections for this town. Let's keep our priorities straight, yes?"

Annalise bit the inside of her cheek. Then her tongue. Would slapping the town's mayor across the face be a bad idea? Yes. Probably.

"I've kept my priorities straight for many years, Nicole." Annalise looked past the woman at Garrett. "*All* of my priorities."

For a moment, a shadow flickered in his eyes. He had the decency to look down and distract himself with his coffee. Funny, how twelve years later, Nicole was still speaking for her brother. The orange T-shirt he wore stretched across his taut muscles as he lifted his cup to his mouth. His carved lips took a sip of the brew.

Annalise swallowed, her face burning. She remembered his mouth. Why didn't some sensory things fade with time? Garrett looked back up, and for a moment there was a plea in his eyes. The kind of pitiable plea that was fast hidden by the need to cover it, to be plastic, to carry on as though nothing ever hurt them.

"I've things to do. Nice seeing you both." Annalise waggled her fingers as she veered back toward her office on that monumental lie. *Nice* wasn't ever a word she could associate with them, unless she went way back into her vault of memories to the time when it was just Garrett and her, and a dare that turned into friendship. Before it shattered into a million irreparable pieces.

—⟋⟍—

Annalise fumbled with her phone to read the text Brent sent. She swallowed one of those lumps that lodged in a person's throat when they didn't want to cry and didn't want to acknowledge emotion. But, Garrett's presence had stirred up a hornet's nest of feelings inside her, stinging hurt that swelled and throbbed in a rhythmic reminder of pain. Now this.

She stared at the text.

Hayes's death will hit paper today. Ongoing investigation. You may be named if Tyler gets wind of the pictures. Chin up, A. We got your back.

Tyler Darrow. He had the local newspaper just teetering on the verge of being a gossip rag, and he loved to pick at town secrets. If Tyler nosed his way in, having this story front and center for the town to read would be dreadful. A destitute elderly man dying just as Annalise was pushing the town to donate property for a shelter and to invest in those very souls? That could be beneficial to her cause, if she were heartless. Proof that Gossamer Grove needed to wake up and see the homeless!

But then there was the issue of her pictures, splayed all over Eugene Hayes's run-down trailer. And she? She was nowhere to be found. No aid. No assistance. No record of Annalise Forsythe ever

47

helping the poor old soul. She didn't practice what she preached, and the food pantry was a sham for her to skim off the top to make her coffee shop more lucrative.

Lies. All of them. But Annalise knew Tyler well, and Tyler would spin it that way in a heartbeat. In the words of her very eternally focused Aunt Tracy, *"Lord Jesus, come quickly!"*

Annalise recited the words in her head. She actually didn't mean them. If Jesus came now, it might have a good effect on a few, but biblically speaking, it meant an apocalypse for the multitude. She wouldn't wish that on anyone.

Annalise shot back a quick OK to Brent in text form. What more could she say? She leaned forward and reached for her second coffee of the day, perched on the desktop calendar on her desk. Her office was her sanctuary, her respite, her place to collect wayward thoughts and put them in some semblance of order. It was her—

"Q?"

Her coffee sloshed through the sip hole of its lid as Annalise jumped. She snapped her head up, sucking a puddle of coffee from her hand that was dripping down to her wrist.

Annalise's eyes met Garrett's. So much for her private sanctuary. "Yes?" She tipped her head and waited.

Garrett's arms were crossed, his forearms heavily corded from hours of climbing. She could see chalk dust embedded in the corners of his fingernails. The desk stood between them. A cornfield, no, an ocean would have been preferable.

"I thought you deserved to know why I came back."

So much for her ocean.

"I do know."

Garrett's brow raised in question. His strong jawline curved toward a chin with a crease down its middle. He hadn't shaved in maybe two days. Chestnut brown hair was floppy on top with sides haphazardly trimmed. The guy was sloppy, but he sure smelled good. Nutmeg, or apple pie, or something.

"You came back to help Nicole ramp up the tourism economy

in Gossamer Grove. Make yourself a happy little place for all your climbing buddies to hang. Literally." Annalise crossed her own arms, but her right hand gripped her coffee as if it were a lifeline.

Garrett shook his head. "Nope. Nic doesn't need my help. And professionals wouldn't come here to climb." He didn't say it arrogantly, just as fact. Apparently, the resort wouldn't be professional climbing caliber.

Annalise took the moment to sip her coffee. "Okay, then why?"

Garrett shifted his weight and jammed his hands into the pockets of his shorts. She couldn't help but notice his calves. Built. The guy was built. Better than her senior year of high school. This must be what over ten years on the professional climbing circuit did to a man. Rock solid—no pun intended.

"Larson contacted me for my expertise in helping design and run his wilderness center. He wants to put in a climbing gym and a zip line. Maybe lead bouldering tours—there are great boulders in the woods near the park. I'm not getting any younger."

"Thirty-one is old?" Annalise raised an eyebrow.

Garrett shrugged. "In competition? It's getting there. I'm competing against nineteen-year-old brutes. Their climbing skills are sick. I need a plan for the rest of my life."

"No more sleeping in decked-out vans and climbing cliffs in Switzerland?" Annalise took another sip of her coffee.

"You followed my career?" Garrett asked.

Annalise choked. Darn it. "No. Yes. I mean, it's hard not to when you're practically the town's pride and joy. Garrett Greenwood, continuing the great line of Gossamer Grove Greenwoods. Medaling in competitions and exploring Europe and Asia. You're hard to ignore."

"I'm hard to ignore?"

Annalise closed her eyes and forced herself to take a deep, controlled breath. When she opened her eyes, Garrett's expression was searching.

"I don't want trouble, Q. Neither does Nic. We just want to

go about life fair and square, okay? The wilderness center will be good for the town, for the people who visit for our outdoor elements here in Gossamer Grove. It'll get people into physical stuff and away from technology."

It dawned on Annalise. Very clearly. The decision for the property and the wilderness center had already been made, just not formalized. There would be no land for a shelter, no acknowledgment of the great need shared by those who'd been ostracized by the community.

"I understand." Her voice came out in a whisper, squeezed by the tension of tears.

"Listen—"

"No. I'd rather not." She made pretense of organizing paper clips in the tray on her desk. She needed him to go away, before tears slipped out and shamed her. Before Garrett discovered how wounded she still was, and how the past was anything but resolved.

"Q . . ."

She sniffed and pushed the paper clips into a pile. "The great Greenwoods. Always looking out for Gossamer Grove." She bit her lip as it quivered, glancing up at him. "And ignoring the little people."

Annalise Quintessa Forsythe may sound lofty, but her parents had failed miserably. Owning a reputable law firm still hadn't been enough to compete with the Greenwoods' hierarchy of banking, industrial factory, and four generations of mayors.

She reached for her planner and a pen, under pretense of returning to work. "Goodbye, Garrett."

There was no resolution in ignoring him as he left her office, silent and without apology.

CHAPTER 8

"Can I get into the trailer?" Annalise knew Brent would tell her no, but she had to ask anyway. "Well?" she pressed him.

"No." Brent crossed the linoleum kitchen floor, his plaid flannel pajama pants matching his ruffled hair.

Annalise swung her attention to Christen, who sat on a stool at the breakfast bar.

"Why can't she?" Christen challenged her man.

Brent leaned against the counter. "You two are like bulldogs. Let up, okay? I don't have the authority to let you into Eugene Hayes's private property, and we don't know COD yet."

"You said he died of a heart attack," Annalise argued.

Brent shrugged. "Sure, that's what the ME thinks. But until we have it official, we don't know."

"Oh gawsh, you don't think he was murdered, do you?" Christen squirmed on her stool, peeling her breakfast orange.

Christen's question may have been flippant and offhanded, but Annalise chilled at the idea. She sank onto the stool next to Christen.

Brent cleared his throat and gave them both a stern eye. "Listen, you two. I can't discuss the case details with you outside of what I've already questioned you on. I'm not even the lead investigator. And I absolutely cannot grant you clearance to snoop around the

51

old man's trailer—not that you'd want to. It stinks like nothing else."

"I want to," Annalise said. "I want to see if I can figure out why he was photograph-stalking me. Doesn't that unnerve you? It's not *normal*. Brent, how did Tyler find out my pictures were plastered all over Eugene's place? This morning's paper was practically an exposé. And that random obituary paper-clipped to my *senior picture*?" She emphasized the last two words in hopes Brent would get her insinuation. Christen didn't know the repercussions of Annalise's eighteenth year, and Annalise preferred it that way. But Brent did. And the picture paper-clipped to the obituary of some dead Greenwood ancestor could not be coincidental. The old man had linked her to the Greenwoods, though why a dead one was important, she had no clue.

Brent looked away. Good. He'd gotten her point. She couldn't afford to have the newspaper digging into the significance of that.

"Well?" Christen broke the awkward silence. "How *did* the paper find out?"

Brent swung his attention to his wife. "I don't know. Someone probably unintentionally leaked it. Gossamer Grove is a small town. It happens."

"Sue for libel." Christen snapped her fingers.

Annalise rolled her eyes and sighed. "That'll make it all better."

"Well?" Christen shrugged. "Tyler needs to know he tiptoes on the edge of slander."

"So does the *National Enquirer* and they've never been stopped," Brent muttered.

"They're still in print?" Christen's tone was incredulous.

"I think so." Brent popped an orange slice into his mouth.

"Oh. Well, I read *People*, so . . ." Christen left her sentence hanging.

"Point made. That type of journalism isn't going away." Annalise leaned forward, trying to soften the panic in her voice. Her old friend met her gaze, and she knew Brent recognized the anxiety that rested there. "I can't have my name smeared through the mud—not before I put up a fighting chance against Doug Larson for the town property." Not that it would make a difference now. "This is important to me. For people like Eugene Hayes who need recognition in this overly proud community. We have a homelessness issue, and it's growing."

Christen shifted in her seat to address Annalise. The citrus scent of her orange drifted into Annalise's nose and refreshed her senses, if not her nerves. "Why does it really matter, Annalise? People know your intentions are good. It's not like you're hiding anything, right?"

Annalise looked down at her fingernails.

Brent choked on the glass of water he'd just swallowed. He set his glass on the counter. Diversion. Christen swung her attention back to him.

"If I were you, Annalise," Brent said, controlling the conversation, "I'd look into who Harrison Greenwood was. The man mentioned in the obituary. That's what the newspaper would do first. See if there's any tie to you, or why Eugene Hayes would've had reason to try to link you to that man specifically."

"Linked to an old obituary?" Christen shivered and plopped an orange section into her mouth. Chewing, she continued, "That's super freaky. I mean, ghost freaky."

"There's no Greenwood ghost haunting me," Annalise mumbled, then bit her tongue. Well, it depended on if one meant actual spirits. The image of the man outside her bedroom window washed over her. She met Brent's eyes. Fine. Slipping off the stool, Annalise nodded.

"Okay. That makes sense." She accepted the clue Brent was subtly handing her. If Eugene Hayes was fascinated by her—which the pictures of her more than implied—then he had to have somehow connected her to a yellowed old obituary and a tent revival.

Annalise could read the message in Brent's eyes. *Find the answer before the paper does.*

"That's all I can do for you." Brent's statement chilled Annalise. All he could do? The newspaper edging its way into her past, random old artifacts that appeared to mean nothing, and Garrett Greenwood returning to town? She needed something—a miracle. Her regimented world was collapsing by the second, and her only option was to research what Harrison Greenwood, the man who died in 1907, had to do with her? More than likely, he had more to do with Garrett, and that made it all so much worse.

CHAPTER 9

Libby

A low fog settled over the grassy lawn by Gossamer Pond, with the moon a half slit in the sky. Within a few days it would be a moonless sky, like the pall the funeral earlier that day had left over the town. The evening breeze sent a chill through Libby as she paused. The outline of a large tented structure rose alongside the pond, its frame imposing and new. Dusk outlined the rectangular tent, its canvas a dark gray with the front doors pulled wide and fastened back to invite souls inside. Ropes stretched from the corners and midpoints of the structure to wrap around metal posts hammered into the ground. It was almost like a circus tent, only this wasn't the Big Top, and the entertainment was a different kind of show. It was spiritual.

Residents of Gossamer Grove lined up their various forms of transportation in the field just west of the tent. Motorcars, wagons, carriages, and some lone horses. Men, women, and children alike all gravitated toward the tent's entrance. Libby knew they were a mixture of curiosity, faith, and trepidation. Tent revivals had been sweeping the nation the last few years and had finally made their way to Gossamer Grove in the form of Jedidiah and

Jacobus Corbin. Since the mid-nineteenth century, people such as D. L. Moody and Billy Sunday had been shaking up people's eternal security. Some, like Moody, seemed well received, with church revival spreading rampantly. Others, like Sunday, were stirring controversy with unscripted tirades from a mouth straight from the baseball field instead of the seminary.

Mitch had told her one paper he'd read said Sunday was so "raw" that they refused to print his words. He used language unfit for feminine dispositions, and even some men were so stricken by his preaching, they were taken from the tent on stretchers, having swooned like a female whose corset was tied too tight.

Libby narrowed her eyes, attempting to catch a glimpse of the Reverends Corbin through the bright lantern-lit inside of the meeting place. Supposedly, the twin brothers had traveled with Sunday for a while and now had struck out to evangelize on their own. Hopefully, tonight's female attendees had loosened their corsets—assuming the Corbin brothers had picked up on Sunday's bad habits.

The smell of kerosene from the lamps was pungent as she neared the meeting place. Libby searched for Mitch, but there were so many in attendance, she couldn't find him. The message he'd left with Paul to have her join him at the tent revival meeting left her scrambling to help finish proofs on the articles going to press that night. She gave Paul a timid reminder to be prepared for Mitch to come busting through the doors at midnight with a special report on the revival. Paul's sneer told Libby all she needed to know about how he felt about that.

Libby caught a glimpse of Old Man Whistler, the town drunk. She was taken aback that he would even be here, and yet it stood to reason, she supposed. The Corbin brothers were a curiosity.

Whistler brushed alongside her, his shaking elbow knocking into her arm as his knuckles gripped the bulbous end of his cane.

"Come to get yerself saved?" he cackled, and Libby tried to hide her repulsion toward the old man and his musty breath.

"I already am, thank you." She moved a step away.

Old Man Whistler chuckled. "I've a feeling we all will be after tonight. Unless we want to hang along with Deacon Greenwood. Even the good can't hide their sin forever, you know."

The elderly man gave her a sideways glance before leaving her behind. Libby swallowed hard. Hide their sin? She watched him wobble toward the tent's doorway. Old Man Whistler probably should not be underestimated. He was a wanderer, and wanderers saw things—*knew* things. His remark struck close to the obituary's heart. The insinuation of hidden sins. But, Deacon Greenwood's slate was so clean, even Mitch had never been able to find a speck of dust on it.

Libby startled as a grating shriek erupted from inside the tent. Gracious, there was an organ! The music began to play, and the shivering tones and airy puffs from the pump organ blasted from the door. Row upon row of attendees lined two sides of the tent with an aisle down the middle covered in sawdust. Libby should have come earlier to find Mitch. There was no way she would now. She stretched up on her tiptoes, but the sea of bowler hats, feathers, bonnets, and bare heads made identifying anyone nearly impossible. The sun had almost completely gone down, and even now, little children were being shushed as ushers made their way up the aisle indicating they were not to disturb with whining and crying.

Libby moved to the other side of the tent, hoping she could edge her way inside and find an unobtrusive spot to stand along the canvas wall. It was hot inside the tent, stuffy with the smells of perfume, sweat, and fresh sawdust. She fumbled with the neckline of her blouse, tempted to remove the cameo brooch and unbutton the lace at her throat.

The organ music whined to a halt.

Silence.

Someone coughed. A child whimpered and was quickly shushed. Libby strained to see the front. A modest stage, a pulpit, and . . .

"Sin!" The deep voice branded the atmosphere with authority.

"It will deceive you. It will drag you to the depths of hell with the claws of demons leading the way."

Libby froze. The vivid picture the Corbin brother drew had the entire meeting place holding their collective breath. Trepidation spread uninvited through the shelter.

Jedidiah Corbin was a man of medium height, with lamb-chop whiskers along his cheeks and wavy brown hair parted down the middle. He couldn't be much older than Libby. His early thirties perhaps. The flyer advertising tonight's event identified this twin as the eldest. His brother, Jacobus, was very obviously missing from attendance.

He stalked across the platform. "The darkness that festers in our souls is like a poison that, but for the grace of God, cannot be squeezed from our hearts."

Libby scanned the crowd around her, twisting the material of her dress in her hands. Running was implausible, but preferable to being here. There was no comfort—no conviction—in the words. Merely impending doom and destruction. Jedidiah Corbin might as well have combined his message with Edgar Allan Poe's poetry, and the congregation would have barely been able to tell the difference.

She jumped as Corbin's foot stomped on the platform.

"But the grace of God is real!" Corbin's gravelly voice rose with intensity, and he flung his arm forward as if throwing a baseball. "It is the damnable misrepresentation of theology that allows us to sin and wait until we lay on our deathbeds, gasping for our last breaths, to lay penitent before the Lord. That a whore can continue in her sin with a backward confession to cover the last evening's errancy. That a drunkard may swallow his liquor along with a prayer. That a thief can pocket coins from the offering plate while admitting other sins to his priest. This hypocrisy is from the pit of the lake of fire and must cease before we hang ourselves from the rafters of a house built on lies!"

An audible gasp arose from the crowd. Whether from the language of curses and vulgar frankness mixed with grace or the reference to hanging, Libby wasn't sure. Murmurs and heads turned toward each other. Libby's throat closed with the claustrophobic reality that Reverend Jedidiah Corbin danced on the circumstances of Deacon Greenwood's death.

"May we not die a sinful wretch unforgiven!"

No more. Please, no more.

Libby shoved through the people toward the tent opening. Her breaths came in short, suffocating gasps. The black sky outside, with only the tiny shaft of moon to light the banks of the pond, held little escape from this sense of being squeezed. She hurried to the pond's bank, staring into glowing waters.

"Libby."

She shrieked. Spinning around, her arms wrapped across her chest, she squinted in the darkness at the form that had come up behind her. She glanced toward the pond, a deep gray reflection rippling in the water. Being trapped between the water and the shadowy form was intimidating.

The man tipped his head, and as he did, his face turned into the shaft of moonlight.

"It's you." Libby's breath released in a *whoosh*. She stepped toward him, away from the bank.

"Who did you think it was?" Elijah frowned. "I was almost certain you intended to launch yourself into the pond."

"The thought did cross my mind, but of course that would be nonsensical, and it wouldn't help a soul." Libby abruptly ended her nervous chatter. Her skin had broken out into little bumps.

"I noticed you escaped the revival." Elijah looked back toward the tent. "I had to as well."

Libby nodded. "It was quite . . . well, I wasn't finding myself drawn to salvation. Maybe if I'd stayed I would have. I mean, it's not that I'm not saved as it is, but if I weren't—if I didn't believe in God—I mean, the crucifixion and resurrection of Christ—then I would be going to hell, I suppose." She stumbled to a halt. Elijah was not standing before her to inquire about the state of her eternal soul.

"Why are you here?" She sought for an avenue of escape from her scattered thoughts.

Elijah took a step closer to the pond, and he watched its dark outline for a moment. "My father was to give the closing prayer." His quiet voice, so matter-of-fact, explained why a grieving son would attend a revival meeting on the day of his father's funeral. Not that it would have been enough of a reason to give Libby the compulsion to attend, but Elijah was, after all, a Greenwood. They stood on principle, not feelings.

"Elijah—"

"Don't, Libby." His voice dropped an octave, thick with memories and truths long buried between them. Elijah turned to her. His dark eyes were troubled, his newsboy cap tugged down over his hair. "I need to clean up after my father's affairs. To take over the mill and get it in order. I cannot—" He seemed to struggle to find words. "I cannot pick at an open wound with suggestions of foul play over my father's own cowardice toward life."

"That's unfair," Libby dared reprimand him. Elijah gave her a sharp look. "One never knows why a person determines to end his life before God chooses. Perhaps there was heartbreak, a sense of lost direction, or maybe—*maybe*—burdens weighted him down. You mustn't speak with such judgment toward your father."

She floundered. But it hadn't been suicide, had it? She knew it. So, if he were honest with himself, did Elijah.

Elijah's jaw worked back and forth in the darkness. She could see the sharp outline of his chin, the cleft there, and the sad lack of joy at the corners of his eyes. Libby tried again, mustering the courage to confront the man she far preferred to stay in the shadow of.

"The obituary—"

"No." Elijah held up his hand.

"But, you cannot discount it!" Libby insisted. "Why would you want to discount it? If it means your father's life was taken against his will—if someone determined to remove him from this world for feelings of ill will or perhaps a personal vendetta?"

"Oh, the questions! Don't forget, Libby, what of the note? In the straw? Did my father have secrets? What man doesn't, I ask? Must he die for them? Or take his own life for them?" Elijah's voice rose, and he stifled his outburst by running his palm across his mouth and looking beyond Libby toward something unseen. Finally, he met her eyes, the moonlight reflecting in his pupils. "I'm not in a place where I can—where I can contemplate it."

How very selfish! Libby swallowed back her ire and tried to temper her voice. The words came in a nervous stutter. "W-whyever not? You're willing to risk another life if they were to strike again by pretending your father's death was not by another's hand?"

Elijah tugged his hat down and sniffed. An awful silence was covered by the sound of the impassioned speech of Corbin in the distance and frogs peeping their night song at the pond's edge. Then the organ started playing, its shaky tones wafting eerily over the night sky with the confessional tune of "What a Friend We Have in Jesus."

She wished Elijah would say something—anything. But he pushed his hands in his trouser pockets instead. Libby couldn't read his face in the darkness of the night. His shoulders were tense, but finally he drew a deep breath in through his nose and let it out through his mouth. His words were grave, his tone deep, telling, and all too knowing.

"When, dear Libby, have you ever been concerned how others' lives may be affected by another's choice?"

It was an unfair question. Hurtful. But burdened with truth all at the same time. Elijah leaned forward, his breath against her face, and his mouth inches from her nose.

"This is what we do. We continue on. We forget what has happened and look toward the future."

"This is . . . is, well, it's *murder*. That's what it is! To pretend it's nothing is *cowardice*!" Libby knew she should not have said the words the moment they filtered from her lips.

Elijah's eyebrows shot upward. His hand lifted, and he brushed the back of her cheek with his knuckles. "And we both know that you and I are the worst sort of cowards."

His whispered words hung between them, bringing the horrid truth into the moment and damning their souls in the echoes of the tent revival.

CHAPTER 10

On any other almost pitch-black night, Libby would have been at peace to walk home alone. The warm spring air, the crickets chirruping, lightning bugs flickering as the road took her from the outskirts of town toward the center. But tonight their two-story home with the gables and scalloped trim and stained-glass windows would be a welcome sight. Restlessness gripped her, along with guilt. They were feelings she didn't want to explore—*hadn't* wanted to explore since her fifteenth year of life. Almost nine years later, just a whispered word from Elijah and it set her heart astir. So much. So much had gone wrong, and yet so much had thrust her into Elijah's life. Including the death of his father. The *murder* of his father, if he would only admit it, and if she'd not given him the obituary to secret away or destroy.

Libby clutched her dress, lifting it higher so she could hike faster and make it home. With the darkness pressing in, the imagery of Deacon Greenwood's body grew more real. So did the gravel beneath her shoes, the shivering branches of the trees, the shafts of moonlight that illuminated shadows she'd not have seen if the moon weren't peeking from behind a cloud.

Whoever had left that obituary at the paper had to know it'd been found. Had to know *she* had found it, for after all, it wasn't a secret she was the one to have discovered the body. It was simple deduction. The police might rule it a fluke, but not the killer. Not the person responsible for kicking the stool from beneath Deacon Greenwood's feet.

Libby hitched up her skirt and hurried faster. Alone on the country road from Gossamer Pond was not a place she preferred to be. Mitch must have scurried away from the revival meeting without her. He'd have a "stop the presses!" proclamation to sour-faced Paul, who would glare at his eccentric partner as Mitch slapped his indecipherable article on the desk. Elijah had disappeared into the throng. Townsfolk had already filtered past her, motor vehicles bouncing by, leaving her in a cloud of exhaust and dust. Carriages rolled past, wagons, and then Libby was very much alone. Lights from the tent behind her dimmed and went out. Someone was still there, yet no one she knew. It seemed everyone was so affected by Reverend Corbin's preaching that they hadn't the decency to pause and offer her transport.

Libby froze as a cat scurried across the road, its tail bushy and the fur on its back bristled as if escaping a foe. She fisted the green material of her dress, the flash of her white petticoat the only bright spot on the darkened lane. The trees rose thicker on either side of the lane, and although Libby could see fields to the east and the river winding to the west, the branches of the clusters of trees reminded her of skeletal arms poised to snatch her.

She picked up her pace, eyeing the bats that swooped and criss-crossed the lane in front of her. Their little black-winged bodies were catching mosquitoes, but Libby cringed as she hurried. They were like a bad omen, of something dark, someone evil, someone with intent to kill.

A squeaking tinny sound came out of the darkness behind her. Libby whirled on her heels and peered into the night from where she'd just traversed. The outline of a man astride a bicycle became clearer. His dark jacket billowed behind him as the wind picked up. The bicycle wobbled and metal clanked as the man neared her. A hat was tugged low over his face. Libby picked up her pace, spinning back toward town and stumbling over the uneven road.

But, within a moment, the two-wheeled contraption was beside her, rolling along, slowing pace to match her strides.

"Miss?"

She stumbled over a stick.

"Miss?" he repeated. His voice sounded familiar, but Libby had no desire to stop and identify who he was by squinting in the darkness.

"Please. I intend you no harm at all."

Of course not. Every killer probably said that before stabbing, shooting, or—heavens—*hanging* their victim.

The bicyclist stopped and lifted his leg over the seat. Libby reached up to snatch the hatpin from her hat. Let the hat fall to the ground and be trampled, she was not going to die without a fight. A hatpin could inflict damage if necessary.

"Stop!"

The command, the tone, the voice.

Libby froze.

Reverend Jedidiah Corbin was tall. She recognized the voice now. Recognized his frame in the dark. Or was it his brother, Jacobus? His lanky form reminded her a bit of a branchless sapling. The craggy lines of his face, the whiskers that frizzed from the chops that bordered his face, and the deep-set eyes were not particularly friendly. He seemed ageless yet also not old.

Libby shivered and wrapped her arms around herself. "Reverend." She acknowledged him but cast a wary glance around her. She readjusted the hatpin in her hand.

The reverend tipped his head, gripping the handlebars of the bicycle. "Jedidiah Corbin, miss."

He'd known she was wondering, although it was more than likely a common question considering he was an identical twin.

"You're alone. Quite disconcerting in this darkness." An eyebrow lifted as he read her fear like a book propped open for perusal. "And unwise," he added.

"I'm fine, thank you." Pitiable response. Libby stiffened her shoulders. She would not cower beneath the imposing judgment of a hellfire-and-brimstone preacher.

Shouldn't one feel safe in the presence of a godly man? And where was the man's twin? Rumor had it they were inseparable, riding a tandem bicycle everywhere. This was a single bicycle, however.

"Allow me to escort you home." Jedidiah Corbin tilted his head as if trying to see her features in the night.

"Thank you, but no." Libby resumed her pace. She squinted, trying to maneuver over the ruts in the road that she could barely see.

He ignored her dismissal but kept beside her, wheeling his bicycle over divots and stones in the path. "I would not be doing God's work to keep the weaker vessel safe if I allowed you to walk alone."

The weaker vessel? Libby considered using the hatpin still poised in her hand just to prove she wasn't helpless. But then, she wasn't convinced she *wasn't* helpless.

"I've heard rumblings about town this week as I prepared for tonight's service. My brother, Jacobus, indicated there was a death of one of your church leaders. Jacobus is ill tonight and could not be with us."

Libby wasn't concerned why the other twin wasn't there, but she did stifle a shiver as Jedidiah Corbin referred to Deacon Greenwood's untimely death. She let the revivalist's words remain unacknowledged. Maybe Libby was imagining it, but the grit in his voice seemed to take on a warning tone of a prophet who knew things everyone else did not.

"The circumstances around your deacon's death, of the question surrounding who he really was. It does not bode well for the future of this town. Without a foundation of confession and grace, it will all fall."

"I don't believe anyone is questioning who Deacon Greenwood really was," Libby muttered.

"No? I always believed that one who took his own life was a cavern filled with untold mysteries that drove him to that point."

"Perhaps." Libby didn't want to think on it. Didn't want to allow Reverend Corbin's words to remotely justify the insinuation in the obituary that Deacon Greenwood went to the grave with some sort of untold secret.

The reverend reached out, forcing her to stop. Surprised at the sudden grip, Libby stumbled and shrugged off his hold. Corbin released her, but his eyes, the pools of shadows around them, speared her like a ghost risen from the grave who had seen the pit of Hell. His hand rose and he pressed it against her cheek with the unwelcome burning of his palm.

"Unconfessed sin will always lead to death," he whispered. "May this not be so for you."

CHAPTER 11

Annalise

I f the dingy, gray, shingled siding on the trailer home wasn't bad
omen enough, the litter and debris piled on the built-on porch
was enough to send her back to her car. She really shouldn't be
here. But when she'd mapped out her schedule for the day, she'd
penciled it in. Yes. Always good to pencil in prospective trespassing onto one's list for the day. This was a dumb idea, but knowing
who Eugene Hayes was seemed just as important as finding out
about Harrison Greenwood from 1907. Who were these men and
how, or why, were they connected to her?

Annalise rolled her eyes at her hesitation and swatted a mos-
quito that buzzed its high-pitched warning in her ear. She took
determined steps forward, climbing the first step and avoiding a
hole in its wooden structure. She snuck across the sloping porch,
holding her breath at the pungent scent emanating from inside.
A mixture of old alcohol, filth, and rotten food made her gag.
Peering in a foggy window, Annalise squinted into the darkness
of the deserted trailer.

An old sofa, bowed in the middle, sat across the room under
a window with a long crack running through its top pane. A pile

of newspapers at least three feet high perched on one end of the couch, and next to them, books upon books littered the cushions and the floor. Annalise took her sweatshirt sleeve and wiped the glass, hoping to clear away some of the cloudiness on the window.

The floor was carpeted, and it looked very soiled. Although it was hard to tell, Annalise thought she saw patches of where it had worn thin, but even that was debatable with the floor covered in piles of magazines, newspapers, books, and garbage.

Annalise wasn't sure if she was appalled or horrified for the one who'd died in this infested hole. Eugene Hayes, whoever he was, couldn't possibly have deserved to pass away in this hovel, alone and surrounded by garbage. Even if he did have some weird fetish with her life, with her pictures, with her.

Cringing, she lifted her gaze from the floor to the walls and stiffened, like a stone gargoyle on a rotting porch with gaping mouth and wide eyes. Annalise lifted her hand and splayed her fingers across the glass, scrunching her face and pushing close until her nose kissed the pane. The thud of her heart echoed in her ears, and for a brief, unedited second, she cursed at Officer Brent Drury. He hadn't told her. Not this. The scope was far beyond a desktop.

Annalise's breath quickened as she swept her alarmed gaze across the inside of the trailer. Papered on the walls were photograph after photograph of Annalise. Her childhood, her teen years, her at the library, and, if Annalise was making it out clear enough through the filthy window, several of her with Garrett. This was a trailer turned into a nine-hundred-odd-square-foot bulletin board of her life!

She stumbled away from the sight, tripping over a bucket of rotting vegetables and fruit. The momentum took Annalise flailing through a spider web that stretched from a metal chair to the top rail of the porch. She barely cleared the steps in her backward catapult off the deck. Spinning, Annalise sprinted to her car, her eyes burning and her breaths coming shallow and fast.

Eugene Hayes's trailer was a shrine to her life. Her very candid, very photographed life. Annalise scurried into the front seat of her ride and slammed the door. She stared at the trailer, its decrepit state, and then twisted the key in the ignition. She needed to get away. She never should have come here. She never should have snooped, or looked, or tried to figure out what the connection was between her, a recluse, and a century-old obituary she read briefly on Brent's phone.

Her tires peeled in the gravel as she spun down the driveway toward the main road. If she hadn't come—hadn't *trespassed*— she could have forgotten. Maybe. At least that was probably why Brent hadn't told her the scope of the old, dead man's fixation. Did Tyler at the paper even have a clue how dramatically worse it was, even than what he'd reported on? This was far more than an old man she'd somehow overlooked in her mission to save Gossamer Grove's down-and-out. This was more than an elderly reject who was bored and made clip art for his scrapbook.

Annalise gripped the steering wheel as she turned onto the as- phalt and sped away from the gravel drive, the sequestered trailer, and the memories. This was personal. Far more personal than she'd considered. This was about her. About Garrett. All about a past she had carefully hidden away in a numerically coded date file in her memory. To be left untouched. Until Eugene Hayes ripped open the seal the day he died.

—◊—

The knock on the front door startled Annalise. She turned her attention from her laptop and the scanned newspaper document to glance at the wall clock.

Seven-thirty in the morning. Saturday. It wouldn't be Christen. She always played with her kids on Saturdays and cleaned the house. Annalise tugged her gray T-shirt over her hips as she padded to the door. She didn't need visitors. Her restless evening scouring the internet for anything she could find on Eugene Hayes, Harrison

Greenwood, and even the revival meetings in Gossamer Grove in 1907 had melted into a fitful sleep. Dreams of the dilapidated trailer and being trapped inside were only made worse by opening her eyes and staring at her dark ceiling, knowing real photographs of her still wallpapered the dead man's house.

Annalise pressed her eye against the peephole in the door, then squeezed it shut. Groaning deep in her throat, she flipped the lock and yanked open the door. "Yes?"

Garrett didn't even have the heart to try to appear sheepish. He lounged against the doorjamb as if he'd wait all day for her to open and let him in. Infinite patience. Well, she knew better. Garrett Greenwood had never been patient. He'd been reckless, bold, and—

"I ran out of coffee."

—and stupid.

"Well then." Annalise crossed her arms over her chest. "There's a super nice coffee shop downtown that makes a killer latte. Or a Target about three miles from here. They sell Folgers."

"Folgers? I'd rather drink mud."

"Oh, you have that too, in your backyard. I think you're well supplied." Annalise moved to close the door, but Garrett's strong grip shot out and grabbed hold of it. His brow furrowed in that half begging, half patronizing way he had that always melted her.

"C'mon, Q, don't be mean. I can smell it. You have Guatemalan brewed, don't you?"

"You can tell the flavor?" Annalise tried not to be impressed.

Garrett shrugged. "It's not hard. You always liked Guatemalan, and you never change habits."

Annalise bit her tongue, then stepped to the right so he could enter. She noted the way he glanced around as he made his way through the Victorian home's foyer and into the kitchen where her laptop was still open on the table. Annalise edged past him and shut the lid.

"I had no idea you were still living here." For once there was a note of apology in his voice, as if Garrett wanted her to believe he really hadn't meant to infringe on her privacy when he returned and bought the significantly less impressive house beside hers.

Annalise reached into the cupboard and pulled out a red mug. "Mom and Dad moved to Arizona. I offered to buy them out."

"They made you buy your own house?" Garrett asked.

Annalise ignored the flip in her stomach. The one that always made it ache when she considered it too long. Not even a discount or a *We're sorry we can't afford to just give it to you*. No. It had all been a business deal. As if they weren't her parents and she their only child. It'd been that way ever since. . . .

Garrett's question went unanswered. Annalise poured him a cup of coffee and handed him the mug. Garrett took it, and his fingers grazed hers. They both stilled. Annalise met his eyes, brown and unguarded. He searched hers as if looking for answers to long-buried questions.

She snatched her hand back. "You can take the mug with you. Just leave it on the porch and I'll get it later."

"Just like that?" Garrett's eyes shuttered.

Annalise swallowed and pressed her palm on the table next to her to steady herself. "Yes. Just like that."

His eyes never left her face as he tipped the mug to his mouth. Bringing it down, he nodded. "So much for neighborly."

Neighborly.

They'd crossed that boundary line years ago.

"I asked you to leave me alone." Annalise sank into the chair and pulled her laptop toward her, lifting the lid. "I have work I need to do." Her words didn't come out as firm as she'd hoped. In fact, she heard the wobble in her own voice.

Garrett, in typical Greenwood fashion, must have determined to do his own thing regardless. He pulled out a chair and swung it around next to her, plopping onto it and staring at her screen before she had the sense to slam it shut again.

"Researching my great-great-grandfather?"

Annalise's gaze shot to his. "I like to study history."

"Greenwood history." It was more of a statement with doubtful undertones than an actual question. A strand of deep brown hair the color of coffee fell across Garrett's forehead, mimicking the way his muscular body straddled the chair. Relaxed, confident, and haphazard.

"Are you trying to dig up dirt to use against us?"

"What would that accomplish?" Annalise sighed and flipped open her computer. Anything to avoid looking at him. "I'm not sure anyone in Gossamer Grove gives two hoots about anyone from 1907, even if they were a Greenwood."

"It's no secret you're up against Doug Larson for your shelter, and Nicole is the one who'll tip the balance in the decision-making process. Tyler's newspaper article about that old guy's trailer and your pictures make it sound like you just might be profiting off the food pantry more than looking out for those in need."

Of all the nerve! Annalise reared back and leveled her most incredulous look on Garrett. "If you knew me at all, you'd never suggest that!"

Garrett slurped his coffee, completely unaffected as he stared at the laptop. "I never suggested it. My mom mentioned it."

His mom? Oh. Right. Annalise relaxed only slightly. She'd run into Mrs. Greenwood yesterday after her chaotic dash back from Eugene Hayes's creepy old trailer. The woman had been standing in line behind Annalise at the library and heard her inquiring about genealogy archives. Annalise tried to block the black-dagger glare from her memory.

"Well, your mom has always loved me." The irony in her voice wasn't missed by Garrett. He shifted in his chair. The first sign of discomfort.

"There are a lot of people in Gossamer Grove who agree with you—that a homeless shelter should be built instead of Larson's wilderness center."

Annalise didn't respond, but began to scroll down the web page featuring an article from some archive about Harrison Greenwood and the start of his flour mill in 1890.

"You're not trying to do any damage to Nic, are you?"

Annalise's head flew up. "Me? Digging up stuff from 1907 to smear Nicole's name, and what? Get her impeached for not giving land to the homeless shelter?"

"Can you impeach a mayor?"

"Seriously, Garrett. I'm not giving up hope your sister hasn't already signed on the line for Larson to take that property. But I wouldn't stoop so low as to dig up dirty secrets on your family."

Not to mention, she wouldn't have to dig very far.

"Then why're you researching my ancestor?"

"You must have read the paper." Annalise danced around his question. "My pictures were all over the trailer. Your ancestor's obituary was there, along with other historical documents." She alt-tabbed the browser and stared at the Greenwood family tree she'd begun to create on the popular website. A leaf dotted the top right corner of Harrison Greenwood's name. All those historic documents she had already perused and yet none of them seemed to help her draw any conclusions as to why his death would some-how be linked to her in the mind of Eugene Hayes.

"Eugene Hayes was an old man, Q. He probably just had ran-dom stuff littered all over."

"And seven hundred pictures of me," she mumbled. Annalise clicked on one of the graphics stating *Obituary* by Harrison Green-wood's name. She ignored Garrett, and they sat in companionable silence. Her eyes skimmed the words, though something pricked in the back of her mind. Annalise zoomed in on the obit.

"Weird," she muttered.

"What?"

"Harrison's obituary. I swear the one online in the public records system is different from the one Brent showed me in the picture from Eugene Hayes's home."

Garrett peered over her shoulder. Well, if that wasn't disconcerting. Annalise edged away.

"Looks like a regular obit to me."

She nodded. "It does. Straight. Factual. To the point."

"'Deacon Harrison Greenwood, owner of Greenwood Mill, and active member of the First Baptist Church, died yesterday at his home. The respected church elder and local business owner will be remembered with fondness for the solidarity he shared with Gossamer Grove citizens.'" Garrett finished reading and gave her a quizzical look. "I don't see a problem."

Annalise slipped from her chair under pretense of getting herself more coffee. "The problem is . . ." she said, watching the liquid brew slosh into her pottery mug, its hues of teal and emerald green swirled in the dark gray hardened clay. "The one Brent showed me was more prolific. Full of prose. Like a creepy early Victorian obituary."

"What'd it say?" Garrett leaned casually back in his chair.

Annalise took a drink of her coffee and toyed with a dish towel. Maybe sharing this with Garrett was a bad idea, but then, if he could fill in some of the holes, maybe she could put this whole mystery to rest sooner rather than later. And dispel the imagery in her mind of the trailer, a dead man, and shadows in the bushes.

"I don't remember what it said exactly. But they weren't the same. I know it." That discrepancy, along with her pictures, and the yet barely researched revival meeting had Annalise's brain spinning in a thousand different directions with zero chance of arriving at any solution that would make her feel better.

"So, don't take this wrong," Garrett said and set his empty mug on the table, "but I don't think you should waste your time researching it. Historical records are known for being inconsistent. Who cares if your picture was alongside my great-great-grandfather's? I mean, Eugene was probably just trying to cause more trouble between our families. If he was following you and your mission for the pantry and the shelter, maybe *he* was the one trying to dig up dirt to undermine my sister. You *are* kind of going up against Nicole. Brilliant move."

The sarcasm in his last comment made Annalise's guard rise to full height. She flipped the dish towel away from her and stalked over to where Garrett had set his mug on the table. Snatching it, she marched back to the sink and plunked it down. "Brilliant move because all your sister cares about is the Gossamer Grove economy and tourism and how we can make money."

"That's bad?"

"It is when people like Eugene Hayes, people with pasts and things that have held them back in life, are overlooked!"

"Like you?" Garrett's words speared her, and Annalise bit down on her bottom lip. Hard. But emotion made her chin quiver, and she shook her head.

"One of the pictures of me in Eugene's trailer?" Annalise paused to make sure she had Garrett's attention. "It was the night of your campfire. Remember that night?"

Color leached from Garrett's face. He shifted his feet.

Annalise shook her head and pursed her lips against any feeling other than sheer defense. "It all means *something*. Harrison Greenwood, that revival meeting in 1907, and me. Eugene Hayes was watching me. Watching *us*."

Garrett's silence communicated more than if he'd whispered a word. Annalise discarded her coffee mug in the sink next to his and stared at the two cups. Together, but starkly different. One pottery and one plain red. Yet their contents had been the same. Shared. Like her and Garrett's memories.

CHAPTER 12

Mathematics made sense to Annalise. She appreciated that two plus two always equaled four. There were no variables, no curve balls, no being blindsided by a random number winging its way into the equation. People often said she should have been an accountant, but if she hadn't gone into business for herself, she would have chosen to be a librarian. Not for the books either. It was the Dewey Decimal System that inspired her. It was orderly.

Too bad life didn't take a lesson from it.

"I don't understand." Annalise ran her fingers through her wavy hair, sending red flyaway strands tickling her eyes. She smoothed them back and shot Brent and Christen a glance. Christen probably reflected what Annalise herself looked like. Pale, stunned, and more than a little confused.

The lawyer exchanged looks with Brent but addressed Annalise. "Eugene Hayes has no family listed in his will. His full estate has been left to you."

Annalise shook her head. "I heard you the first time. I just—I just don't understand why a stranger would plaster the walls of his trailer with my photographs and then leave me his belongings."

Brent frowned. "How did you know about the photographs on the walls?"

Annalise stilled. Oh boy. She'd blown her trespassing. "Umm . . ."

"Never mind." Christen waved off her husband, ever the cop. "I'm with Annalise. This is verging on ludicrous. Was the old man a stalker?" She twisted in her wooden chair in the police station conference room and faced her husband. "Was Annalise in danger from him? Is she still in danger?"

"Whoa, whoa." The lawyer held up his hands. "Let's not get ahead of ourselves."

Annalise leaned against the wall and crossed her arms over her chest. This after-work meeting with the lawyer was not at all what she'd expected. It was blindsiding.

"I agree." She needed to reel in the conversation, capture the facts, and somehow process it all through a logical lens. Not this emotionally enhanced fear of a dead man and his obsessive legacy. Annalise pushed off the wall.

"Why me?" she asked.

The lawyer shook his head and rearranged the papers in front of him on the table. "Mr. Hayes didn't specify. Only that his entire estate—which isn't much, I might add—is to be left to Annalise Quintessa Forsythe."

"When was the will composed?" Brent interjected. Annalise was thankful he was here, that Christen was here, that she wasn't alone.

"A few months ago."

"And his previous will?" Brent pressed.

The lawyer shrugged. "It doesn't appear he had one. No living relatives. No next of kin. Nothing. He created the will through an online agency."

"But should she be afraid?" Christen speared her husband with a look that stated she'd commit crimes on Annalise's behalf if necessary.

Brent shook his head. "Chris, you're not helping."

"Eugene Hayes is dead, and Annalise says his trailer is a veritable shrine to her. You don't find that the least bit weird? For crying out loud, you're a cop." Christen slugged Brent's arm, but there was also a hint of a tender, teasing smile that touched her lips.

Annalise let Christen fight her battle. Her brain was spinning in circles with no clear beginning or end.

"Listen." Brent shifted in his chair. He was about ready to go on duty, his police uniform evidence of the fact. "It was determined Mr. Hayes's COD was natural causes. His heart."

"But everything about him is suspicious, honey," Christen said. "His trailer was wallpapered with Annalise's face."

"Which you've stated at least two times already, and which the info about the pictures on the wall was never released to the public." Brent gave Annalise a look that told her she should be brought up on trespassing charges—if she didn't own the property. "Don't be a conspiracy theorist. He might have been an old man with a weird obsession with Annalise because of the food pantry."

But the squint of Brent's eyes told Annalise his words were merely glossing over his own doubts and suspicions. Their eyes met. Annalise held her old friend's gaze until he dropped his.

Annalise directed her attention to the lawyer. "So, the trailer is mine now?"

The lawyer nodded. "Yes, ma'am. And the half acre it sits on."

"That was all Eugene Hayes owned?"

The lawyer folded his hands and met Annalise's eyes. "I'm sorry, but he didn't have anything of real monetary value outside of the tiny piece of land. Even that isn't worth much."

"No, of course not." Annalise noted the key that the lawyer extended to her. It lay in the palm of his hand, and she reached out to take it. "I can go back, then—I mean, I can go to the trailer?" She directed her attention back to Brent.

His brow furrowed. He studied her face for a moment, then gave a slow nod. "You can. But I'd advise caution."

"Why?" she asked. If he knew something—anything—that he wasn't telling her about the man's death, he needed to bring her in on it. Now.

"It's never smart to go to secluded places on your own."

"Case closed?" she challenged.

Brent stretched his neck from side to side, and she heard it crack. He gave her an imploring look. "The case is closed on Eugene's death. Yes." His words were laden with meaning.

"Thank you." Annalise stuffed the key in her pocket. She slung her purse over her shoulder and offered the room's occupants a hesitant smile. "I'll see you later."

"Annalise, wait!"

Christen's cry and the *clap-clap* of her tennis shoes against the linoleum floor followed Annalise. Outside the conference room, Annalise hooked her thumb around her purse's shoulder strap and waited.

Christen hurried up to her, her glasses askew on her face. "What are you going to do?"

"I'm going to go home, get some sleep tonight, and then go to Eugene's trailer in the morning. I'm going to find out what he knew about me, who he was to me, if anything, and what it all has to do with Harrison Greenwood and 1907." Annalise heard the decisiveness in her voice. She sounded way more confident than she felt.

"What if you can't find anything?" Christen's voice dropped, resonating the nervous energy Annalise was trying to suppress.

"I'll find something." Annalise's mind raced to the picture of the campfire at Garrett's house. "I'll dig until I do."

"What about your job? The food pantry? Your proposal for the shelter?" Christen argued.

Annalise adjusted her purse and leveled a determined gaze on her friend. "None of it will mean anything once this hits the *Daily Democrat*. The destitute old man not only collected photographs of me but left me his home? That's irony in and of itself. Tyler will twist that into a desperate last effort by a dying man to give the pilfering benefactress one last stab. Not only did I do nothing for him, but he died of neglect and abandonment right under my nose. I can bid farewell to any supporters who may still back the food pantry and my proposal. I can't let Tyler or anyone else twist anything more than they already have."

Christen rested a comforting hand on Annalise's arm. Her expression softened, searching Annalise's face. "What more could they uncover about you?"

Her words might have intended to be rhetorical and reassuring, but they weren't.

Annalise blinked. This was why she needed to research this alone. "Tyler will make up a story from practically anything."

—◆◆◆—

Annalise hit the garage door opener as she exited the garage, playing with her keys in the dark to identify her house key. She hiked up the brick walk to the front porch, the height of the Victorian house casting a gothic shadow over the yard.

"Lawyers," Annalise muttered. She really felt like dropping an extensive line of cusswords right now. Her purse slipped off her shoulder, and she yanked it back on, dropping her keys on the bottom porch step. A curse slipped out.

She needed to get herself under control. She was a mess. Snatching the keys from the step, Annalise hurried onto the porch and opened the screen door. Her life was spiraling completely out of control, like Dorothy's tornado on *The Wizard of* . . .

Annalise halted, her key poised to insert into the doorknob, but the door was already ajar. The opening of a few inches revealed the blackness of the interior of her home. She always left the light on in the foyer. Always. Not to mention she'd double-checked the door was locked before she left.

Tendrils of fear curled around her, and Annalise's heart increased its pace. She looked over her shoulder and did a quick survey of the yard, the bushes, and the shadows. Nothing. But the distinct feeling, that unnerving prick in her gut, made her speed up her mental assessment of what steps she'd taken before she left the house and compare that to how it looked now.

The door hadn't been pried open, and there was no sign of damage. Annalise distinctly recalled flicking on the entryway light switch and tugging the door shut with a firm latch that morning before work. It was her habit. Every morning. She was predictable, like Garrett said, and her habits rarely shifted.

She stepped back and let the screen door slam shut. Fumbling in her purse, Annalise found her phone. Was this a 911 scenario? Annalise backed away from the door. There wasn't any sign of anyone being inside now. It was pitch-black. Outside too. The moon was a sorry excuse for a light source tonight.

Annalise jogged back down the steps and the walk toward her garage. She stopped. What if someone had been in the garage when she pulled in? What if they were skulking behind the garbage can? She spun on her heel. This feeling of being watched, studied, *surveyed* was enhanced by the vision of Eugene Hayes's wall covered with her photographs.

Without a second thought, Annalise hurdled over the low bushes and sprinted into Garrett's yard and onto his porch. The much more modest house boasted a porch light—turned on even!—and a doorbell that begged to be rung. Annalise rammed her index finger against it while eyeing her house, as if some hulking figure might emerge from the inside.

Garrett's door opened. He looked like he'd just woken up, but then he always did. His hands were covered in chalk dust.

"Q." He stared at her. She'd caught him off guard this time. All was fair in love and war.

Annalise pushed past him into the living room.

Garrett shut the door, a confused expression plastered on his face. "What's going on?"

Annalise tossed her purse onto his couch and hugged her arms across her body. "I think someone broke into my house."

"What?" Garrett's brows went up quizzically, and he crossed the room to the kitchen window to glance outside toward her porch.

Annalise explained the open door that had greeted her on her arrival home. The dark interior with the entryway light no longer on.

Garrett rubbed his chalky hands down his tattered shorts, leaving white splotches against the black. "Let's call the cops." He reached for his cellphone.

Annalise leaned against the back of the couch, waiting. So maybe she wouldn't have been overreacting to call the police? She should have done that rather than engage Garrett's assistance. He'd think her helpless or that she needed him.

He ended the call. "Cops are on their way. We need to stay put until they get here." Garrett motioned toward the couch. "Have a seat. I was just in the basement on my salmon ladder. I need to go shut off the light."

"Your salmon ladder?" Annalise inquired, if only to distract herself.

"Yeah. Ever watch *American Ninja Warrior?*"

"No."

"*Arrow?*"

"Huh?" Annalise wasn't following.

"Never mind." He shook his head. "It's a ladder I use to build upper body strength."

"Oh." Annalise had no idea what he meant.

Garrett disappeared for a minute. On his return, he was pulling a sweatshirt over his head. His eyes were soft as he addressed her. "Let's head outside. The police will be here any second."

Annalise nodded and followed him outside. A cop car pulled up as they exited Garrett's house, and Brent stepped out along with his partner.

Thankfully, Brent happened to be on duty tonight and was the one who came. Welcome to Smalltown, USA, population four thousand—where everyone knew everyone, and the police force was just a handful of people.

——◊◊◊——

"Annalise, what the heck?"

"I don't know," she shrugged. "I got home and the door was open. I thought maybe I was just a bit too jumpy after tonight."

"After tonight?" Garrett interjected.

"So you went to Garrett?" Brent asked in disbelief at the same time.

Both men eyed each other. Annalise shifted on her feet. This was awkward. Brent gave her a look that said *What were you thinking?* And Garrett's shoulders stiffened.

Annalise waved her hand toward the house, frightened, tired, and exasperated all at the same time. "Can you just see if I'm going to be murdered tonight or if I can go into my house?"

Brent shot Garrett one last big-brother glare and then addressed his partner. "Check the perimeter. I'll check inside."

He approached the front door. In a few moments, lights popped on inside.

"What happened tonight?" Garrett asked, his hands in his pockets and his eyes on the lights turning on in the second story.

He wasn't going to let it go, was he? Annalise sighed through her nose. "Eugene Hayes happened."

Garrett had no reaction. Another light popped on in what would be the upstairs bathroom. "So, he's not going away, even though he's dead?"

"Nope." Annalise watched Brent's silhouette move past the window.

"What now?"

Annalise gave Garrett a sideways look. In the darkness of the night, his features were still strong, still attractive, and still so much trouble. "I inherited his property. He left it all to me."

Garrett's frown made him turn his head and stare at her. "Why?"

"I don't know."

"You're safe to come in!" Brent hollered from the front door, and Annalise pushed past Garrett. She nodded her thanks to Brent's partner, who returned to the police cruiser.

"I don't see anything that screams intruder." Brent assessed the house as Annalise entered. She hung her purse on the antique hall tree and eyed the entryway. Nothing off here.

"Do you see anything missing?" Brent followed her into the front parlor that doubled as her study. Annalise surveyed the room. Garrett entered behind them, silent.

"Everything looks fine here." Annalise moved past them, and they continued to check each room. Nothing. No damage, no vandalism, just . . . nothing. Annalise almost wished someone had poured sour milk all over the furniture and graffitied the walls. The *nothing* was more terrifying than if it had been *something*.

The three of them hiked up the stairwell and paused outside of Annalise's bedroom. She glanced at Garrett. Brent edged between them and again raised an eyebrow at Annalise. She ignored it and entered her room.

Her queen bed was undisturbed, the comforter in hues of greens and grays still pulled neatly in its place with the pile of solid-colored pillows carefully arranged just as she'd left them that morning. The curtains were pulled back and the shade pulled up. She remembered doing that first thing when she woke up, to see the sunrise and—if she were honest—to stare down at Garrett's bedroom window, and remember. Just for a moment.

She turned toward the men. Brent was alert and on guard, his stance stiff, and Annalise wondered if it was because of Garrett or because of the potential intruder. Garrett was impassive, his hands still in his pockets, and his eyes lidded and unreadable.

"Everything looks fine." Annalise wondered how she would ever sleep tonight. Both eyes would be open. Had Brent checked under the bed? She took a step away from it and eyed the dark chasm that lurked below the bed frame. An intruder brought a whole new meaning to the idea of a bogeyman under the bed. She glanced at her dresser, trying to recall if her pepper spray was still in her underwear drawer.

An empty spot on top of the dresser snagged her attention. Annalise stared, her chest weighted down with horror. She rushed past Brent and Garrett to the dresser.

"No." Her whisper was much louder than she'd intended. She

palmed the top of the dresser. Her earrings, her journal, her box of Kleenex. All still there. The jewelry tree with various necklaces dangling from it, the bookmark Christen had given her for Christmas, and next to it a glaring absence. The intruder, for there had been one, might as well have come inside and stabbed a knife through Annalise's pillow.

"What is it?" Brent's question echoed through her subconscious as she stared at the empty place.

She didn't answer—*couldn't* answer.

"Annalise?" Brent again. Insistent. His tone indicated that he knew she'd noticed something awry.

Annalise touched the empty void on the dresser.

"Annalise!"

She snapped out of her stupor and turned to Brent. "It's gone."

"What's gone? What's missing?" Brent urged.

Annalise looked beyond him and locked eyes with Garrett. His brows were pulled deep in question, and his eyes crinkled at the corners as if silently coaching her to tell them.

"They took it."

Garrett stepped toward her. "Took what, Q?"

His voice pulled at her. His eyes reminded Annalise of every moment, every look, every *everything*. She remembered the first and the last, she remembered the smiles and then the tears. Worst of all she remembered the tearing apart when her soul was torn into shreds.

"It's gone," she choked out, drilling her gaze into the man who had once meant everything to her. "They took the only one I had. They took the picture of our baby."

CHAPTER 13

Libby

"How did this get printed?" Paul smashed the morning's paper on the desk in front of her. Libby startled and for once was glad Mitch was beside her. She could tell Paul was fuming.

"How did what get printed?" Mitch didn't so much as flinch. He straightened from his position beside Libby where he'd been explaining a few of his unreadable scribbles to her for transcribing.

Paul stabbed the column with his index finger. "This—this nonsense about the Petersons!"

Mitch blinked as if bored and rested his hands at his waist. He eyed his partner with a bit of disdain, and once again Libby found herself pivoting between the two like watching a game of catch.

"It's the truth," Mitch shrugged.

Paul blustered, spun on his heel, took a few steps toward the office door, then whipped back around. He shook his finger at Mitch. "You're making a spectacle out of them!"

"I believe Mr. Peterson made a spectacle out of himself."

Libby had no idea what the two men were sparring about. She leaned over the paper and quickly read the short column.

Mr. Lowell Peterson was fined $25 for assault and battery com-
mitted against his wife. As told to the authorities, Mrs. Peterson
stated she desired to be in attendance at the revival meeting of the
Corbin twins, and Mr. Peterson heartily objected. The words led
to some slaps and a little choking, which provided her a reason for
her husband's subsequent arrest.

Libby lifted surprised eyes. Spousal abuse over the attendance
of a Christian revival? The idea was ludicrous, but considering
her disturbing walk home, not at all strange. Jedidiah Corbin's
message and his subsequent interaction with her was enough to
make her believe he was capable of twisting even solid minds awry.

"The violence ensuing because of these two preachers is worth
being written about," Mitch argued.

"Violence? What violence? A man has a right to refrain his
wayward wife without making the paper!" Paul snapped in return.

"The man was arrested." Mitch snatched the paper out from
under her as he glared at Paul. "Not to mention, I've noticed
quite a few columns I've written lately have suspiciously *not* been
printed. Are you censoring my paper?"

"*Our* paper." Paul clenched his teeth. "You're supposed to be
the editor, not the reporter, and yet you're gallivanting around
town writing those ridiculous pot-stirring stories. It's shaming the
Democrat and what I established this paper to be about!"

"You established it to be about news. This is news." Mitch
tossed the paper in the air.

Libby ducked as the paper swooped, nearly missing her face.
She cowered, waiting for the men to cease arguing. Her nerves
stood on end, raw and aggravated. She would almost consider
purchasing a train ticket and leaving this madness behind had
she anywhere to go.

"News should be about *community*," Paul groused. "If I didn't
pull certain rabble-rousing articles of yours, this paper would go
under, and this town would self-combust in tension and turmoil.
No one wants their secrets splayed on the front page!"

"This was printed on the third page," Mitch muttered, derision dripping from his voice. He was thumbing through the paper he'd snatched from where it'd fallen, then stopped when he spotted something. His brow furrowed. "What is this?"

"What's what?" Paul barked.

Mitch eyed the paper, glancing at Libby before leveling a glare on his partner. An eyebrow rose and disappeared into his graying mop of curls. "Did you write this and print it without my knowledge?"

Paul blanched.

"This list of *good* things the Corbin twins are doing?" He shook the paper and read out loud. "'The Corbin brothers' recent message both at the Friday evening revival meeting and several church meetings earlier this week at the Baptist and Presbyterian churches has led to many converts. The honesty in the Corbin twins' approach is both refreshing and necessary to bring about a change in one's soul.'"

"Your stories needed counterbalancing," Paul said, shoving his spectacles against his face.

Mitch laughed. "Speaking of controversy! Your article is at war with mine. You're undermining your own mission to build community."

Libby folded her hands in her lap, wishing she could both disappear and that she had the resourcefulness to tell them they were making the newspaper into a tug of war. No one would know what to think if they continued to compete for print space.

Mitch threw the paper back on the desk. "Well then." He turned to Libby. "The next time I give you my articles to transcribe for print, please be certain you return them to me so that I can oversee they make it into the paper."

Libby nodded.

Paul blew a puff of exasperated air through his lips and stomped from the office. Mitch stared after his partner's retreating form. Libby said nothing, knowing any words but his own would irritate Mitch in this moment.

Finally he spoke. "I can make this paper grow. I will print news whether Paul likes the content or not."

Libby didn't reply. He gave his head a little shake and widened his eyes, as if feeling guilty in her silence.

"It's going to get worse before it gets better, you know. Those Corbin brothers are as devoted to the Word of God as they are to collecting fame."

"Then why help them achieve fame?" Libby ventured, remembering the worrying interlude with Jedidiah Corbin the night before and the condemnation in his words. "Why print anything at all?"

Mitch gave a small sniff. "Because that's what makes news interesting, Libby. That's what sells papers."

———

Libby finished transcribing her father's scribbles, notes, and articles. Laying the pen on the desk, she caught a glimpse of her reflection in the shine of her father's silver-plated pencil case. She lifted it and stared at herself. The distorted image of her dark hair in wisps around her face and her almond-shaped eyes stared back at her. The conversation with her father replayed in her mind like the repeated circular motion of the newspaper press.

The twist on the news sold papers, no matter who it hurt, shamed, or exploited. Mitch wasn't particularly wicked, but his discretion rivaled Paul's insistence that the paper take the position of extremely conservative. Pleasantries, feed prices, almanac weather predictions, and the like. Sensational versus boring, and the *Democrat* had evolved into an unpredictable mess.

Libby replaced the pencil case to its spot.

She pushed back in the desk chair, its wheels squeaking against the wood floor. Standing, Libby shook the wrinkles from her gray skirt and adjusted the watch pinned to her soft, pinstriped blouse. She needed to walk, to clear her mind.

Libby closed the office door behind her, the mechanism clicking into place. She waved at the pressman, then slipped into the hall toward the front desk. The broad glass windows had the words *The Daily Democrat* painted black and backward so as to face the front. She reached for the brass door handle and glanced at the mail slot in the green door. It was where the obituary had been slipped, falling to its resting place on the scratched wood floor, staring up at the ceiling until she'd arrived to discover it.

Mitch would be furious if he found out she had kept it from him. News fodder. Libby slipped out the door and onto the sidewalk.

A brisk walk down the street brought her senses alive. A few carriages rolled by, with a bouncing automobile on high, round tires pretending it had the right of way. She passed a few ladies who were out for an afternoon stroll, their wide hats perched on their heads like crowns that competed for greatness. The cigar shop was to her left, the courthouse in the middle of the square. Libby relished the familiarity of her hometown. Were its citizens void of sin and shame? No. Certainly not, but she agreed with Paul that they didn't deserve to have it splayed in the paper.

"Miss Sheffield!" The friendly voice captured her attention, and she lifted her eyes to meet the kind gaze of Reverend Mueller, Calvin's father. Her smile of recognition waned as she noted the Corbin brothers flanking him. She recognized Jedidiah immediately, only because he gave her a cold smile and nod of familiarity. His beady eyes fixed on her, as if he could see into her soul. It wasn't a place she wished him to visit. The other brother, Jacobus, appeared less intense, yet it was difficult to differentiate her emotions when the men were so remarkably similar.

"How are you this fine afternoon?" Reverend Mueller stole her attention back. She shifted her focus to their old family friend.

"I'm well." She should be ashamed to lie in front of three ministers. "And Calvin? I haven't seen hide nor hair of him since . . ." Libby let her words drain away.

Reverend Mueller's countenance fell, and his mouth took a downward turn. "Ahh, what a horrific thing for the two of you to come upon. Calvin is shaken, but he's been spending quality time fellowshipping with these two good men. It's a turbulent period in Gossamer Grove, to be certain."

"A reckoning day will come," Jedidiah Corbin said, his eyes narrowing. It was as if he knew, or was *trying* to know, all about her.

"Jedidiah," said Jacobus, "now isn't the time for proselytizing."

Libby cast him a surprised look. She hadn't expected the other twin to put the aggressive one in his place.

"Of course," Jedidiah nodded, his lips straightening with his attempt to soften his expression apparent but not at all genuine. "Miss Sheffield, do accept our condolences about Deacon Greenwood's death."

"He wasn't *my* father," she blurted. "I mean, I do care about his passing, but condolences shouldn't be given to me. Well, I did find his body hanging—" She clapped her hand over her mouth.

The Corbin twins exchanged glances, and Reverend Mueller held up his hand. "Yes, yes." Calvin's father gave her a gentle smile, calming her fluster. "However, we know you are close with the Greenwood family, and you also bear the memories. Therefore, we say prayers on all your behalf."

Libby nodded, her eyes darting to the twins, both staring at her as if she were a mystery to be analyzed and solved. It was remarkably disconcerting and unnerving.

"Well then, we must be on our way. We're having a meeting with some other church leaders and gentlemen of the community." Reverend Mueller tipped his hat, and the Corbin twins followed suit.

Libby looked over her shoulder as they moved beyond her, and Jacobus Corbin glanced back. Their eyes locked for a moment, and if she wasn't careful, her imagination would have read concern and almost an urgent warning in them. But he turned away and left her with only a sense of restlessness, of unanswered questions, and not a little foreboding.

CHAPTER 14

L ibby looked up as the tin bell jangled above the door. The
front office of the newspaper held little space for visitors,
and the Corbin twins' presence filled it as they entered. Their
narrow eyes were dark, their wavy hair ruffled from the wind, and
both had muttonchop whiskers bordering their angular faces. The
meeting with the "other church leaders," as Reverend Mueller had
referred to them, must be over.

Libby eyed them with unease.

"Miss Sheffield, may we have a moment of your father's time?"
A mole by Jedidiah's mouth moved as he spoke. She tore her eyes
away from it and met the stark gaze of the much quieter brother,
Jacobus. He did not have a mole. For some reason, it made him a
tad more attractive, in an angular, pale sort of way.

"My father is occupied at present," she answered, quite proud
of herself for not babbling some long, ill-worded attempt at excus-
ing Mitch. He hated being bothered by "unannounced visitors."

"It's quite important." Jacobus's voice was firm but less sharp
than his brother's. Strong, with a tone capable of slicing through
a crowd but with an element of control that made him either more
stable or more dangerous. His eyes were stormy and perhaps a
little bit treacherous at the same time. She squirmed beneath the
searching contemplation. It was difficult to look away. He arrested
her with a simple stare.

Either way, she wasn't keen on entertaining the Corbin twins alone. She glanced over her shoulder at the hallway that led to the office and then into the print room. The air closed in on her, thick with the smell of ink and the bay rum of the twins' cologne.

Jedidiah snapped his fingers as if to regain her attention. "We've news the editor may be interested in."

Lord knew, the years had not been kind to her, and she'd retreated further and further into herself. But pluck was there somewhere deep inside, and now Libby mustered it as best she could.

"Mr. Sheffield has asked not to be disturbed." Her voice quivered.

Jacobus's eyebrow quirked, and for a moment Libby saw a flash of humor pass through his eyes. But then it was gone, replaced with a direct stare that made her shift her feet and reach for papers on the desk to shuffle merely for something to do with her hands.

Jedidiah continued to argue. "Come now, Miss Sheffield. We're about the Lord's business, and matters that concern the church, concern the town, which in turn concern the newspaper."

It was a riddle she didn't wish to solve. Libby stood, her dress brushing the tips of her shoes. She gripped the edge of the desk. So much for pluck. "I'll get Mr. Sheffield right away."

This wasn't a discourse she wished to engage in. Libby preferred to let her father deal with the revivalists. They were practically a circus on a bicycle but more intimidating than clowns, and rather reminding her a bit of barely restrained tigers.

Mitch was not pleased when she knocked on his door. His growl might have overwhelmed her another day, but now there was a familiarity behind it that brought her some comfort.

"The Corbin twins are requesting to speak with you." Libby shouldn't have been surprised when Mitch stood with a flourish and waved his arm, but she was.

"Why didn't you say so?"

Of course, he'd welcome them. They were, after all, only the leading news story next to Deacon Greenwood's death. How silly of her to procrastinate when Mitch was half launching himself down the hallway.

Paul stepped from his own office as Mitch's shoes clomped down the hall toward the front. His eyebrows drew together in disapproval, and Libby ducked her head as she passed him. He wouldn't be pleased she'd allowed the bombastic revivalists into the newspaper office to speak with Mitch. Her father would take whatever these men had to offer, mix it with lurid exaggeration, and call it truth.

"We've some grave concerns." Jedidiah Corbin began the moment Mitch entered the front office. No greeting, no handshake.

Libby glanced beyond them and out the window toward Fourth Street and the brick road lined with oak trees. A motorcar bounced by a carriage, and the horse tossed its head. Two women with broad hats stacked with flowers and tied with ribbons strolled by, their purses dangling from elbows covered in puffed sleeves. Their skirts buttoned to the sides of their waists, and their capes reminiscent of a magician's.

Magicians, circuses, and revivalists. All of them ranked in the category of the unbelievable for Mitch. The unbelievable, but the ever so intriguing.

"Grave concerns, eh?" Mitch's voice broke into Libby's thoughts. He'd pulled a notepad out, and a pencil was poised above the paper. "How may I assist?"

Jedidiah Corbin pulled an envelope from his inside jacket pocket. "We received an anonymous letter today. Of course, we've already reported it to your local authorities, and they will be on guard. However, it warns my brother and me to be on the lookout at our next gathering. We believe the public should be made aware of the possible threat."

"Threat? The lookout for what?" Mitch asked. He completely ignored Libby, and she preferred it that way. She fixed her eyes on her Bible that lay on the desk just inches from Mitch. It would be her luck for one of the Corbin twins to notice, inquire about her religious affections, and in turn send her down a blustering trail of half-truths. Standing before these men made the idea of coming before a righteous God perhaps the most terrifying idea she'd allowed herself to consider since . . .

Jedidiah Corbin unfolded the letter and handed it to Mitch. "Cowardice, really. They daren't sign their name to it."

Mitch's lips pursed as he skimmed the letter, perhaps both impressed and shocked. Libby strained to see over her father's shoulder. Mitch handed the paper back to the minister before Libby could capture any more than a cursory glimpse of the handwriting.

"It appears you've made some enemies," Mitch affirmed.

"Enemies? Most certainly." Jedidiah stuffed the letter back into his pocket. "Understand that people in the past have threatened to blow our brains out. But there's little way we could retaliate, for if we tried it in return, nothing would happen. They have no brains to be spattered!"

Libby cupped her hand over her mouth as a little yelp escaped.

Jedidiah ignored her. "Regardless, violence is not our choice of response. This death threat needs to be brought to the attention of the people. For their safety. For ours. To call a bluff to the imbecile who dared to threaten the working of God's hand within the community of Gossamer Grove."

Libby's eyes went wide, and she shot a glance at the very silent other brother. Jacobus appeared placid. Unaffected. Almost bored.

Awkward stillness separated Libby and her father from the Corbin twins. If they were trying to stir up further trouble by bringing an anonymous threat to the newspaper, it would well succeed. Yet, one could hardly argue that if they'd already reported it to the police, perhaps they truly *were* looking out for the best interest of the locals.

She lowered her hand, which was trembling. Libby attempted to hide it in the folds of her dress, but she caught the eye of Jacobus, who didn't seem to ever blink. She looked away. A handwritten threat to the reverends, delivered anonymously, was similar to the typewritten obituary for Deacon Greenwood. Yet she could hardly tie them together with the only common denominator being violence. One committed, one merely threatened.

Mitch cleared his throat. His face was awash with fascination. "I do say, something such as a threat against men of the cloth must be published in warning that the congregations not only defend you but also stay within the boundaries of Christian character."

Libby blinked. Her father was parroting her mother's pious tone, as though trying to garner kinship with the revivalists. He was engaged with their cause now, if not for the salvation of souls, for the selling of newspapers.

"The sender is obviously disturbed and in need of divine intervention." Jedidiah Corbin patted his chest where the letter was hiding in his jacket. "But, by the grace of God, we will continue to spread the wonder of grace in view of confessed sin."

"Certainly." Mitch nodded. "I shall pen a report regarding this threat and your imminent safety."

"Wonderful," Jedidiah replied.

"Thank you for your time," Jacobus added, his eyes shifting between Mitch and Libby, finally resting on her face. "We covet your prayers for protection, not only for us but also for those in attendance who so desperately need to hear the Word of the Lord."

"Certainly," Mitch assured.

After one more long stare, the Corbin twins departed, leaving Libby very unsettled in their wake. While Deacon Greenwood's obituary was unlikely to be connected to the reverends' letter, Libby couldn't be sure. The ministers appeared to be intent on cleaning up those they felt held little intelligence toward things of a spiritual nature. But what did that have to do with the death of a church deacon?

Nothing. They were unrelated. At least that was what Libby tried to convince herself of.

—◊—

Libby slipped out the rear door of the office, dusk settling over Gossamer Grove and the brick buildings, casting shadows over the alley. A cat scampered by her and disappeared in the stairwell leading to the basement of the newspaper office building. Libby had never been in the basement. She'd never had a desire to go there. She'd caught a peek inside once, however, and it was dank, tomblike, with spider webs blanketing the ceiling between the wooden rafters.

She crossed her arms over her chest and rubbed them with her hands. Peering down the alley, she squinted into the fast-growing darkness.

"Libby?"

Libby yelped at the whisper that arrived just as a cool breeze lifted loose curls against her cheek.

Elijah slipped from the narrow pathway between the newspaper building and the next-door hotel. He eyed the cat in the stairwell even as he mumbled, "I didn't mean to startle you."

Libby hugged herself even tighter. "That's all right." She was relieved he'd come after receiving her message delivered by one of the newsboys. All afternoon she couldn't shake the desperate feeling that circumstances were spiraling out of control. Too much was being overlooked, ignored, or not dealt with. Starting with Elijah's father, his death, and the obituary forever etched in her memory.

Elijah's features were shaded by his fedora. His form in a dark jacket and trousers cut a striking figure, but in the dark, even Elijah seemed a tad intimidating to Libby. The Corbin twins had certainly done a number on her nerves.

"We cannot stay silent, Elijah. We must face this." Libby whispered her rehearsed words, although truth be told, it wasn't really necessary. Their meeting was covert only to avoid drawing attention to the reason why they were meeting. Perhaps they should have been less dramatic and met over tea.

It was too late for second thoughts.

"Do you still have possession of the obituary?" Libby asked.

Elijah pushed his hat back on his forehead, and his eyes narrowed as he gave her a distant once-over, as if trying to convince himself why he was even here. Finally, Elijah reached into the pocket of his trousers and withdrew it. Libby eyed the offensive paper with derision. For a split moment, she'd hoped he burned it, destroyed it, or otherwise disposed of it. If it didn't exist, maybe it hadn't happened. But that was sheer foolishness.

"I don't like this, Libby." Elijah handed it to her.

She opened it and gawked at the undeniable message, indicative of a very different motive behind Deacon Greenwood's death. Not to mention, its allusions to some secret sins Deacon Greenwood harbored were a horrific claim to make in the wake of the man's sudden death. Whoever had written it had a vendetta. The same as whoever had written threats against the Corbin brothers. As if—

"It's as if they want to mete out righteous judgment on us all," Libby mumbled.

"Pardon?" Elijah tilted his head.

Libby lifted the obituary. "This—this prophetic telling of your father's death. Secrets and sins. The meting out of justice. Then there were the death threats made against the Corbin brothers, as though their way of bringing about conviction wasn't being effective enough." Libby shrugged, her thoughts tumbling from her mouth almost faster than she could think them. "As if people were being converted and baptized, but there was no public confession of sin? Maybe that's it. Or maybe they have nothing to do with each other."

Elijah appeared bewildered, trying to follow her jumble of words.

Libby pushed the obituary toward him. "I don't know. But we must take this to the police, Elijah. Someone killed your father. You cannot be in denial of it."

Elijah glanced over his shoulder as the night breeze picked up and blew a lone page of newspaper their direction. It tossed across the ground, rolling and wafting, then tucked away in the shaded corner of the stairwell. He shifted his attention back to the obituary. His frown deepened in the shadows, and in the dimming light Libby could still make out the troubled darkness in his eyes. She read the doubts there.

"You have to believe me, Elijah. My father and I didn't concoct this to create news. My father doesn't even know it exists." Libby dared to reach out and rest her hand on his forearm. He glanced at it. "*I* wouldn't allow that if it was even a consideration."

Elijah had taken the obituary from her, and now he ignored her pledge of loyalty. "This line here. 'No more shall his secrets wound. No more shall his secrets shame.' That isn't Poe, I don't think. Whoever wrote this composed that line to imply my father had some sort of shameful secret."

"Yes." Libby breathed a sigh of relief. Elijah was coming out of his grief-stricken daze. Logic and the horrible truth were finally coming to light.

"My father didn't *hide* any sins, Libby Sheffield." The thickness to his words, the untold truth behind them, was what speared Libby.

Like we hide ours, he seemed to add. Only it came from his expression, his eyes, and the tilt of his mouth in cynical shame.

"Still, we cannot hide the obituary," Libby argued. Lord, forgive her for her own secrets even as she attempted to expose another's. But he was already dead, gone, surely that counted for something? It wouldn't affect Deacon Greenwood were the accusation true, should he have something hidden worth being brought to some righteous end. But what about his family? *They* would bear the agony of those secrets if they were to come to light.

"I know." Elijah's admission was low and dragged from him against his will. When their eyes met, instead of his distant disdain, Libby saw the reflection of the boy she'd once known.

"I am willing to take the obituary to the police."

"No. No, I should." Elijah folded it and returned it to his pocket. "It's my father."

Maybe the police would believe him over the daughter of the newspaperman.

"You *will* report it?" Libby pressed. Logic exposed the fact a killer with a frightening ability to premeditate was still free in Gossamer Grove. Yet, she could still see the all-too-familiar flecks of a question in Elijah's eyes. What would be unearthed about his father?

Yes. What?

If Elijah held those doubts, then his earlier outburst that his father held no secrets was merely a shroud to cover the horrid reality that Elijah believed it possible, after all. Possible that Deacon Greenwood hid some horrible sin. Sin that required recompense. Death. The grave.

"I want to help." Her voice came out strained. She reached out her hand, silently pleading that Elijah hand the obituary back to her. Without it, she was nothing but the rambling daughter of the local gossipmonger. With it, she at least had something tangible to argue that the newspaper hadn't made it up for sensational reasons.

"I know you do." Elijah rubbed his hand over his mouth, agitated. "But, it isn't safe. I don't want to be responsible for anything happening to you."

A coldness settled in Libby's stomach. Being responsible for another's fate was understandably a large burden. It was one she bore every day. "You must show the police the obituary," she urged one more time, "or we may be responsible for the fate of one not yet dead." It was horrible to think the killer might be determined to bring another sinner to task and fill yet another grave.

"I've got to go." Elijah patted his pocket. "Be safe."

As was his custom on the rare occasion they were alone and it all came rushing back to them, Elijah's expression softened, and he lifted his hand to palm her face.

"Be safe," he whispered again, then spun on his heel and disappeared into the fast-approaching blackness of the evening.

Libby stood in the doorway of the newspaper building, the door held open in her hand. She stared into the alley where Elijah had vanished. Vanished with the obituary. It should have relieved her to reach a tentative agreement that it must be taken to the police, but instead she was unsettled.

"What are you doing?"

Libby startled, letting the door slam shut behind her. The hallway was illuminated by electric lamps, but its dim glow haloed Paul's form. He glared at her, a wisp of hair flipped opposite the balding on the top of his head and standing upright like a devil's horn.

"N-nothing." Libby hated herself for stuttering.

Paul studied her, then stepped aside as Libby hurried past. She could feel his eyes boring into her back and then heard the door shut behind him as he exited the building. She'd done nothing wrong. Nothing. But Gossamer Grove—home—had become such a dark place. Everyone seemed suspicious of something now.

An envelope was perched on the front desk beside her Bible and reticule. Libby pushed it away as she gathered her things. It was another evening she would need to walk home alone. Mitch never bothered to pay attention to where his daughter was or whether she made it home safely for dinner. The paper was going to press, and she could hear the nighttime workers in the printing room. She was the last to leave the office, and by the time she returned home, night would have settled with a cemetery-like stillness.

Libby slipped the strings of her purse over her wrist. Her gaze fell on the envelope, and this time she took more notice of it. A thousand fears flooded her as she reached for it. Nothing boded well when another anonymous missive was left at the paper.

She ripped it open and tugged out a square note card. The typed print burned into her vision with the ominous familiarity of Deacon Greenwood's obituary.

> Paul G. Darrow. Born November 2, 1861. Died May 14, 1907.
> His secrets held, his secrets lost, shall rise again on
> tempests tossed.
> His spirit while it laid to rest cried for mercy, then
> for death.
> Be silent in that solitude,
> Which is not loneliness—for then
> The spirits of the dead, who stood
> In life before thee, are again.

Paul. Libby clutched the premature obituary. She held his obituary, and yet, just moments before he left the paper, he had glared at her. Tonight he was very much alive. Libby cast her eyes back toward the page. But tomorrow? Tomorrow he would be dead.

CHAPTER 15

Annalise

He was following her. Annalise glanced in her rearview mirror as she shut off her car's engine. The rusty, dented pickup truck pulled onto the gravel drive behind her. Its headlights illuminated the inside of her vehicle and cast a glow over Eugene Hayes's abandoned trailer.

Annalise yanked on the handle and swung open the door. It was irritating as heck that Garrett Greenwood chased after her, pretending to care. Within moments of discovering the missing photograph, Annalise had sprinted from the house. Nighttime held no terror over her, for the most precious belonging she had was taken. The only thing Annalise could blame was this trailer. This pit of rotting mysteries that had somehow started a series of events that sent her on a downward spiral that would never stop.

The woods around the trailer were silent. All animals and insects had been frightened into stillness with the arrival of the two vehicles. Annalise slammed her car door shut. Now that she was here, some of the angry compulsion had drained away, leaving her very aware of her rashness in jumping in her car and making a mad dash to find—what?

She'd locked up impulse years before, when that first pink-positive appeared on the pregnancy test. But now? The world—*her* world—had tipped on its axis.

Annalise climbed the slanting wood stairs to the rickety deck attached to the trailer. Garrett left his truck running with its head-lights on. She could hear him approaching from behind her.

"What do you think you're doing?" His half shout ricocheted off the tin roof of the trailer home.

Annalise ignored him, inserted her key, and twisted the door-knob, opening the front door. Her breath caught as the rancid smell of a hoarder's home assaulted her sinuses.

"Q!" Garrett's fingers closed around her arm. Annalise tugged from his grip and leveled a glare on him that she was sure would sink a lesser man right through the trailer's carpeted floor.

"I owe you *zero* explanation." She hoped he felt the pain of her scowl. Annalise pushed her way past him into the black hole of the trailer. She pulled her phone from her jacket pocket and tapped on its flashlight app.

"You owe me a *massive* explanation." Garrett was practically on top of her. Annalise spun around, her nose almost hitting his chest. She lifted the phone so that the beam of light hit the bottom of his unshaved chin.

"Listen." Oh, she'd had it. Completely and entirely had had it. "You left. End of story."

He pushed the phone away so he wasn't blinded. "Everyone said to get on with my life, and I did."

Wow.

"Must have been nice." Annalise shook her head and turned away. There was a place for memories like that. Locked up and stored away. A sideways glance at Garrett told her he wasn't going to allow her that luxury.

"They told me *you* said I should go."

Annalise didn't answer. Never. She'd never said that. But if she was thinking at all rationally, she could wager a guess it was her parents who'd communicated that on her behalf. Separate the two before worse things happened. Like they actually got *married* or something!

"Did you?" Garrett said over her shoulder as she made pretense of sweeping the trailer with her phone's light.

"Did I what?" Annalise snapped.

"Say I should leave?"

Annalise blinked away those annoying type of tears that weren't from sadness or sensitivity but from anger. Sheer, unadulterated anger.

"Why would you ever think I'd be okay with you leaving for Switzerland while I had to cope with your parents thinking I was a pariah and my parents weeping over their lost dreams of a perfect child? While I had to wobble around on swollen feet and sit on a blow-up seat cushion like I was an eighty-year-old with hemorrhoids?"

Silence.

Yes. Answer that, Garrett Greenwood.

But he didn't. For whatever reason, Garrett was silent. Annalise stood in front of the dark wall, silhouettes of photographs taped to it. Photocopies of old newsprint. A revival flyer copy.

"What did she look like?" His question stilled Annalise's sweeping of the room with the flashlight. The beam settled on a lamp in the corner, its shade cockeyed and stained from cigarette smoke.

What did their baby girl look like? If the picture hadn't been stolen, she might have shown him. *Might* have.

Annalise's eyes burned with unshed tears, and the wash of emotion at the idea that her one link to their child was gone threatened to release the floodgates. She blinked furiously.

"She was beautiful," Annalise whispered. Without any more explanation, she shone the light in the direction of the desk still littered with papers and photographs. "I want her picture back. It's all I have."

She should have made one zillion copies of it and filed them in safe places. She could have done it all online and no one local would have had to print the photograph of the Greenwood baby no one knew existed. But it was a calculated move Annalise had always been reticent to take. There was control in one photograph, one memory. Comfort in knowing it was solely hers.

"You think you're going to find the picture here? In the middle of the night?"

"No." Annalise lifted some photocopied pictures off the desk. Vintage photographs like the ones in an antique photo album displayed as décor in her house. She turned to Garrett and waved the papers at him. "But, I'm going to find out what is going on. It cannot be coincidence that her picture was stolen the same day I inherit Eugene Hayes's trailer complete with a museum of pictures of me and"—she shook the papers again—"some dead guy you're related to."

Garrett took the photocopies from her hand and bent to look at them. "Shine the light over here." His tone was clipped, almost landing somewhere between irritated and hurt. But she could never tell with Garrett. He wasn't expressive unless he wanted to be.

Annalise did so, and the photograph lit up on the page. The black-and-white man stared back at them, his eyes bright as if he were somehow still alive. His arms were crossed over his chest as if challenging their inquisition into who he was. Well-trimmed beard and mustache emphasized the now-dead man's cheeks, and his top hat was perched on his head as if to hide secrets he kept stored away in his mind. His presence in the picture portrayed him in an almost ubiquitous fashion. As if at any moment he would appear in real life here while his image remained stationary and frozen in time.

"He looks familiar." Garrett squinted and motioned for Annalise to lift the light higher.

"It's Harrison Greenwood. Your great-great-grandfather."

"How do you know?"

"Because Eugene wrote his name on the top of the page." She stabbed at it with her fingertip.

"Yeah, well, I climb. I don't study genealogy." Garrett handed the page back to her.

"Or read, apparently," Annalise mumbled.

"Who *was* Eugene Hayes?" Garrett ignored her insult.

"I don't know," she whispered, willing the crossness from her. Garrett didn't deserve all her bitterness. In some way, he was as much a victim as she'd been. Their parents had been forces to deal with—big hurricane-like forces.

Annalise tried to muster an element of commonality. "That's what bothers me. Who was Eugene Hayes to all of this? To me?" *To our daughter* were the words Annalise couldn't voice.

She swung the flashlight around the room. A blown-up photograph of Harrison Greenwood surrounded by smaller copies of other Edwardian-era people hung on the wall opposite the one wallpapered with her own images.

"And who are these people?" Annalise bent and studied them. A woman, a younger man with eyes suspiciously like Harrison Greenwood's, and a photograph of twin gentlemen astride a tandem bicycle, of all things. Garrett's shoulder brushed hers as he bent in the darkness to peer at the wall. The shadows illuminating the pictures brought them to life somehow. Their spirits seemed to beckon both Annalise and Garrett until their own pasts became moot compared to the mystery these individuals represented.

"I think that's my great-grandfather, Elijah Greenwood." Garrett's finger landed on the younger man's photograph. "I remember my mom showing me a picture of him when I was a kid."

"Do you know who she is?" Annalise traced the face of a pretty young woman whose dark curls framed her features and whose expression seemed timid, almost nervous.

Garrett shook his head. "No clue."

Annalise focused on the revival meeting poster taped crookedly next to the picture collage. Where had Eugene dragged up all these artifacts? That old obituary? It was as if he'd raided a Greenwood family museum.

She straightened, drawing in an intentional breath. "Tomorrow I'm going to come back here and take down every single photograph, newspaper print, and photocopy, and put them in chronological order as best I can. Then I'm going to find out who Eugene Hayes was and why he felt connected to me. I need to know what I have to do with all this historic mumbo jumbo. Most of all, I'm going to find out who took my baby's picture, and why."

Her determined proclamation echoed through the trailer, followed by an uncomfortable silence that either insinuated she was teetering on the edge of sanity or remarkably in charge of the situation. More likely the former.

Garrett sniffed, then jammed his hands in his pockets and stood so close that Annalise almost put her hand out to push him away. Her heartbeat sped up, and she could make out the lines of his face in the dim light. Her flashlight beam bounced off the floor as her hand lowered.

Garrett tipped his head, and his words were soft against her tempestuous emotions. "I'll help you find her."

Find her. The words clipped her breath, and Annalise bit the inside of her upper lip. No, he meant the picture. The picture. They would never find *her*. Their baby was gone forever. Closed case, sealed files, compliments of parents and her eighteen-year-old insecure self.

"I will help you uncover what all this is about."

Annalise hated the way she leaned toward him. The old magnetism, the way her body remembered everything about Garrett Greenwood, and the forgotten sense of how his sensitive side—not often seen—made her feel. As if only Garrett would ever be able to know her. Really, truly know her. That was perhaps the worst part of it all. Only he could understand her pain, if he chose to meet her there.

—⁘—

The long folding table was littered with papers and photographs. Annalise's laptop was propped open on her desk to the login page of a popular genealogy site, and the smells from the coffee shop drifted into her office. She took off her glasses and squeezed the bridge of her nose as Christen floated through the doorway, bringing with her two mugs topped in cappuccino foam and the persistent temperament of a woman who wanted answers.

"Okay." Christen set a mug in front of Annalise and sank into a chair opposite Annalise's desk. She sipped her cappuccino as her gaze swept the room. "You slept here, didn't you?"

She fixated on the quilt bunched in the corner with a pillow on top.

Annalise busied herself with logging in to the website.

"I don't blame you," Christen nodded, her eyes wide and earnest. "'Cause after yesterday? That was freaky. Inheriting Eugene Hayes's shrine to everything you and then having your house broken into? Brent wouldn't tell me what was taken. He said it was police business."

The roll of Christen's eyes told Annalise that she was not going to get off so easily.

"So?" Christen leaned forward in the chair and rested her mug on the desk. "Was it bad? Did they take a lot? Are you installing a security system?"

Annalise had forgotten her password to the site with all Christen's prattling. She closed the lid on the laptop. "Yes, it was bad. It was an invasion of privacy. No. They didn't take much." Just her sanity, her most treasured possession, and maybe worst of all, the distance between her and Garrett.

"And the security system?" Christen pressed.

Annalise nodded. "I'm looking into it."

"Did you put a stop on your credit cards?"

"My what?" Annalise blinked. "Oh no. No, they didn't get anything financial."

"What'd they take, then?"

Annalise looked away and sighed. Garrett was going to be here in a few minutes. His text indicated she had little choice in the matter. The baby's picture had been stolen, so this affected him too. His own ancestors lined the walls of her newly acquired squatter's trailer. And, they both had dibs on the property his sister, Nicole, had major influence over. So, they needed to talk.

"Well?" Christen said.

Did it matter anymore? Annalise was sure it would all come out sooner rather than later. Garrett and his sister certainly wouldn't say anything, but now that the baby's picture had been stolen? Someone knew. Someone—*something*—bigger was going on that threatened not only Annalise's peace but also her future.

"They took a picture from my dresser." Annalise probably should have told Christen ages ago.

"A picture." Christen's eyebrow rose.

"Yes."

"Oooooookay. That's weird. A picture of who?" The concern in Christen's voice was almost Annalise's undoing. She would be better off if Christen's peppy personality was paired with snark. Instead, her perky determined nature was compassionate and protective. It was hard to build a wall against it.

Annalise drummed her fingers on the desk.

"Annalise?" Christen's expression of worry encouraged Annalise for a split moment before every fear rushed back. What would Christen say? It was the twenty-first century after all. Stuff like this happened all the time, and most unwed mothers were thrown baby showers like any married mother. So why did Annalise feel as if someone had pushed her back into 1907, to the front aisle of that revival meeting where she was to beg for her soul?

"I had a baby, Christen," Annalise blurted. "Years ago. When I was eighteen. They took the only picture of her that I had."

Silence.

The clock on the wall ticked loudly.

Hissing from the steamer in the coffee shop filtered through the door.

Christen remained still. Mum. This was not like her.

"Well? Say something." At this point, Annalise would be all right with condemnation. This silence from Christen was awful.

Then the chair Christen sat in scraped backward against the floor as she rose with a flourish. Rounding the desk, Christen wrapped her arms around Annalise, both stunning her and knocking her glasses askew.

"Oh, love!" Christen crooned in Annalise's hair. Part of Annalise wanted to melt in the instant forgiveness of her best friend. Another part wanted to bristle and stiffen. She didn't deserve it. She'd bowed to her parents, to Garrett's parents, and given up the baby. Her life was a measuring cup filled with all sorts of wrongs.

Christen pulled away and blinked rapidly behind her glasses. "Garrett's the father, isn't he?"

Christen was also smarter than people gave her credit for.

Annalise nodded.

"Oh. My. Gosh."

Annalise held her breath.

"Does Brent know this?" Christen's face shifted from utter disbelief to narrowed eyes. "He does, doesn't he? He's always known, hasn't he?"

"He was Garrett's best friend."

"Was." Christen returned to her seat and slumped back in the chair. "Goooooooot it. That's why Brent was acting weird about Garrett moving back to town." More silence. And then, "I'm sorry, Annalise." Her voice leveled out, and her eyes softened. "I had no idea."

"No one does." Annalise reached for her cappuccino. "But now?" She eyed the table covered in stuff she'd taken from Eugene Hayes's trailer. "I have to believe all this is tied together somehow. It's too coincidental not to be."

"Did you name her?" Christen's question came out of nowhere and stole Annalise's breath. She locked eyes with her best friend.

"Christen."

"It's okay, Annalise. You don't have to tell me."

Annalise swallowed the gargantuan lump in her throat.

Christen reached across the desk and laid her hand over Annalise's.

Annalise stared at Christen's hand. A gesture of friendship, of understanding. Not one of judgment or condemnation or of someone who'd walked a higher moral ground.

Annalise stared at Christen's red fingernails and whispered, "I called her Gia."

"Wow." Christen squeezed her hand. "Does Garrett know?"

"I do now." Garrett's baritone filled the room.

Startled, Annalise jerked her head up to meet his eyes, haunted and hurt. But it was the sight of his sister beside him that made Annalise shrink back into her chair. Nicole glared at her. The kind of ice shooting from the blue eyes of an older sister who would fight to the death for her baby brother. She flipped straight, razor-cut bangs from her forehead. Her high cheekbones blushed as she locked gazes with Annalise.

"You *named* her?" Nicole's chest rose and fell. "You never told us," she accused.

Annalise glanced at Christen, who was staring at her fingernails as if they'd suddenly grown ears. She searched Garrett's face, but only the muscle in his jaw twitched.

"I—" Why should she apologize? *She* was the one who'd given birth to Gia. *She* was the one who'd handed her away for the last time. *She* was the one who stared at Gia's picture every day for the last twelve years and prayed to God that whoever had adopted her loved her and cared for her.

Instead of apologizing, Annalise squeezed her eyes shut for a long moment before opening them and giving Nicole a direct look in return. "After the baby was born, it was as if nothing had ever happened. Gia was *my* memory, not yours."

"But she was our baby too," Nicole blustered. A sheen was over her frosty gaze.

"She was *never* yours!" Annalise choked out. Because Gia had been given away. Because she had taken another name, one they didn't know.

Annalise's gaze drifted to Garrett. For a moment, it was as if they understood each other, perhaps for the first time ever. Gia could never have been theirs. She was meant for more than they could give. That alone was why Annalise had released her baby girl that day and swept the shattered pieces of her heart into a dusty corner. She was willing to meet her future alone, because in the end, her parents were right, even if their motives were only to save face. It was what was best. Regardless of Gossamer Grove, and reputation, and Garrett or the Greenwoods, it was what was best for Gia.

CHAPTER 16

The door to the newspaper office swung open, and in typical small-town atmosphere the tin bell that hung from a string announced her entry. Annalise greeted the man at the front desk. The desk itself had to be from the turn of the century, marred with scratches and pen marks but rich with history. News story after news story had passed across that desk, and the long, narrow building that housed them wafted with the stale breath of ghosts and stories lost in time.

"Annalise!" Tyler Darrow did everything at his paper. He ran the front desk, the editorial desk, and cleaned the bathrooms too, so it was told. He was savvy but also overconfident. He had, after all, printed the story of Eugene Hayes and her pictures. He tended to be biased and supported whatever Garrett's sister Nicole wanted to push through as the mayor. Probably because he'd had a thing for Nicole since grade school. Too bad Nicole was in a long-term relationship with Brian Faucett, owner of a car dealership. Fitting. Politics and car sales.

Annalise welcomed any smidgen of humor. The last few days had been wretched. Distracted by the recent circumstances, she'd hardly slept, even after having an alarm system installed in her house. Her heart hurt—physically hurt—it seemed. The coffee shop was running fine, but the food pantry had been short-staffed, so she'd volunteered her time there in hopes of setting her brain to rights. A bit of reality shoved into her surreal life would maybe put things in perspective.

It didn't.

So here she was.

"Tyler." She was going to have to vet her words carefully. Tyler was, after all, always scouting out a story, and she was a walking Pulitzer Prize.

"What brings you in?" His blue eyes twinkled, and he pushed straight blond hair off his forehead. Very Nordic. Very cool.

"I wanted to find out what you may know about this obituary." Annalise slid Harrison Greenwood's old obit across the desk. She wondered if it had touched the same desk years before and passed through the hands of others who'd run the *Daily Democrat*. Regardless, she wasn't sure she was glad it was in her possession now that Eugene Hayes's belongings had been released to her from the department.

Tyler gave it a cursory glance, shook his head, and handed it back to her. "That's old. I'm not up on Gossamer Grove history." He gave her a crooked smile.

Annalise took the obituary back. "You don't have records, old files, or maybe books of news stories from that era?"

Tyler tapped his index finger on the desktop. "You could check out the archives at the historical society. They have a lot of the old *Democrat* papers there. The library probably has them on microfiche."

"I checked the library already. This was about all I could find on him." She didn't mention that the obituary at the library and online was worded significantly different.

"Is that Harrison Greenwood in the obit related to Nicole?"

Of course he'd ask. Annalise slipped the obituary into the manila envelope and stifled a sigh. "Yes."

"Where'd you get it?" Tyler asked, understanding dawning in his face. "Ahh! That's the obit Eugene Hayes died with, isn't it?"

Annalise knew she didn't need to answer. Tyler had connected the dots just as she'd suspected he would. But she had to start somewhere, and the closer to the actual source the better. Now that she knew most of the papers were archived at the historical society, she wished she'd just stayed away altogether. There was no going back now, though, so she might as well dive in. Pulling out the revival meeting poster, she passed it to Tyler.

"Oh, yeah, so this and that obituary and your picture were all in his hand when he died?" Tyler fished.

Annalise bristled. "Those weren't the exact details."

Tyler sniffed. "Well, regardless, it's creepy." He read the poster before handing it back. "I vaguely remember hearing about the revival in 1907. Some of my relatives were *saved* in it or something. I dunno. But I do recall family tradition stating there were two of them."

"Two?" Annalise pushed the poster back into the envelope.

"Yes, two revivalists. Twins."

Annalise brightened. There was the picture of the two identical-looking men on the tandem bicycle she'd taken from Eugene's house! But the poster didn't list two preachers. She studied it for a moment. It didn't list any names, just not-so-veiled threats of eternal hellfire. She blinked.

"Do you remember the names of the twin revivalists?"

Tyler drew in a deep breath and let it out slowly, his eyes narrowing in thought. "Wow. You're testing my memory. It's not as if anyone cares anymore."

"I care."

Tyler smiled, a lopsided one that made him come across cockier than kind. "Sure. Anything to link to the Greenwoods and dig up dirt, eh?"

Annalise drew back. "Why would finding out the history on the revival have anything to do with the Greenwoods?" She tried to sound bewildered, but Tyler saw through it. It was obvious that if the revival were linked to the Greenwoods' ancestor, which in turn was attached to her picture, something was amiss.

"Who knows. Maybe the preachers dug up some nasty scandal. Something you can use to undermine Nicole and get your way with that land and the homeless shelter."

"I don't play that way," Annalise scowled. "That's dirty."

"You know that in Gossamer Grove the Greenwood name is gold. Mess with it and you get trouble in return."

Oh, how she knew that already! Annalise glared at him as a renegade thought crossed her mind. She sidestepped his insinuations and tugged out the obituary again. "Does this look as though it was printed by the *Daily Democrat?*"

Tyler shrugged and stuffed his hands in the pockets of his dark-washed jeans. "Hard to tell. It doesn't look like a paper clipping, though. I mean, there's no header on it, and the print is larger. The paper isn't consistent with newsprint."

"Okay." Annalise flipped an errant strand of wavy red hair from her eyes. "Do you think the newspaper may have printed the revival posters too?"

Tyler raised an eyebrow. "I honestly don't know, Annalise. My family has owned this paper since the early 1900s, but I'm not an archivist. You'd be better off asking those questions at the historical society. Or go online to see what's been documented in public records."

"Are you saying there are no past records here at the paper?" Annalise had to ask one more time. She found it a bit hard to believe Tyler was that naïve about a paper that had been in his family for eons. Although it was Tyler. He was present day, present story, and all about featuring Nicole on the front page as often as he could.

"Maybe in the basement." Tyler pursed his lips and wagged his eyebrows. It was obvious he wasn't taking her all that seriously. "I haven't been down there since I was ten. It's a hoarder's paradise."

"Like Eugene's trailer," Annalise muttered. She raised her eyes to meet Tyler's. For all his casual appearance, they sparked with curiosity and an intensity that made her wonder if Tyler was more interested in the answers to her questions than she was. "Did you by any chance know Eugene Hayes?"

His expression remained impassive. "Nope. But he must have had a penchant for you and your cause to help Gossamer Grove's homeless. I mean, why else would he leave his trailer to you? But it's not like you could build a decent shelter on only half an acre."

Tyler's keen gaze pierced her. Disconcerted, Annalise rammed the manila envelope into her bag. "How did you . . . ? I never told anyone—I just found out about that myself."

"Word travels fast in Gossamer Grove." Tyler's eyes narrowed, and friendliness drained from his tone, replaced with suspicion. He rubbed his hand over his mouth. "You know this town. Always up for a juicy scandal. And it's been quite some time since anything this interesting has happened around here."

Annalise adjusted her purse on her shoulder, Harrison Greenwood's obituary and the revival meeting poster safely tucked inside it. "I expect you'll stick to reporting *truth*."

Tyler gave her a disingenuous smile and shrugged. "You're safe from the press, Annalise. You know I like you."

His tone sent a chill up Annalise's spine. The coolness in his eyes made it evident that he didn't like her so much as he liked a good story. If he found one, Annalise had little doubt he'd spew it all over the newspaper's front page.

—⁂—

Thunder rolled overhead with raindrops squeezing from overstuffed storm clouds as Annalise left the newspaper building. She hurried down the sidewalk, her heart palpitating with every step. Christen said once that God had a sense of humor. Annalise was beginning to believe that it was a jaded sense of humor. Her faith had become a shadow of what it once had been, as a child in Sunday school hearing the stories of Daniel in the lions' den and David slaying Goliath. That stuff just didn't happen anymore. Instead, it piled on and piled on. Her bandaged life had been a decoy all these years. Now that Garrett was home, she was bleeding again, and the brutality of recent events had left her emotionally battered.

Annalise fumbled in her purse for the key remote. Rain came harder now, and a clap of thunder jolted Annalise into a jog. Her hair hung in wet strands around her face as she came up on her car parked at an angle in front of the karate studio. She opened the driver's door and hopped in, tossing her bag in the passenger seat.

Key in.

Engine on.

Reverse.

There was a weird thudding sound, and the car seemed to flop backward. Annalise braked and shifted it into park. A jagged flash of lightning cut across the sky and disappeared behind a stretch of two-story brick buildings constructed in the mid-1800s. The historic section of Gossamer Grove was fogged by the deluge.

Biting back a curse, Annalise wrestled with the door and sprung out, her feet landing in a puddle on the street. She peered around the door to see what might have obstructed the front tire. The flattened tire glared up at her as if irritated she hadn't noticed when she'd hurried past it to get out of the rain.

"No. No, no, no." Annalise spun and looked at the rear tire. Another flat. She splashed around the back end of the car to the passenger side, and the sadistic reality set in. The other two tires were both flat, one obviously slashed.

In midday.

She smeared her hair back from her forehead, plastering it against her head. Rain pelted her face and stuck to her eyelashes. The street was remarkably barren. Everyone had either gone home for lunch or taken refuge inside somewhere. Her only option was to wait out the storm in her car, calling Christen for a ride and then calling the police. This was vandalism, right on the heels of the breaking and entering.

Hurrying back to the driver's door, Annalise got back in. She slammed the door shut, barring out the rain, and released a pent-up growl. She reached for her bag to retrieve her phone. The bag had fallen to the floor. She paused. The manila folder had slipped out, and from it the revival flyer declaring the need for repentance from sin. The top portion of Harrison Greenwood's photograph peeked out from beneath the yellowed flyer. His face and lifeless eyes stared back at her. In them she saw Garrett. The shape, the slant, and even the tilt of the man's head.

It was as if the dead man were speaking to her from the grave. *Sins never stay buried.*

They always rise from their crypt.

She didn't need to be reminded of that—didn't *want* to be reminded of it. Basic Christian faith stated that God forgave sins and forgot about them. So then why couldn't everyone else? Or did she have something wrong and there was a catch to it all?

Leaning over, Annalise scooped up the manila envelope and stuffed its contents back inside it before getting her phone to contact the police. Eugene Hayes's fascination with her and the long-dead Harrison Greenwood was linked by the implication that both she and Harrison had secret shames. Perhaps Eugene Hayes had one too. Regardless, the revival of 1907 hadn't reformed or redeemed the town of Gossamer Grove, and even now someone seemed intent on making sure she knew her mistakes were no longer her own private disgrace.

CHAPTER 17

Aboot to her behind might have had less impact than the patronizing smile and raised brow of the police officer at the front desk of the station. With an offhanded wave, Libby was all but escorted from the building. The man's hand palmed the door as he opened it for her, and she twisted in the darkness of the evening to stare up into his face with disbelief and not a little bit of panic.

"But you cannot dismiss this!" Libby insisted.

"We've already been over this, Miss Sheffield," the officer said. "We'll look into it, but please be advised, if this is something your father has any part in manufacturing for a story, he'd best be cautious or he'll be facing charges of slander."

She wished she was feisty and bold. She'd hiss a *How dare you* at the policeman. Instead, she quailed beneath his firm expression. Libby lifted Paul's obituary, her hand shaking. It'd taken all her courage, all her tenacity, to bring it to the authorities. Especially in the waning daylight that had now become full-on nighttime.

"I'm trying to save a man's life!"

"As you attempted to save Deacon Greenwood's?"

"I told you, I didn't believe it myself at first. As you can see, it's unfathomable."

"It's insinuating we've a repeat killer on our hands, Miss Sheffield. In a place like Gossamer Grove, I would find that to be an exaggerated claim. We are a small and safe community. The medical examiner even deemed Greenwood's death as caused by the deacon's own hand."

"The man—the examiner—the *doctor* had no reason to look for anything other than that," Libby argued, rather surprising herself, as well as the officer if the expression on his face were any clue. "You must understand that my intentions are good. This obituary isn't fabricated. My father didn't write this. Someone else did!"

"Mm-hmm." The policeman stepped out onto the sidewalk, making Libby step back a few paces.

She gripped the obituary to her chest and tilted her chin. "Do you not care to save a man's life? Isn't that your duty as an officer of the law?"

"Miss Sheffield, as I told you a few moments before, we'll investigate into Mr. Darrow's well-being. But I will not be organizing a militia to charge his doorstep. Now please be on your way. Leave this to the police."

The promise of an investigation did little to appease Libby's angst. She folded the obituary and jammed it into her handbag. "You will come with me then? To check on Mr. Darrow's welfare? Now?" She looked over her shoulder, as if the writer of the obituary leered from the shadows, snickering at her conundrum. How difficult should it be to inspire a policeman to run to the aid of a potential murder victim? Must she deliver them another dead body to prove her point? Libby shuddered. God help her. She'd hoped the obituary would create a sense of urgency, and at best it'd created only a sense of duty.

"Leave it to the police, I implore you." With that, the officer closed the door.

She stared at it. He hadn't even asked to keep the obituary.

Perhaps he was simply trying to de-escalate her panic and in truth really was already gathering his things to check on Paul. But, a niggling sense inside Libby told her he wasn't going to move in any sort of expedited fashion.

"Good night," Libby mumbled, very belatedly. She turned on her heel and headed back toward the main street. Her hands shook as she clutched her purse. She would never sleep tonight, never be able to close her eyes. If Paul was attacked, somehow subdued, hoisted over a wooden beam and hung—

"Miss."

"For all that's holy!" Libby shrieked and spun, whipping her handbag and slapping it across a broad but lean chest.

The man cleared his throat. Muttonchop whiskers were outlined by a streak of moonlight peeking from behind a cloud. Libby squinted to see his features. Long nose, deep-set eyes, angular cheekbones, thin lips, and . . . no mole. This would be Jacobus, not the more intimidating Jedidiah. Although, now that this revivalist brother stared down his nose at her, she wasn't entirely sure there was much difference between them.

Jacobus ran a hand over his chest, the suit coat he wore a dark outline against the shadowed building behind him. "Your purse is quite the weapon, Miss Sheffield."

Libby coiled the purse strings in her hand. Perhaps she would use it again. She eyed him.

He eyed her back.

"Well, excuse me then." Libby tried to sidestep him, but he stepped along with her.

"May I escort you somewhere?"

She didn't miss the irony that his brother had asked the same only a few nights before.

"No, thank you." Libby clutched her purse closer.

"Lollie?" A familiar male voice came out of the darkness and from the alleyway between the police station and the brick building that housed a men's suit emporium. The endearing nickname, and the way he dragged out the syllables, brought instant peace to her soul.

"Calvin!" Libby tipped her head and was able to make out the features of her friend.

"Ah, Mr. Mueller." Jacobus Corbin gave the young man a nod, and for a moment Libby was thankful the revivalist didn't give Calvin special treatment due to his more simplified approach to life.

"Hi-ya, Preacher." Calvin's face split into a grin. They shook hands, man to man, and then Jacobus turned his attention to Libby.

"I see you're in capable hands."

Calvin grinned.

Libby nodded. Yes, please. Go away. She needed assistance, needed someone who would understand the earnestness of the situation and not dismiss it. Calvin would understand. He had been there. He had seen Deacon Greenwood hanging. Jacobus Corbin had not.

Presumably.

Libby eyed the man, his odd features.

"Good night then." Jacobus tipped his hat and his long legs strode away toward the corner where the saloon doors were open and music and raucous laughter filtered onto the sidewalk. Fancy going into the saloon, a preacher who'd just hours before had reported death threats against himself. Libby blinked to clear her thoughts. There was little logic left in this town.

"What are *you* doin' alone?" Calvin challenged her with a cock of his head and a lopsided smile.

Libby reached for her friend's hand. His fingers curled around hers in a boyish familiarity, one with the promise of lifelong devotion and nothing more.

"I must find Elijah. Quickly, Calvin. I believe he's the only one who will listen to me."

"I'll listen." Calvin seemed hurt, and his childish smile waned.

Libby squeezed his hand. "I know you will, and I will explain. But we must go to the Greenwood home. Will you go with me?"

Calvin wagged his head back and forth. "That man died, Lollie."

"I know." Her throat clogged. Explaining death to Calvin was something she'd prefer to leave to his father. Reverend Mueller had always doted on him, before and after the accident that trapped Calvin in the world of a child. He would be the best person to explain such things. But she could certainly empathize with Calvin. "Yes, he did."

Calvin's eyes widened, and Libby could make out the whites of them in the darkness. "Swung to and fro. Remember?"

She couldn't get it out of her mind.

Calvin was too fascinated, and Libby's empathy shifted. "Calvin, you mustn't speak ill of the dead."

"Oh, I'm not." He shook his head with fervor. "I'm just sayin' the truth. One notch tighter and the rope woulda cut off his head."

She was going to be sick. And now? Paul. Libby pressed her hand over Calvin's wrist. "Please." It was all she could say. Praying Calvin saw the desperation in her eyes.

"Okay." Calvin nodded, the fascination draining from his face, replaced with a softer gleam of affection. "I'll walk with you. You can't be alone, Lollie."

His hand stayed wrapped around hers. In another life, in another world, perhaps it would have been different. Two beloved friends growing up side by side and walking hand in hand through life together. Now . . . Libby stole a sideways glance at Calvin. Now she walked with him under the pretense he could and would protect her. But he was captive to a mind forever damaged by tragedy. He was forever a boy.

CHAPTER 18

I'm not going to die tonight!" Paul Darrow threw his hands in the air, exasperation lacing every intonation of his voice. He glared first at Elijah, then at Libby, then gave a perplexed glance over her shoulder at Calvin. The light from inside his home lit the doorway and deepened the shadows on his bony face.

"You don't know that!" Libby insisted. Though she lacked a fondness for anything Paul, she certainly didn't wish him murdered.

Elijah held the obituary up for Paul to read. The newspaperman snatched it from Elijah's hand and crumpled it.

"Drivel. Sheer drivel." He wagged his finger at Libby. "Stuff your father would want to print, especially in lieu of that ridiculous article about anonymous death threats against the Corbin twins."

"Death threats against the twins?" Elijah shot Libby a concerned glance, and she gave her head a small shake. This wasn't the time to expound on that story.

"Now, I ask that you leave me alone tonight so that I may sleep in peace, mind you, not *rest* in peace."

Elijah tried again, this time with more conviction to his voice. "Mr. Darrow. Consider my father. You heard of the obituary that Libby received, and assuming it wasn't concocted to create some news story, then someone out there has sinister intentions."

Paul's skin turned ashen, and he shifted his attention over their shoulders into the black night. When he brought his gaze back, his eyes reflected a very distinct glimmer of anxiety. His voice dropped to an assertive hiss.

"I'm telling you, leave it alone. Leave *me* alone. There is—I've no intention of being slain tonight. You also have no business nosing into this any further."

Paul made a move to close the door, but Elijah's foot stopped it. His chin was set, and even in the glow of the lamplight, Libby could see Elijah's jaw flex. It was firm and unemotional, his expression calculated. One that seemed to add up the circumstances and find them lacking.

"It *is* my business." Elijah leaned in, effectively edging out Calvin and causing Libby to take a step sideways. "My father's legacy is now as a man with a weak-willed constitution whose only way to cope was to end his own life. But, these obituaries speak otherwise. If my father's life was taken by another's hand, I would be a fool to deny it."

Elijah pressed his hand against the doorframe. Libby moved to her tiptoes to see over his arm. Elijah ignored her and leveled a look on Paul.

"Whoever wrote my father's obituary must have written yours."

Libby noted Paul's knuckles whiten with his grip on the door.

Elijah did not back down. "I will not have my father's name stained with scandal and his killer taunt us days after as though we were playing pieces in a game of chess."

Paul blinked and then pushed his spectacles up his nose. His lips were set in a thin line, and his chin jutted out as he raised it. "Your father's name will always be stained with scandal, whether by his own hand or another's."

"What are you insinuating?" Elijah demanded.

"Haven't you read his obituary? *My* obituary?" Paul jammed the crumpled obituary touting his impending death against Elijah's chest. "We have sins that must be paid for. One can only outrun their sins for so long. There is nothing you can do."

The door slammed in their faces. With it came a shroud of darkness as Paul snuffed out his lamp.

———m———

Morning dawned, a gray fog floating low against the earth. Sleep was as elusive as a wandering spirit haunting an old house. Libby held the collar of her coat against the breeze that blew into her face as Mitch drove them toward the newspaper in his Orient Roundabout motorcar. She bounced on the long seat that resembled a buckboard wagon, the thin white-rimmed tires vibrating against the brick street. The padding on the seat made it cushion-like, but the open-air carriage didn't shield her face from the breeze. It may have the simplicity of a bicycle, as the advertisement touted, but today it complicated matters. Mitch enjoyed shifting between its two speeds, and in the fog and mist, in town no less, it felt danger-ous. Disconcerting. Libby was not a fan. Neither, for that matter, had her mother been when Mitch plopped down four hundred twenty-five dollars for it.

She shifted her hand from her collar to her hat and pressed down as the wind from the ridiculous fifteen-miles-per-hour speed con-tinued to play on her nerves. But Libby didn't try to slow Mitch's driving. For as much as she preferred to walk, she was anxious to get to the paper. Nothing would bring relief like the sight of Paul's annoyed face, balding head, and pinched expression. She'd spent most of the night praying, hoping the police had offered Paul protection whether he desired it or not. That they had taken the obituary seriously and, at the very least, humored the panicked, silly girl of the local newspaperman.

Another motorcar sped toward them, two men perched on its seat. The driver waved at Mitch. They both slowed, and Libby noted the paleness of the driver's face. It was Reverend Mueller, his graying hair flipping in the breeze as he applied the brake. Beside him was the studious Jacobus Corbin, less his twin brother, cloaked in his bland expression.

Their eyes met. His were sharp. Libby dropped her gaze.

"Reverend Mueller! Reverend Corbin!" Mitch's smile of greeting waned as he too noticed the pallor of Calvin's father. Reverend Mueller ignored the greeting. He gripped the steering wheel that extended in front of him on a long metal rod.

"You'll want to follow me, Mitch." Reverend Mueller was grave, and his eyes lacked the smile and warmth Libby was accustomed to. He didn't even acknowledge her presence, which was unusual for him.

"What's happened?" Mitch asked the question, but Libby already knew the answer.

She laid a gloved hand over her mouth. Paul. If only he'd listened!

"They found a body this morning. In Gossamer Pond. I'm headed there now." Reverend Mueller pointed in the direction from whence they'd just come. The pond was located just on the outskirts of town, past the Greenwood Mill, about a mile away.

Without another word, Reverend Mueller shifted and set his vehicle into motion with a puff of exhaust and a jolt. Jacobus adjusted in his seat and turned to look at them. Libby stared after him as if some unbreakable thread connected them. As if he'd compelled her to follow with just a look and not a word. She was convinced. He did read souls.

Mitch's voice brought reality crashing into her. "You'll have to come with me. I'm not waiting to get there."

Libby clenched her hands all the way to the pond. There had to have been something more she and Elijah could have done to stay this dreadful course of events. But, they'd warned Paul! Warned him and he'd refused to take heed. What sin could be so great as to justify murder?

The word echoed in Libby's mind as the trees along the roadway cleared and open field bordered them. The car hit a rut in the hard-packed dirt, causing Libby to bounce on the seat and lean into Mitch's arm. He ignored her and kept the speed where it was as the automobile cut through the fog. The emerald green of spring's new growth almost glowed with dew, and Libby could make out a cluster of motorcars and wagons on the side of the road up ahead.

Gossamer Pond was only an acre, not large at all, and its edges were already patchy with algae and lily pads even though summer hadn't yet brought its suffocating, humid warmth. The medical examiner's wagon was positioned at an angle, and Reverend Mueller had already alighted from his seat and stood next to Dr. Penchan.

Two rowboats had been launched into the pond. Shouts drifted across the fog. Mitch brought the Roundabout to a shuddering halt. For a moment, he cast Libby the concerned look of a father rather than a newspaperman.

"You'll want to stay here, I'm sure." He patted her knee, and then intrigue entered his eyes and he jumped from his seat.

She might be timid and even squeamish, but Libby had no intention of staying in the motorcar. It was as if the body in the pond drew her. She was bonded to it for no other reason than she had more likely than not been one of the last people to see Paul alive.

Libby's shoes sunk into soggy earth at the pond's embankment. A man's hand gently wrapped around her arm and drew her back.

"Libby, you'd best not look." It was the calming voice of Reverend Mueller. But she couldn't give him attention, couldn't even meet his concerned gaze, for her own eyes were fixated on the body still floating in the water.

She took a few steps forward, away from Reverend Mueller. A presence moved beside her, but this time it wasn't the reverend. Jacobus Corbin stood to her left, his hands clasped behind his back. His hair curled in the morning mist, whiskers outlining his strong jawline.

"Death is mesmerizing," he said, his voice splitting the morning. The sounds of men yelling across the pond provided an eerie background noise. Jacobus turned to stare down his nose at her. "Don't you agree?"

How could she argue the morbid truth? She could barely tear her eyes from the activity in the pond. The men in rowboats were reaching for the body, one of them trying to pull it toward their boat by hooking an extra paddle on the other side of the body.

Her breath caught. It wasn't Paul! Long, dark hair floated around the corpse and a white chemise gown, almost sheer from being wet, draped over the body like a funeral shroud. Pale fingers, bare feet, and the face. The face was still in the water, concealing the victim's identity. Libby squeezed her eyes shut against the sight.

"Open your eyes, Miss Sheffield." Jacobus's words compelled her compliance. But when she did, he commanded her attention. "Deep breaths and we shall focus on those here who will need our help."

"It's not Paul," Libby mumbled. She realized her error at Jacobus's furrowed brow.

"Who?"

"I thought it may be someone else. Somebody I knew. I mean, know. Well, there's—it's not them." She fumbled to a halt. She needn't explain her thought process to anyone. Especially a virtual stranger like a Corbin brother.

Jacobus surprised her and reached out to touch her arm. "Are you all right, Miss Sheffield?"

She nodded. But their eyes locked once again. She lost her breath for a moment as he studied her. A slight smile touched his mouth.

"Yes. You're quite all right. Good woman."

His words bolstered her strength in a way she hadn't expected. He seemed pleased she wasn't swooning at the sight of the body.

Libby focused on the pond and the poor drowning victim. Another rush of relief that it wasn't Paul was fast replaced by a horrible fascination with who it was in his place. An older woman by the looks of the plentiful gray among the brunette strands. The rescuers finally grasped her body and struggled to pull it from the water.

Footsteps jogging from the road and down the embankment startled her. Jacobus stepped away, and she didn't miss his lean form walking through the mist like a tall mirage.

"Look away, Libby," Elijah commanded, a protective note to his tone. She did so, but only to meet Elijah's eyes.

"It's not Paul," Libby whispered.

"Shhh." Elijah took her hand and led her toward the road, away from the sight. Libby found herself scanning the banks for Jacobus Corbin, but he'd disappeared.

"How did you know to come?" Libby asked under her breath, casting a backward glance at the pond just in time to see the body fall to the bottom of the rowboat.

"Oh, Lord, have mercy." She clapped her hand over her mouth and spun toward Elijah. He leaned closer, looking over her shoulder toward the grisly scene while he spoke.

"I saw Paul at the paper. I went there first thing this morning. I couldn't sleep last night."

"Nor could I," Libby breathed.

Elijah's dark eyes locked with hers. It was evident he was questioning the obituaries again. While his father's may have come to fruition, it seemed, if last night's obituary was authentic, the killer had killed the wrong person. "Paul is very much alive. But he shouldn't be, and he seemed to imply that when he told me a body had been found here. Do we know who it is? Why this person and not Paul?"

"I don't think someone intended to kill Paul and somehow mistakenly took the life of a woman!" Libby whispered hoarsely. She glanced around to be sure no one was eavesdropping.

Elijah's shoulders rose in a heavy breath. He shoved his hands in his pockets. "You're assuming this even has anything to do with the obituary. And now all credibility is lost with the police, you know."

Libby winced. She'd not thought of that. But something inside of her, something raw and sure knew that the body being rowed to shore was in no way a mistake, nor was it unassociated with the obituary aimed at Paul.

A shout came from the boat in the pond, and murmurs started through the onlookers of the constable, Dr. Penchan, Mitch, making its way to Reverend Mueller, who approached them while shaking his head in grave solemnity.

"It's Dorothy Hayes." His grim tone traveled across the morning air with a weight of finality that chilled Libby to the bone.

"Isn't she—?" Libby couldn't complete her question, but the stunned look that settled on Elijah's face threatened to shatter what little calm she had left.

"Aunt Dorothy?" Elijah's expression was one of shock.

Libby turned as the men scraped the rowboats' bottoms along the shore. She saw the body of Elijah's aunt, his mother's sister, splayed on the floor of the boat. Her body drenched and pallid. Her eyes open, as if she stared into death's eyes before taking her last breath.

Libby closed her own, seeing the writing of the obituary, word for word, as it'd been intended for Paul.

> His secrets held, his secrets lost, shall rise again on tempests tossed.
> His spirit while it laid to rest cried for mercy, then for death.

Cried for death. Libby remembered Paul, fear in his eyes, but insistence that nothing would happen. Almost—almost as if he were afraid, not of death but of *truth*. Secrets. Once again, secrets. And yet, in the wake of an obituary that seemed to taunt him with the escape from them, lay Elijah's aunt.

> Be silent in that solitude,
> Which is not loneliness—for then
> The spirits of the dead, who stood
> In life before thee, are again.

Death was a reuniting of souls in the afterlife. Deacon Greenwood and Dorothy Hayes were family—through marriage, but family still. Both dead. Silenced for eternity.

Libby shivered and wrapped her arms around herself as she watched Elijah stumble down the embankment toward the boat that held his aunt's body. It was Elijah's family that was being singled out, and Paul who was being goaded by the promise of escape from his secrets. Somehow they were tied together.

She'd been right. Libby sensed the strength leave her knees, and she sank onto the bank as men scrambled to hoist the woman's body from the boat. Dorothy Hayes *had* stared into the eyes of Death's abyss, and Death had laughed at the cruel game it was playing and the riddles it left behind as Dorothy slipped into the hellish blackness of night.

CHAPTER 19

Annalise

G arrett was at the round corner table in the coffee shop—
her personal favorite—with the worn white paint and its
farm table-style legs. The mismatched chairs were occupied across from him. Nicole, her significant other, Brian, and . . .
oh no. Annalise's attention was snagged before she could collect
her thoughts regarding the fourth person at the table. She forced
herself to focus on the customer at hand.

"I'll have a large double caramel latte."

Annalise mustered a smile and punched in the $4.25 and then
repeated her smile when the customer stuffed a five-dollar bill
in the homeless shelter fund-drive jar. She glanced back toward
Garrett, whose rapt attention was on table occupant number four,
Doug Larson, the contractor for the prospective wilderness center.
Or rather, Garrett's attention was on the blueprints Larson had
stretched across the table. Maybe it would be odd to some that
they would be doing business at the local coffee shop. But, this was
Gossamer Grove, after all. People here preferred the hometown
atmosphere to meetings at a stale office. Either way, it was gutsy
of Larson. He knew well and good that she owned the coffee shop,

that she had petitioned the town board for that land, and yet here he was, as if it had already been determined.

In the end, her vision rested on Garrett. He appeared well rested, if not a bit reminiscent of Shaggy from Scooby-Doo. It irked Annalise that he could sleep, plan his future, and carry on when her desk was covered in pictures and photocopies and vintage newsprint all recovered from Eugene Hayes's trailer. It stung even worse that he would agree to meet Larson here, with Nicole and Brian. A family affair, it seemed, at the expense of those in the town who needed grace, intercession, and someone to just simply give a darn. It was all so . . . Greenwood of them.

Annalise turned away, blowing air through her lips. She bumped into one of her baristas, who wobbled a cup of coffee in her hand, a bit of the hot brew splashing from the opening in the cover.

"I'm so sorry," Annalise mumbled. She met the gracious gaze of her employee, who handed her the cup with the glossy smile of a teenager.

"You need this. You look exhausted."

To say the least.

Annalise took the gift and gave her young protégé a quick hug, watching as the teenage girl flipped her hair over her shoulder and bounced away to flirt with the college-aged male barista. Sighing, Annalise prayed the girl would be smart and not taken in by young emotions that led nowhere fast.

"Good coffee today, Annalise." Doug Larson's deep bass broke into her bad memory. She turned, the rubber soles of her sneakers silent on the shop's barnwood plank flooring.

Annalise sipped from her cup. It was searing hot, and the tip of her tongue burned. But she preferred this distraction over the disconcerting expression on Larson's face. In his mid-fifties, the man was fast making his place as the richest man in historic Gossamer Grove. Yet he didn't look the part. His blue jeans were worn and permanently stained with the evidence of manual labor. His T-shirt was frayed at the neckline, and the flannel shirt over it had seen better days. The steel blue of his eyes drilled into hers, and Annalise was sure that if every freckle on her face could scamper up her forehead and hide in her red hair, they would.

"Heard about your break-in. And your tires were slashed?" He clicked his tongue. "Shame. Hope the police are following up on that."

Of course. Small town. News spread fast. Annalise nodded, trying to remain civil in the wake of Larson's semi-plastic concern. "They're looking into it."

Larson's blue eyes flashed as he finished taking a drink of coffee. "Looking into it? If you were my daughter, I'd be on top of them to make sure they caught the culprit."

She wasn't his daughter. Annalise blinked behind her glasses, not even sure what to say to the contractor.

"How's your father?" Another awkward question.

Annalise knew he was trying to get under her skin, communicate in some chauvinistic way that he was smarter, more savvy, and more capable than she was. Everyone in Gossamer Grove knew there'd been a falling out between her and her parents several years before. They just didn't know why. They weren't aware that Annalise had finally told her parents she hated herself for giving up Gia, resented them for pressuring her as a teenager to give away her baby. It was the final wedge. A year later, Annalise was buying her childhood home and her parents were shaking the dust of failure from their shoes and leaving Gossamer Grove to make their mark in an Arizonian retirement community.

Larson cleared his throat, and Annalise jerked her attention back to him.

"Fine," she mumbled. "My father's fine."

Larson gave a thin but knowing smile. "Well, honey, if you need anything, you just call me. I know it's hard being a single woman on your own."

Annalise bristled. He had no right to—

Larson kept talking as if they often discussed life over the coffee shop counter. Unfortunately, no one was behind the man in line to give Annalise an excuse to shut down the conversation.

"I've been chatting with Greenwood over there." Larson lifted his cup in the direction of Garrett, still in deep conversation with his sister. "That man just slays me. He has such tremendous plans." Larson clicked his tongue again as if completely in awe. "All the years climbing overseas served him well. He's immersed in that culture, and it'll speak to a lot of climbers and more extreme athletes. A good draw to the area." He took a long sip of his coffee. His eyes spoke volumes.

I've won.

Annalise refused to be cowed by Larson. His veiled hint was clear. Garrett equaled revenue. Annalise equaled charity.

"I still stand by my conviction, Mr. Larson. We need to care for Gossamer Grove's citizens even more than we do those coming into our town to visit."

"Of course! I agree!" He nodded with enthusiasm as though to emphasize how right she was. "Job potential awaits them all if they clean themselves up and interview with my wilderness center. I've plans to build this summer, and all the investors are lined up and ready to go. Vintage cabins that inspire fishing and outdoorsy things like hunting and hiking. We've the forest land that Garrett says is ideal for climbers to—what he'd call it?—go *bouldering*? I don't know. Regardless, it all means more jobs. More opportunity. You should be pleased Garrett is back in town."

It was a backhanded comment. Sneaky, really. Annalise narrowed her eyes at Larson whose own stared back at her, unblinking. She stilled, her fingers tightening around her coffee cup. She managed a platonic smile. "Gossamer Grove is always pleased when a Greenwood comes home. But sometimes we wish they'd stay away and let the monarchy fade."

Larson drew back, but his jaw clenched and then relaxed. He gave her a forced smile that came nowhere near meeting his eyes. He patted the countertop. "You have a good day, okay?"

Annalise stared after Doug Larson as he wove between tables and exited the coffee shop. She glanced at Garrett, who happened to look up. A shadow of question flickered in his eyes, then dimmed before he returned his attention to Nicole—who seemed to purposefully ignore her. She smiled at something Brian said, reaching up and brushing light brown hair from his temple.

Annalise escaped into her office, toward the mystery splayed across her desk. A deep sense of disturbance filled every nuance of her spirit. She rested her coffee cup on the desk. Lifting the photograph of the Edwardian-style woman, she stared into her eyes. They were dark, framed by elegant eyebrows, her cheekbones high and her features beautiful. Wavy brunette hair framed the young woman's face and swirled around her head in a fashionable Gibson-girl style.

"Did you ever walk in the Greenwoods' shadow?" Annalise whispered to the nameless woman, even as she glanced beyond it to the photograph of Harrison Greenwood that lay haphazardly atop the picture of an eighteen-year-old Annalise. She returned her gaze to the mystery woman. "I have a question."

The woman in the photograph stared back as if captivated by Annalise's words, waiting, listening.

Annalise spoke softly. "Without compassion, without grace, what do I have left? What do any of us have left?"

She tossed the picture on top of Harrison Greenwood's, but the woman's fixated gaze didn't leave Annalise's face.

———

The twin doors of the fieldstone house that was headquarters for the Gossamer Grove Historical Society creaked as Annalise opened them. A draft caressed her face, the inviting smell of vintage goods tickling her nose. Old papers, polished wood furniture, cracking leather newly oiled, and a pleasant citrus scent lingering in the air all spoke to the caregivers who worked here. The front hall was trimmed in dark walnut, thick and imposing.

Annalise's footsteps echoed on the floor as she stepped off the wool carpet runner and toward the door on the left. What used to be a parlor now doubled as the registration room. It was significantly brighter here. The windows were tall and wide, sunshine streaming in and bouncing off pale-yellow walls. An angular woman sat behind the registration desk, which was probably relocated from the study, if one judged by its bulk and manly ambience. Books stacked in piles and a few index boxes sat in front of her, along with rows of photographs. Her fingers tapped a medley on the desktop computer's keyboard.

Clearing her throat, Annalise waited. She tried to appear patient, but her foot timed a rhythm on the floor that was probably more attention grabbing than her tentative cough.

"Annalise Forsythe!" Brown eyes lifted and peered through metal-rimmed glasses. Gray hair was pulled back into a low ponytail, and the curator ceased typing to stand. Moving around the desk with hands extended, she grasped Annalise's.

"I'm Gloria Fairchild." The woman, Gloria, squeezed Annalise's hands.

"Hello." Her face must have communicated her confusion.

Gloria squeezed her hands again and then released them, crossing her arms over a silky blouse with a very 1980s-style bow tied at the collar. "Gossamer Grove is just getting too big. I was your Sunday school teacher when you were a little girl. I believe it was first grade."

Oh yes. Gloria Fairchild. *Mrs. Fairchild*, as she called her as a child. Annalise adjusted her messenger bag on her shoulder that was loaded with folders of clippings and photos she'd taken from Eugene Hayes's trailer. "You might guess why I'm here then."

Gloria tipped her head and smiled with a nod. "I have a suspicion. The town has been all abuzz. I've heard all about Eugene's trailer and the strange pictures and news clippings. What a shame. And how curious! But, dear"—Gloria leaned closer and patted Annalise's arm—"I don't believe any of those rumors that somehow you disregarded him. Your work with the food pantry is honorable."

Annalise smiled gratefully.

They both jolted when the front hall doors banged shut.

Garrett loped in, eyebrow quirked and a question stretched across his face. His eyes captured Annalise's, and he gave his head a shake. "What are you doing?"

"Um . . ." Annalise gave Gloria a smile, then turned to spear Garrett with a wide-eyed look that said *Not now*. "Research."

Garrett's eyebrow rose even higher. He shrugged and palmed the air. "Why didn't you tell me your tires were slashed?"

"Not here," Annalise muttered. "Did you follow me?"

"Of course I did." Garrett had no shame. "You left the coffee shop like a bat out of—" he glanced at Gloria—"I wanted to make sure you're okay."

"Oh, dear," Gloria said, the wrinkles on her face soft and deepening, "He's concerned about you."

"Thanks." Garrett tossed the older woman a smile that reached his eyes and creased his cheeks and caused Gloria to lift her hand to the bow at her throat with a self-conscious chuckle.

Oh brother.

Annalise had forgotten how charming Garrett could be when he wanted to be.

She held up her hands. "My tires . . . the police are working on that."

"Yeah, I know. Brent said there weren't any clues as to who did it. Not even a street cam."

"A street camera in Gossamer Grove?" Annalise quirked her own eyebrows. "This isn't the big city."

"Obviously," Garrett mumbled.

"What can I help you with?" Gloria inserted herself into the conversation like a pleasant little peacemaker in the middle of thwarted lovers.

Who was Annalise kidding? They *were* thwarted lovers. The

thought brought warmth to her cheeks, and Garrett noticed, like he noticed everything about her. He narrowed his eyes in question, and Annalise shifted her attention back to Gloria.

"My first question is in regard to Eugene Hayes. I find it interesting he went so long unnoticed on his property, with back taxes even, and no one seems to really know who he was." Annalise sensed Garrett take a step closer. He wasn't going away, that much was clear.

A sigh fell from Gloria's lightly glossed lips that wrinkled with age at the edges. "The people who care about him know who he was. But they're few and far between. Come. Let's go sit down in my office."

They moved to a room off the parlor with overstuffed red velvet chairs, a coffee table with a tea set on it, and more sunlight streaming in from windows nearby. Gloria settled into one of the chairs and waved her hands for Annalise and Garrett to do the same.

Her eyes sparkled with sadness. "Eugene Hayes," she breathed in a slow sort of recollection. "We went to school together, actually. Way back in the late fifties. Elementary school, then the upper grades, although Eugene left when he was in tenth grade to work on his father's farm. I lost track of him then for quite some time. We were from different worlds, although the same town. He was a farm boy, I an independent young woman, so in the sixties it was off to the university for me."

Annalise exchanged glances with Garrett. At least someone in this town could finally give them a starting point. Some answers maybe.

Gloria drummed her fingers on the arm of the chair and smiled. "The next I heard of Eugene, he had been drafted into the war and was stationed somewhere in Vietnam."

"When did he come back to Gossamer Grove?" Garrett asked.

Gloria shook her head and adjusted her glasses. "Oh, I don't know. By the time the war ended, I was married and we'd relocated to Minnesota for my husband's job. It was years later before we moved our family back to Gossamer Grove, and by then Eugene was a mystery to most. An alcoholic, a recluse, and for all sakes and purposes, one of those people you're so set on helping, Annalise. God bless you for it."

There was an awkward shift of Garrett's body in his chair. He looked ridiculous in a Victorian wing-back chair.

Gloria continued. "I knew in the nineties that Eugene was living in an old trailer. But for the most part, he wasn't the focus of anyone's attention, least of all mine. On occasion, he would come into the library. I worked there for several years before I came here. He would spend hours on the microfiche when he did visit."

"What was he looking for?" Annalise asked. She scooted to the edge of her seat.

Gloria bit her bottom lip. "That's one of the reasons why he still sticks out in my memory. He read old papers, old archives, things the library had scanned that this historical society had not. I even heard that he used to scrounge around in the newspaper's basement. Tyler Darrow's father allowed it, more because Eugene was harmless. But I wouldn't be surprised if Eugene carried off old artifacts from that basement. He was curious, that man. He had a proclivity, it seemed, for history. One of his favorite time periods to read about at the library was when Gossamer Grove was blessed, so to speak, with twin revivalists. The Corbin brothers."

Garrett cracked his knuckles.

Annalise couldn't help herself. She reached out and laid a hand over his to keep him from fidgeting. It was a move she made in error. He flipped his hand palm up and captured hers so that they sat across from Gloria, holding hands. Garrett's fingers interlinked with Annalise's.

She tugged.

He tugged back.

Her lips tightened and she gave one more tug.

Garrett's mouth tilted up in a smile.

Gloria's eyes twinkled, as she hadn't missed the exchange. She

144

chose to ignore the not-so-subtle spat in front of her. "A rowdier, more controversial set of twins you'll never hear of again."

"How so?" Garrett asked.

Gloria frowned, considering for a moment. "Things like barroom brawls. They would go into the saloon and start preaching. If you read the newspaper articles from the *Daily Democrat*, the Corbin brothers weren't afraid to stare sin in the face and cause quite the stir, but they still had an impactful ministry, it seems."

Gloria stood, smoothing her shirt over her straight hips. "Let me show you. I have some scrapbooks with newsprint about the Corbin brothers. Maybe something in there will help you understand why Eugene Hayes was so enamored with them. It's really a rather forgotten but sensational series of events in Gossamer Grove."

They followed Gloria into a dining room converted to research room. Garrett finally released her hand, and Annalise massaged it with her other hand. She could still feel his callused skin and strong grip.

"Here we are." Gloria laid a large rectangular scrapbook on the table, its corners bonded with worn leather triangular guards. The black cover was embossed with the faded gold word *Memories*.

"We found this old book in the home of Margaret Darrow about five years ago after she died. You know Tyler's grandmother, don't you? The *Daily Democrat* has been in their family for well over a century." Gloria opened the scrapbook, and a musty scent permeated the air. Long strips of newspaper clippings were glued onto black paper pages. She pointed to one. "This clipping tells of the Corbin brothers' partiality for tandem bicycling. Apparently, they rode from saloon to saloon to preach the Good News during the evening hours."

"Didn't they have tent revival services?" Annalise peered down at the article. She vaguely recalled reading about the old-time religion ceremonies. Of Billy Sunday preaching under canopies. Even the early days of Billy Graham and congregants flocking to sit beneath a tent to hear the Word of God preached.

"Oh yes." Gloria gently flipped a few pages in. "This article tells of an evening revival where Jedidiah Corbin presented such a rousing sermon it stirred up the people. I'm not sure that it was a positive stirring. Oh, let's see . . ." She turned the book and squinted to make out the fine print. Reading aloud, she continued the tale. "Well, the title itself is quite telling: 'Insults, Epithets, Vituperation Vomited Forth by Twin Blasphemous Grafters.'

"'The *Daily Democrat* has refrained from outright discussion in regard to the circus that has been holding its acts in tent services by the pond and outside saloons. Also in question are the church organizations that allow the Corbin brothers to trail the teachings of the Meek and Lowly into filth and slang bordering on obscenity. The women of Gossamer Grove have been insulted by the brothers' language. When confronted by a local church leader as to whether content of the sermon was appropriate, Jedidiah Corbin was quoted as responding, 'Some of you don't like it, do you? You'll twist your face into a corkscrew and your head into hell.' In summary, the Corbin brothers' message of the Gospel is being taken into question as to whether it truly is upholding the church of God.'"

Gloria stopped, her eyes wide and a slight smile on her face. "I do believe even now that would be, um, a fairly controversial approach within the church regarding evangelism."

"And yet they're still credited for bringing revival to Gossamer Grove?" Annalise could understand why Eugene Hayes might be intrigued by the stories, as they were quite theatrical.

"Apparently so." Gloria closed the scrapbook. She tapped the top of the book with her fingertips. "There are more news stories in here, not only of remarkable amounts of baptisms but also of changes in the community. Good changes. The Baptist church went from a dwindling congregation to well over a hundred strong."

"That's not the First Baptist Church still up on Walnut Street, is it?" Garrett interjected.

Gloria nodded. "Interesting, yes? That men this conflicting and this divisive were still so key in bringing life and faith back into a dying church? And for it to affect generations over a hundred years later?"

Annalise reached for her bag. The Corbin brothers were an interesting piece of history, but how or *if* they related to the obituary for Harrison Greenwood was yet to be seen. Not to mention how they related to her. She wasn't Baptist. She wasn't really *anything* of late.

She pulled out Harrison's photograph along with the sepia-tone print of the unidentified woman. She laid them atop the scrapbook.

"Do you know what Harrison Greenwood might have had to do with the revival?"

Gloria focused on the photo, and a warm smile lit her face. She turned to Garrett. "My, my, you are the spitting image of him."

Garrett offered an awkward smile.

She furrowed her brow. "Hmmm . . . I'm afraid I don't have the answer to that question." Gloria lifted the picture of the mystery woman and studied it.

"What about her?" Annalise tapped the photograph of the woman.

Gloria shook her head. "No. I don't recognize her at all. You're welcome to browse our photo database. Although"—Gloria pushed the scrapbook in Annalise's direction—"you may have to do all of this the old-fashioned way, dear."

Annalise stared at the book. Then her eyes widened as Gloria reached down and hefted a banker's box, dropping it on the table next to the scrapbook.

"Dig, read, take notes, and dig some more," Gloria finished with a grin.

A wonderful thought, Annalise mused, if she could avoid more recluses dying, house break-ins, and slashed tires. She glanced at Garrett. He met her eyes. The fact that he read her thoughts and understood with a nod of his head was disconcerting.

"We can search my family history online too," Garrett offered.

The Reckoning at Gossamer Pond

"Mom has a whole family tree built in her online ancestral account. Maybe that woman is one of my relatives."

Annalise grimaced. Yes. Garrett's mother. Getting the username and password to log in to her account made scaling the Great Wall of China seem like a simple game of hopscotch. She couldn't help but give Garrett a look of desperation.

"I'll help," he said.

They were the same words he'd used in Eugene Hayes's trailer the night of the break-in at her house. The implication planted butterflies in her stomach and caused old memories to surface at all the wrong times.

Garrett's eyes, so dark, so unconcernedly self-assured, stared into hers.

Annalise bit her bottom lip, then released it as she responded, forgetting Gloria witnessed it. "You'll help, until you're just not there anymore. Like before."

Garrett withdrew, his expression unreadable. His words in response stung. "And you'll take my help, and more, and then blame it all on me when it falls apart. Go ahead. I've spent a lifetime getting used to it."

CHAPTER 20

"You know you live in a creepy old house, don't you?" Christen stood from her chair at the kitchen table and retrieved the bag of mint Oreos from the counter.

Annalise gave the room a quick inspection. "It's not creepy."

"It has so many nooks and crannies. I swear, the Victorians sure knew how to add angles into their architecture. Shadows are everywhere. So, yes, considering recent events, it's creepy."

Christen raised an eyebrow as she came back to the table and plopped the Oreos down. Fingering one from its row, she waved it in a circular pattern as if selecting the items splayed out on the table. "Made more so, I might add, by the plethora of disturbing artifacts as seen here in Exhibit A."

Annalise smiled a little at her friend's overdramatization. But her vision drifted to the piles she'd created early in the evening after she escaped Garrett and the historical society's laundry basket of research.

"So, explain all this to me." Christen munched on the cookie. She'd dropped by after her kids were in bed, needing a break from home. Annalise was thankful Brent had an occasional night off.

Annalise drew a deep breath and reached up to adjust her ponytail, tucking wisps of hair behind her ears. "Okay. Pile one is newspaper articles photocopied by Eugene Hayes about the Corbin brothers' revival in 1907. Pile two is obituaries, although it's not

149

really a pile so much as a few obits. Pile three is old photographs Eugene had on his wall and desk. Pile four is pictures of me."

Christen nodded and swallowed her cookie, reaching for another. The packaging crinkled as she fumbled for an Oreo. "And we are assuming all of this is tied to you, and he's not just a really dead, weird old man?"

"Well, considering there are at least fifty different pictures of me here, I think that fact has been established for some time now."

"Hmm." Christen adjusted in her chair. "Fine. So we know this is Harrison Greenwood?" She pulled the man's picture from pile three.

"Correct." Annalise reached for a few older photocopied pictures. "These are two photographs of Harrison Greenwood as well. One with some family members, I assume, and another in front of his church."

"Was he a religious man?" Christen inquired.

Annalise gave her a wry smile. "Aren't all Greenwoods?"

"Pardon me." Christen rolled her eyes. "Was he a man of faith, not just pious and churchgoing for show?"

Annalise shook her head. "I'm not sure. But what I am sure of . . ." She reached for her iPad and flicked the screen on. "I logged on to that ancestry site and started researching Eugene Hayes. I need to understand why he felt connected to me, and frankly the Greenwoods. I found information that substantiated what Gloria at the historical society told me. I also found out some about his lineage."

"Like?" Christen had depleted half a row of Oreos.

Annalise shifted in her seat. "Well, Eugene was only twenty when he fought in Vietnam. He was born in 1948, and his father, Lawrence, was fifty-two when Eugene was born. So he was an older father, which may or may not be important. It also means that Lawrence was only eleven years old when the Corbin brothers were in town for their revival."

"Okay." Christen sealed the cookies before she could eat another row. "So maybe Eugene started researching his own family tree and that's one of the interesting time periods here in Gossamer Grove that his father lived through?"

"Maybe. But look at this other obituary Eugene had in his trailer." Annalise reached for pile two. She set Harrison Greenwood's obituary aside and lifted a copy of another obituary. "This was from the same year as the revival, 1907, and the same month of Harrison Greenwood's death."

"And?" Christen pulled her feet up onto the seat of her chair and wrapped her arms around her knees.

Annalise adjusted her glasses. "Dorothy Hayes. Lawrence's mother, and Eugene's grandmother."

"Okay, now that's weird!" Christen breathed.

"I know." Annalise nodded.

"And is it all Edgar Allan Poe creepy like Harrison's obituary?"

Annalise smoothed the page on the table. "It's not." She dropped her gaze and read. "'Dorothy Hayes. Born September third, 1854, passed from earth into God's loving arms on May fourteenth, 1907, after she was found in Gossamer Pond. Medical Examiner Dr. Rutherford Penchan has identified Dorothy as a victim of a tragic case of drowning. Funeral services will be held—'" Annalise stopped. "Blah, blah, blah. It's bland and boring."

Christen sniffed. "What'd you want? Another gloomy poem about buried sins and shameful secrets and the grave swallowing them whole?"

"No, but look at them." Annalise placed the obituaries side by side. "Harrison's is typewritten. Dorothy's even has the header of the *Daily Democrat* on it. So, what if Harrison's is fake?"

"Like a prank?"

Annalise shrugged. "I don't know. I showed it to Tyler at the paper, and he said it probably wasn't an obit run in the *Daily Democrat* because theirs of that time had an entirely different typeset."

Christen reached for the iPad and pulled it toward her.

Annalise eyed her friend, whose nose was scrunched up in

contemplation as she typed into the tablet. She grew antsy waiting for her unnaturally silent friend to say something.

Christen leaned closer to the tablet. "I wonder . . . what if the reason Eugene Hayes is so interested in Harrison Greenwood is because . . . bingo!"

"What?" Annalise hurried around the table to look over Christen's shoulder. They both stared at the iPad's screen.

"I just kept connecting the dots to suggested relations in Dorothy Hayes's family tree and look what happens."

Annalise frowned as she studied the online ancestral tree for Eugene Hayes. She blinked and leaned closer until her nose brushed Christen's hair. "Is that—?"

"Yeah," Christen breathed. She leaned away from Annalise, staring up into her face. "Eugene Hayes's grandmother, Dorothy, was Harrison Greenwood's sister-in-law."

"Which means . . ." Annalise moved to the sink and gripped the edges of the stainless-steel bowl. She stared out the window into the evening's blackness as a few pieces fell together in a very perplexing way. She turned back toward Christen, whose expression might have mirrored her own. Bewildered.

"Eugene Hayes is a distant cousin to the Greenwoods."

"Yeeeeeep." Christen dragged out the word, ending it with an exaggerated pop.

"Technically, then, Garrett's great-great-grandfather died in the same month as Eugene's grandmother."

"Same month. Same town. Same family attending both funerals."

Annalise bit the inside of her bottom lip. "With the probability that Eugene's dad, Lawrence, was at both his mother Dorothy's funeral and Garrett's great-great-grandfather's funeral."

The iPad slowly dimmed to black, and Christen picked at a fingernail while Annalise contemplated what it all might mean.

"Gossamer Grove gets smaller and smaller every day, doesn't it?" Christen broke the silence with her quiet mutter.

Annalise tried to take a deep breath, but the weight on her

chest made her breath shudder. "Smaller and more suspicious."
She caught Christen's look of empathy and shook her head. "I
should have left Gossamer Grove years ago. I could have avoided
all of this."

"Would you still have Gia if you had?" Christen asked the question that made the air in the room feel heavy.

Annalise didn't answer. She couldn't. Gia was a door she had
refused to open for years. Until Eugene Hayes's death busted it wide
open by force, leaving her exposed, weak, and very, very vulnerable.

CHAPTER 21

Libby

S he was helpless, utterly helpless. The only other time she'd felt
that way was years before. Libby remembered the gut-clenching
pain, the breath-stealing panic, and the screams that tried to
rip from her throat. Elijah had been there too. It was their secret,
their shared agony, and now . . . Libby watched him stagger as he
climbed down from his carriage. They shared distress a third time,
with the second, his father's death, barely having collected dust.

Even though he had the gentlemanly instinct to circle and help
her down, the feel of her hand in his failed to excite her as it once
had. She saw the grief etched into Elijah's face, the stoop of his
shoulders, the bow of his head. He was merely escorting her back
to the paper, but his mind was far away with his father and now
his aunt. Leave it to Mitch to abandon her at the pond and make a
mad dash back to the newspaper. Poor Elijah. Libby blinked away
the memories, the guilt. He was always rescuing her.

Libby opened the front door to the newspaper, surprised when
Elijah followed. She paused in the lobby, her shoes echoing on the
wood floor. Pulling her gloves from her hands gave her something to
do as she addressed the man that life had beaten. It had all started

with her, hadn't it? After all, she'd been the first person Elijah had tried to save, and since then . . . he'd lost too many.

"Can I do anything?" she murmured helplessly, wishing she could squelch the stark vision of Dorothy Hayes floating facedown in Gossamer Pond.

Elijah tugged off his hat and raked his fingers through his hair. He leveled shocked eyes on Libby. She tried not to look away, to hide from the reality of what had happened.

"I need to tell Mother." His broad chest rose with a deep sigh, his stare shifting out the window toward the morning bustle of Gossamer Grove's main street.

Libby reached out to lay a comforting hand on his arm, hesitated, then drew back. "I'm—I'm sure the police will tell her."

"The police?" Elijah's gaze swung to her face. "I should be there. She'll be crushed."

"Yes. Of course."

"It should have been Paul."

Libby knew Elijah didn't truly mean it. But the anxious panic that kept them both awake during the night, the desire to somehow intercede for Paul's life as foretold in the cryptic obituary, had now transferred to a blinded wish that it indeed had come true.

"You don't really mean that." Libby stepped forward and this time carried through with laying her hand on his arm. The touch seemed to startle him.

Elijah stared at her hand, then lifted his eyes to connect with hers. "No. No, I don't."

"Well, that's good." Paul's voice cracked the silence as he marched down the hallway from the back of the paper. He waved a telegram-sized paper in his hand. His eyes were buggy, his voice shaky, but the nasal tone still held hints of assumed superiority. "Another obituary was delivered."

Libby's hand flew up to cover her mouth. Elijah collapsed onto a chair by the front window.

"This is asinine," Elijah muttered. He leaned his elbows on his knees and ran his hands over his face.

Paul lowered his voice, casting anxious glances around the front lobby as if someone were eavesdropping. "Please tell me who died. I know they found someone in Gossamer Pond, but Mitch isn't blabbing anything to me."

"Paul—" Libby started.

"Tell me!" Paul demanded, his fingers crinkling the obituary in his hand as he fisted it in her face.

"D-Dorothy Hayes," she blurted with an uneasy peek at Elijah.

"No . . ." Paul breathed, his face whitening. He thrust the paper toward Elijah, who took it. With a solemn expression, his dark eyes skimmed the words. Libby could see the indentations on the back of the page that indicated it had been typewritten. She edged closer to Elijah and looked down over his shoulder where he sat.

> Dorothy Hayes. Born September 3rd, 1854. Died May 14th, 1907.
>> I heard all things in the heaven and in the earth. I heard many
>> things in hell. How, then, am I mad? Hearken! and observe
>> how healthily—how calmly I can tell you the whole story.
> Her shame exposed, a vacant soul
> Death knocks at one door, then knocks no more
> She floats on waves made of fire
> But on her lips a cry of horror

Libby leaned against the picture window, her knees weak and her heartbeat thudding a cadence against her rib cage. She'd been right. Death had knocked on Paul's door, teased and taunted, but moved on to take the life of another victim. One with implied shame—just like Deacon Greenwood.

"Whoever wrote it has a fondness for taking Poe's writings and massacring them with their own attempts at morbid, putrid, godforsaken *rubbish*!" Paul snatched the obituary from Elijah's hand, balled it in his fist, and launched it at the wall.

Elijah's jaw clenched, and his mouth twitched. He looked at

Paul, not standing, as if his legs wouldn't hold his weight yet. "The police already believe it to be an accident."

Paul seemed to rethink his furious toss, and he scurried to retrieve the obituary. He spread it open against his leg, attempting to smooth out the creases. "Then I'll take this to them. I'll show them. It's evidence of murder, that's what it is. And where is mine, from last night? They must have that too."

"They already saw it," Libby supplied. Her throat was dry and her voice weak. Trembling started in her calves and moved up her torso. She hugged herself close, feeling cold as the realization of helplessness grew into a deeper sense of utter powerlessness.

"And?" Paul insisted on an answer, his eyes snapping.

"And . . ." Elijah drew in a long, agonizing breath before pushing himself from the chair as if he were a stiff old man. "You're alive." He gave Paul a pointed look. Then Libby. "Which means your obituary, Paul, was a hoax. Go ahead, take my aunt's obit to them. They'll laugh you off now. A disgusting, concocted scheme by the paper to monopolize on my family's deaths. That's how they'll see it, considering who delivered it. In fact, I'll bring you my father's and yours and you can try your hand with them. Then keep them for your collection."

Elijah ended with a glare that skewered the newspaperman.

Paul wasn't ruffled. "Yes. Do. I will make sure the police see all three."

Elijah turned to Libby, a blank look on his face. "More disturbing to me is whoever wrote these obituaries is convinced Dorothy, like my father, hid some egregious sin."

He moved to the front window, his hands at his waist, his jacket shoved back exposing a shirt that upon waking must have been crisp and starched. Now it was soiled from being at the pond, from the moment he'd bent over his aunt's corpse and steeled his expression as he pushed drenched hair from her pallid face.

"What sin?" Elijah demanded, spinning to face Libby and Paul. "What could my father possibly have done to *deserve* being hung from the rafters of his own carriage house? Or my aunt? Drowned?"

A suspicion nagged within Libby, and she couldn't help but cast a wary eye toward Paul. "And why were you suddenly shown mercy? What sin have you committed that you so quickly found justification for it?"

Paul blustered, shoving his spectacles up the bridge of his nose in his familiar fashion. "I do not like what you're implying, Miss Sheffield."

"Of course not." Libby swallowed. "But if you wrote that obituary yourself, you would therefore deflect all suspicion with the creation of Dorothy's. How could anyone assume you took her life when you yourself were targeted for your own appointment with death?"

"I did not murder Dorothy Hayes!" Paul bellowed, just as the front door of the paper opened.

Mitch stood in the doorway, a bewildered expression on his face as fresh air rushed into the lobby, along with the busy sounds of the street behind him.

Elijah rubbed his hands over his eyes as if he'd seen and heard quite enough. Paul choked back whatever words had been about to erupt from his mouth, and Libby bit down hard on her bottom lip.

"Ahem. Yes. Well," Mitch began, taking in the three of them, their words hanging between them all in the front of the newspaper building. "Now that we have that out of the way, I'd like to get to publishing the news." His dismissal capped the tension with an invisible but indelibly bold exclamation point.

—m—

The town was stirring with rumors and rumblings. Deacon Greenwood and Dorothy Hayes, both dead within the span of a week, both related, though by marriage, and both such odd ways to die.

Libby hurried down the boardwalk, leaving the newspaper

behind as she ran an errand for Mitch. If only she could tell her father no for once. Just once. But the black cloud of obligation to do her duty, to watch out for others, never lifted. Mitch needed a new tie for Dorothy Hayes's funeral. To which, Libby could almost place odds he'd not been invited to the service. No press would be or should be. Still, her own mother was sure to attend, as the support for Elijah's mother. Therefore, by default Mitch had an automatic opportunity to sidle in and disguise his news-sniffing curiosity with condolences.

It was only this morning that the medical examiner deemed Dorothy's death as natural with no physical evidence to support a claim of foul play. As Elijah had predicted, the police had given Paul a distrustful brow-raise when he offered them Dorothy's morbid obituary, along with the others Elijah had given him. Paul had scurried away in haste, attempting to avoid any suspicion of blame being thrown in his direction.

The police stated that regardless of the examiner's conclusions, they were attempting to find out why Dorothy Hayes had been at the pond in her chemise in the middle of the night. Her husband had last seen her when he went to bed, stating she had remained awake to read a novel. The next morning they were fishing her body from the pond. She was a lady, a mother of one son, Lawrence, and a widow who was upright, faithful to her local church and ladies' society, and if nothing else, very, very proper. The setting of her death did not suit Dorothy Hayes's reputation.

A real obituary had been submitted for Dorothy as well by Elijah's mother, and that was the one that went to print. The cryptic obituaries had disappeared somewhere in Paul's clutches, and Libby had a sneaking suspicion he'd disposed of them or filed them away, not to be seen again.

She edged around a mother, who was leaning over a baby carriage and cooing at her baby. They had parked just outside of the drugstore, which was kitty corner to the haberdashery. With a glance in all four directions, Libby hustled across the brick road, pausing as a motorcar puffed by, leaving behind a plume of exhaust. She skirted a pile of horse droppings and hurried toward the haberdashery whose large picture window boasted at least fifteen hats on display, a tailored suit, and the name *Hamilton's 'Dashery* painted in bold scrolling letters across it.

"Out of the way!" A shout startled Libby. She looked up to see a riderless horse barreling down on her. A body slammed into hers and shoved her out of the way of the wild-eyed animal that charged past with a screeching whinny. Her rescuer held her against a slender frame, and for a second they remained frozen on the walk outside of the haberdashery.

"Are you all right, Libby?" a gentleman shouted from across the street, dodging a carriage. Reverend Mueller held his hat to his head with a hand as he stared after the horse being corralled by other concerned citizens. Calvin jogged not far behind him, his smile almost silly, stretching ear to ear. Libby twisted in her rescuer's hold and drew back to see Jacobus Corbin's long face and narrow nose.

"Oh, gracious. I beg your pardon. Never did I imagine that I—you put yourself in danger on my behalf, and well, that was heroic. No. No, not heroic. Well, it was, but then you're not particularly a hero, are you?" Libby caught a glimmer of humor in the placid face of the evangelist. She stopped trying to ease the awkwardness and instead focused on disentangling herself from his embrace. She equated the fluttering in her stomach to the terror she'd just experienced, but she couldn't help a quick glance at the revivalist twin. He met her eyes with a slightly raised eyebrow, causing a blush to warm her face.

Reverend Mueller and Calvin were almost upon them. To the east, striding toward them, Jedidiah Corbin.

"Are you hurt?" Reverend Mueller hurried to her side.

"No. I'm quite all right." Libby frowned. Almost run over by a renegade horse? What with the odd deaths of late, she had to convince herself not to jump to a conclusion that it had somehow been frightened into a frenzy for the very purpose of trampling her to death.

"Lollie." Calvin edged around his father. He blinked, and then blinked again as if clearing some fog from his mind but was unsuccessful. "Want to get a soda?" He pointed to the drugstore.

"Not now, Calvin." Reverend Mueller patted his son's arm and shared an understanding look with Libby.

"I am fine. Truly." Libby mustered a smile. It wouldn't offend her if they all went about their business. The attention was disconcerting, and the fact that she'd been swept to safety by the enigmatic Jacobus Corbin made it all so much more bewildering. She wasn't certain why, but when she caught him looking at her—those icy-blue eyes inscrutable—Libby was sure she'd never felt as safe and never felt as threatened at the same time. It was a conundrum she daren't explore further. The man and his brother were proving to be nothing less than firebrands to Gossamer Grove.

"You put the fear of God into me." Reverend Mueller swiped his hat from his head as he addressed her. Wisps of graying hair fluttered in the breeze.

"The fear of God should already be in you." Jedidiah Corbin's bold voice sliced through the moment as he came upon them.

Calvin's face broke into a smile. "Hi, Preacher!"

Jedidiah looked down his nose at her, his eyes narrowing. Had he spooked the horse with intent to harm her? Libby took a step away from him, but that, unfortunately, only put her closer to Jacobus, who remained rooted where he stood. It didn't calculate properly, and Libby attempted to erase away all her suspicions. That Jedidiah would have orchestrated spooking a runaway horse was absurd. That would be just shy of breaking one of the Ten Commandments. "Thou shalt not murder." The thought of it stole warmth from Libby's face. Murder. Cleansing of those with shameful sins. If the Corbin twins couldn't rid the town of sinful practices, perhaps they could eliminate the sinner?

"I best be on my way," Libby mumbled, catching the more

161

comforting warmth of Reverend Mueller's concerned gaze. "I truly am fine. Thank you. All of you."

Libby nodded in Reverend Mueller's direction. Calvin sidled up to Jedidiah Corbin, who glowered down at him as if he were too simple to understand enough theology to successfully be saved at all.

"I will escort you safely back to the paper," Jacobus inserted.

Libby started as his hand curled around her elbow. She eyed his long fingers.

"That would be good," Reverend Mueller nodded.

"But I—" Libby cast a helpless glance at Calvin, who didn't sense her discomfort or come to her aid.

"Come." Jacobus urged her from the haberdashery.

Jedidiah Corbin strode away, a jabbering Calvin following in his steps like a loyal disciple. Reverend Mueller tipped his hat and continued his way, leaving Libby alone with Jacobus.

"Please." Libby pulled back.

Thankfully, Jacobus released her. She didn't wish to play tug-of-war with her elbow.

"I need to purchase a tie for my father."

"Your father should purchase his own tie," Jacobus stated blandly. "It's unsafe for you to be unescorted."

It was daylight. It was also 1907. Ladies were doing many things unchaperoned now.

"I'm capable of seeing to myself," Libby maintained under her breath, rather afraid to be so bold as to speak her mind out loud.

Jacobus gave her a sideways glance. "It's not your capability I question, Miss Sheffield. Rather, I find you very accomplished. Intelligent as well. But, only a fool would argue the idea that two are better than one. It's biblical, after all."

Libby didn't argue.

Safely across the street, Libby stepped onto the walk with Jacobus having reclaimed her elbow with a loose grasp. She stopped and mustered more pluck. He stared down at her with a raised brow of question at her pause.

"Reverend Corbin," Libby said and forced just the right amount of firmness into her voice, "thank you for your generosity and fine care. I am well enough to be on my own now."

Jacobus's eyes narrowed but for a moment, and Libby saw in them something she hadn't seen in his brother's. Kindness, perhaps?

"I mean well, Miss Sheffield."

"I'm sure," she acquiesced, studying the strings on her purse. Trying to maintain a very proper and cool composure was about as simple as convincing Paul he needed to stop arguing with her father. "But, I—I much prefer to be on my own."

Curse her wobbly voice. The reverend might just be capable of wilting her with one narrowed study of his eyes.

Jacobus tugged on the lapels of his jacket. "Miss Sheffield, I must say, I've experienced and witnessed many traumas in my life. I wish to impart something to you." He paused.

This was not going well. Escaping this man—this *revivalist*—whose entire posture mimicked a wickedly intelligent professor rather than a vibrant hellfire-and-brimstone preacher. He exuded a confidence that was just shy of arrogance due to a humble restraint one might credit to the man's devotion to God. Regardless, Libby knew she was trapped by her own obligation to etiquette and polite discourse, this versus a snub and spitfire toss of her head as she turned her back to the disquieting man.

Jacobus cleared his throat. She blinked. He was well aware of how she was scrutinizing him in her mind. He had to be. He'd waited to impart his wisdom on her, as if allowing Libby time to contemplate. Now he blinked—finally—and continued.

"No amount of mystery in one's soul can escape the ever-watchful eye of God. One may carry guilt and shame with them for years, only to discover that while they attempted to dodge God's judgment, they instead cheated themselves of His forgiveness."

Jacobus had a curled strand of hair that fell down the middle of his broad forehead. Libby focused on it. His voice was hypnotic, reaching into a place deep in her spirit she'd locked away even though

163

she wasn't entirely sure what he was talking about. But she compre-hended two words quite well: *guilt* and *shame*. Old feelings bubbled up inside her as if tamped down for too long. She tried to ignore them by conjuring up current events, the shock of Dorothy Hayes's death, anything but revisiting the deep remorse that lived inside of her. Lived there since she and Elijah had ceased discussing it.

"Do you believe in grace, Miss Sheffield?" Jacobus moved out of the way of two gentlemen passing them on the walk. His move-ment urged Libby to take a step closer to the drugstore window.

She blinked in surprise. "Pardon me?"

"You believe in wrongdoings, but do you believe there is grace?"

Libby nodded. "I do."

She didn't. She wanted to. Or perhaps she did believe in grace of some sort. The eternal, distant grace offered her in exchange for repentance.

He stepped closer to her and lowered his head so he could study her. The lines by his eyes were not harsh like his brother's, but there was still something about him that made Libby question whether she could trust him. Maybe it was his brother, or maybe it was the way her nerves stood on end whenever he was near. As if the man had known her for years, known her heart, known her secrets. As if he could reason through her mind and conclude who she was simply based on the facts he found there. It was a disconcerting feeling, be-lieving someone could administer a verdict about you and be correct.

"Your sins, Miss Sheffield, can be forgotten by the Lord. He will not hold them against you if your heart is contrite. But it is a horrible place to wallow when you cannot forgive yourself."

He knew. Somehow, Jacobus Corbin knew everything.

Libby could sense the warmth leaving her face, and Jacobus tipped his head.

"Be careful, Libby," he whispered. But it wasn't threatening, as she might expect. Instead, it was telling. Very telling. As if he knew of dangers she had yet to discover and was giving her a warning, to save her, as Elijah once had.

CHAPTER 22

Annalise

Annalise left the door to the trailer locked, opting against fresh air in exchange for a modicum of safety. The trailer still reeked, but she had ceased trying to pinpoint the exact smell. What with the empty liquor bottles, piles of dried-out cans from soup dinners, and a few mouse carcasses she'd discovered, this place needed to be torched. But, here she was, pilfering through junk to try to uncover more clues regarding what had been going on in the mind of Eugene Hayes in the days before he died.

She paused to pull out her cellphone. Christen was supposed to meet her over ten minutes ago and she hadn't arrived yet. Annalise could feel Brent's glare from a mile away and hear his admonition.

"You've had a break-in and we've found no answers as to who slashed your tires. You do not go to that trailer alone."

Of course, on further thought, even if Christen did show up, he probably wouldn't approve of the mother of his children being her bodyguard.

Running late. Sorry. Babysitter got held up. Didn't have heart to tell her to hurry.

The Reckoning at Gossamer Pond

Annalise smiled. Christen did try to be all things to all people.

She turned her attention back to the task at hand. She'd already cleared off most of the desktop, gathering more photographs of herself and random scribbled notes that really made no sense to her. The walls were empty now since she'd unpinned the photographs. But with the new revelation that in a roundabout way, Eugene Hayes was cousin to Garrett, Annalise had to return to the trailer. In case she'd missed something. Somewhere.

Two deaths in 1907, one a Greenwood and another a direct relation to a Greenwood. That couldn't be happenstance. It was too convenient. A supposed suicide and a drowning. Neither were normal deaths by any means. It wasn't as if there'd been an outbreak of smallpox or even a bad flu. Something happened in the Greenwood history, and it seemed Eugene Hayes was connecting more dots than even Annalise could see now. Then why would it be her pictures displayed across the trailer wall of the recluse instead of Garrett's? Or Garrett's father, or for that matter, the entire Greenwood family? She had no ties to the Greenwoods, except for her one confidential, guarded secret. That Eugene Hayes would have figured it out was hard to believe. He'd have had no reason to even look.

Annalise knelt on the floor, glad she'd worn her oldest pair of jeans. Puffs of dust in the carpet tickled her nose, and she was almost certain that the carpet was damp. Reaching for the top newspaper on a pile of papers, Annalise browsed the headline to make sure it had no significance before she threw it in the black garbage bag next to her. It was from 2013. She reached for the next and the next until half of the pile was depleted. There went 2013 into the trash. Annalise tried to recollect that year, but like many others, they all melted together in her mind, always with Gia in the forefront.

The image of her infant daughter was never going to stop crowding out life. The guilt ridiculed Annalise daily. Better choices, better care, better responsibility. She should have been . . . better. And, she was trying, wasn't she? A penance of sorts, especially her work in the food pantry. Helping those who needed saving. Those who needed grace. Someone had told her once—maybe it had been someone at church when she used to attend—that grace couldn't be earned. It was given. Annalise had yet to find that present wrapped under her spiritual Christmas tree. Maybe she was doing something wrong. Something she hadn't put her finger on yet.

She attempted to rein in her tempestuous thoughts. Lately, her brain was on a virtual merry-go-round of emotions, facts, questions, and bullet-pointed lists. Oh, for more bullet-pointed lists and less emotions! She was a thinker—an overthinker, truth be told—and she wanted to be in control. But this chaos? It was enough to send her to a therapist.

She reached for the next newspaper. Moving backward to 2012. Her eyes dropped to the remaining one-third of the pile, and her chest tightened. A few fast blinks and Annalise knew she really was seeing it. Hidden between 2013 and 2012 was another picture. This one of a very pregnant eighteen-year-old Annalise. Her breaths came in quick staccato intakes and exhales as she reached for the photograph. It was the only one ever taken of her pregnant, and it'd been taken by her Aunt Tracy. She remembered the moment the picture had been snapped. It was as clear in her mind as if it'd been yesterday.

Fingering the bent corner of the picture, Annalise sat back on her heels, tears burning the backs of her eyes. There she was, eight months' pregnant, in the garden outside of her aunt's home in Connecticut. The place she had gone to hide, as if she lived in 1950 and bore the full shame of an overtly promiscuous girl. It didn't matter that it was really 2006 and most pregnant eighteen-year-olds just registered for college anyway, or got a job and started single-parenting. No. The plane ticket had arrived, and Annalise was flying her way east before she could think for herself.

It was in that moment she'd almost been convinced God had completely washed His hands of her. If it hadn't been for her mother's older sister, Aunt Tracy, she would have been. But Tracy had some sort of crazy faith that she took with her to the grave. Annalise wouldn't have minded lambasting God for every bad dish she'd been handed, including Aunt Tracy's stage-four breast cancer. But, it was Tracy who claimed that God had enough grace to cover her through her dying process, and Annalise needed to give Him a chance.

The memories invaded like old ghosts long locked away. The picture shook in Annalise's hand. Fresh air. She needed fresh air. Grasping the arm of a chair, Annalise hefted her way off the floor, her toe kicking the remaining pile of newspapers and sending them sliding across the floor. She stumbled to the door, her throat sore from holding back unwanted tears. She'd gone almost twelve years being numb, finding a semblance of sanity during torturous memories. Now, from the grave, Eugene Hayes had the audacity to dig it all up with a picture he shouldn't even possess.

She cleared the three rickety steps of the trailer's porch and hiked a few yards into the woods, taking deep gulps of air. The breeze rustled the new leaves on the oak and maple trees. Glowing almost emerald green with vegetation, the forest was beautiful. Like life should be if one could only look ahead and forget the ruins they'd left in their past.

Annalise ran her thumb over the image of her eighteen-year-old face. Three weeks after the picture was taken, she'd heard Gia's cry. Muted, short, and wobbly. The vision of her tiny little arms flailing their way out of the swaddling blanket, fighting, as if to tell them all she would not be held down, but she would fly.

The day the picture was taken was the last day she'd allowed herself to consider being a mother. It was the day her future and Gia's future permanently changed.

Brushing away the tears that wet her face, Annalise glanced around her. No one was there. She needn't be embarrassed mourning for a child few knew she'd had. The trees crowded around her and were suffocating. Undergrowth tangled around her ankles.

Annalise turned toward the trailer. Christen hadn't come yet, she was a mess, and Brent's warning kept coming to mind. Inside the trailer was one thing, but here? She was too exposed.

Without thought, Annalise crumpled the photograph in her hand as she took a step back toward the trailer. It wasn't a memory she wanted, and it wasn't one Eugene Hayes should have ever seen. Annalise drew her hand back to throw the picture into the woods. She glanced at it in her palm and stopped. There was ink on the back of the photograph. Probably a date, but it was enough to give Annalise pause. She lowered her arm and un-crinkled the picture.

Annalise Forsythe
Garrett Greenwood
Harrison Greenwood
Libby Sheffield
Corbin twins
Dorothy Hayes
Dad (Lawrence)
Me

The list of names had been penned in the same handwriting as other notes in Eugene's trailer. It was as if he'd created a character playlist on the back of her picture. Libby Sheffield? That was a new name, but the fact he'd penned "Me" gave Annalise more pause than anything. Eugene *had* connected himself to all of them. Somehow.

She smoothed the picture on her leg, emotions calming with the diversion of the mystery yet to be solved. Annalise looked up when a rustling sounded in front of her. Her searching eyes landed on a black squirrel that scampered from one branch to another. She took a few more steps toward the trailer, then glanced down at the photograph as she walked. Something else had been written under the list of names, but it had obviously at one point been set in water and smeared. The handwriting—from what she could see of it—seemed different. More cursive and loopy.

Annalise stopped, lifted it closer to her face, and squinted. "Save?"

she muttered to herself, thinking she'd deciphered the first word. She adjusted her glasses and tilted the photograph toward the light filtering through the treetops.

Save Annalise

Her mind registered the fateful words just as a twig snapped behind her. Annalise spun, her feet rustling in the fallen leaves of last summer. A scream choked in her throat just as an arm swung at her, a fist colliding with her face. Catapulting backward, Annalise's backside slammed against a tree root. Her attacker leaped on her, pushing her shoulders into the ground. As the face covered with a ski mask blurred in Annalise's vision, blackness filled in as if her eyes were closed.

"Eugene was wrong about you." The words hissed in her ear as the weight of the man pressed down on her body. "You don't deserve to have anything."

His callused hands were on her naked skin at the waist of her jeans where her shirt had slipped up.

Dear God . . . No. The prayer screamed from her subconscious. For now, in the abandoned property of Eugene Hayes, it was only God who could hear her screams.

—m—

She blinked, clearing fog from her vision. The room was dim, a rhythmic beeping greeted her ears, and the smell was a mixture of bleached sheets, sterile air, and beef stroganoff.

"Annalise?" Christen's voice came from the blur. Annalise turned toward the outline of her friend, and slowly Christen's face gained clarity. Worry in her expression was the first thing Annalise noticed. Second was the sprawling body of Garrett, draped across a hospital room couch behind her. He was sound asleep.

Annalise swung her attention back to Christen. The woods. The picture. The hands groping her body. She clawed at the sheets scrambling to sit up. Christen's calming hand on her shoulder pressed her gently back down.

"Shhh, honey. Don't make sudden moves. You have a concussion."

Annalise could believe it. Her head pounded as nausea sprung up, eliminating any interest in the beef stroganoff being served up in the hallway to patients. She assessed her body by concentrating on where she hurt. Her backside felt bruised, her shoulders too, and her head felt like it weighed three tons.

Christen's murmur interrupted Annalise's frantic mental assessment. "You were attacked at Eugene's trailer. Do you remember?"

"What happened?" Annalise whispered hoarsely.

"It could have been worse. Much worse." Christen lifted a plastic water bottle and positioned its straw in Annalise's lips. Annalise took a long draw of cool water and closed her eyes.

For a moment, she was petrified it'd been an assault of worse proportions. A rustling sound caused her to open her eyes, and when she did, her gaze collided with the concerned brown eyes of Garrett looking over Christen's shoulder.

"Hey." His voice was gentle, and Christen shifted so he could edge closer to the bed.

"He's been camping out here," Christen explained, pointing her thumb at him, a *Be nice* glint in her eye.

Annalise offered him a neutral smile before diverting her attention back to Christen. She didn't know what to make of Garrett standing sentry over her while she'd been out.

"How'd I get in the hospital?"

Christen tipped her head and raised her eyebrow with a stern arch that had no impact because of the sheen of anxious tears that glossed her eyes. "My babysitter finally showed up."

"Huh?" It was all so cloudy, so confusing.

"I was supposed to meet you at Eugene's trailer and I was running late. When I finally got there, you were lying on the ground just outside the trailer. Brent thinks my car must've chased away your attacker."

That was a little too much for her brain now. Annalise let her eyes slip shut, and she listened to Garrett and Christen mumble.

A nurse came in and took her vitals, fingertips cool against her skin. Then, after what seemed like hours, the room was quiet.

Annalise braved opening her eyes, sensing even Christen had departed now. The room was dim, lights having been lowered. The hospital room curtain was pulled to shield her bed from the doorway beyond. Annalise released a shaky breath.

"You okay?"

The deep voice gave Annalise a start and she yelped, swinging her hand up as if to strike her attacker. Garrett's fingers curled gently around her wrist as he stepped from the shadows.

"Hey, I'm sorry. I didn't mean to scare you."

"Or make me rip out my IV?" Annalise rubbed where the taped needle penetrated her skin at the back of her hand. "Why are you here?"

It came out almost as a plea. A part of her she really didn't like was touched he'd been holding vigil by her bed. But, it wasn't as if she were dying, although that might have been the outcome if her attacker had more devious intent. Still, Garrett had no business being here. None. At least she tried to convince herself of that.

Garrett pulled up a chair with wooden arms and orange pleather-covered cushions. It squeaked as he lowered his weight into it. Annalise took a moment to study him. At some point since the last time she'd seen him at the historical society, he'd had his hair trimmed. This time he looked less like Shaggy and more reminiscent of—well, a man who cared to comb his hair. His creased chin was clean-shaven, and he wore a button-up, blue plaid cotton shirt. The sleeves were rolled up to his elbows, revealing corded forearms that now rested on bare knees as he leaned forward. He still wore ratty shorts, with strings hanging off the coffee-colored material.

If she were brutally honest with herself—and maybe when she had a concussion wasn't the best time for that—she had never, ever been attracted to anyone the way she was to Garrett Greenwood. Yet something in his demeanor had changed since high school. Maybe he'd just become even more laid back, more than he'd even been in high school. Or maybe it was something else. Maybe he was at peace.

That created a tiny twinge of jealousy she was hesitant to explore.

"You didn't answer my question," Annalise ventured before she could stop herself. "Why are you here?"

Garrett shrugged. "I told you I'd help."

"Help with what? I successfully achieved having my tires slashed and engaged in a one-sided fight that wound me up here." Annalise attempted a laugh, to lighten the mood, to sound less bitter and unfriendly. But she winced as a wave of throbbing pain shot across her head. "I think I'm handling things just fine," she mumbled.

Garrett's mouth quirked up in a sideways smile, but his eyes narrowed with feeling. He didn't address her poor attempt at snark. Honest transparency reflected on his face. "I wasn't here twelve years ago. So, I'm here now."

Annalise turned her head away. A lone tear burned a trail down her cheek. She swiped at it, careful not to rip the IV cord from her skin. Her bottom lip quivered as she responded, even while she stared up at the ceiling.

"It's a little late, don't you think?"

The pleather squeaked again as Garrett shifted his weight. Annalise didn't look at him—*couldn't* look at him. Whatever happened between them twelve years ago had come full circle. The consequences were still being meted out, this time in terrifying form.

"I know you think I just—left." Garrett's voice was raspy.

Annalise studied the paint bumps in the ceiling.

He continued. "It looks like I took off for a great career and left you here to—to have the baby alone."

"Actually, I was in Connecticut with my Aunt Tracy." Annalise grimaced at the memory. "So no one would know the Forsythe girl had seduced the Greenwood boy."

"It was the other way around," Garrett said.

"Right?" Annalise nodded, her eyes widening to affirm her point. A wave of pain sliced through her head again and she closed her eyes. "You came after me."

"On a dare," Garrett muttered.

"A dare," Annalise affirmed.

"I was a jerk."

"Totally."

"But I fell for you anyway."

"I fell for you too." She opened her eyes.

Neither of them had more words. Just memories.

The entire football team had dared Garrett Greenwood to go after the straitlaced Annalise Forsythe. The boyfriend-less girl who liked calculus because it made organized sense. What no one knew was that when Annalise cared for something, or someone, she gave her all. Everything. Passionately. In the same way she'd ploughed her way through community college, convinced the bank to give her a loan to start her coffee shop, convinced her parents to sell her their house, and started a pro bono food pantry. The same way she dedicated herself as surrogate aunt to Brent and Christen's kids. The same way she would have given her soul for Gia . . .

"She had dark eyes. I bet they turned brown." Annalise's throat tightened.

Garrett needed to know how much she'd loved their daughter. How much had been stolen from her.

"Yeah." It was a resigned word. As if somehow he knew the infant girl would have looked just like him. Did he also guess she'd had a distinguishable crease in her chin or that her toe next to her big toe was longer, like his?

"My parents promised me they'd look after you," Garrett finally admitted.

Annalise watched him link his fingers together, his elbows still on his legs. He stared down at his fists.

"I'd worked hard, and when the sponsorship was offered to climb in Switzerland, they wanted me to take it. I mean, it was only supposed to last a few months and then I'd have been back. For the baby to be born."

"But you didn't come back," Annalise stated boldly.

"No." Garrett looked up and locked eyes with her. "I didn't. I wanted to. I called my dad and told him I was going to. But—"

"But you didn't. They made me give Gia away." Annalise's whisper was crowded with tears. They escaped her eyes, and she had little control over her words. Maybe it was the concussion, the terror from the day, or maybe it was finally just time to be honest and pick at the infected emotional wound that had been festering since she was eighteen. "Your parents and my parents *talked*. They told me the best thing to do was go to Aunt Tracy's, have the baby, give it up for adoption, and then come home. It would save your climbing career and keep your pristine image."

"Q—"

"No." Annalise pulled the hospital blanket up to catch her tears. "No. I had no one to bounce my decision off. No one who wasn't biased. My parents wanted me to go to college and said a baby would inhibit my future. So there I was, in a hospital in Connecticut, having a baby girl who looked just like you. I heard her cry. I held her. Touched her feet, her hands, and kissed her—I kissed her little lips and then she was gone!" Annalise's voice rose to a whimper she couldn't control. "She was gone, Garrett! And you were climbing rocks in Europe like a nomad, while I came home with nothing. Nothing but a heart shattered into little pieces so tiny they can't ever be glued back together. I was given instructions to 'put it all behind me.' So I did. For everyone. For you, for your family, for my parents, even for Gia. But I was left with just me, my memories, and this insatiable need to show people in my community who are broken that I am too."

Voices in the hallway of the hospital drifted into the room. A toilet flushed in the room next door. Annalise dragged the corner of the blanket across her face, under eyes, and gently around the bruise left by the fist that had knocked her down.

She didn't know whether she still wanted to scream bitterly at Garrett or recognize the wounded expression on his face and ask him what secret pain he might have suffered too.

Annalise chose silence.

Garrett leaned back in the chair and stretched out his legs, hooking his fingers behind his head, elbows sticking out. "I stink at life, Q."

He averted his eyes to the curtain beyond her, as if reliving his own memories, his own mistakes.

"But it's like climbing. You rip the skin off your knuckles. You hold your weight up, pinching a grip less than an inch in depth. Every push higher makes you gut-scream, which echoes across the valley beneath you. One wrong move, one miscalculation, and it's over. The climb is finished. That free fall? One second feels like years when you're a thousand feet above solid ground. You screwed up. There's no coming back."

Annalise was transfixed. She'd never seen Garrett introspective. His words resonated in her soul, even though she fought against it. She didn't want to relate to Garrett, didn't want to let him reach any place inside of her ever again. Yet, he did . . .

His eyes moved back to hers. There was a quiet confidence there, mixed with regret. "As you fall, you pray that anchor you set in the crevice holds. When you wedge that tiny piece of metal in that crack in the rock face and you clip on, you're trusting it has the grace to catch you if you fall."

"Did you fall?" Annalise whispered.

"Yeah," Garrett whispered back.

"Were you caught?" She couldn't even blink.

Their eyes were locked.

Garrett nodded. "Yeah. By the grace of God."

CHAPTER 23

Libby

This day was too similar, too stained in suspicion and fear, like the day they'd buried Elijah's father. While the parlor walls and décor were in hues of blues instead of yellows, it had still housed a casket, shrouded in funeral crepe. The stifling scent of flowers perfumed the air, mirrors cloaked, pictures facedown. The body of Dorothy Hayes lay silent, hands crossed over her chest before they'd taken her to be buried at the cemetery. Libby had stared at her, every nuance of her mind trying not to concoct what Dorothy's last moments might have been like. What she might have endured. The terror of staring into the eyes of her killer, accused of some secret worth having her life stolen, being plunged beneath Gossamer Pond, needing to breathe, with her hands clawing at the one who held her under the murky water. . . .

Libby shook her head to clear her mind. Concocting visions of violence would result in nightmares. She'd had enough of those the past few nights and had no wish to repeat them when awake.

The home of Dorothy Hayes was now clear of mourners, leaving behind a few stragglers like Libby's and Elijah's mothers. The women worked soberly and efficiently to tidy the house. This time, unlike with Elijah's family, there was no mother left behind to put things to rights.

"Libby?"

Grateful for the interruption to her unwelcome but unstoppable thought progression, she jerked her head up at the sound of Elijah's voice. A boy shadowed him.

"This is Lawrence, Dorothy's son. He'll be staying with my family for a while until . . ." Elijah glanced over his shoulder at Lawrence's father, the bereaved widower who slumped in a chair in the corner of the room. "Well, until my uncle can sort through her affairs."

Libby gave the blond boy a smile. He ignored her and looked up at his cousin with sad eyes. Elijah held his shoulders, muttering instructions. Lawrence nodded, brushed away a tear he was too embarrassed to let fall, and hurried away.

Watching the boy disappear through the parlor entry, Libby wondered what kind of future he would have. Losing a mother so young would impact him for the rest of his growing-up years.

"We need to speak."

Libby nodded. Yes, they did.

Elijah led her down the hall into a small room. Gauzy white curtains filtered the sunlight that cast pleasant rays over a desk whose feminine curves from its legs to the scalloped edge of its top led Libby to conclude this must have been Dorothy Hayes's personal study. A doily with delicate tatting of yellow-and-blue threads adorned the mantel over the small, cold fireplace. A porcelain statue of a raven-haired Southern belle was centered on the spot of homemade décor. Libby noted a few volumes of books, hardcovers embossed with gold flowers with titles printed in a golden swirl.

Elijah closed the door and brought Libby's appreciation of the simple beauty of the room to a shuttered halt. The room became suffocating. Like being in a casket with the lid closing and latching over her. She wrapped her arms around herself, her fingers toying with the satin-covered button on the cuff of her black dress.

Elijah's eyes bored into hers. There was distance between them, as there always had been, in spite of the truth they shared. A truth Elijah would never speak of. She wished he would. There was so much of Elijah that spread silky cobweb-like dreams in her heart, and yet, like a cobweb, they were fragile and spoke of neglect. The Elijah of her memories was less and less the Elijah who stood before her.

His voice was toneless. He crossed the room and stared through the filmy curtains. "The authorities are still trying to figure out why my aunt was in Gossamer Pond. The only thing they can conclude is that she went for a nighttime walk."

"In her undergarments?" Libby's eyes widened at her own loud exclamation of surprise.

Elijah shook his head. "They found her dress in the bushes. Like she'd removed it so she could swim."

Libby pursed her lips. "In the middle of the night? Your Aunt Dorothy would have done no such thing." Even Libby knew that, and she wasn't well acquainted with the woman. Her reputation preceded her.

Elijah blew out a puff of air that lifted the hair falling over his forehead. His face seemed gaunter, his skin paler. Grief was a weight no man should have to bear.

"I can only assume she was lured from here. After my uncle went to bed. I don't know why, or how, but—perhaps whoever wrote the obituary wrote her a note to compel her?"

"And the police won't even believe you? About the obituaries?"

"They believe *something* happened. What, is unclear." Elijah raked his hand through his hair and released a growl. He lifted a brass letter opener from the top of his aunt's desk. The blade glistened in the sunlight. For a brief, strange moment, Elijah seemed ominous to Libby. Unpredictable.

Elijah set the letter opener back in its place. "Unless I find something to substantiate the obituaries' obtuse claims and the remarkable timing of your trying to convince them Paul was going to die

179

and then Paul showing up the next day attempting to convince them my aunt was murdered . . . it's all just something they're still 'investigating.'"

Libby eyed the desk. Perhaps it was wrong of her, but the need to press for the truth persuaded her. If she didn't, her father might be permanently branded a mudslinger, and if word of the obituaries got out as falsified reports, it would ruin the paper's credibility. She might not have a conventional relationship with her father, but Mitch still deserved her loyalty as a daughter.

"Perhaps we should search your aunt's things."

Elijah drew back. "For?"

"For whatever lured her from the house. A note, anything. Isn't it odd that both your father *and* your aunt have—well, have died? And don't you think it strange they both have something shameful and yet are so well respected?"

His eyes flashed. "What are you implying, Libby?"

Libby sucked in a gulp. Well, she knew what she was implying, but she had no desire to speak it aloud. It was scandalous, moreover, and the actual saying it to Elijah would be awful.

"I'm saying," she paused, twisting her hands and wishing it was anyone but Elijah standing here. Anyone at all. "What if your father and your aunt—"

"No." Elijah's word split through Libby's suspicion.

"And what if, whoever is writing the obituaries lured your aunt from the house with the threat he would—well, I mean, consider it, however painful it could be—if I were your aunt, I wouldn't want my husband to know, my family to know!"

"Of course you wouldn't." Elijah's voice was stern. Convicting. Resigned.

A coldness ran through Libby as she realized her words. The memory so rife between them rose like a ghost in the room, snatching any warmth and leaving in its wake a sickening guilt.

"Elijah, please." Libby looked away, biting her upper lip against the tears.

He leaned closer, his breath against her ear, his hand lifting a curl to brush her cheek. "I'm so tired of secrets, Libby. I have no compulsion, no energy to seek out those of my father and my aunt." Elijah's hand cupped Libby's upper arm. Gentle, almost with longing but also with regret. "We've enough of our own, don't you think?"

Libby turned her head to the side and then looked up at Elijah. Yes. Yes they did. Every day since she was fifteen, they had eaten tiny pieces of her soul.

"We must find out, Elijah. What if . . . ?" Libby hesitated, a greater fear in her heart. "What if whoever knew your father and aunt's secret, knows ours? What if—what if we're next?"

Elijah's shoulders sagged. He rubbed his eyes, squeezing the bridge of his nose. With a barely suppressed groan, he crossed the room and pulled open the drawer of his aunt's desk. Libby watched him tug out bunches of blank writing paper and fan through them. He shoved them back into place. A bundle of letters was next. Elijah studied each one, finally returning them to the drawer as well.

Libby swiped at tears as they trailed down her face. Tears of guilt, tears of fear, and tears of what had been ruined.

The drawer slammed shut, its little brass pull tapping against the drawer from the movement. Elijah straightened.

"Nothing. I found nothing. What am I supposed to look for?" Elijah took a step toward her, his brows drawn in frustration with a look she was certain mimicked her own.

"I don't know," Libby whispered. Helpless. All she'd ever wanted was to protect Elijah, just as he'd done for her all those years ago. She was failing miserably, and yet it wasn't her fault. She hadn't done this. Someone far more devious and wicked had. Someone who believed they were bringing God's justice down on the deserving.

Elijah gave her a short nod. "I'll go look in her dressing room. Perhaps—" he paused and swallowed as if choking back emotion— "perhaps I'll find something there."

The door shut behind him. Libby sank into a stuffed chair beside a table with hardcover books on it. She wiped at her cheeks, her chin still quivering uncontrollably.

She absently picked up a book with a burgundy cover and straightened a crease in one of its pages. A bookmark tilted out from the back third of the book, and Libby straightened it. As she did so, she noticed handwriting. Curiosity overtook her.

The bookmark had a purple ribbon at its top. Its edges were straight, and a violet was embossed on its paper. But it was the script at the bottom that made her frown.

> *Our love never lost, though silent for now.*
>
> *H.*

Libby ran her finger over the inked words. While a delicate bookmark, it was not a womanly script. The lines, the slant, even the shake of the handwriting insinuated it was male. But the *H*? Harrison.

She fumbled through the pages of what must have been Dorothy's favorite book. A small paper fell from it onto Libby's lap. Typewritten. So familiar. She unfolded it and sucked in a breath.

> Be sure your sins will find you out. Secrets can never be silenced.

It said nothing about Gossamer Pond. Nothing that would even be enough to convince the police that she was murdered. But it was enough for Libby. The killer knew and he'd told Dorothy so. It was enough to drive her from her home into the night. Perhaps that was all he'd been counting on. He followed her, waited, and then enacted a righteous judgment against unconfessed sin.

Libby's hands shook with fervor. She would show Elijah, and in turn he would show the police. But that wouldn't stop this person. A self-appointed judge was at large, whose personal vendetta reached across the boundaries of the Ten Commandments and well into the dark places behind "Thou shalt not murder."

CHAPTER 24

Annalise

I'm fine." Annalise adjusted herself on a stool in the stock room of the food pantry.

Christen shot her a dubious look as she stacked canned peas from a donation box on a shelf.

Word of Annalise's attack had spread as soon as Tyler Darrow learned about it and printed it as front-page news. Some claimed it was a publicity ploy for more attention for her social cause. Annalise chose to ignore them. Her bravado didn't include sacrificing herself to bodily harm.

"I can finish unpacking this box, but then I need to get home. Brent has to get to work, and I need to watch the kids." Christen lifted a can of black olives and wrinkled her nose. "Ew. If I were homeless, I'd still pass this up."

"No, you wouldn't." Annalise was sorry her tone was so grave and serious.

Christen cast her a sheepish glance. While Annalise spent much of her time in the coffee shop running the business end of things, she still helped the volunteers during the hours the pantry was open. She'd seen the faces of people like Eugene Hayes who were hungry, alone, and needy. She'd even handed out food to people she knew were taking advantage of the system and too lazy to get a job. But, she couldn't judge them. Life's circumstances could be disabling sometimes. Without guidance, help, grace, it was hard to crawl out of that pit.

Christen straightened and rubbed her hands down her jeans. "So, um, I meant to ask, but have your parents called at all?"

Annalise raised an eyebrow, and Christen met her with open frankness. Annalise grabbed a can from the crate of donated canned peas and set it on a bottom shelf. "Yes. My mom did. Well, first it was a text—*Heard you've run into some trouble*—but then she called when I didn't reply."

"Well, at least she was concerned." Christen, always trying to find the good in things, God love her.

Annalise gave her a soft smile. "Yeah." She nodded. Her mother had been concerned, a little. But more than anything, it had been very awkward, stilted, and Annalise was willing to bet her mom was as relieved as she was when they'd ended the call.

"Brent isn't telling me much about the investigation, but then again, he hasn't been around much either." Christen eyed Annalise as she placed the last can of olives on a shelf higher up.

Annalise wished she had more to tell Christen too. She'd spent several hours chatting with the police, recalling as much as she could so they had something to go on. "It's so hard," Annalise admitted. "Crimes shouldn't be this difficult to solve, and yet all I know is it was a man in black—and not Johnny Cash, mind you—with a ski mask and a husky voice."

"No fingerprints on anything?" Christen pressed gently.

Annalise frowned. "There was nothing to leave prints on and it's hard to lift them off skin. I know they took my clothes for DNA processing, but nothing conclusive seems to have come of it."

Christen squatted at eye level with Annalise, who still sat on the three-legged stool. Her big eyes were wide behind her glasses.

"Yet. Nothing's come of it yet. Brent is like a bulldog. He is hell-bent on finding whoever did this to you."

Annalise swiped at a sudden renegade tear. She gave her friend a watery smile. "I don't know what I'd do without you two."

Christen patted her knees and stood. "We'd all be lost without each other. Now, I need to get going, love. But, please, don't open the pantry this afternoon. I know it's only for a few hours, but you're getting over a concussion."

"I have help coming," Annalise assured her. In fact, a few people from the Baptist church had called to volunteer. Regulars. They knew what to do. She was planning to go home, recheck her alarm system fifty times, and rest her eyes all while clutching a can of pepper spray. But she didn't tell Christen that. Sometimes her best friend was too motherly. She needed to learn to stop worrying. Besides, the police would do periodic drive-bys. That was something.

"'K." Christen gave Annalise one more dubious look before taking her leave through the side door that led into the coffee shop.

"Grab a latte on your way out," Annalise called after her.

Christen lifted her hand in a wave. "Yeah. It'll help me when the kids wake me up sixteen times tonight!"

Silence invaded the pantry. Annalise slid off the stool and left the stock room to enter the main area. A few chairs and tables. Shelves with supplies like towels and blankets, coats, hats, clothes organized by sizes. Donations came in regularly. Why would anyone give her a tough time about wanting the town to support a homeless shelter?

The connecting door to the coffee shop opened, and Annalise looked up as the smell of coffee wafted in. She met Nicole Greenwood's frosty blue eyes, and her spirits plummeted. Nicole took a cautious step into the pantry, her eyes skimming the room as she did so.

"I've never been in here before," she stated.

"I know." Maybe it was the knock to her head, but Annalise didn't feel like trying to play politics or win Nicole's favor.

Nicole walked to one of the shelves and pulled off a gray towel. She gave Annalise a frown. "It looks used."

"That's because it is. We rely on donations, and most people don't go out and purchase brand-new and then donate the stuff."

"Oh." Nicole nodded and replaced the towel on the shelf. She turned, her red heels clicking on the wood floor. "How are you feeling?"

That was strange. Nicole wasn't normally . . . nice.

"Better. Thanks."

More clicks as Nicole neared her. She crossed her arms over her chest. Nicole had a great manicure. Annalise couldn't help but glance at her own nails, half chewed with all the stress of late.

Nicole cleared her throat. She shot an agitated glance toward the coffee shop door, then returned her focus to Annalise. "Listen, I—I don't know if your attack had anything to do with the bid on the property or not. I know rumors are circulating, but I want you to know I've been contemplating your proposal regarding the shelter. For some time now. I just haven't made that contemplation public, and I've confided in only a few people."

That was unexpected.

Nicole continued, concern etched at the corners of her eyes. "Please tell me you didn't use Mr. Hayes as a platform for your cause."

Annalise shook her head in disbelief. "As if I would use people and ruin them to better myself."

"Well?"

"Well what?" Annalise shot back.

Nicole stiffened. "You did it to Garrett."

All fight drained from Annalise. That empty, helpless ache gripped her. The kind there was no healing from. She squeezed her eyes shut and drew in a deep breath. When she opened them, Nicole still stood there, waiting.

"How did I use Garrett, Nicole? His life went on. His career. He's been successful."

"He's had to bear the secret that he has a child," Nicole argued.

"And I haven't?" Annalise detested the watery shake to her voice. "I agonize over it every day. And now? Garrett is back. I'm having to revisit it. And with the circumstances around Eugene Hayes, around the shelter? I don't see how this is all my fault. I gave up my baby, *our* baby. Garrett helped create her, you know. Willingly."

Nicole colored and turned her head away, contemplating, her arms still crossed over her chest and her left toe tapping the floor. She sighed, her lips pursed. Finally, Gossamer Grove's mayor met Annalise's gaze. They stared at each other for a long moment. Annalise knew the line in the sand had been drawn years before when Garrett's mother identified Annalise as a "tramp." Nicole had been away at college, defensive of her beloved younger brother, and distant from the actual circumstances. She'd drawn conclusions after hearing only one side.

Now Nicole nodded. She uncrossed her arms and reached into her purse that was slung over her shoulder. A nice Coach purse with white polka dots and a red background. Pulling out a check, she handed it to Annalise.

"What's this?" Annalise reached for it. Everything in her told her to be cautious, but curiosity made her look at the check. It was a modest amount on a personal check, signed by Nicole. Certainly not enough to raise any eyebrows as a political bribe or payoff of some kind.

"Why?" Annalise lifted her eyes.

Nicole swallowed, and for the first time a tiny glimmer of kindness flickered in her eyes. "Regardless of the current situation, I want you to know I do believe in taking care of the citizens of Gossamer Grove. *All* citizens."

"Thank you." Annalise wasn't sure what she was supposed to say. Was this a white flag? An extension of peace? Or was Nicole trying to come across as generous right before she announced her support for the town to sell the land to Doug Larson and make the wilderness center official?

Nicole closed her purse and adjusted it on her shoulder. "I didn't mean for—" She stopped. Shook her head. "Never mind." The self-contained steel in her eyes had returned. "Have a nice afternoon, Annalise."

Hurrying toward the coffee shop, Nicole almost seemed to be trying to hold herself back from running, as if she were attempting to escape.

"Nicole?" Annalise called after her.

Nicole froze.

"You didn't mean what?" There was no way she was going to allow Nicole to brush off her comment and not explain herself.

Nicole looked over her shoulder. Annalise noticed a tiny quiver in her chin.

She shook her head. "Leave it alone."

Annalise took a few steps toward Nicole. The mayor turned, her hand on the doorframe of the coffee shop.

"Is there something I should know?"

Nicole drew in a shuddered breath and blinked fast as though fighting back tears. She looked at the ceiling to compose herself. "Just that . . . I didn't mean for you to suffer all alone these last several years."

It was a flimsy answer. Annalise studied Nicole's face. There was more. Behind the blue eyes and the confident façade, Nicole had unrest written. Indecision.

"Stay safe, Annalise," Nicole whispered. In a flurry of red and perfume, she was gone.

Annalise stared after Garrett's sister, left alone to determine whether Nicole had meant her parting words out of genuine concern or a veiled caution that more was yet to come.

—⟊⟊⟊—

Rage was a wicked emotion, but coupled with betrayal it turned into an entirely different beast. Annalise barely kept it under control, although overreacting would get her nowhere.

So she set her jaw until Tyler emerged from the back office of the newspaper. A quizzical lift to his brow told Annalise he was going to play dumb.

"What's up?" he asked casually, sauntering to the front counter. His hair was mussed stylishly, and his wire-rimmed glasses gave him a very hipster appearance, sans the beard. Tyler looked nice. Looks were very deceiving.

"This." Annalise set the 8.5x11 piece of paper on the counter and withdrew her hand so Tyler wouldn't see it shaking. She had sat in her car for over thirty minutes, planning out what she would say, what her demands were, what she needed to accomplish.

Tyler skimmed the page. His smile stayed pasted on his face as he lifted the sheet of paper. "She's beautiful," he observed. It was patronizing. It was infuriating.

Annalise had tried all morning to convince herself she should be grateful he hadn't printed it front and center. That Tyler had sent an employee to her coffee shop with a manila envelope with this page inside it. But his Post-it note was less a friendly gesture and more a threat.

Got this at the paper. Was thinking of printing it, but figured I'd run it by you since it's pretty outlandish.

—Tyler

"Why? How did you get it?" It was all Annalise could ask. Her structured agenda was blurry in her mind. Emotion clouded it, rendering it nonexistent. She watched Tyler set the paper down. The photograph of Gia, the one Annalise had treasured on her dresser top, was printed on it. "How did you get the photo?" Annalise demanded in a hoarse whisper.

Tyler shrugged. "Someone mailed it anonymously. It had a Post-it note on it with your name as the mother, the date of birth of the child, and the state of Connecticut for where she was born."

"So you printed it? Based on a Post-it note?" Annalise was incredulous.

"I didn't print it!" Tyler drew back, holding his palms up and out. "I thought about it—obviously." He waved at the page. "But in the end it didn't feel right, so I sent it to you. I know everything that's been going on, your concussion. I love my news, Annalise, but that's just low, even for me. Someone has it out for you."

Annalise calmed, but only a bit. "Still. You researched me first."

"It's in my DNA. I'm sorry. I vaguely recalled you had an aunt who passed away awhile back who lived in Connecticut. It was a dot-to-dot, and the facts lined up after I did my research."

Annalise didn't respond. She couldn't. Her throat was clogged with horrified tears. She tried to swallow around them, but one slipped out. Swiping it away, Annalise gathered up the paper she'd set on the counter. Her picture. Her baby. Her Gia. She sniffed. Natural deduction would have led Tyler to Garrett. She'd never dated a single man since. At least not long enough to be remembered by anyone.

"You can't print it."

"Sure. No." Tyler shook his head.

"And you—please. It's been years, and no one knows, Tyler." Great. Now she was begging. Annalise drew in a shaky breath.

"I won't print it." Tyler's flippancy disappeared. He glanced over her shoulder out the window toward the main street, then back to her. "I wouldn't do that to the Greenwoods either."

So he *had* made the deduction.

They stared at each other for a long moment until Annalise was relatively confident Tyler's infatuation with Nicole was in her own benefit.

"This picture"—Annalise shook the paper at him—"was *stolen* from my home."

Tyler nodded. "I figured. But I didn't take it! Like I said, it was mailed to me."

"I want the envelope. I want my picture back," Annalise demanded. Of course, having gone through the postal system, there

190

were probably a hundred fingerprints on it, and if the thief had any smarts, they wore gloves when they handled the photograph. Still.

Tyler gave her a short nod. Annalise watched him walk toward the back offices. She hated to admit it, but she really didn't believe Tyler was guilty of anything except receiving the anonymous picture and having an insatiable curiosity that had a severe lack of healthy boundaries.

Tyler returned and tossed the brown envelope her direction. It slid across the counter, and Annalise picked it up. The postmark was from some town three hours away with a population of over twenty thousand. Two days ago. The address was a printed label, no return address, and the envelope was self-stick. She opened the flap and pulled out the photograph, her hands shaking. Gia. Gia's beautiful little face. But instead of her picture, Annalise held another color photocopy.

"Where's the original?" She cast a desperate look in Tyler's direction.

"That's all there was. I promise."

She pushed it back into the envelope. Her next stop would be the police precinct. It was evidence, and at this point she needed any evidence she could get. The well-mapped world she lived in had exploded into shrapnel that spanned centuries. It had created a puzzle that was missing many, many pieces.

Annalise turned her back to Tyler and walked to the front door of the paper. He cleared his throat and called after her. When she looked at him, his gaze was searching.

"I always wondered what happened between you and Garrett," he stated.

She answered by slamming the door shut behind her.

CHAPTER 25

When Brent and Christen had asked her if she wanted to stay at their place for a while, Annalise insisted she'd be fine at the house alone. But she had been overconfident. Annalise pulled all the curtains closed against the night sky, rechecked the alarm system to make sure it was activated, and patted her pajama bottom's pocket to make sure her phone was handy. She hadn't told Christen she'd gone and bought six cans of pepper spray. One for the front entrance, hidden in the plant on the entry table. One for her bedroom, of course. Another for the kitchen, the living room, the basement, the garage. That didn't count the one she'd already owned that was stuffed in her purse.

Annalise curled up on the couch, a pad of paper in hand, and tried to ignore the pounding in her head. Whether a continuing side effect of the concussion three days ago or the stress of Tyler's news, she wasn't sure.

She began a bulleted list.

Possible motives to hurt me:
- *Someone is afraid I'll uncover something Eugene found out from the past*
- *Someone doesn't want me to convince Nicole to build the homeless shelter*

- *Someone is angry at me for having Garrett's baby*
- *Someone thinks Gossamer Grove should be rid of rejects and sinners*

Annalise paused and almost laughed. They all seemed outrageous. Perhaps the most plausible was the homeless shelter point, but even then, what did that have to do with Eugene? And why would someone hiss in her ear after attacking her that "Eugene was wrong." No, it was more personal than that. Yet it still felt connected. Somehow.

The doorbell pealed, and the pad of paper flew out of her hands as she jumped. Her pen had flipped to the end of the couch. Annalise paused to catch her breath. She glanced at the clock on the wall: 8:00 p.m. It was an old antique clock she had to crank with a key every morning before work to keep it ticking. Eight o'clock really wasn't that late. Still. Who just dropped by unannounced?

Annalise padded into the entryway, the light already on, as was every other light in the house. She fumbled in the plant and wrapped her fingers around the pepper spray. Annalise peeked out the peephole in the door. Her shoulders sagged with relief, even though the image of Garrett on the front porch wasn't what she preferred. She shoved the pepper spray back into the plant and flicked the bolt lock on the door, then twisted the lock on the doorknob and remembered to disarm the alarm just before she pulled the door open.

"Man." Garrett eyed her.

She must cast quite the sight. Pink fuzzy socks, varsity-style pajama pants, and a baggy yellow T-shirt with a chest pocket and V-neck. Her hair was pulled back into a red pile on top of her head that was anything but a Pinterest messy bun, and her chunky black glasses framed her makeup-less eyes.

Annalise squirmed. Exposed.

"You look awesome," he stated, brushing past her.

She wrinkled her nose, perplexed as she pushed the door shut.

When she turned, she almost smacked into Garrett's chest, which was almost as disturbing as the gentle expression in his eyes.

"You doing okay?"

She'd texted Garrett a picture of Tyler's note . . . and Gia's photograph. He deserved to know, especially if Tyler decided to talk about it.

Annalise ducked her head and pushed past him, retreating to the living room. She'd known it was inevitable he'd confront her with it.

"Did you show your sister? Your family is probably in an uproar," she mumbled, dropping onto the couch.

"Meh, just a bit."

"I'm sorry." She looked at him. Not knowing why she was apologizing, but feeling she needed to for some reason. Yes, he'd left her, and yes, she'd agreed to let him go when his parents acted as liaison and presented the argument that if she loved him, she'd let him pursue his dream. But Gia's picture made it all so raw, and perhaps the rawest of all was that deep down, Annalise knew Garrett hadn't been consulted about the adoption. It'd just been decided when Annalise was flown to Aunt Tracy's three months' pregnant and Garrett put on a plane for Switzerland. He'd lost his baby too.

Garrett sank onto the couch next to her. Annalise pulled back and moved to the far end.

He ignored her apology as if she didn't owe him one. "So, how are you doing?"

"Fine," she lied.

Garrett reached over and flipped a renegade strand of hair over her shoulder. He did look a lot better with the haircut. He flopped an arm over the back of the couch. Annalise couldn't help but notice his fingernails were caked with chalk dust again. He'd been climbing. It was familiar, it was sexy, it drew her, as much as she wished it didn't.

"Are you okay?" She diverted attention from herself. He'd just seen a text with a picture of his baby girl. The first time he'd seen her. *Okay* probably wasn't going to be his word of choice.

194

Garrett shook his head, and his honesty stunned her. "No. I'm not."

Their eyes locked.

"I'm torqued. At Darrow, at the invasion of privacy."

Oh. Annalise could only stare at him. Where had this Garrett been twelve years ago? He lifted his hand off the couch, and his thumb picked at a snag on his index fingernail. Garrett glanced at it, then at the floor where her pad of paper lay. He bent over and picked it up, reading her notes.

"Yeah," he nodded. "I'm trying to figure all this out too." Garrett tossed the notepad onto the couch.

There was so much that he could have said, so much that maybe *should* be said, but Annalise sensed he wasn't ready, and for certain neither was she. She opted for the other volatile topic that somehow, while more frightening, seemed less intimidating. She was reminded of her discovery with Christen a few nights ago, before she'd been attacked and before the paper had stolen her attention.

"Did you know you're related to Eugene Hayes?" she blurted out.

Garrett pulled back. "Uhhh . . . no?"

That went well. Annalise tried not to roll her eyes at herself. She reached for her tablet that sat on the coffee table and flicked the screen. She loaded the ancestry site and showed Garrett the family tree she'd created. He eyed her for a second, then looked back at the genealogy map.

"How does all this stuff get online?" He seemed taken aback that the Greenwood family tree was as exposed as it was, even though he'd already mentioned his mother had her own account on the ancestral site.

Annalise smiled and gave him a *No duh* sort of look. "I know you're one with the earth and all, but you're a bit behind on technology. Any public records are loaded online, because they're public. So old censuses are some of them. Then any cousins, distant relatives you have, they all can upload birth certificates and such too. Even if your family wanted to keep this under wraps, they can only do as much as they can control."

Garrett gave a quick waggle of his brows. "I don't know why anyone would want to study this stuff."

Annalise bit back a chuckle. "Well, some people are history buffs. Others, like us, have other reasons to look it up."

"Truth." Garrett redirected his attention back to the table. "So, Eugene's a cousin?"

"Eugene's father, Lawrence, would have been your great-great-grandfather Harrison's nephew." Annalise nodded. "Perhaps that's why Eugene was researching Harrison. Me, even. I mean, he must have figured out I'd had your child."

"But how? And why?" Garrett's face reddened.

"He had a photograph of me when I was pregnant at Aunt Tracy's in Connecticut. Tracy took that picture and it was the only one that existed."

"Then why not have pictures of me in his trailer?" Garrett frowned. "Why Harrison Greenwood? And how did he know your aunt?"

Annalise rolled her eyes. "And why did someone hit me over the head at his trailer? And why did he also have pamphlets of a revival that took place the same time frame that your great-great-grandfather died?"

"No joke." Garrett reached into the pocket of his jeans. "I'm going to call Mom. I wonder if she knows about our relation to Eugene."

"You're going to get her involved?" Annalise shrank back. The idea was akin to asking Godzilla for a favor. No. Not Godzilla. Lord Voldemort.

"If she knows half this stuff, why take forever to get the answers by combing through piles of junk at the historical society?"

He had a point.

Garrett tapped the speakerphone icon on his cell and held a finger to his lips to indicate she needed to stay silent. The phone rang, and Garrett's mom answered, her tone decidedly warmer than when Annalise last saw her.

They exchanged a few brief comments and then Garrett went straight to the point. "So, do you know anything about Harrison Greenwood?"

Silence. A sigh. "Is this because of Annalise?"

Annalise reached for a blanket folded over the arm of the couch and pulled it over herself like a shield.

Garrett glanced at her, then back at the phone. "It's because of everything."

Another sigh. Her voice chilled, dropped in volume, and sounded resigned. It was as if she couldn't tell her baby boy no, yet had no desire to give him what he wanted.

"That's the Greenwood side of the family, Garrett. I married into it, so I only know so much."

"Have you heard about us being related to Eugene Hayes?"

A brief intake of breath expressed her indignation. "Who told you that?"

Garrett answered firmly, "An online genealogy site."

"Oh." Her tone indicated she remembered. "Yes. But it's a very distant relation, and your father wasn't even grieved when he heard Mr. Hayes had died. There's no reason to bring it up."

"According to the website, Harrison Greenwood and Eugene's grandmother were brother- and sister-in-law."

Garrett's mom must have turned on a faucet. Annalise heard water running in the background, and then it stopped. "The Greenwood history in Gossamer Grove can be traced back to your great-grandfather times four. When the town was first settled. The genealogy tree more than likely has branches that span many different families."

"What do you know, Mom?" Garrett might as well have said *Get to the point.*

"What I know is . . ." His mother sounded irritated again. "Harrison Greenwood's son, Elijah, became the first Greenwood mayor

197

in Gossamer Grove. Then your grandfather, your father, and now Nicole. Those are the important people. The ones I recall. Other family members, I've little knowledge of and I know your father has even less. I learned what I know from your grandmother."

She's dead, mouthed Garrett, reading Annalise's quick surge of hope that someone old enough might know more details. Have more knowledge of the past and how it wove its way into their present day.

"Nicole told me about that text from Annalise. The baby's picture and Tyler Darrow?" Displeasure laced every nuance of Mrs. Greenwood's voice. Annalise pulled the blanket higher, staring at the smartphone that lay on the couch between her and Garrett, as if his mother could materialize through the phone. "I don't know what Annalise thinks she can gain by sending it to you. It's inexcusable. If it comes out you were the child's father, it will rip through what remains of your career and have horrific implications on Nicole's position as mayor. I find it—"

"Stop." Garrett's command had instant results. He rarely came across authoritative, and Annalise stared at him. He reached for the phone. "Don't blame Annalise. If you don't know anything else about how we might be tied to Eugene Hayes, then I'm finished here."

A stillness settled over the room. If she could pull the blanket over her head without looking ridiculous, she would. Her head was pounding. She wasn't even certain how to interpret this different side of Garrett. Standing up to his mother, putting his foot down firmly. It was a changed type of self-confidence than he'd exhibited years before. It wasn't cocky or reckless. It was mature. It was definitive.

"I've nothing else." Mrs. Greenwood's response was low, hurt.

"'K." Garrett moved to end the call when she interrupted.

"Wait. No. There is something else you should know." Maybe it was Garrett's forcefulness that made Mrs. Greenwood want to somehow bridge the tension between them, or maybe it was guilt.

"Yeah?" Garrett inquired.

His mother sighed. "Back in the early 1900s, the paper published an obituary about Harrison Greenwood."

Annalise caught Garrett's eye.

Mrs. Greenwood was still speaking. "The owner of the paper at the time apparently had a reputation for being quite blatant in his articles. Pot-stirring and all. He published Harrison's cause of death as a suicide. Later, there were rumors circulating that his death was suspicious."

"You mean a murder?" Garrett asked.

"Yes. At least that's what your grandmother told me. Greenwoods don't like to talk about it, even though it happened well over a century ago."

"Sure," Garrett smiled, but it was sideways and bitter. "Gotta keep that Mr. Clean appearance."

"Garrett," Mrs. Greenwood's voice chided.

He didn't respond.

His mother cleared her throat. "You have to understand, the Greenwoods are a founding family. We set the bar, the standard by which this community thrives. Our economy is built on our community, our reputation, our classical town."

"Yeah." Garrett gave a curt nod. "Grew up hearing all that, Mom."

Mrs. Greenwood reacted, her tone rising in frustration. "Don't be disrespectful. You don't understand."

"I don't understand what?" Garrett cast Annalise a quick look. She could tell he was ticked. A muscle in his jaw twitched, and he glared at the screen of his phone like it were his mother.

"It's important we're discreet." Mrs. Greenwood's words were tight. Firm. Reprimanding. "Whatever did happen to Harrison Greenwood, his death set in motion this chain—a history. Greenwood men have never been *good*, and it's the women who've had to be the strong ones. We're the foundation on which Greenwood men stand. And Nicole? She is our crown."

Annalise stared in shock at Garrett, whose face had gone as

white as his climbing chalk. His jaw worked back and forth until finally he gave a customary flippant response.

"Thanks, Mom."

A flustered breath followed. "I didn't mean—"

"Sure. I know. I slept around. Partied hard. Heck, I even dabbled with drugs, Mom. Is that what you want to hide? That your son smeared the Greenwood name, which was why you wanted me to hit the climbing circuit when Annalise got pregnant? Conveniently disappear for a while?"

"I never said that!"

Garrett didn't let up. "What, did Dad screw up too? Have an affair? And Grandpa? What are you saying? Are all Greenwood men messed up?"

"Your father—this isn't about your father." Exasperation filled the line. "This isn't a conversation to have over the phone."

"Definitely not." Garrett reached again to end the call.

His mother's voice stopped him. "Garrett! Garrett, honey, listen to me. History is—it's messy. It's dirty. It's not who we really are, who we're supposed to be. And Mr. Hayes's death, it's all bringing things to the surface that the Greenwood family has moved on from. Our standing in this community, our good efforts, our faith—that speaks far more to who we are than old stories and past wrongs."

Garrett sniffed. He didn't reply. Annalise wondered if she should breathe or keep holding it in. She hadn't expected this. But then she was certain Garrett hadn't either.

"Faith." Garret sniffed and drew in a deep breath. "Mom, faith is only real faith when it's honest. It seems to me, the Greenwoods haven't been honest for a long, *long* time."

"Garrett—" His mother started again, but this time Garrett interrupted.

"Good to know we have a thick armor-proof front, Mom. 'Cause apparently the idea of authenticity hasn't been a brand of the Greenwoods for years."

His finger swiped the phone and ended the call.

CHAPTER 26

Libby

When had she personalized the murders? Libby wrapped the cord of her purse around her gloved wrist as she minded her steps down the walk. The first obituary had inspired in her a horrific concern for Elijah and his family. For Deacon Greenwood's reputation. But then the obituary written and subsequently retracted for Paul caused Libby to question everything with bewildered confusion. The type of confusion that, when analyzed, the stark truth lay beneath it all, although the mind and soul were desperate to deny it. Dorothy's death was the final push that launched Libby over the cliff of question and denial. Now the obituaries, along with their insinuations, had evolved into something darker, repetitive, and frightening. It was the repetitive element that had Libby's insides quivering with an uneasy compulsion to look over her shoulder.

Libby stumbled on a crevice in the walkway. What if she had been assessed? Repentance was an imminent demand. But to confess, she would open so much hurt and pain, not just for herself but for Elijah and for . . .

Her skin crawled with the sensation of being watched. She

looked down the street, lined on one side with two-story buildings with narrow alleyways between them. A mix of red brick and
crème brick brought warmth to the community. Familiar shopping
places, a street where one might run into a neighbor. To the left
was the town square. A courthouse rose in the middle, constructed
of white granite, which was rather marvelous. A cannon honoring
Yankee soldiers from Gossamer Grove sat in the courthouse yard,
along with a park bench of cast iron. A block down and to the
right of that was the newspaper building.

But this was what she could *see*. Seeing the world around her,
one would conclude Gossamer Grove to be welcoming and peaceful. For the most part, it probably was. Filled with good people,
and people who needed saving by the message the Corbin brothers were attempting to bring. But to Libby, Gossamer Grove had
seemed dark. Ever since she was fifteen.

She squeezed her eyes shut as she walked, blocking out memories. Libby had no ability to judge one's soul. To dive into another's
spirit as if to understand what sins were hiding there that were an
affront to God. So then, who in Gossamer Grove identified enough
with God to believe they could read souls? That they could pass
judgment on others? Death was a terrible thing to come face-to-
face with. She certainly wasn't ready. She wasn't willing to die.
She didn't want—

"I don't want to die!" The words tumbled out of her as she
careened into a hard chest and collided toe-to-toe with a pair of
black shoes and long legs. Libby raised her head knowing the full
weight of her fear was reflected in her dark eyes. After all, it had
been a week since Dorothy's death. If the judger of souls moved
in a pattern, wasn't it time for another obituary? And if so, then
she was terrified it would be hers.

Libby stepped back, mumbling an apology. She stared up at the
tall man. He didn't respond. Jacobus Corbin's blue eyes blinked.
That was all. They just blinked at her. Libby swallowed hard,
almost as if she had a gumball lodged in her throat. But it was

unadulterated fear. Fear of being alone, of being ashamed, of being dead.

He was one man who seemed to read her soul. Trusting Jacobus Corbin as a man of God made Libby wonder if she were staring into the eyes of the serpent of Eden himself.

Jacobus studied her. His face narrowed at the chin, his almond-shaped eyes shrewd and scrutinizing. Finally he spoke, ignoring the bustle of passersby, who murmured their greetings to the revivalist twin who just last night had helped his brother baptize seventeen parishioners from the Presbyterian church. Like tick marks on a chart of holy successes.

"One should always be ready to die." His words were grim with no inflection to his voice. "It's a reasonable assumption that it will come sooner rather than later. It is foolish to leave such a future to fate."

She should run. Flee. Fly away as fast as her feet would take her. Yet, Libby froze in place. As much as he terrified her, Jacobus Corbin compelled her at the same time. His eyes drew her in. The kindness—feigned or authentic—that hinted at their corners caused Libby to trip over her sense of caution and instead question whether in fact she was desperately wrong and that being with Jacobus Corbin was the safest place to be. They were irrational emotions. She wasn't thinking clearly. But then she could never claim she ever had.

"Excuse me." Libby made an effort to continue forward, to a place she'd rather not go.

Jacobus stepped in front of her, tilting his head up and eyeing her down the length of his nose. "May I help you, Libby?"

Libby. It was informal. Personal. She'd never invited him in.

She tried to muster some of the ever-elusive courage. It was just long enough of a pause for Jacobus to lean his tall frame toward her, his gaze magnetizing. He was dangerous. Whether a wicked or good dangerous was yet to be determined. But something in his expression told Libby that inside of this man boiled a fire that, once released, would explode and consume all those around him.

"You needn't do this alone, you know." It was a statement, not a question.

Libby shook her head. "No. No, I'm fine."

Jacobus didn't move. "What must I do to earn your good faith?"

"Good faith?" Libby's startled expression betrayed her.

Jacobus cleared his throat. "I mean you no harm. I know your father is quite taken with the stir my brother has aroused in Gossamer Grove. I must assure you, my brother—*I*—have our spiritual passions, but our methods of delivery are normally at odds. I stay with Jedidiah merely to try to keep him under some form of control. Please, do not draw conclusions about me, and I . . ." He raised an eyebrow, and for the first time there was a tiny flicker in his eyes. "I will not draw them about you."

Libby swallowed. A threat, or perhaps a reassurance? She moved closer to the storefront window of the drugstore, allowing a clear line of escape without Jacobus blocking her way.

"You will not draw conclusions about me?" she managed to ask. "Is it your right to cast judgment?"

Jacobus's smile was thin. "Cast judgment? No. Throwing the first stone is not my forte. Although there are some—many—who will."

"But doesn't God condemn?" Libby couldn't help but challenge him, though the wobble in her voice belied her courage.

Jacobus's face softened, and he drew in a deep sigh. "Ahh, yes. The ever-condemning God. Mankind's excuse to turn their backs on Him because He dares to enact discipline and consequences for sin."

His hand reached out and for a brief second brushed her upper arm. It was as if he warred between remaining aloof or coming near her and showing genuine care.

Perhaps, Libby mused briefly, he was torn as tumultuously as she was. "But who would follow a God who judges?" she whispered.

Jacobus ducked his head and smiled, the corner of his mouth

tipping up in a wry chuckle. "Oh, Libby Sheffield. There is a balance to be struck between justice and grace. I say justice rather than judgment, although sometimes one comes hand in hand with the other. We cannot cheapen God's righteousness by familiarizing Him to such a degree that His grace becomes a ticket to wanton freedom. Yet we cannot discount His forgiveness under the assumption He creates only to destroy."

Libby blinked.

Jacobus must have seen the confusion in her eyes. He ran his fingers through his hair as if perturbed he was unable to connect with her. It ruffled from its careful style, and for a moment Libby was struck that in spite of his angular features, he posed an oddly striking appearance. One moment bordering on vaguely handsome, and the next not at all what one would consider eye-catching.

He sighed. "Let me rephrase. The consequence of sin is death, but the grace of God brings us life. One must fear God for what He *can* do, while loving Him for what He *doesn't do*. A contrite heart results in the withholding of discipline in exchange for mercy—and love."

"Love?" Libby muttered, before realizing she had been completely taken in by the hypnotic lake-blue of his eyes. Intense, unblinking, philosophically wise. Now not at all wicked, but still dangerous. She despised what this man did to her mind.

"Love." He nodded while not breaking their staring at each other, their connection. "Grace."

"Forgiveness?" Libby countered, almost unwillingly, but as if the word were dragged from her in a hesitant whisper.

"Precisely." Jacobus snapped his fingers.

Libby jolted at the sound. As if he broke the hypnosis and brought her back to herself.

"I cannot believe that God would forgive the worst of sinners," she breathed. Testing Jacobus. Studying his face to determine, once and for all, if he had taken the mantle of God's reaper of justice or administer of grace.

Jacobus's eyes narrowed. He raised his hand and hovered his palm over her cheek, as if he ached to touch her but dared not be tempted by the seduction of a sinner's soul.

"Denying God's ability to forgive," he responded in deep baritone, "is denying oneself the ability to live."

His answer left Libby with no satisfaction. Worse, she hated herself for regretting when the preacher dropped his hand without touching her and turned his back and walked away.

———⁕———

Calvin fingered through a wooden box of marbles as they sat on the floor of the Mueller home. Libby stared at the marbles, like little eyeballs rolling around, trapped. She blinked, breaking her stare.

Reverend Mueller sat perched in an overstuffed chair, his legs crossed at the knee, a large book in his lap.

So went the customary afternoon when Libby took time away from her day to spend with Calvin, on his level, doing what interested him. Often enough, he trailed after someone in town. Lately it had been the Corbin brothers, but before them, it was Elijah or herself. Libby watched him pick up a red marble. He grinned.

"You love red, don't ya, Lollie?"

"Yellow," she corrected him gently. He smiled wider and handed her the marble anyway.

"Well, you always look pretty in red to me."

The words increased the ever-growing sharp pain in her heart. She'd worn a red shawl that night, nine years ago. Her throat hurt as she swallowed back tears, her gaze caressing the beloved features of Calvin's face. So much could have been different. So much *should* have been different.

"Miss Sheffield is a good friend to you, Calvin," Reverend Mueller interjected. "You should see if there's a yellow marble in your box. She could use that as her shooter."

Yes. Shooting marbles had been one of their favorite pastimes as children, and now it would stay with them forever.

"Did you want a yellow one?" Calvin asked.

Libby reached out her hand. "No, red is fine."

His smile reached deep into his eyes. A loyalty and an honesty that made Libby care even more for him, and hate herself even greater.

"I saw the police at the Hayes home this mornin'." Calvin's voice was casual, almost disinterested.

Regardless, Libby perked up. "You did?"

"Yep." Calvin made a circle on the carpet with some string. "I heard them sayin' she might got herself killed, not drownded."

"Calvin." Reverend Mueller broke into the conversation again, closing his book. "We mustn't discuss the grief of our neighbors with others."

Libby watched Calvin. His long limbs curled underneath him like a boy's. Overalls stretched over his shoulders, and his shirt-sleeves were rolled up, revealing the toned arms of a man. She bit her lip. So very much a man, and yet he'd never grown up.

Calvin looked up at his father. "I wasn't gossiping. Just sayin' truth."

Reverend Mueller offered him a patient smile. "I know." He looked down at Libby. "And how does Elijah fare?"

She sniffed back some unbidden emotion from her perusal of Calvin and met the reverend's inquiring gaze. "He's—it wasn't easy taking the information we found to the police."

"No." An empathetic tone entered Reverend Mueller's voice, and he pressed his lips together in thought. "That had to be difficult. The implications of his father and Mrs. Hayes are . . . unfortunate."

Libby nodded. Not many knew of the suspicions surrounding Harrison and Dorothy's relationship, but Reverend Mueller was the Greenwoods' minister.

"No one knows who killed her," Calvin inserted as he dropped ten marbles in the center of the string circle. "I heard 'em say might not be true. Just a rumor." He turned to Libby, frowning. "That's an awful rumor if it's true. Wouldn't find me kissin' someone who ain't my wife."

Libby blushed.

Reverend Mueller half choked and half chuckled. "Well then. Let's see about this game of marbles." He lowered himself onto the floor.

The game proceeded, but Libby fought distraction. Calvin's words, the implications of them, rang in her mind. For so many years she'd convinced herself that Gossamer Grove wasn't much better than a cesspool of humanity hiding secrets she was partially privy to by working at the newspaper. But instead it was she, made evident by the guilt she had lodged in her throat, threatening tears. By the fear she was attempting to assuage by making sure she was around people she felt were safe. And by trying hard, so very hard, to forget the day a stolen kiss changed the lives of those she cared about the most in Gossamer Grove . . . forever.

CHAPTER 27

Annalise

An earsplitting alarm jolted Annalise from sleep. She glanced at the clock as she vaulted out of bed—2:00 a.m. Her bedroom was dark save for the shaft of moonlight that floated through the lace curtains at her window and cast patterns across her blanket. She scrambled to grab her pepper spray from her nightstand and snatched up her cellphone, thumbing 911.

"Nine-one-one, what's your emergency?"

Annalise clutched her phone tight to her ear. "My house alarm has been tripped. I think an intruder may be inside."

"I'll dispatch police, ma'am, if they aren't already on their way. Please stay on the line."

Stay on the line? Because if the intruder burst through her door, then the 911 dispatcher could record the sound of her being murdered? Annalise hesitated, holding the phone to her ear as she took a few cautious steps toward her open bedroom door.

"Ma'am?"

"Yes?" Annalise hissed, the operator's voice startling her.

"Police are on their way. Ma'am, where are you now?"

"In my bedroom," Annalise answered, stepping into the hallway.

She peered down it, the darkness making it appear like a tunnel of doom in a house of horrors.

The shrieking of the alarm tortured Annalise's ears. She paused in the doorway of her bedroom. A crash sounded downstairs. Annalise sprinted forward, flipping the hallway switch that shed blessed light through the upstairs. She hurried down the hall, turning at the landing to look down the glossy wood steps with the thick banister. The landing below was empty as well. She flipped on another light switch. Lights everywhere. They would have to scare an intruder away if the alarm hadn't already pierced their eardrums.

"Ma'am? Ma'am?"

The 911 dispatcher's voice was distant. Annalise realized she'd lowered her hand that was holding the phone to her ear. Quickly she lifted the phone again. "Yes?"

"Stay in your bedroom, ma'am. Do not attempt to confront the intruder."

Too late. She was already down the stairs to the next light switch, brightening the entryway. To her left was the doorway into the kitchen. In front of her stretched the living room where only hours before she'd listened to Garrett's mother all but insult the entire family tree of Greenwood men. To her right were the Victorian parlor and the main entrance.

A small table had been upended by the front door, a blue vase smashed on the wood floor. The door was partly ajar.

Annalise punched her code into the security system to silence the alarm. She heard police sirens in the distance, but she still held her pepper spray in front of her, fully prepared to release stinging havoc on whoever had invaded her home. But there was no one. Her bare foot slipped on something that fluttered across the floor. An unfamiliar blue note card glared up at her.

Her chest constricted. Balancing her phone and pepper spray, Annalise snatched it from the floor. The fact that it was here, foreign-looking, made the card as intimidating as finding a land mine in her house.

A man's voice collided with the sudden silence of the alarm. A scream ripped from Annalise's throat, and with no further hesitation she lifted her pepper spray to unleash it full throttle.

"Stop!"

Brent's command brought reason back to Annalise. She dropped the pepper spray, and it rolled across the floor. Brent waved at his partner, who began to survey the perimeter of the property, her gun and flashlight held high. He took the phone from Annalise's hand and spoke to the dispatcher before ending the call.

Annalise felt numb. She began to tremble all over.

Brent urged her to the front step as another cop car pulled up the driveway. "Sit here. I'm going to check inside."

"There's no one inside." Annalise blinked rapidly to try regaining reason.

Brent nodded. "Probably, but let me check anyway."

His partner rounded the corner of the house. "Nothing," she stated, coming to stand at the bottom of the steps. They were joined by the other two officers who'd pushed into the house on Brent's behalf. He gave them a grateful nod and then sank onto the step beside Annalise. She was grateful he was on the scene.

Annalise pushed her hair over her shoulder, glancing up at the night sky. Stars. Moon. It was very clear out. Crickets chirruped in the bushes as though nothing out of the ordinary had occurred.

Brent reached for her hand. "What happened?"

Annalise gave a short laugh, more out of stunned disbelief than anything. "I woke up to my house alarm. Then I heard a crash." She looked over her shoulder and back into the house. "The vase, the table—they were pushed over."

"Probably when the intruder ran," Brent said.

Annalise nodded.

The porch light at Garrett's flicked on, and Brent cast a glance toward it and grimaced. "Looks like we woke up your ex."

"Stop it." Annalise nudged Brent with her shoulder. He was fiercely protective of her, partly due to their longtime friendship

211

and partly because of Christen. Regardless, Garrett didn't deserve Brent's animosity. Not now anyway.

"What the heck is going on?" Garrett jogged up to the front steps.

Brent stood, leaving Annalise sitting there on the stoop.

"Q?" Garrett ignored him.

"I'm fine." Annalise attempted a wobbly smile.

"Her security alarm went off," Brent offered by way of explanation. "Someone broke into the house."

"No way." Garrett stared over Annalise's head into the house, which was fully lit now. One by one, the police officers made their way outside.

"No one to be found," one of them said. "We're going to canvass the street. See if the neighbors saw anything suspicious."

"Told ya," Annalise muttered.

"You didn't get a look at the intruder by any chance?" Brent's partner asked.

Annalise met the woman's eyes and shook her head. "No. I didn't see anyone."

Suddenly, Annalise remembered the blue note card. She still clutched it in her right hand. "Oh!" She held it out. "I did find this. On the floor by the front door."

Garrett grabbed the note card before either police officer had a chance to respond.

Brent snatched it away from Garrett, holding its corner with a Kleenex. "Give me that. Between the two of you, you've probably smudged all the prints."

She hadn't thought of that. Annalise couldn't control the shiver that passed through her. She wrapped her arms around herself. Her feet were cold against the wood plank of the old step.

Brent flipped the card over. His brows went up, and he held it out so they could all see.

"Is that an obituary glued to it?" his partner asked. She looked between them. "I don't get it."

212

"I do." Annalise rose to her feet. She peered down at the card illuminated by Brent's flashlight. "Someone doesn't want us to forget," she stated.

"Or maybe the opposite," Brent said. "Maybe that's exactly what they want you to do. Forget about it. Forget about everything."

An old obituary, with yellowed edges and typeset, stared back at her. Beneath it, scribbled in pen at the bottom of the card, were words that sliced through the moonlight into Annalise's soul.

We weren't meant to come back from the dead. Leave us alone.

———

Annalise was no longer to be left alone. Period. Brent's orders. She'd packed a bag under Brent's guard and moved into the Drury home. A police report was filed, documentation was submitted as evidence for investigation, and Annalise was left with only photographs of the newest obituary to join her previous collection of Harrison Greenwood's and Dorothy Hayes's online record. But, the dooming handwritten note left below this obituary didn't need a photograph stored on her iCloud to be remembered. The words were etched into Annalise's psyche with the indelible mark of a nightmare.

It was all she could do not to take Garrett's hand. But it was daylight now. She was safe. Annalise glanced at Garrett. His confident stride was more alert than normal.

"You okay?" He gave her a sideways glance.

"Yeah," she lied.

They hiked up the sidewalk, maple trees arching over it in quaint style, enhanced by old-fashioned iron lampposts on every block. A robin cheeped and a squirrel scampered across their path. As usual, Gossamer Grove looked unstained by anything remotely dark or sinister.

"So. Paul Darrow." Garrett's words snapped her from her

internal, anxious thoughts. He gave her a slight smile. He knew she was overthinking everything. Turning a mountain into an asteroid. Annalise stepped around a piece of gum stuck to the sidewalk.

"I wonder if he's related to Tyler," Annalise mused, seeing Tyler's self-satisfied smirk in her mind. The image of the blue note card with its obituary glued on it had been riddled with Edgar Allan Poe. This one was also like Harrison Greenwood's. Typewritten. Undated. No byline at the top, like Dorothy Hayes's, indicative of being printed in the newspaper.

Paul Darrow. Apparently, another man in 1907 had been doomed to die. But then he wasn't a Greenwood. The addition of another old Gossamer Grove family name only muddied the waters further. Who had written such cryptic and morbid obituaries?

Garrett pulled open the door to the historical society, and Annalise entered. Their footsteps fell on the invisible prints left behind by those who'd once lived in the old house.

"You're here!" Gloria's voice was shakier today, belying her age. Her seventy-plus form appeared more fragile too. She met them with a smile and outstretched hands. "I'm so happy to see you both again."

Gloria's phone call had arrived this morning, right on the heels of finishing out the night at the police department. Gloria's message stated she had found something interesting about Eugene Hayes and she thought Annalise would want to know.

Gloria led them into the original dining room, where a long oak table was used to lay archived works on, old books, and photographs.

"We had a few questions for you as well," Annalise ventured.

Gloria smiled. "Of course! Would you like to go first?" The older woman pulled out a chair, motioning for Garrett and Annalise to do the same.

"I guess—" Annalise cleared her throat and started again. "I was wondering if you were familiar with the name Paul Darrow?

I'm estimating from around the same year as Harrison Green-wood—1907."

Gloria's thin, gray eyebrows rose. She tapped a finger to her chin. "Of course. The Darrows have been a part of Gossamer Grove for decades."

"Tyler Darrow is related to this Paul Darrow?" Annalise asked.

"Yes. Let me see how they were related exactly." Gloria eased out of her chair. "One moment." She left the room for a long moment. Silence pervaded until her footsteps announced her return. She held an iPad in her hands. A smile tilted her lips. "I hate these things. An old lady like me shouldn't have to learn how to use them when I'm seventy-one!"

Regardless, Gloria seemed adept, if slow, and soon she turned the tablet so they could see the genealogy tree. Gloria pointed with her index finger.

"Paul Darrow. He would have been Tyler's great-great-grand-father. And . . ." She tapped on Paul's name. A document loaded. Vintage. A census. "This is a census from 1915. It states Paul's occupation as 'newspaper owner.'"

"So, Paul Darrow owned the paper in the early 1900s?" Garrett asked.

Gloria nodded, setting down the iPad. "It makes sense. Tyler is just the next in his family to continue the business."

"Wait." Annalise looked down at the iPad. "The census is from 1915."

"Yes?" Gloria gave her a questioning look.

Annalise tapped the tablet. "The obituary I saw stated he died in 1907."

"No, that's not possible." Gloria shook her head. "I remember seeing Paul Darrow's name in several bylines that covered stories from the First World War. He was quite prolific during that time."

"How could that be?" Annalise cast a bewildered look in Garrett's direction.

Appearing as lost as she was, he shrugged. "Maybe the obituary wasn't real. Maybe it's the same as the other one that doesn't match my great-great-grandfather's Mom referenced."

"Why are we interested in Paul Darrow?" Gloria interrupted. "I thought you were inquiring about Eugene Hayes?"

"We are." Annalise fumbled for words. Garrett caught her eye with a small shake of his head. Fine. She'd keep the disorganized details to herself. They were driving her crazy, let alone overwhelming an elderly historian with the toxic story. "I'm just researching all sorts of family trees."

Lame, but Gloria bit. She smiled and nodded. "Oh, they're so fascinating! I love them. It's good to know where we came from, and Gossamer Grove has such a rich and beautiful history. The unity, the community—it's inspiring."

Not the words Annalise would have chosen. But Gloria was still speaking and drawing a scrapbook to rest in the middle of the table.

"I was working on scanning in some photographs from this old scrapbook. I wanted to add them to the database of historical pictures of Gossamer Grove."

Annalise drew her attention to the scrapbook as Garrett positioned himself next to Gloria.

"I found a photograph of Eugene." Gloria bent over the scrapbook and pointed. Annalise edged closer, and the three of them focused on the page. Gloria continued, "This scrapbook is a hodgepodge of pictures taken at a Gossamer Grove Fourth of July celebration in 1965. There he is."

Annalise squinted to see the faces better. There were at least three couples in the photograph. The sky was blue, the grass a yellowed green from the photographic development. Two of the men wore white T-shirts. One of them had a long braid reminiscent of Willie Nelson. They had their arms draped over women in miniskirts and V-neck blouses. The third man was shirtless, his frame muscular, with a tattoo that spread across his chest and an eagle's head framed in the middle of his pecs. He wore dog tags, his eyes were narrowed, his dark brown hair mussed from the wind.

"Dog tags," Garrett mumbled. "Didn't we send troops to Vietnam in '65?"

"We did." Gloria's nod of affirmation was grim. "Eugene was already in the military by then. This must have been shortly before he shipped out. I remember someone—I don't know who—mentioning when he came home a few years later, he was very unpredictable and very defensive of the time he spent there. You know"—Gloria glanced between them—"GI's who fought in Vietnam weren't praised when they returned home. Eugene flaunted his war wounds and made it known he'd done his duty, whether it was appreciated or not."

Annalise frowned. She leaned closer and studied the woman who was huddled against Eugene's side. Her brown eyes were dewy, her flaming red hair twisted into a knot on the top of her head with a bandanna tied around it. Her dress was long and bulging in the front. She was obviously pregnant. Obviously coupled with Eugene. It stood to reason, it was his child.

Confusion ripped through Annalise, the kind that shortened her breaths and made her step back.

Garrett shot her a look of concern. "You okay, Q?"

She shook her head. A sick feeling in the pit of her stomach.

"Honey?" Gloria turned and laid a hand on Annalise's arm. Her eyes were knowing. "You saw it too, didn't you?"

"Saw what?" Garrett glanced between them.

Annalise focused on Gloria's earnest, caring gaze. She nodded. She hadn't expected this. Not this.

"What?" Garrett pressed. Annalise shifted her focus to him. Greenwood men. She could hear Garrett's mother on the phone. The women in their lives were their foundations in their times of indiscretions. Eugene Hayes was practically a Greenwood himself. Like Garrett, like who knew who else in their male family lineage?

"My grandmother." Annalise stared at the picture. "That's my grandmother."

Garrett bent over the photograph. "Wow. Yeah. She looks a lot like you."

"She was pregnant." Annalise's words slipped from her mouth like an accusation.

"But Eugene is not your grandfather," Gloria said.

"No. He's not. My grandmother was happily married. She—she had my mother in 1967."

"So . . ." Garrett let the word hang between the three of them. So it only meant one thing.

"You'd best talk with your mother, dear." Gloria patted Annalise's hand.

The last thing she wanted to do.

"I'm so sorry, Gloria, but I need to go," Annalise choked out. She hurried from the room toward the front door. She heard the echo of Garrett's voice calling her name, but she ignored him. Her grandmother had had a relationship with Eugene Hayes? It was insanity. No. No. It was small-town secrets, that's what it was. Family secrets. Secrets everywhere.

Annalise sprinted down the steps outside the house. She was going to open them. Every last one of the secrets. She would exhume them all from every grave if necessary, and there was no way—she thought of the warning written on the note card with Paul Darrow's ominous obituary—there was no way she was going to give up. If Gossamer Grove was willing to murmur and scuttle about her own scandal and secret child, then Annalise was going to uncover everyone else's.

It was time for answers, for retribution, for tearing down the façade and exposing Gossamer Grove for what it was. A town like every other town. A town filled with broken people.

CHAPTER 28

Dusk had settled over Gossamer Pond. The mist rolled off its surface, making the mossy green algae glow in the moonlight. The meadow grasses, the sound of the canvas tent shifting beneath the evening's rather brisk wind—it all brought a sense of peace crashing into chaos. With the spring night's humidity, the wisps of fog reminded Libby of spirits hovering over the waters. Of Dorothy Hayes, somehow locked between worlds in a struggle for her soul. It was wrong that the revival continued in the shadows of her watery grave.

"Utterly thrilling." Mitch's voice wobbled with excitement, its sharp tone snapping Libby from her haunted musings. She glanced at Elijah, who flanked her other side. Though her hand rested in the crook of his elbow, this was anything but an evening out as a couple.

They neared the tent, joining with throngs of both familiar and unfamiliar faces. Libby caught sight of the town drunk, Old Man Whistler, who sidled up to Mitch. His clouded blue eyes flashed with a vigor that made Libby raise her eyebrows.

"Here to twist them words again, Sheffield?" Old Man Whistler spit a stream of tobacco juice as he nudged Mitch's arm.

"Don't tell me you've been converted." Mitch's snide response brought a scowl to the other man's face.

"And if I were? Might do you a lick of good too." Whistler cast them all a stern look.

Elijah cleared his throat. "We are faithful followers of the Lord."

"Huh." Old Man Whistler eyed him. He tipped up his chin in a challenge, white whiskers sticking out from it like porcupine quills, thick and ugly. "Might need to step it up in that regard. Don' seem to be shared by the rest of your family."

Libby felt Elijah's arm tense. She gripped his elbow tighter, watching his jaw set. His brow furrowed, and his expression turned dark.

Mitch intervened. "Ease off the boy."

Whistler held his palms up to them, widening his eyes in a pretentious and inauthentic wide-eyed apology. "I'm just sayin'. A saved man ain't goin' to string himself up like a dead deer, and a saved woman ain't goin' to wander around half nekked in the dark."

Elijah's arm jerked, attempting to shake off Libby's restraining hold. She was sure if she released him, Elijah would strike the old man. Libby glanced around them. The people entering the tent were oblivious to the tension.

Old Man Whistler scowled at Elijah. "Can't stop thinkin' it's mighty strange those two died within days of each other. And so odd-like." He gave Elijah a long look, as though he too had surmised something scandalous, something hidden behind closed doors. The elderly man turned on his heel and sauntered into the tent with the rest of the townsfolk.

Elijah took a determined step forward, half dragging Libby with him.

"Stop, Elijah," she urged.

He looked down at her, his eyes stormy.

"Let him go. It's not worth arguing," she whispered.

"Brazen idiot," Mitch muttered and wandered away.

Elijah worked his jaw back and forth. The mist rolled over the meadow, beneath their feet, bringing with it the pungent smell of pond water. "Everyone knows, don't they? It's gotten out, I suppose. My father. My Aunt Dorothy." He looked down at her, and the look in his eyes made Libby ache even worse than she already did.

"They were adulterers," he said aloud.

Libby didn't respond. There was no glorying in being right.

Elijah turned his back to the pond and surveyed the revival tent. Organ music crooned through the open doorway. He breathed deep through his nose and set his shoulders in a straight, determined line. "God help us all."

———〰———

The twin revivalists stood at each end of the makeshift stage. Wooden risers made their already-tall forms tower over the crowd. Hay bales and wooden benches served as chairs. Sawdust ran down the middle in an aisle that beckoned newcomers to come and be saved.

Libby's breath was snagged by the scents of the hay and sawdust. Along with perfumes of women, sweat from men who'd worked all day, the kerosene from lanterns lighting the innards, and even some lingering smells of liquor and tobacco that clung to the rabble-rousers in the crowd.

Jedidiah Corbin's booming voice and swinging arm led the attendance in a hymn. Libby's shoulder brushed Elijah's as they found seats on a hay bale. The straw poked through her dress into her thigh. It was uncomfortable. Hot. She longed for a cool breeze that made the canvas of the tent sway in and then collapse out as the wind removed its breath.

The hymn drifted away, and Jedidiah began to pray. It was earnest, not as condemning as she'd heard him in the last tent meeting. Perhaps he was less assertive tonight since it was Jacobus who was going to preach. Jacobus.

Libby opened her eyes. She froze. His were open too. Fixed on her with an expressionless face. His iridescent blue eyes pierced her. She couldn't look away, feeling magnetized as he didn't avert his gaze in a gentlemanly fashion, not seeming to consider that he was supposed to be in prayer.

"Amen." Jedidiah finished the prayer, and heads around them lifted.

Jacobus didn't break his stare.

Libby saw Elijah's head move from its bent position. He shifted beside her, but she couldn't look away from Jacobus.

"Grace." As the word left Jacobus's lips, he blinked and their connection was broken. He scanned the crowd slowly. "In spite of our sin, there is grace. But sin must be recognized. It must be admitted or freedom will linger in the shadows ever out of your reach. Ever mocking the hollowness in your soul as you hide your shame and you try to find peace where it does not exist."

Libby squirmed, and Elijah glanced at her. Was he remembering too? She couldn't help but skim the faces in the crowd before her eyes fell on Calvin, who was seated beside his father, Reverend Mueller.

"Jesus said, 'Come to me, you who are weary.' Are you weary tonight? Weary of bearing sorrow and pain?"

Jacobus's eyes rested on her. There was gentleness in them in that moment. He fell silent. His delivery was so different from his brother's, who seemed to want to terrify people into salvation from the pit of hell. Jacobus believed there could be relief from the darkness that lingered in one's soul—in *her* soul.

Elijah frowned and looked between Jacobus and Libby. No one else seemed to notice who Jacobus was looking at, but the silence in the tent grew thick. Palpable. Someone coughed. A child whined.

"That is grace," Jacobus finally said, his voice lowered but his tone slicing through the stillness. "That is forgiveness." He seemed to plead with her, something desperate in that moment, something haunting that he was trying to communicate over the heads of those gathered.

A shout outside the tent startled the audience. People murmured, looking over their shoulders toward the tent flaps tied open in the back of the meeting place. Another shout, and it shook Libby from her stupor. Elijah twisted where he sat as more yelling echoed through the tent. It sounded riotous, dangerous, and not at all complimentary to the meeting.

Reverend Mueller stood, as did Mitch, as did Elijah and a few other men. Jedidiah hopped onto the platform beside his brother, almost shoving in front of him. His face was ruddy, irritated.

"They don't wish to hear the truth of the Word of God!" Jedidiah shouted.

"It's Ralph Hayes! He's rounding up a posse of no-good heathens!" a yell informed the tent's occupants. Several more men jumped to their feet.

Ralph Hayes? Dorothy's husband? Libby had no time to react as Elijah launched himself past her into the aisle just as snapping and tiny explosions ripped through the night.

"Cannon crackers!"

There were screams from some of the women. Libby stumbled as a few shoved to get by her to the aisle where they could flee with their children.

"And eggs! The boys are throwin' eggs!" Old Man Whistler seemed to summon every ounce of youth in him as he waved his cane in the air like a flagman heading into battle. He ran toward the back of the tent. "The Corbin twins don't deserve this madness!" he hollered.

Frantic lunacy erupted around her. Libby's toe caught on her skirt and she fell forward, her palms slamming into the hay bale, stalks of straw stabbing her skin. She looked in every direction. Elijah had disappeared, and Mitch was pushing his way toward the door, determination on his face to witness every gory detail. She shot a desperate look toward the platform. Reverend Mueller had hold of Jedidiah's coat sleeve and was urging him through the back of the tent to safety. Jacobus stood, indecision on his face. When he spotted her, he bent and said something in Calvin's ear. Calvin nodded, his eyes round. He ducked his head and charged after his father and Jedidiah.

Jacobus hopped off the platform, pushing people out of the way, heading toward Libby. His hand closed around her arm. "Come with me. Out the back," he urged.

"I can't." Libby pulled in the opposite direction. "Elijah!"

"He'll be fine." Jacobus almost sounded as if he growled. She tugged against his hold.

"It's Ralph Hayes. He's Elijah's uncle. We can talk sense into him, I know it."

Jacobus considered her words, then gave a quick nod.

They made their way out of the tent. Jacobus pulled her down into a crouch as an egg flew toward them, hitting the tent over their heads.

"They're mad!" Libby yelled at Jacobus. It was as if Ralph Hayes had recruited every teenage boy and miscreant in Gossamer Grove. She scanned the crowd, people dispersing toward wagons and motorcars. The pond lay still behind them, its waters a glittering background to the chaos. She saw some men attempting to calm the teenage vigilantes. Mr. Thurgood, the night watchman, along with a policeman brandishing a stick.

"Where are the twins?" Ralph Hayes wove through the mob, his fist in the air.

Elijah's head and shoulders bobbed over a few of the young lads.

"Elijah!" Libby shouted. But he didn't hear her. He was moving in the opposite direction of his uncle, apparently not having caught sight of Ralph Hayes.

Libby jumped forward, away from Jacobus. He reached for her, his fingers grazing her sleeve. She didn't pause to think about his safety, one of the twins the crowd was shouting about.

"Mr. Hayes!" Libby panted, out of breath as she reached his

side. His arm swung out and shoved her away. "Mr. Hayes, you must stop!"

"Where are the twins?" he shouted. A man beside him brandished a pistol and shot it into the air. Screams. People ducked. More gunshots sounded at the opposite side of the meadow near the main road.

"Don't do this! The Corbin brothers have done nothing wrong!" Libby hung on Ralph Hayes's arm. He tried to shake her off.

"Nothing? They drove away my wife! Drove her to leave the house and drown!"

Libby's own suspicions about them, especially Jedidiah, raced through her mind. But there was no time to consider. "Mr. Hayes, you must bring this to an end. This won't resolve anything."

His eyes were wild as he hissed in her face, spit dotting her cheeks. "My son is motherless. Dorothy wasn't the same after she went to one of these meetings. Said she was 'convicted.'" Rage filled his eyes. "It would've been better if they never came and stirred things up. I wasn't going to say nothin' or do anythin'! We were fine the way we were! She didn't need to leave me. Didn't need to get herself drowned!"

"Libby!" Elijah appeared from the mass. He edged between her and his uncle. "You need to go, Libby. It isn't safe."

He spun toward his uncle. "What are you thinking?"

Libby answered for Ralph Hayes as the man glared at Elijah. "He thinks the twins' message started everything. Made Dorothy feel convicted, and then she left him that night. The night she drowned."

Elijah's glare drilled through her. "I told you to get out of here!"

Hurt and shock stunned her. "But, he needs to know about your aunt Dorothy. That she was going to meet the kill—"

"I said go!" he shouted.

Arms wrapped around her from behind, pulling her against a solid chest. Warm breath filled her ear as a firm voice spoke directly into it. "He's right, Libby. You've done what you can. You must be safe."

Jacobus.

She twisted, her face only inches from the intense eyes.

"It's madness here. Reason will be ineffective." His lips moved against her ear as his logic sank in. Jacobus steered her behind him.

"You!" Ralph Hayes's growl filled the air. He launched himself past Elijah and at Jacobus.

Libby saw the glint of a blade in the darkness. The moon's reflection momentarily warning her. The man intended to kill Jacobus Corbin.

She shoved in front of Jacobus. A searing pain coursed through her. She heard Elijah's shout, sensed Jacobus's arms, and then the night went black—as if the moon had been snuffed out by evil itself.

CHAPTER 29

Annalise

Nicole and her boyfriend, Brian, were picture-perfect. Annalise bit the inside of her bottom lip as she handed them their coffee. Brian's stylish haircut, tailored cotton shirt, and straight-legged olive-green pants made him appear as though he'd stepped out of *GQ* magazine.

Annalise avoided looking at Nicole as Brian inserted his credit card into the chip reader.

"Here you are." She ripped off the generated receipt and handed it to him.

"Things going well?" Brian asked as he signed it.

Annalise tapped her fingers on the counter, eyeing the credit-card machine. "Mm-hmm."

"Garrett told me you found some interesting information at the historical society." Nicole's words made Annalise's insides curdle. It was natural Garrett would tell his sister.

"He didn't tell me what, though," Nicole finished. Her tone was hesitant, as if she hoped Annalise would offer it up.

Not a chance.

"Sometimes messing with the past isn't worth it," Nicole stated.

Annalise finally looked at her. The frigid eyes irritated her. "But, sometimes it's necessary," she retorted.

Brian handed the credit-card slip to Annalise. He placed the pen back in the cup on the counter. "You've got a lot on your plate right now." He smiled. "What with the food pantry and the coffee shop. I know it's been tough."

"I'd rather not comment."

Brian had the graciousness to look apologetic. He tipped his head toward a table and spoke to Nicole. "I'll just take the coffee over there."

Nicole nodded. When he walked away, she leaned closer to Annalise. A whiff of jasmine perfume teased Annalise's nose. Nicole offered her a grim smile, her attempt at camaraderie.

"Tyler Darrow had no right to even research the picture of the baby." Nicole glanced over her shoulder at Brian, then back at Annalise. "I hope no one finds out the baby is . . ." She let her sentence hang.

There it was again. Don't tell. Don't ruin the Greenwoods. Don't let on that it was Garrett's baby.

Annalise rolled her lips between her teeth. She grabbed a washcloth and busied herself wiping the counter down. Illegitimate children seemed to run in the family. The image of Eugene Hayes with his arm draped over a younger version of her grandmother ate at her.

"They won't find out," Annalise muttered.

"You're certain?" Nicole might as well have asked what she really meant, which was *You won't tell?*

"I know you don't like me." Annalise took little satisfaction from the way Nicole paled. "I know you want Gossamer Grove to keep being pretty, vintage, *nice*. For the magazines and for tourists. No scandal. Nothing dirty. Nothing controversial. I get it. The town's economy is important. But so are *people*, Nicole. You can have your Norman Rockwell life, if you want, but it's not real. Our town has broken people in it. Many of them come to the pantry every day." Annalise waved a hand toward the food pantry door. "You can choose to try to hide them, like you hide me, and my baby, and Garrett's mistakes. But we're there. Always there."

Nicole blinked. She adjusted the bottom of her blouse. "Are you trying to sway my opinion regarding the homeless shelter versus Doug Larson's wilderness center?"

Annalise palmed the countertop and breathed in deep. It went so much deeper than a piece of property. How did she get anyone to recognize the broken people under their noses? That each of them was living out ramifications of bad choices and tragedies. That life wasn't *pretty*.

"You will never get it, Nicole, until you hurt." Annalise met the woman's eyes. "Until you understand what it is to be destitute. Whether financially or emotionally or spiritually."

Nicole said nothing, but turned and walked away. Toward Brian, toward her coffee, toward her carefully ordered world. Annalise had spent years building her own well-ordered world too. Order from chaos, she'd hoped, yet the broken pieces of her could never walk away.

Annalise hurried into her office and slouched in her chair. She reached for her messenger bag and pulled out the folder that held obituaries, photographs, and revival flyers. The photo she'd found of herself, pregnant and alone at Aunt Tracy's. She flipped it over, staring at the names she could only assume Eugene Hayes had penned. All of them were familiar but one.

Libby Sheffield.

Who was she? What had she to do with this story? This unsettling conglomeration of people spanning well over a century.

Annalise fumbled through the photographs, pulling out the picture she'd asked Gloria about on her first visit. The unfamiliar young woman with the brooding dark eyes and hair, the pale skin. She studied her. Was this Libby? How did she fit into the Greenwood family tree? Or didn't she?

Her eyes narrowed as something in the photograph captured her attention. Annalise frowned and leaned closer, but it was tiny and the picture quality blurry. She tugged open her desk drawer, neatly organized into compartments. Paper clips, rubber bands, pens—blue ink in one compartment, black in another—a ruler, scissors, and . . . She reached for the magnifying glass and held it over the image. Holding her breath, her heart began racing until it pounded in her chest.

A small watch was clipped to the woman's blouse. Heart-shaped, with gold filigree, and tiny hands with the time frozen for eternity at what looked to be 8:36 p.m.

Annalise shoved the papers and pictures back into the folder and jammed it in her bag. She needed to go back to her house. The jewelry box, upstairs in her bedroom, filled with cheap baubles and a few inherited pieces. Her grandmother's watch, handed down to her mother, then to her. A heart-shaped timepiece, identical to the one in the photograph. But it was broken. It had never worked. Time had stopped at 8:36 p.m. and never started again.

—⁓⁓—

"Where are you going?" Garrett braced a sheet of plywood against an angled frame he'd built against his garage. One sheet of plywood had already been screwed down. A box of climbing holds sat in the yard. He was building a climbing wall. Annalise didn't care.

She hurried by him toward her home. Since the historical society debacle yesterday, she'd avoided him, choosing instead to escape to Brent and Christen's and play with their kids.

"Hey!" Garrett jogged up to her. His T-shirt had sawdust scattered across it and had holes in the sides under his arms. "You can't be alone, Q."

"I'm fine." She wasn't. He was right. Her heart palpitated just looking at her front door.

"I'll come in with you." Garrett tugged at the stocking cap he wore as if he were going skiing.

She tried to ignore him, tried to ignore the way he followed her up the stairs to her bedroom. The way he filled the space with the most intoxicating and yet uncomfortable mix of emotions.

Annalise ran her fingers over the empty spot on her dresser. She longed for Gia's picture. The real one. Not the photocopy of it, reminding her someone was still out there. Still trying to hurt her.

Garrett shifted behind Annalise. He probably didn't intend to make her this aware of his presence, but she was. All because of Gia, and *before* Gia. They'd conceived her together when they were only eighteen years old. Annalise remembered how nervous she'd been, the butterflies in her stomach when the popular Garrett Greenwood approached her that day by her locker. She wasn't unpopular, but she wasn't popular either. Annalise had blended in, on purpose, except for her flaming red hair. Unlike her parents' ambitions, she only wanted to reach her goals, bullet point by bullet point.

Garrett Greenwood and his eyes. They were what appealed to Annalise. The other girls oohed and aahed over his hard muscles from climbing. His abs, his hair, his charm. But in his eyes, Annalise found a vulnerability hiding behind the quiet swagger. She'd been drawn in.

Never mind she found out later that he'd been dared to win the affection of a nobody girl at school. Why he'd zeroed in on her, she didn't know, didn't care. By that time they were "a thing." A couple. Going anywhere and everywhere together. A kiss, another, and then more. Until the night of Nicole's campfire. His older sister home from college. There'd been underage drinking, but neither Garrett nor Annalise could blame their behavior on that. They didn't have a sip. They were intoxicated—with each other. As the night drew deep, the campfire warm, they'd snuck away. For a kiss, Annalise thought. But it had grown into much more than she'd ever intended. His bedroom, the comforter, the pillows, the smell of his spicy deodorant, and the lull of music in the background. She'd memorized him. He'd memorized her.

Annalise swallowed and drew a fast breath, blowing it out between her lips. Twelve years ago. She hadn't forgotten him.

"You okay?" Garrett's voice invaded her thoughts.

"Yeah."

"I don't believe you." He was good at seeing through her.

"I'm looking for something." She rummaged through her jewelry box, her fingers finding the heart-shaped watch with its pin in the back to attach to a shirt or jacket. Annalise rubbed her thumb over its face. 8:36. Turning, she held it out to him. Anything to shift the subject of her thoughts. She was tired. Alone. Garrett shouldn't be here.

He took the watch, his callused fingers brushing hers, reminding her that he'd left to spend twelve years on the climbing circuit. She caught a glimpse of green ink that wound around his bicep and disappeared beneath his shirtsleeve. More tattoo peeked out through the wide holes in his ratty shirt. The man had turned into a vagabond, a successful climber with numerous endorsements and money to spare.

Garrett gave her a quizzical look. "What is it?" He turned the watch over in his hand.

"It was my grandmother's," Annalise explained. "And it's identical to one in that picture of the young woman I found in Eugene's trailer."

Garrett raised an eyebrow. "You think it might be the same watch?"

Annalise nodded.

Their gazes collided.

She swallowed.

He took a deep breath.

She made pretense of crossing the room to look out the window.

Annalise heard him set the watch on her dresser. A moment later, she sensed him behind her. Neither said a word. She could hear him breathe, smell the sawdust on him. She wished things could go back to the way they'd been. Before he'd come back to Gossamer Grove. Before Eugene Hayes. When Gia's picture greeted her every morning. She'd pray for her and then go about her day pretending everything was all right. She was okay with pretending. She had done so for twelve years now.

Annalise wrapped her arms around herself as she stared out the window toward Garrett's house below. Maybe she wasn't okay with pretending anymore. Now that the wounds were opened, maybe now she just wanted to heal.

"I'm sorry." Garrett's voice rumbled behind her.

Annalise didn't turn.

Garrett moved from behind her, his hands jammed in the pockets of his shorts. He stared out the window as well. They looked down over his house, the deck, the electric saw and sawhorses, the box of climbing holds.

"I never should have listened to my parents. Leaving you was a stupid move."

"It wasn't all your fault," she finally admitted. "I could have fought harder." Annalise looked over at him. "I could've *asked* you if you wanted a say in anything."

Garrett shrugged. "I don't know if it would have changed anything. I was stoked to hit the rocks. You know? But I did care, Q. I did."

She wiped away a tear. Hoping Garrett didn't notice, Annalise wrapped her arms back around herself.

"I've thought of her every day." His words. So quiet, so low, Annalise barely heard them.

"You and me both," she muttered. Only she'd birthed Gia, carried her for nine months, held her after she was born, handed her off to a nurse, signed papers, listed the father as "unknown," and never once ventured to ask if Garrett had an opinion. She hadn't wanted to ask. She'd been frightened, hurt, and angry. She'd also been just as wrong as he was. Each one's mistakes weren't greater or lesser than the other's. They were just . . . mistakes.

Annalise turned toward him, her shoulder brushing his.

Garrett's lashes were damp and he looked away, worked his jaw from side to side, and blinked.

One word whispered in her heart.

Grace.

She hated that word, in this moment, more than any other. For to give grace, forgiveness was required. Forgiving herself, forgiving him. It was her war cry for all the destitute of Gossamer Grove. Authenticity! Why hide the shame, the grief, the trauma? A community should extend grace and love and care. But it was so hard to practice. Especially when she knew it wasn't all Garrett's fault. It was hers too.

"Did you ever . . . ?" Annalise hesitated. It wasn't worth asking. Did he ever have another relationship? Think of getting married to someone else? Or had what happened ruined him like it had her? Burned her, made her gun-shy. A loner.

Garrett must have read her mind. He shrugged and blew out a sigh. "Yeah. I hung with a few women. I mean, I was in Europe. It's part of the lifestyle, unfortunately. Climb, hang out, mess around. It's a rush, you know? Until you crash."

"You crashed?" Annalise hadn't. She'd never allowed it. Only right choices from then on. Order, control, wisdom, and responsibility.

Garrett nodded. "Oh, I crashed hard. It was sick."

"Did you fall off a mountain?"

He smiled, a vague smile that told Annalise her question showed her ignorance about climbing. That his crash hadn't been physical. Of course not. She would've heard about it.

"Nah. I didn't fall." Garrett gave her a quick glance. "A guy I climbed with did. But he took routes free, no ropes, no anchors. Dude scaled El Capitan that way."

"Oh." She didn't really know what he was talking about.

"No, my crash was about three years ago. I met this guy named Matt. He was a climber from Colorado. He tagged along with a few of us for a while, but he wasn't up to our category. He mostly did 5.11s, 5.12s."

Annalise nodded. She understood that from when she'd dated Garrett. The pitch. The scale. The climb difficulty. 5.10 was considered good. 5.12 really good. Anything over this was champion stuff. It was Garrett.

Garrett gave a small laugh. "One night," he went on, removing his hat and balling it up in his hand, "I'd had too much to drink. I passed out in an alley outside a little joint in Innsbruck, Germany, and Matt found me. Hauled me back to the hostel where we were staying. The next morning I wasn't fit for climbing, so the rest of the guys took off and Matt stayed back with me."

"What happened?" Annalise asked.

Garrett met her eyes. His narrowed, emotional, deep. "I told him—everything. About you. About the baby. I don't know why, but I did. You know what he told me?"

"What?" Annalise bit her lip.

Garrett's eyes dropped to her mouth, then rose fast to her eyes again. "He told me that to understand grace, you have to fall. Crash and burn."

They weren't the words she was expecting, or wanting, to hear. They didn't even really make sense.

Garrett's hand came up, and his fingers trailed down her cheek. "I hadn't crashed yet, Q. But I did that day. Hard."

"What do you mean?" she whispered, leaning into his hand, into the feel of him, into the comfort that came from his touch when it shouldn't.

"That was the day I faced you." His gaze caressed her face. "What I'd done. Who I was. That was the day I hated what I'd become. That was the day I crashed but realized there was grace to start over. To try again. To become different."

His fingers pushed through her hair, tucking it behind her ear. Her breath caught and held as he lowered his face. The vulnerability in his eyes staggered her, taking her off guard and completely erasing the anger she harbored toward him. They'd both been prey to their own choices, both been at fault, and yet, somehow, Garrett's healing seemed far beyond hers.

Annalise kept her eyes open, locked onto his as he palmed her face with both hands, tilting it up toward him. His lips pressed against her forehead, taking her breath away more than if he'd kissed her mouth. It was the first kiss he'd given her that spoke of newness, of grace. He held his lips there for a long moment before drawing back.

Garrett let his hands drop to her shoulders. "When I climb a route and hit the crux, it's painful. But I push, Q. I push past it and it's a total rush when I stand at the top. It's like coming back to life. The climb is still there. But I conquered it."

"How?" Annalise searched his face.

"I gave myself the grace to admit I'd fallen. Then by the grace of God, I started to climb again. It's a beautiful view from the top, Q. It's beautiful."

His answer burrowed into her soul, making her forget everything but the idea that she might be able to let her heart beat again. Really beat. To live, without regret.

CHAPTER 30

Libby

The pain in her shoulder was almost unbearable. Voices screamed. A hand pressed something against the knife wound. She saw stars—literally—from her position flat on her back, blinking up at the night sky. Her head was cradled between two hands.

"Come back. Come back." The murmur was low. Even. Comforting somehow.

Shouts.

A hand patted her cheek. "Don't go. Stay with me." She could almost open her eyes again. Almost. Her body jostled and she screamed, the pain searing her shoulder muscle.

"Get her to the motorcar!" someone shouted. Distant. Commanding. Elijah.

Arms shifted and lifted her. She sensed the man who hoisted her against his chest stumble beneath the awkward weight of her body.

"Help my daughter!"

Mitch.

"Papa . . ." she muttered. The old endearment so rusty, so rarely used.

237

"Shhh." Mitch's voice in her ear. But then he moved away.

The chugging of the automobile. The grinding of gears. Whoever held her cradled her head in the crook of his elbow while pressing down on her knife wound. The body beneath hers absorbed most of the bouncing from the motorcar hitting ruts and crevices in the dirt road.

Her vision went black. The stars went out.

—⦚—

It was the night everything changed. Libby knew that now, and she imagined years later she would look back on the fear, the trauma, and wonder if things might have been different in another life. She had done something she had never done before. This time she'd not run, not abandoned. Instead, she'd saved. The knife wound in her shoulder was the throbbing reminder that she'd saved Jacobus Corbin's life.

Now she rocked in the rocker on the front porch of her home. Her mother had brought her a quilt and wrapped it around her legs. A cup of tea sat on a circular end table. In her hand, Libby fingered her watch. The one she'd pinned to the tailored jacket of her dress the night of the tent meeting. The one that had deflected Ralph Hayes's knife, making her injury a deep cut instead of a gouging stab that would have damaged her far worse.

Libby stared at the face of the watch. The hands had stopped at 8:36 p.m. The frame was dented where the knife had struck. There wasn't anything particularly special about the watch, yet it seemed as a treasure to her now. It told her the moment she'd saved Jacobus Corbin's life. The man who seemed to know everything about her—though even Libby wasn't quite sure why she was so certain Jacobus knew her darkest secrets—and yet, still, she'd saved him.

Libby was not heroic. She never had been. Her fingers closed over the watch. Somehow, at 8:36, she'd become as indelibly linked to Jacobus Corbin as she had been to Elijah Greenwood that evening at dusk so many years before.

The screen door opened, and her mother exited, her skirts swishing against the whitewashed floor of the porch. Stiff, crisp navy blue, with a starched white blouse with little adornment. She was the dichotomy of Mitch. His impulse and headstrong passion ran into his wife's pious righteousness like a motorcar crashing into a brick wall. Libby still didn't understand how they'd ever married, or how Mitch had ever convinced her mother to front a large portion of her dowry to buy out Paul Darrow's paper.

"You haven't touched your tea."

Libby glanced at the teacup. It was cold now. She was cold. Gossamer Grove had evolved into a dark place.

"I'm sorry." Her apology seemed to soften her mother. The woman sighed and reached for the cup.

"Well, I must say, you're looking better this morning. Such a fright from two nights ago."

Libby watched a carriage roll by on the brick street. The white picket fence that lined their yard was like a border. If she crossed it, she would return to chaos. Yet, staying here, staring at the rose-bushes, the green lawn, the violets and dandelions springing up between the grasses . . . it was an illusion of peace. It always had been. Libby had just become very good at ignoring the shadows.

She looked up at her mother. "I—"

No. Confession to her would not end well. There would be no grace. It was why Libby had fostered the secret deep inside for years, why she'd idolized Elijah for his own silence, and why Jacobus's words had opened the scab that had grown over the infected wound.

"Did you read the paper this morning?" Mother ventured. Apparently, she hadn't heard Libby's attempted start. Libby sealed her lips and shook her head.

"Your father and Paul—they will forever be at odds. That horrible paper." With rigid posture, Mother moved back inside, taking the teacup with her.

A robin hopped in the yard, distracting Libby for a moment. The screen door opened again, and her mother left the house while snapping open the paper.

"I don't know what those two men are thinking! I'm certain your father will not be pleased after today's issue. Paul undermines him every step of the way."

"Well, it used to be Paul's paper," Libby mumbled, a momentary pang of sympathy extending to the shrewish newspaperman whose financial straits had led him to selling the bulk of the ownership.

Mother stared down her nose at Libby. Libby matched her stare. Finally, Mother pursed her lips and redirected her attention to the paper.

"Your father wrote an article about the twins' behavior causing riots, and Paul printed letters to the paper in defense of the Corbin twins. Thank the good Lord." She snapped the paper again as if it would portray her angst to the newspapermen who printed it. "I have personally attended several of the Corbin twins' services and find them of great value and much needed in this town. But apparently your father wishes to continue riling the citizens against them."

"What did he say?" Libby knew her mother wanted her to ask. She was too tired and too sore to withstand her.

Her mother began to read. "Your father writes, 'The decent and self-respecting citizens of Gossamer Grove deem it time to put a halt to the Corbin twins' meetings, specifically after the debacle that left a few injured, several arrests, and the Corbins afraid for their lives. One might suppose, though, that the brothers have lent to the outcry against them due to the forthcoming and vulgar preaching from the once-respected pulpits of this community. Nearly every woman has been insulted with their language—language so low it would be ill of this paper to print it and would make this paper liable for publishing obscenity.'"

Mother stopped. Libby didn't even know how to respond. Mitch's article, while sounding properly offended, had a double entendre. He was stirring up the town, and Mitch knew it. Selling papers on outrage when only days before he'd monopolized on the deaths of Deacon Greenwood and Dorothy Hayes, the front page also splashing the announcement of death threats against the Corbin twins.

"It's outlandish." Mother's voice cut through the silence. "And then, the letters to the paper. This one is from Old Man Whistler himself, whom I never believed would take the side of a preacher."

Libby raised her head to look at her mother as she turned the page. "What does he say?"

Whistler was the elderly version of her father. Rabble-rousing, gossiping, and doing whatever he could for attention.

"He writes to the paper—quite uneducated, I might add—'Yo mene dirty editor, I hope the twins will brake yor hed.'"

Libby's brows rose, and she met the censoring gaze of her mother's eyes over the paper.

"You see?" Mother snapped. "This paper will be the death of us. I'm sure Paul allowed this letter to go to print." She continued to read. "'Them twins don my sole good. If yo sey any mor mene things about them twins, yo paper best be lookin' out.'"

"A threat? Whistler threatened the paper?" Libby frowned. It was all getting out of hand. Fast. If her father ever saw the obituaries for Deacon Greenwood and Dorothy Hayes—the ones submitted but never printed—it would make matters even worse. This righteous crusade was going to cost more lives if her father—and Paul—didn't stop waging their own personal war against each other and stirring up a tornado of trouble.

Mother closed the paper. "As I said, this paper is filled with opposing views."

Libby hesitated. Jacobus. He didn't seem vulgar. He didn't use words that offended. Unless one countered that "being damned to hell" was offensive. It certainly did rattle the senses, but so did truth. Why did Jacobus even side with his brother? They were so different . . . weren't they?

"Anyway"—Mother's voice broke through Libby's thoughts—
"it's a blessing Calvin knew what to do the other night. Considering his . . . condition. The boy is slow, but he certainly is devoted
to you, Libby."

Confusion riddled through her. "What are you talking about?"

Her mother's eyes widened. "Calvin," she stated, as if Libby
should know, should remember. "He carried you to the automobile. He held you all the way to get help. He pressed the cloth to
the wound to stop the bleeding."

"Are you certain?" Libby breathed, her throat closing. Calvin,
saving her life. Holding her, tending her. It made her eyes sting
with tears. Guilt-ridden tears.

Mother folded the newspaper. "Of course I'm certain. They
could hardly get Calvin to leave your side."

It was as if the nightmare had become worse. Calvin. He was
ever her faithful friend, her companion. And she didn't deserve
it. She had made him who he was today. She had stolen his future
from him, and yet he'd given hers back.

—⁓—

Libby eased onto her chair at the newspaper. Mother had argued
that she wasn't fit to return to work. While her shoulder was still
stiff, the fact the knife had not buried into her muscle but rather
slashed the skin had been a relief to all. It wasn't devotion to her
job, to the newspaper, or even to Mitch that drove Libby to return.
It was guilt.

She hadn't slept last night. The shaky sensation in her body
from lack of rest only compounded the feeling of swollen, achy
eyes and a stomach twisted into anxious trails of theories and
assumptions. Not to mention the memories. The cold fingers of
reality that squeezed her heart, bringing back all the terror of that
night. The terror, and then the dread, and then the years of guilt.
Guilt, every time she heard Calvin call her Lollie. Off-putting her
shame into hero worship of Elijah for shielding her had worked.

For years. Now Libby sensed it was all crumbling, and when it did, she would be exposed.

Libby turned to the pile of mail on her desk. Apparently neither Mitch nor Paul wanted to mess with menial tasks. She opened the first two. Letters to the editor. Skimming them, she cringed. One was threatening to burn down the Baptist church if the Corbin brothers didn't leave town. The second was lauding the message the Corbin twins had brought to Gossamer Grove and stated it was time that the sinful practices of the town be brought to task.

They would need to go to Mitch's desk.

Libby stifled a sigh. She was reaching for the next letter when her fingers stilled. Stopping the tremor in her hand was impossible. The envelope. The typeset. Her name.

Libby Sheffield

Sliding the letter from its casing, Libby's breath quickened. She skimmed the words, her heart beating faster.

> *Sins must be atoned, for God requires blood.*
> *Only now do I see you have danced around the edges of your own darkness.*
> *Be assured.*
> *Your sins will go unpaid no more.*

Libby shoved the paper away, across the desk. The words mocked her. Yes, she danced around the edges of darkness, just as she'd danced when she was fifteen in the Newmans' abandoned barn with Calvin. Just as they'd shared their dreams, young love, with Calvin gently stroking the back of her hand. Just as she'd closed her eyes as he kissed her, then more passionately, and then Elijah Greenwood had found them. Their scramble apart, the hurt on Elijah's face when he saw her with Calvin, and her elbow knocking over the lantern, lighting the hay on fire. She'd been so torn, even at fifteen, with her infatuation with Elijah that seemed to be mutual, but her deep friendship with Calvin that warred against it. And that night? It had been Calvin, only Calvin, until the fire. The dry straw and hay in the old barn had burned with fury. Elijah and Calvin, teenage young men exchanging punches, and her screaming that they needed to run as the barn became enveloped in flames.

Libby's eyes slid shut against the memory, but that only made the images in her mind brighter, more ferocious. Calvin landing a solid fist into Elijah's gut. Elijah stumbling back and then leaping aside as the barn's wall *whooshed* into flame. Their shouts ensuing. Elijah, grabbing her arm and urging her to run. Calvin yelling her name. Elijah hadn't looked back, but she had. She had! Calvin's overall strap was snagged in the back by a hook on the stall's wall. He'd yelled for her to help. Elijah had shouted for her to duck. In that moment, that split decision, she ran. And then came the crash. The horrible crash as a falling beam struck Calvin in the head, changing the course of their lives forever. *His* life. Her best friend, and he was gone, in that moment, as she ran from him. Left him. Hours later, after Elijah had braved the fire to drag Calvin out, Libby was already home, in her room, in the dead of night hiding her shame. No one knew she'd been there that night. Only that Elijah had rescued poor Calvin Mueller, whose head injury had almost killed him. She'd planned to apologize when Calvin regained consciousness days later, to beg his forgiveness. It was then they knew. The entire town knew. Calvin Mueller would never be the same again.

Now Libby scrambled for a handkerchief, fighting back a sob. The inkwell tipped in her frantic grasp for the cloth, and instead of wiping the tears that coursed down her face, she tried to blot the ink from marring the desk permanently. She pushed the offensive typewritten note away. It floated back and forth before finally resting on the wood floor.

Whoever had selected the paper to be their voice of judgment knew her shame. The years of harboring the horrible guilt was coming to an end.

———m———

The door to the back alley behind the newspaper was already open. Libby surged through it, gulping in deep breaths of fresh air. It was laced with the scent of must, and manure, and the dank moisture that collected in an alleyway. But the brick buildings rose above her, the cobblestone path beneath her feet, and a row of trees parallel to the newspaper office. Shelter. It was a hiding place of sorts.

Libby closed the door and looked to her left, down the short flight of stairs leading to the basement. The basement door was open, its green paint chipped and worn. It was never open. She took a step toward the first stair out of curiosity, then paused, her toe hovering. Libby withdrew. The chilly air from the open basement doorway drafted up the stairwell like the breath of a ghost. There was nothing inviting there.

Libby startled and leapt back from the stairwell as a crash from inside the basement echoed up the stairwell. A muffled curse. A bang. Another curse.

Paul.

She hurried down the steps as if obligated to ensure he was all right. Ironic. Libby blinked. If she had only realized her obligation to help Calvin . . .

Libby braced her hand on the doorframe. Her nose twitched with the thickness of dank mold. The foundation was fieldstone and insulated the cavernous inside with cool air. It was pitch-black save for a small spot of light in the far back corner.

"Paul?" Libby ventured. She lifted the hemline of her dress. Its practical green cotton didn't deserve to be dragged across a filthy floor. "Paul?" she called again. This time she could hear her heart pounding in her ears.

She crept deeper into the basement, toward the light. Wooden filing drawers rose on either side of her, creating a maze of walls that blinded her to the basement's vastness.

"What are you doing down here?"

Libby screamed, clamping her hand over her mouth and stumbling into a cabinet. The jarring of her shoulder against the wood sent a spear of pain through her wound.

Paul stepped from the shadows, a kerosene lamp lofted so he could see her. Its light made pockets of shadows on his face, turning his eyes ghoulish, his twisted mouth mean, and his cheeks hollow.

"I asked what you're doing here," he repeated, hissing through his teeth.

Libby backed away toward the door, toward freedom and the daylight that promised escape. "I—I heard a crash."

Paul stepped toward her and she retreated some more. She'd never been frightened by him before, but now she trembled.

"I dropped a crate," Paul reasoned. The whites of his eyes were huge and glaring. "You shouldn't be here."

"Why?" Libby held her arm across her waist, supporting it with her other arm and trying to ease any stress on her wounded shoulder.

"Because," Paul said. "Now go!" He waved her away.

"But why—?"

"Get out of here!" Paul's sharp command made Libby spin and flee for the door.

She burst into the light and ran up the stairwell. Her shoulder was pounding. Her heart was keeping time with the beats of pain. Libby didn't stop. She half jogged, half walked as fast as she could down the alleyway. The heels of her shoes made her ankles twist on the cobblestones, but she didn't care.

When she finally reached the end of the alley and broke out onto the street and the boardwalk, Libby looked both ways. Motorcars, carriages, and a few bicycles wove in and out amongst each other. The sun broke through the clouds as if to taunt her. It reflected her own life. Her own secrets. The dark basements of her soul she wanted no one to see into compared to the bright sunshine of a pleasant disguise. It masked the truth of what lurked in the shadows. But by three o'clock this afternoon, the sunshine would illuminate the alleyway, exposing it. If it hid anything, it would be discovered in the light.

Sometimes the daylight was more frightening than the dark.

CHAPTER 31

Annalise

"This is absolutely nuts," Annalise hissed as she tiptoed behind
Christen. "You're going to get us killed."

"Hardly killed," Christen shot back over her shoulder
with a smile. "You trust me, love. I know you do."

Christen was right. Annalise did trust her, but sneaking through
the back alley of a row of historical brick buildings had not
been on their BFF bucket list. The night air was cool. Crickets
chirruped as if to cheer them on, and a frog hopped across the
alleyway. Annalise's foot almost landed on it. She jumped to the
side, avoiding the inevitable *splat* that would have followed.

Christen hurried through the darkness like a woman on a mission.

"Where are we going?" Annalise dodged a bucket of cigarette
butts at the back door of one of the buildings.

"You'll find out," Christen said.

She wove around a metal dumpster to the back door of the
newspaper. Reaching out, Christen tugged on the doorknob. "It's
locked."

"Ya think?" Annalise sidled up to her, cellphone out with the
flashlight turned on. Christen had taken a dive off the deep end.

"Seriously, what is going on?" This skulking about back alleyways between old brick buildings was ridiculous.

Christen cast her an apologetic look. "If I told you, you wouldn't have come." Christen rattled the doorknob again. Her dark sweatshirt made her almost blend into the shadows.

"Why wouldn't I have come?" Annalise pushed for more than a vague answer.

Christen released the doorknob and turned. Her eyes were bright behind her glasses as Annalise lifted her phone's flashlight. "It involves Garrett." She held up a hand as Annalise opened her mouth. "I know, I know. The other day with him weirded you out, and I get that. But avoiding him won't bring you resolution. He asked me to bring you here."

"In the dead of night?" Annalise said.

"Seriously! Point that light somewhere else." Christen pushed the phone aside so it wasn't shining in her eyes. "And stop being so stubborn. Between you and Brent, you're so jaded you can't see what a stand-up guy Garrett is."

"I've never heard that term applied to Garrett Greenwood."

"Well"—Christen's voice dropped its sharp edge—"people can change. You of all people should know that."

Annalise shook her head. There it was. The call to offer grace. But wasn't forgiving and accepting Garrett's presence in her life playing with fire all over again?

Christen moved from the back door to a stairway that led down to the building's basement. She twisted the doorknob of the basement door. Victory lit up her face as she looked up at Annalise. "Ah-ha! It's unlocked!"

"No!" Annalise looked over her shoulder down the dark alley, half expecting Brent to flood it with headlights from his patrol car and arrest them for breaking and entering.

Christen waved Annalise in. "C'mon!" She stepped into the basement beneath the newspaper offices. Annalise released a sigh of exasperation.

249

Christen's head popped out of the doorway. Her glasses framed huge eyes. "C'mon!" she repeated before disappearing again.

Annalise aimed her phone's flashlight down the steps. The last time she'd succumbed to impulse and peer pressure she'd wound up on a plane to Connecticut to have a baby. Rolling her eyes, she heaved another sigh and bounded down the steps, her orange leather Naturalizer shoes silent on the concrete.

She poked her head inside. A light bobbed at the far end of the room. The thick smells of damp cement and mold toyed with her nose. Bank boxes were stacked against the walls just inside the door. Annalise shone the light down at her feet and noticed patches of wet flooring with cracks running through the aged foundation.

"Helps if you two turn on a light."

Annalise screamed. She swung her arm around and behind her. "Garrett?" Her voice squeaked as light flooded the basement. "Tyler?" She hated the way her voice rose another octave. Tyler stood at the metal light box mounted just inside the door. Garrett was beside him, holding a carryout cup of coffee from McDonald's. Any other time Annalise would feel like lecturing him about cheap coffee. But not now. Not when she'd just experienced another fright—an unnecessary one at that.

Christen scurried from the back of the room, excitement etched in her face. "Oh! You made it!" she said to the men.

Annalise crossed her arms and looked between the three of them. Christen looked marginally guilty, with Garrett looking oblivious to any internal struggle Annalise might be having. And Tyler, he appeared to be irritated.

"*Why* are we here?" Annalise chose to level her question on Garrett. The memory of being in her bedroom, the feel of his lips on her forehead, made her want to run. She couldn't—*couldn't*— soften toward him. It was survival. He was dangerous.

Garrett gave her a knowing smile, sad but understanding. He directed his attention to Tyler and didn't answer her question. "Thanks for letting us come tonight."

"Yeah. Sure." Tyler blew out a sigh. "But I didn't exactly want to come down here. Not after what happened."

"What happened?" Annalise looked between Garrett and Tyler. Tyler raised an eyebrow toward Garrett. "You didn't tell her?"

"Tell me what?" Annalise demanded. The dreadful sinking feeling in the pit of her stomach wasn't about to go away. Annalise realized she was turning into the perpetual pessimist. For good reason.

Tyler gave a small smile. "Figures." His expression was so frank, so unguarded, Annalise knew immediately she wasn't going to like what he had to say. "I received another anonymous submission today."

Annalise chilled. Her skin prickled beneath her sweatshirt.

Tyler continued. "There weren't any more pictures of your baby." Then he had the audacity to pause. Annalise wanted to put a chokehold on him. If he was enjoying dragging this out for sensation's sake, she was going to—

"It claimed Garrett was the father." Tyler shrugged. "Of course, I'd figured that out, but whoever sent it probably didn't know I would."

That threw a damper on Christen whose expression dropped. She must have thought this clandestine gathering was something to help Garrett and Annalise reconcile. In Tyler's moldy newspaper basement? Not likely.

Annalise swept her attention to Garrett. He didn't seem surprised at all. "You knew about this? The submission?"

"I called him." Tyler smirked. "I needed to check my sources."

"And you admitted it?" Annalise couldn't hide the tears in her voice. Of course he had. It was an easy deduction. She hadn't had a meaningful relationship since.

"I'm tired of hiding it. I'm not ashamed of our baby, Q."

Not ashamed.

Those words were both healing and scarring at the same time. He was twelve years too late to not be ashamed. But, she'd also waited twelve years to hear him claim Gia as his.

Annalise looked at Tyler. "Well, are you going to print it?" She exchanged a quick glance with Christen, who mouthed *Sorry! I had no idea!*

"It *is* an interesting story," Tyler said.

"It's slander!" Annalise blurted.

"She'll sue!" Christen inserted.

"Hold up." Garrett stepped between them. Christen half hid behind his shoulder. He leveled a strong look on Tyler. "You're better than that, Tyler. Besides, you know that would be a dumb move."

"Okay, so what's the whole cryptic *meet us in the basement of the newspaper* bit then? Some attempt to talk me out of it?" Tyler jammed his hands in the front pockets of his jacket.

"Not really." Garrett took out his phone and flipped through some photos before turning the screen toward Tyler. "This."

Tyler's eyes skimmed it. He blinked. "Where'd you get that?"

"It's at the police station right now for evidence. Annalise's house was broken into a few nights ago." Garrett's words were laced with insinuation.

Tyler held up his hands. "I did *not* break into her house."

"He's not saying you did," Christen jumped in. Her hands swept the air as if to remind Tyler where they stood. "But that obituary is of your ancestor. Which means Paul Darrow is somehow tied to all this ruckus, and that means *you're* tied to it as well."

Garrett nodded. "Paul Darrow, your great-grandfather, used to be part owner of this paper."

"Part owner? No." Tyler frowned. "He owned it. It's been in the family for years."

Garrett shook his head. "Not in 1907."

Annalise's head shot up. How did he know that?

Christen moved to her side, and Annalise felt her friend's hand slip around hers. She leaned into Annalise and whispered in her ear, "Let Garrett do this. For you."

Garrett was still speaking. "Gloria and I did some research on

Gossamer Grove as it related to events that occurred here in 1907. We found out this newspaper was sixty percent in the ownership of a man named Mitch Sheffield."

"Sheffield?" Annalise interrupted. Libby. Libby Sheffield. The woman in the photograph she'd assumed was Libby. The watch. The time stopped at 8:36.

"That's crazy." Tyler shook his head. "I've never heard of him."

"Apparently, your ancestor had some problems with money." Garrett let the words hang.

"Okay." Tyler tapped his foot and sighed. "So, where are you going with this?"

"Do you know how Paul Darrow died?" Christen interjected. She seemed to know what Garrett had in mind, though Annalise had to admit she was as confused as Tyler.

Tyler shot Christen an incredulous look. "No. That was over a century ago." He backed up and leaned against a tall wooden filing cabinet. Antique-looking. He crossed his arms. "C'mon. Lay it out straight for me. What are you getting at?"

Garrett took a long drag from his coffee, then set it on top of a banker's box. "There's a series of obituaries that have surfaced. One of them was in Eugene Hayes's trailer."

"That one you showed me?" Tyler asked Annalise. "For Harrison Greenwood?"

She nodded, but then bit her tongue, letting Garrett take the lead.

"We found another one online, for a Dorothy Hayes," Garrett continued. "That one was printed by this paper. It had the same masthead."

"It didn't include any Edgar Allan Poe poetry either," Christen added.

"Hmm . . . that's odd." Tyler's interest seemed piqued. "Dorothy Hayes? Was she related to Eugene Hayes?"

Annalise nodded. "His grandmother probably."

"Huh." Tyler shrugged. "Okay. So her obit was printed by us."

"The third obit is your ancestor's. Paul Darrow," Garrett concluded, as if Tyler should get it.

"In the vein of Harrison Greenwood's," Christen said. "All creepy Poe-like."

Tyler gave them all a blank look. "Still not following."

"Paul Darrow owned the paper, right?" Garrett asked.

"Yeah," Tyler answered.

"He owned it *well after* 1907." Garrett made a point to emphasize his words. "*After* he was supposed to have died, according to the obit."

Tyler's eyebrows winged upward as realization dawned. "Oh . . ." He raked his fingers through his hair.

Annalise was finally connecting the dots as well. "If the only person of the three obituaries who actually *lived* past 1907 was Paul, then—"

Christen snapped her fingers. "Then Tyler's how-many-times great-grandfather was hiding something."

"Swell," Tyler groused. He palmed the wall, bracing himself against it. "My great-great-grandfather, what, wrote weird obituaries? You can't prove he wrote them. Dorothy Hayes's obit doesn't imply anything either. The woman died. Happens all the time."

Garrett leaned into the doorjamb as if prepared to hang out in the dank basement all night. "Well, Dorothy Hayes and Harrison Greenwood both died within days of each other. Paul Darrow has an obit but didn't die until decades later. According to Dorothy's obit, she died from drowning in the pond just outside the town."

"Gossamer Pond." Tyler nodded, as though following Garrett's line of thinking thus far.

Garrett went on. "The obit for Harrison Greenwood that was printed by your paper claims he committed suicide. But the other obit that Eugene Hayes had implies he was murdered. Why two obituaries, one published, one not? What if Paul Darrow had something to hide so he printed Harrison's obit and skewed it as a suicide?"

"A cover-up!" Christen snapped her fingers again.

"You're insinuating my great-great-grandfather murdered your great-great-grandfather?" Tyler narrowed his eyes at Garrett, then at Annalise. "You've both lost your minds. If Paul killed anyone, why would he write obituaries he never printed? What would be the point?"

"Don't you think we should find out?" Garrett pressed.

Annalise sank onto a crate. Her knees were quivering. If she had her way, she'd yank Garrett's coffee from his hand, cold or not, and guzzle it right now.

"Is that why you wanted to meet here? In the newspaper's basement?" Tyler kicked at a box. "You think somehow we're going to figure out what happened with our grandparents? No one is concerned whether Paul Darrow from 1907 committed murder or printed falsified information. No one cares who wrote those weird obituaries."

Garrett shrugged. "Someone cares. Annalise has been attacked, her house broken into twice. The police are tracing a few leads, but so far we've got nothing. If Eugene was this fascinated with history, something back then still affects today. Gloria said Eugene used to dig around in this basement. I'd say odds are good this is where he found my great-great-grandfather's obituary and maybe where Paul Darrow's came from."

"Oh, c'mon!" Tyler gave Garrett a look of disbelief, as if what Garrett was proposing was outlandish.

Garrett didn't respond. It was as if he'd used up all his words. He took a long draw from his coffee. Tyler stared at him, but Annalise could tell he was battling through the logic versus theory of the argument. Christen took a seat on the crate next to Annalise. They waited.

Finally, Tyler let out a sigh. "Fine."

"So you'll help us? You'll let us look through your records here?" Annalise surveyed the room. The rafters were thick wooden beams with blankets of cobwebs between them. She didn't look forward to rummaging through old papers and documents to solve a century-old mystery.

Tyler threw his hand in the air. "Have at it! If you want to dig up the past, well it's right here. Dust and all."

"Help us find out what happened," Garrett urged the newspaperman.

Tyler raised an eyebrow. "I don't have much interest in digging through all this."

Garrett chuckled, and Annalise envied him as he took another drink of his coffee. "Keep telling yourself that, Darrow."

Annalise hid a small smile. Garrett was counting on Tyler's natural curiosity.

Tyler gave a tight nod. "Let's start with finding out exactly who this Mitch Sheffield is."

Annalise followed Tyler, Garrett, and Christen as they made their way to the northwest corner of the basement. To the old filing cabinets there. To antique stories that threatened to disclose a sordid tale Gossamer Grove had kept hidden for years.

CHAPTER 32

Libby hurried down the street, away from Paul, away from the basement, away from the newspaper. It was at least a minute before she realized townsfolk were passing her walking fast, a few slapping reins over their horses' backs, urging carriages forward. She looked across the street. The Methodist church with its white steeple rose up among a grove of trees. A few people hurried from that side of the road, jogging across, pointing and fixating on something she had yet to see.

Trapped between returning to the alleyway or pressing forward, Libby stopped in the middle of the sidewalk. Immobile. Her dress fluttered in a breeze that wafted the scent of crabapple blossoms through the air. The clouds, white and puffy, floated lazily overhead in the vibrant blue sky. But around her, tension boiled.

A shoulder slammed into her, stunning her for a moment as she cried out, reaching for her arm. Her wound throbbed, and she shot a pained glare at a teenage boy who raced by her, his shoes clomping on the cement walk, his hand slapping the brick of the two-story building on her left.

Libby sidestepped another passerby and leaned against a lamp-post. Wincing, she checked the blouse of her dress with a tentative touch to see if she was bleeding in case her wound had reopened. Seeing no blood, she looked up as a hand gripped her elbow.

Elijah's dark eyes were haunted. Exposed. They tore into Libby with such fervor, such pain, that she sensed the world around them fade.

"What is it?" she asked. She laid a hand on Elijah's upper arm. The coarseness of his wool jacket reminded her that what seemed gentle, what seemed warm and inviting, still scratched and stung.

Elijah glanced at her hand. His face pale, he locked eyes with her. "My father. Aunt Dorothy."

"Yes?" Libby prodded. Elijah took her by the elbow and ushered her through the growing crowd. They moved back toward the alley, dodging people. "What's going on?" Libby stumbled, trying to keep up with Elijah.

They left the sidewalk, stepping into the alleyway. Once again the sun was darkened by the shade of the building and the over-hang of trees.

"I visited Uncle Ralph in jail. I had to understand why he would start a riot at the tent meeting, why he would—" Elijah stopped and cleared his throat—"stab you. Or rather, try to stab Jacobus Corbin."

"And?" Libby asked breathlessly, the sound of Jacobus's name doing odd things to her attempt at calm.

Elijah bent, his face almost nose to nose with her, his eyes drilling into hers with a type of accusation and admission all rolled into one. "He told me that not only did my father and my aunt Dorothy—my mother's *sister*—have an affair ten years ago, but my cousin Lawrence is *not* my cousin, Libby. He's my half brother!"

Libby blinked. Stunned. She'd not imagined that boy at the funeral was Elijah's little brother. "Oh, Elijah, I'm so sorry. No, not sorry. I mean, it's wonderful you have a little brother, but—well, the circumstances are horrible."

258

Elijah ran both hands through his hair, leaving them positioned on the top of his head, his hat falling onto the ground. "Uncle Ralph said he'd known all this time. But when the Corbin brothers came to town, Aunt Dorothy was *convicted*. Uncle Ralph told her not to say anything. Not to confess, or be baptized. Then she disappeared and that's when—"

"She was murdered," Libby finished.

Elijah's gaze snapped back to hers. "Someone played on her guilt! Knew she'd leave the house when she found that note. A threat to publicly expose her sins? It would have ruined our family. Ruined us!"

Elijah bent to retrieve his hat. He slapped it against his leg as he rose. "I have to go back and tell the police. I left Uncle Ralph and just hightailed it from the jail. I had to think. I had to—" he paused, then gave her a quick look—"I wanted to find you. It will give more credence to the note we found. Even the obituaries. And I have to tell my mother—"

"No!" The word escaped Libby before she could hold it back, before she could think it through.

"What?" Elijah stared at her, incredulous at her outburst.

Libby swallowed. "No. She's already grieving. She's lost her husband and her sister within weeks, and now you want to tell her they'd also had an affair and a—a child?"

Elijah let out a deep sigh. A few shouts from the sidewalk echoed into the alley, reminding them that something was fast gathering the town.

Libby shook her head. "Perhaps it's unfair of me to suggest you not tell your mother, but at least maybe wait awhile longer? Until we understand what the obituaries mean? Let the authorities make serious work of this now."

"But why kill them?" Elijah pleaded for some explanation to justify why his family had been slain. "Why not just expose it? The affair? And I still don't understand why Paul received an obituary! What is gained by taking their lives and mocking Paul with his?"

"He frightens me," Libby admitted.

Elijah frowned.

"Paul does," she explained.

Elijah glanced over his shoulder in the direction of the back alley and the newspaper office. "The police need to interrogate him. He could be behind everything."

Their eyes met.

A dog barked and bolted from the backyard of a house across the alley. It bounded past them and after the people congregating along the street. An urgency filled the air, rising within Libby.

Elijah's jaw worked side to side. A firmness settled in his eyes, at war with the gentle tone of his voice. "I'm tired of carrying secrets, Libby."

"I'm sorry," she whispered. Dare she tell him she was almost sure that Jacobus Corbin seemed to know what she'd done to Calvin? That somehow the man had figured it out? If Jacobus had potentially uncovered her story, had he also found out about Deacon Greenwood and Dorothy's? Maybe Dorothy *had* gone and confessed the sin and it resulted in . . .

Her thoughts trailed away as Elijah's hand lifted to rest on her cheek. He lowered his voice. "Everything happened so fast that night. I was angry, but I wouldn't have left Calvin if I'd known he was caught."

Libby nodded, frozen by the warmth of his hand on her face and the knowledge that Elijah had gone back for Calvin and she had not. His eyes searched hers.

"I'd been so fascinated by you, Libby. That night I couldn't believe my eyes when I found you two. I'd followed you. I thought maybe we would . . . well, that I would be in Calvin's shoes. But no. And then I—I just lost it. I cared for you, yet I also knew you were Calvin's. So I punched him, then the fire, and then when you ran from Calvin, when I saw what you did, I just—I wanted to protect you. To keep you from being blamed for Calvin's condition."

Elijah was her hero. Libby's insides began to quiver.

"But I don't want to anymore." Elijah dropped his hand, and his brow furrowed. The words chilled Libby. She quailed away from him. "There are too many secrets in this town. They've ruined people's lives. *You've* ruined lives."

The accusation spilled from his lips. Tears burned her eyes, and Libby wrapped her arms around herself. Elijah shook his head, his expression both regretful and stern.

Then Elijah left her. Alone. As he stalked away toward the momentum building on the street and disappeared into the throngs of people, all of Libby's daydreams for him shattered into the ashes of a fire that had started years before.

—⟋⟍—

She pushed between bodies, attempting to reach the curb. Arms were held high, fingers extended, pointing at something. Libby didn't attempt to hide the tears that left tracks down her face. No one noticed. No one cared. Gossamer Grove was astir again and she was quite sick of it. Of all of it. If she could get to the curb, she could more than likely edge along the brick street and make her way home. Every part of her throbbed now, not just her shoulder. An ache that was awakened from years of grief, years of guilt, and now the driving dagger of accusation from the one person she'd always believed would protect her.

Elijah.

Stumbling, Libby reached out and steadied herself on a parked motorcar.

"Get your hand off my automobile!" the driver shouted, his knickers buttoned around knee-high boots, and his shirtsleeves dusty from his drive.

Libby snatched her hand back as if the car were boiling hot. She hurried in front of some teenage boys who were doubled over with laughter, raucous and mocking. A woman stretched out her arm and ushered Libby back onto the sidewalk. Her gloved hand patted Libby's.

"It's insanity here," she said with a raised voice. Libby recognized her vaguely as someone who was part of her mother's Ladies' Society. "You must go home at once, child."

Child.

Libby cringed. She was a grown woman who needed to make good her wrongs. More than a weekly game of marbles! More than allowing Calvin to keep her company whenever he wished. She needed to confess.

A man bumped into her, and Libby tripped forward. She lifted her head, her view finally unobscured by people who muttered, shouted, and pointed. The terrible sight was beyond anything she'd imagined. It was so evil, so laden with horrible intent, and so close to the events of late. Two imitations of bodies swung from the lampposts across the street. Their feet were barely a foot above the walk. Straw stuck out from sleeves and pants. The heads of the bodies were coarse and made of balled-up sheets somehow attached and noosed around their necks with old twine used to tie up hay bales. Libby noted the eyes blackened on the sheet with coal, lips drawn on in a straight black line, and black hats perched on the heads. But it was the crosses, the wooden crosses that hung down over the chests of the fake bodies that marked their identities. *Corbin Brother 1, Corbin Brother 2.*

The effigies were of Jedidiah and Jacobus. Blatant, striking, and horrendous.

She had to get away from here.

Libby pushed her way through the crowd. She was almost at the entry to the newspaper. She had no desire to go in, to be confronted by Paul or see Mitch scurrying about like a hungry squirrel who just had a bushel basket of acorns dropped in front of him. It couldn't be a coincidence that the scarecrow-like copies of the Corbin twins hung almost directly across the street from the paper's front window.

Libby dug through her purse as she staggered down the walkway. Pulling a handkerchief from the bottom, she wiped tears from her face and walked directly into a body. The impact jolted her backward, but hands reached out and righted her balance.

"Leave me be, please." Libby struggled to release herself from the grip, her eyes lifting.

Calvin.

The irony that Calvin stood in front of her with the Corbin brother imitations hanging behind wasn't lost on her. Sin and confession, the consequences of bad choices versus the ones who called a soul to confession.

"I'm sorry," Libby whispered. Nausea curdled in her stomach. The gripping sickness of guilt. "Calvin, I'm so, so sorry!" A sob ripped from her throat.

"Are you okay, Lollie?" Calvin's words came out thick, as if he weren't schooled in how to enunciate. His brow furrowed in concern. "Lollie?"

"Yes, yes." She nodded, quick short nods. Apologizing would do no good. He didn't understand, he never would— why they were bonded in such a strange way. Calvin had just always followed her. Since that day, his devotion had been a continued reminder that she must endure the shame of what she'd done.

"Do you need help? Is your shoulder still bad?"

Libby jammed her handkerchief back into her purse. "I'll be fine, Calvin." The lie froze on her lips as she watched him reach into his coat pocket. He withdrew an envelope, the typeset very clear, very much her name on the front of it.

Earnest eyes rose, and he grinned as if he'd been given a privilege, an honor. "I'm s'posed to give this to you, Lollie."

Libby eyed the envelope. She couldn't endure another obituary, another death, another self-righteous attempt from a murderer to cleanse the town of sinners.

"Take it." Calvin smiled and pushed the envelope toward her.

"Who gave it to you?" Libby grasped his wrist. "Please, Calvin, who gave that to you?"

Calvin gave her a comforting, almost patronizing smile, as if she were the one who struggled to understand. He tucked the envelope into her purse. "It's all right, Lollie," he said, giving her a comforting pat on her good arm. "The preacher man says you'll be just fine."

"Did the preacher man give this to you?" Libby waved the envelope at Calvin.

He glanced at it, then at her. A nod. "He said it was only right I be the one to give it to you." Calvin glanced over her shoulder at the effigies and the crowd. His brow furrowed as he turned back to her. "I think he's right. He knows I'll always be here for you, Lollie. It's what friends do."

Libby crumpled the envelope in her hand. Intuition told her what was inside. "Yes, Calvin." Her words hitched. Tears burned paths down her face. "It's what friends do."

His shoulder brushed her wounded one as he passed by, leaving in his wake the throbbing pain of guilt and horror.

CHAPTER 33

Gossamer Pond had once been a place of respite. So Libby had raced across the street that led down the hill toward the woolen mill where Gossamer Pond became the separating point between the town and the countryside. A few times she'd stopped to glance over her shoulder. A nagging sensation told her she was being followed, but each time she looked, there was no one there.

Libby was frightened, and yet, didn't she deserve it? She hurried over the trail through the orchard and finally collapsed not far from where the revival tent had been erected. Its frame tall and long, reflecting on the murky green waters of the pond. Its canvas sides ballooning out and then snapping in as the breeze inflicted wear and tear on the carefully staked tent. If the killer was following her, then he would find her here. He'd been to the banks of the pond before, with another woman—another sinner.

Libby blinked against her mind's images that superimposed onto the pond water. The floating body of Dorothy Hayes. The tired resignation on Elijah's face. The effigies of the Corbin brothers dangling from the lampposts.

Calvin's envelope remained unopened. Libby pulled it from her purse and set it on her lap as she sat on the grass. Water rippled and flowed in front of her. Any other time, any other moment, she would have drunk in the peaceful presence of the warm sun that spread a blanket over the scene. But there was no peace. Not now. Probably not ever.

Libby reached for the envelope, which shook in her hands. She slipped her finger under the seal and opened it, pulling out an all-too-familiar piece of stationery. The words curled around her.

> Libby Alice Sheffield. Born February 18th, 1883. Passed away this morning, the 6th of June, 1907.
> The boundaries which divide Life from Death are at best shadowy and vague. Who shall say where the one ends and where the other begins?
> As poets of yesteryear ponder the grave
> Sinners today are yet to be saved.
> Shame on her shoulders and take to the tomb
> Leave her memory behind, a soul gone too soon.

This was it. Her obituary. She stared at it as if it had come to life and now stood over her, poised with a blade ready to spear her heart and leave her to bleed out as recompense for the sin she'd committed against Calvin.

A twig snapped, causing Libby to twist from her position on the ground. Her heart pounded in her ears. A wicked, hollow thumping like the ticking of a clock. Her hand rose to the watch she'd pinned to her dress out of habit. 8:36 p.m. The night the entire town exploded from its tenuous existence of peace into a chaotic confusion. The moment she had finally done something good for once, something selfless. When she'd saved Jacobus's life.

She released a breath of relief as she eyed his form coming down the orchard trail. Maybe she'd hoped he would come. Whether a bearer of forgiveness or the one who would bring her final judgment, Jacobus's actions and words made her believe that somehow he knew her darkest sin. Knew her most intimate guilt. The man who read her soul.

"If you're here to kill me, please, do it quickly." Libby's voice quivered, watery with tears of fear and shame. She could almost invite death in this moment. Take death's hand and walk away with it. But in her heart, she dreaded what lay beyond.

"Killing isn't something I do regularly." A wry tone filtered through his words. He eased his long frame onto the grass beside her. He was hatless, his brown curls flipping in the breeze. The whiskers that bordered his cheeks made them seem even longer, hollower. But his eyes were alive with intelligence. The kind of intelligence that verified he knew too much but would never reveal as much.

Libby offered him the obituary. He took it and read.

"I'm going to die." She stared out over the pond, almost accepting it now.

"So it appears." Jacobus handed the obituary back to her.

They sat in silence. He was calm, placid, almost boring. Especially considering that someone had hung scarecrow imitations of him and his brother from lampposts. Maybe people did wish the Corbin brothers dead, but more likely they wanted to scare them from Gossamer Grove. Or maybe, more truthfully, it was because no one liked conviction. Whether presented in a harsh, judgmental way, or wrapped in lace and flowers to be as inoffensive as possible. But truth was truth, was it not? Most people knew they would eventually pay for their sins. Most simply did not want to dwell on it.

"How does one die?" Libby's words floated along the tops of the dandelions, carried on the breeze toward the pond, and drowned in the cattails bordering its edges.

Jacobus blinked. "One dies in sheer terror of what is to come, or with the peace of knowing one's soul rests in forgiveness."

Libby swallowed. Her throat hurt. Ached with the tension of tears and now the horrible knowing that unless she fought, escaped, twisted, or cajoled her way, the reaper intent on bringing eternal justice on God's behalf would render it unto her.

"Are you afraid to die?" she whispered. The images of Jacobus's straw-filled body hanging from a noose made her tremble.

He blinked again. "No."

Of course not.

"How does one not be afraid? How do I find forgiveness for trespasses that hurt others more than myself?"

"One must confess."

"Confession." Libby's voice shook.

Jacobus gave her a sideways glance, then plucked a dandelion and twisted it in his long fingers. "It is always relieving when one genuinely expresses repentance." He handed her the weed. "But, confession means nothing without understanding what is given in return."

"Forgiveness." Even the word made Libby cringe. Calvin may—or may not—bestow it on her. He may never understand that out of everyone, he was the one she needed forgiveness from the most. Elijah had certainly moved beyond the word. And Jacobus? Jacobus's opinion mattered little, yet she hated to admit that, in an unexpected way, she preferred he didn't leave her side.

Libby looked down at the yellow dandelion, its almost fluffy petals. Beautiful and yet a weed, one that sucked the life from the other flowers around it. Pretending to be one while inside flourishing until its spitefulness was unveiled as its petals turned feathery and flew away, leaving a gangly stem in its place. Ugly. Colorless. Stubborn.

Jacobus's voice rumbled beside her. "My brother preaches of the consequences of sin. It is true. One cannot escape judgment, and yet one can find mercy. Their case appealed before a holy God by a Savior who paid penalties we shall never survive if we attempt payment ourselves."

In the meadow, under the shade of the tent, Libby found his words less abhorrent and more inviting. Maybe it was because she faced death herself. Desperation caused one to look inward.

"I despise it," she admitted. Lifting her face, she stared at Jacobus until he turned and their eyes met. Let him see inside of her, let him read every word etched on her ugly soul. She had little to lose now. "I cannot bear how we believe if we do enough, *be* enough, we can pay penance and find a way of escape. When we die? Our names are etched into a gravestone, penned onto an obituary, and finalized in eternity. A legacy remembered by words of kindness, while everyone questions who we really were, in our darkest moment, when no one else but God could see."

"Only God's opinion bears any merit." Jacobus did not touch her, did not reach for her. Instead, he took the dandelion from her hand and tossed it into the grass. He pushed the blades of green away and slid his fingers toward their roots. When he drew forth his hand, he held a violet. A flower buried under the surface of deceptive beauty. The violet was delicate, fragile, and sweet. He placed it on Libby's palm, his fingertips touching her skin for a moment before withdrawing.

"Our souls can be made beautiful when grace is accepted. Grace is receiving what we do not deserve."

"What *do* I deserve?" Her question hung between them. She tested Jacobus. In this moment she didn't want tentative threads of platitude and heroics that would only dissolve later and leave her holding her own obituary.

Jacobus gave her a thin smile. He would not hide the truth from her.

"Your soul deserves to die."

A chill ran through her.

Jacobus lifted the violet from her hand and in a slow, gentle motion, tucked it behind her ear, pushing away a dark curl that had escaped her coil. His touch against her ear caused her to lean into his hand. It stilled for a moment, as if surprised. Then he left it there, his fingers caressing her cheek with a featherlight touch. His eyes softened, the blue of them warming as if sunshine had emerged on an icy day.

"But with repentance, God forgives. In Him your soul will live. Therein lies the beauty amidst the weeds."

It seemed too simple in comparison to the shocking and

detestable shows Jedidiah Corbin put on in the tent meetings with Jacobus standing in the wings.

Libby reached up and touched the violet, but when her hand dropped to her lap, it rustled the paper that bore the words of her death.

She lifted the page, then her eyes, to Jacobus. "And if my soul lives, will my body still die?"

Jacobus's eyes shadowed for a moment. He closed his hand over the paper, his fingers wrapping around hers. His silence left her question unanswered, but Libby was not alone. For once, someone finally understood her. All of her. And while there was fear, for a moment there was also peace.

CHAPTER 34

Annalise

Annalise leaned against the doorjamb of the basement door. It was midmorning and, having been up all night, her body was achy and her brain fuzzy. She studied the sky, the fluffy clouds that passed by over the old historic buildings. Tyler rustled about in the basement files, muttering under his breath. Christen had returned home hours before to care for her kiddos. Garrett had run —literally—to Annalise's coffee shop to get a carafe and some mugs. They were going to need sustenance. Annalise had sent her barista a text to throw in a bag of scones to go.

"Hey, Annalise?"

Tyler's voice at her shoulder made her jump. Annalise eyed him. He held out an old newspaper. "I just found this."

Annalise took the paper and read the front page. A story about the Corbin brothers, an inked sketch of effigies hanging from lampposts. She gave Tyler a look of disbelief.

"They hung the imitation preachers in the town square?"

"I know." Like it or not, Tyler was fully engaged now in the quest to uncover the story. "It's so *Scarlet Letter*."

Annalise bit back a sigh. Tyler tended to exaggerate things, but still, it was hard to believe something like this had happened in Gossamer Grove. A ruckus surrounding the Corbin brothers was just an odd piece of history lost with time. Now that they were discovering it, Annalise wondered what it was that had made Eugene tie them to the obituaries and subsequently to her.

She skimmed more of the article. It didn't trigger anything significant in her mind. She handed it back to Tyler. He pushed against her hand.

"No. Open the paper."

"Okay?" Annalise shot him a quizzical look, then carefully opened the aged, yellowed newspaper.

Tyler edged closer to her and pointed. "There. See that?"

Yes. Yes, she did. Annalise leaned forward. "Dorothy Hayes? There was an investigation around her death?"

"It appears so." Tyler tapped the page. "Apparently, there were questions as to whether she'd been murdered. Drowned on purpose. If you read closer, toward the bottom of the article, it seems they were looking into an affair between her and Harrison Greenwood. Perhaps it was a motive for their deaths."

"Wow." So they *had* been considering murder back in 1907. She kept reading. "Dorothy had attended the Corbin brothers' revival meetings. Even spoken to her friend of being baptized, it says."

"Yeah, and look there." Tyler ran his finger over the last paragraph. "Her husband was arrested for trying to stab the one revivalist twin, Jacobus Corbin. Ended up skewering—"

"Libby Sheffield!" Annalise's eyes went wide. "So, Eugene Hayes's grandmother, Dorothy, might have had an affair with Harrison Greenwood. She was coming to terms with that due to the revival meetings, and then after she died, her husband . . . what? Blamed the revivalists somehow?"

"Sorta gets the suspicion thrown off Paul Darrow," Tyler muttered.

"Or raises the bigger question. Why did he have an obituary written about him? He wasn't related to any of this, was he?"

"I'm going back in to see if I can find more papers on this." Tyler scowled at her, obviously not keen that she was still trying to find some link to Paul Darrow and potential murders.

She watched him disappear farther into the basement. Could she blame Tyler? Really? No one liked hearing their family could be tainted. One wanted to remember the nostalgia, the smiles, the successes. Not the sins.

Annalise sank onto a cement stair. She pulled her phone from her pocket. She had no desire to, but now that she had a moment to herself, she needed to summon the courage to call her mom. Garrett was willing to be open about their past, about Gia. Even Tyler was facing the fire and looking into his family's and the paper's own questionable pasts. The image of her pregnant grandmother with Eugene Hayes's arm draped around her shoulder was burned into Annalise's mind, including the penned warning in the obituary for Paul Darrow: *"Let the dead stay dead."* Buried. Both Eugene Hayes and her grandmother were gone, yet she couldn't leave them in their graves. Not when someone was exhuming her own past.

Before she could chicken out again, Annalise made the call to her mom.

"Hello?"

Her mom's greeting filtered through the cellphone's speaker. Annalise's voice caught in her throat. "Hi, Mom," she finally answered.

"Annalise."

Awkward silence. They couldn't even fake pleasantries. Fine. She'd just dive right in.

"Mom, I, uh . . ." Not for the last time did Annalise wish she could press rewind and go back to the days before Eugene Hayes was found dead in his trailer, half buried in pictures of her. There was no easy way to bring up the question to her mother, who had never wanted to speak of Gia or of Annalise's indiscretions. So now she was going to propose that her own grandmother, her mother's *mom*, was guilty of the same thing as Annalise?

273

"What is it?" her mom pressed.

"I've been digging into some old family records at the historical society." There. That was a start.

"Oh?"

"Yeah. And there was a picture in a scrapbook, of Grandma. Grandma Ellen?"

"Yes, I suppose she might've made a few of the photographs around town. My father did own the bank."

Oh yes. The always inserted reminder that they were of the upper class of Gossamer Grove. Good grief, one would think this was Hollywood in 1952.

Annalise adjusted her position on the stair and caught a glimpse of Garrett striding down the alley, a coffee carrier in his hand, a carafe and the bag of scones in his other. She tried to ignore it—ignore him. That was difficult. The sun haloed behind him, making his skin tan, his lean muscles highlighted. . . . She tore her eyes away.

"So Grandma was in a photograph with Eugene Hayes." Annalise hurried on before she lost courage. "Eugene passed away not long ago, and he left me his trailer. I—he had pictures in it, of me."

"Of you?" Her mother's voice turned grave. Low. As if the woman couldn't decide whether to hang up or stay on the phone.

Annalise took a deep breath and blurted, "He had a photo of me when I was pregnant at Aunt Tracy's. Of—"

"Stop."

Annalise did. She'd always obeyed. Dutifully. At the cost of her own self.

"Yes, your grandmother knew Eugene Hayes"—Annalise could tell her mom was gritting her teeth—"but that was years ago. The man went crazy, and it was due to his war memories. Vietnam did horrible things to those men. Anyway, he was probably fascinated with our family and that was why he had your picture."

Annalise knew she was in an intricate dance with her mother.

Going straight in for the truth would have them both crashing to the floor. She chose to tiptoe instead.

"But, Aunt Tracy took the picture of me pregnant, Mom. In Connecticut. It's the only picture anyone took of me pregnant."

"Fine. All right. Well, does it really matter?" her mother snapped.

A whiff of coffee alerted Annalise's senses, and she jerked her attention toward the aroma. Garrett stood by her, the coffee in his hand. She reached for a disposable cup, carefully removing it from the carrier.

"It's black," he whispered. "Just how you like it."

She really needed to not be so predictable. At least where Garrett and coffee were concerned.

"Mom," Annalise continued, her coffee in hand now, "why did he have that photo? Why was Grandma in a picture with him?" Fine. There wasn't any point waltzing around the truth. "And why was she pregnant?"

Her mother cursed through the phone.

Annalise was expecting a gasp or even an abbreviated "shush." But she wasn't expecting her mom to swear, then follow it up with stony silence. She gripped the phone tighter. Garrett's gaze drilled into her. She could tell he was waiting, trying to gather what was being said.

"Mom!" Annalise's voice was sharper than she intended. She shoved the coffee cup back into Garrett's hand, dragging her fingers through her hair until the red strands were pulled tight away from her face. "Mom, tell me whatever you know before Tyler Darrow plasters on the front page of his newspaper that I had Garrett's baby."

It was a fake threat, but it did the job.

Another curse from her mother, then a cough, then more silence.

Finally, Annalise heard the clacking of her mom's fingernails, probably being drummed atop the granite counter in her kitchen.

"Before your grandmother married your grandfather, she had a fling. It was the sixties."

The sixties. Free love. Hippies. Sex and drugs. Got it. Annalise's image of her proper grandmother evaporated.

"She was with Eugene Hayes for over a year. That was when she had your Aunt Tracy."

The knot that had been forming in Annalise's stomach, that foretelling insight just before someone spoke the actual truth, twisted into a permanent stitch. "Eugene Hayes was Aunt Tracy's father?"

Annalise fixed her stare on Garrett's. She had to or she might faint, or maybe just bash her head against the doorjamb to knock some sense into herself.

"Yes." Her mother's voice was tight now. "That's really all I know. Your grandmother never spoke of it—never spoke of *him.*"

"But Aunt Tracy knew?"

"Well, she must have. It's obvious she found out somehow."

Suddenly, the words on the back of Annalise's pregnant picture made sense. *Save Annalise.* Had Aunt Tracy sent the picture to Eugene herself with instructions to look after her? She'd known Annalise needed someone to see Annalise for who she was, not who she could be. Someone who would understand her circumstances. Someone like Eugene.

"Did *you* know?" Annalise asked the question—the elephant in the room.

Silence at first, and then her mother cleared her throat. "I know you think your father and I didn't take your feelings into consideration back then. But now you understand why I pushed for things to happen the way I did with you. Good heavens, you were so naïve. It took years for your grandmother to live down her pregnancy with Eugene. And Tracy? There was an unspoken stigma over her growing up. The child who really was a Hayes."

"Were you ashamed of her?"

God help Aunt Tracy. Help Gia. Why did people stare down their noses at others? Were they without sin? Then throw the stone. Otherwise, toss it in their own faces!

"I was never ashamed of Tracy," her mother snapped.

"Were you ashamed of me?" Annalise clutched the phone, her knuckles white. She locked eyes with Garrett, who drew his eyebrows in concern.

A sigh.

A pause.

Then, "I need to go, Annalise. Your father is calling for me."

Annalise stared at the phone for a long moment after her mother hung up. She snatched her coffee back from Garrett, who eyed her cautiously. She took a gulp and bore it as the liquid scorched its way down her throat.

Annalise swiped her tears with the back of her hand and gave Garrett an honest look. "Well, now you know what it was like when you weren't around. My mom never received the gift of nurturing."

Garrett sat on the step next to her, setting down his load of coffee and scones. Their shoulders brushed in the narrow space.

"Our moms are—they need help."

Annalise gave a watery laugh. "Yes. Yes, they do."

Garrett gave her a lopsided smile. "Considering, we didn't turn out so bad."

Annalise met his eyes. "No," she answered softly. "I guess we didn't. We just did things backward."

Garrett nodded. "At least our daughter has a name."

"And we claim her?" Annalise whispered.

Garrett's eyes grew serious and deep. "Yeah. Yeah, we claim her."

"No more secrets?" Annalise reached for his hand. She couldn't help it. His fingers closed over hers.

"No more secrets."

"Oh my gosh!" Annalise dropped Garrett's hand and lurched to her feet. "Why didn't we put two and two together?"

Garrett reared back, surprised at the sudden shift from their intimate moment.

"An illegitimate child! That's the common denominator! Eugene and Aunt Tracy. Harrison Greenwood and Dorothy Hayes. They had to have had an illegitimate child. It's the only reason why Eugene would have tied them to his story and to our story!"

Garrett just sat there staring at her, stunned.

Annalise waved for him to follow her to the basement. "Tyler found a newspaper. An investigation into Dorothy's death. Rumors of an affair between her and your great-great-grandfather. I swear, Eugene was connecting the dots! I'd place bets that his father, Lawrence, was really a Greenwood—Harrison's illegitimate son with Dorothy. And now"—she looked Garrett in the eye—"our daughter. A Greenwood. It comes full circle back to the Greenwoods."

"You should be an investigative journalist," Tyler snarked from the doorway as he edged past Annalise to reach for a scone from the bag. "Problem is, you've no proof of the affair between Harrison and Dorothy. Just a theory."

Annalise nodded. "But if we work from that theory, then what does Libby Sheffield have to do with all this? And how did Libby's watch end up in my jewelry box? She had to have known someone in Eugene's ancestry. Someone more her age. Like—like Harrison's son maybe?"

"Elijah." Garrett was still on the stair, his elbows resting on his knees.

Annalise turned to him. "What are you thinking?"

Garrett shrugged. "I just remember my grandpa mentioned him once. I remember him saying his father avoided anything religious. Especially church and preachers."

Annalise raised an eyebrow. "Maybe it all comes back to the revival? Libby Sheffield was hurt at a tent meeting, stepping between Jacobus Corbin and his attacker, Dorothy's husband and widower. What if one of these people was so upset at all the filth and scandal, they determined to take God's justice into their own hands and clean up the town themselves?"

"Good grief, that's the craziest idea yet!" Tyler rolled his eyes as he chewed his scone. "Who would be that stupid to write horribly scripted obituaries and start killing people?"

"Paul Darrow." Garrett's grim words silenced Tyler.

He glared at Garrett and shook his head. "No. No. This is conspiracy theory at its worst. You're saying my great-great-grandfather was somehow inspired by the revival meetings and decided to kill them because they, what, didn't confess? And you have his obituary! Why would he be the killer if he was on the list to be knocked off himself?"

Annalise didn't reply. It did sound outlandish. Yet, it also made sense when she thought of it from the angle that Eugene might have. A string of generational sins all mirroring one another and coming full circle. Especially with Garrett's mother's implication that Greenwood men weren't known for their fidelity.

Tyler hiked back into the basement, the scone in his hand leaving a trail of crumbs. Then he turned on his heel, his eyes bright. "Fine. You want to go down this trail? I'll play along. You'll need to talk to Doug Larson. His dad and Eugene Hayes used to hang out at the veterans' center downtown. I remember 'cause I did an article on them. If there's anyone still alive who might be able to answer your question about an affair, then Doug's dad is the one."

Annalise had no desire to search for Doug Larson. His wilderness center had already usurped priority over the broken people of Gossamer Grove. People like Eugene Hayes. Groveling at his feet for information seemed tacky at best and nauseating at worst.

"I can ask him." Garrett's voice sliced through the silence. He sipped his coffee as though it were any normal day. "I need to talk to him about the climbing gym in his plans anyway."

Annalise chose to let that comment slide. "I'll go with you." She glanced at Tyler and gave him a stern frown. "We already know the Corbin brothers had stirred up a lot of emotion in Gossamer Grove. It seems 1907 was a year of pot-stirring and murder." Addressing Tyler, Annalise added, "See what you can find on Libby Sheffield."

"Yes, Sergeant," Tyler groused. "Paul Darrow too. There's no way I'm going to let you pin this conspiracy on him."

Annalise leveled him with a dark look. "Here's hoping. For your sake. But I don't have a good feeling about it."

"I don't have a good feeling about any of this," Garrett muttered.

CHAPTER 35

Libby

L ibby attempted to match Jacobus's long strides. His jaw was
set, even under his muttonchop whiskers.

"You can't go back into town." Libby took two steps to
his one. She hoisted her dress up so she wouldn't trip. "They'll
string you up like a lynching mob."

"No. They did that to my scarecrow," he stated, as if an imitation of himself would appease the haters.

"Why do you stay with your brother?" The words escaped her
before she could stop them.

Jacobus gave her a sideways glance. "Family has no obligation
to you?"

Libby took three steps to his one. "Of course. I didn't mean it
to be rude. Family is important. However"—she was growing out
of breath trying to keep up with the man—"you're not as . . . well,
you see you're different from your brother. He is—"

"Explosive. Unpredictable. Offensive. Tactless. Aggressive,"
Jacobus supplied.

Libby nodded. "Yes. I was thinking that but—"

"Never refrain from saying what you think," Jacobus said firmly.

"To me, anyway," he added. "And I remain with my brother in an attempt to temper his passion and to try to keep him from damaging the message with his asinine approach to evangelism. I prefer to create an effective ministry."

Libby hopped over a rock that had rolled onto the walkway. Her breath came in puffs. Jacobus had no notice of her exertion. "What are you going to do?"

"What are *you* going to do?" he countered.

Libby wasn't accustomed to having the decision, the plan of action, tossed back at her. She'd expected—what *had* she expected? A hero? The man who'd read her soul to save her? She couldn't run to Elijah. Calvin? Her mother had left town this morning by train to visit her aunt, and Mitch had for all sakes and purposes disappeared in the "brouhaha" of recent events—as Mother had called them.

"I don't know what I should do." She was helpless. Helpless in lieu of the obituary, in the memory of Dorothy Hayes's body floating facedown in the pond, and in the shadow of Deacon Greenwood hanging from the rafters of his carriage house. Perhaps Jacobus could help her escape eternal death, but physical death? That was something altogether different.

He didn't seem to hear her. They reached the top of the hill and one of the side streets of Gossamer Grove. Jacobus paused for a moment, and his eyes shifted back and forth as if calculating.

Libby dared to put a hand on his sleeve. He jolted, as if he hadn't expected the physical contact, even with barriers of cotton and wool between them. She dropped her hand, but she finally had his attention.

"What should we do?" she whispered.

Jacobus's mouth twitched. "Miss Sheffield—my dear Libby—God has granted you much more than a soul. He's gifted you with a mind. Use it."

And with that bewildering statement, Jacobus marched toward downtown and the chaos without a backward glance. Abandoned

282

on the outskirts with a death threat in her purse, Libby stared after him, stunned and not a little upset. The angel of death was after her, and the preacher walked away.

His challenge rifled through her, scraping the edges of her timidity, slapping awake her stubbornness, and catapulting her determination into action. Jacobus was right, after all. There was only one person who could be her champion now, and that was herself.

"How did you do it?" Libby burst into the press room, shouting over the mechanics of the press and ignoring the stunned looks of the men running it. Paul's eyes widened, and he handed a wooden clipboard to an assistant, waving his hand toward the door in an impatient gesture.

Once in the hallway, he shut the door behind him and seared Libby with a glare. "Do what?" he snapped.

Libby had found her voice. She shook her index finger at him, the gray of her cotton glove inches from his face. "How did you escape death?"

Paul set his teeth and grabbed her arm. His fingers bit into her flesh, and Libby twisted away from him. "Don't be barbaric," she hissed. "Your hands will stay off of me!"

Paul froze, his expression one of shock. "What's gotten into you?"

Libby reached into her purse and tugged out her obituary. She pushed it toward Paul.

"It's my turn. I want to know how you convinced the killer to allow you to live, because I've no intentions of dying tonight."

"I didn't *convince* the killer of anything!" Paul unfolded the obituary and read it. With a blank look on his face, he handed it back to Libby, turning on his heel and striding down the hallway toward the closet office he called his own.

A momentary twinge of indecision caught her, but the knowledge that she would never live if she didn't fight for herself urged her forward. She needed to know Paul's story, why he'd been spared, and why he'd even been targeted in the first place. He had nothing to do with Deacon Greenwood and Dorothy Hayes.

"I asked you how?" Libby insisted, following him into his office.

Paul shoved his glasses against his face. "I don't know. *I don't know!* One moment you and Elijah Greenwood were knocking on my door with the abominable message, and the following morning, for all sakes and purposes, Dorothy Hayes had taken my place! Maybe I wasn't accessible enough. Gullible enough. Now leave me alone, Miss Sheffield, please."

Libby almost didn't notice it, but then it caught her attention. The tremor in his voice. The tremble in his hands that he hid by folding them behind his back.

"What are you hiding?" she asked.

For a wild and frightening moment, Libby wondered if Paul was the killer himself. It would stand to reason. He had seen, witnessed, and heard many a sight and rumor. Perhaps he knew about Deacon Greenwood and Dorothy Hayes. About their illegitimate son, Lawrence. But, how could he know about that night, when Calvin claimed her first kiss and she left him behind when he needed her the most?

"I'm not hiding anything," Paul spat.

"Please, Paul, in good conscience you must tell me." Tears watered her voice. No. She wouldn't cry. It would help nothing. Solve nothing. "Someone wants retribution for—for my sins."

"What have *you* done?" Paul's eyes narrowed. He crossed his arms over his chest. "Why would the obituary writer target you?"

Libby stared at him. Telling Paul wasn't her preference, but then apparently telling her wasn't his preference either.

"God gifted you with a mind. Use it."

Jacobus's exacting words rang in her ears. Use her mind. Outside, she had felt abandoned, diminished in importance to him. But now clarity pushed its way through her mind as though awakening years of a sleepy, guilt-suppressing haze. Jacobus had empowered her. He'd given her the shove she needed to finally fight for herself, for honesty, and for her own atonement.

"I'm going to the basement." Libby lifted her nose in challenge, then swept around and started down the hallway. As expected, she heard Paul's footsteps chasing after her.

"No. No, you mustn't go down there!" he argued, but Libby tugged open the door and stepped into the alley. A burst of fresh air met her, only to be swallowed by the damp silty air of the basement as she hurried down the steps and opened the basement door.

"Miss Sheffield!" Desperation laced Paul's voice now.

She entered, determined. Her entire life she had hid behind Elijah, stifled the reality of the consequences for her choices, and recalibrated herself into a timid echo of the person she'd been in the process of becoming as a young woman.

Libby lit a lantern that sat on a crate as Paul huffed at her side. The glow of the light, coupled with daylight streaming in through the doorway, made the cave-like room easier to see.

"What are you hiding?" she whispered.

Paul tightened his lips.

Libby lifted the lantern. Crates and filing cabinets crowded the basement. She wove in between them. A trunk with metal corners and an iron latch and hinges sat in the far corner. Swinging around, Libby lofted the lantern high.

In the southwest corner was a table and four wooden ladder-back chairs. A few bottles of liquor were perched on an upturned crate. She shot Paul an incredulous glance before walking toward the sight. He sagged against a filing cabinet, and his sigh of resignation followed her.

Libby neared the table and set the lantern on it. A few glass tumblers, two still partially full of old brandy, rested on the table. Three decks of cards. An ashtray with stubs of cigars in it. Newspapers were piled on the floor against the wall, as if it were an extra stool to squeeze in one more place for a person to sit.

She turned her back on the table and leveled a bewildered stare on Paul. "Gambling? You've been gaming here?"

Paul drew in a deep breath through his nose and let it out slowly. He gave a curt nod.

"But . . ." Libby paused, trying to calculate the situation. Gambling in its raw form—poker and the like—wasn't necessarily illegal, but it wasn't embraced as socially responsible or even remotely Christian. Still, it wasn't akin to having an extramarital affair and fathering an illegitimate child. "I don't understand."

Paul grumbled as he pushed past her and stacked the brandy glasses as if tidying up would somehow help. "I'm not proud of it."

"But, it's—cards." She'd expected worse. What, she wasn't sure of. "Why would someone wish to target you over a game of cards?"

Paul's head shot up, his spectacles sliding down his nose. "Precisely why I didn't believe the obituary to be serious. And, I was correct."

"So you believe Deacon Greenwood and Mrs. Hayes *should* have been killed?" Libby leaned against a wooden filing cabinet, incredulous.

"No!" Paul almost shouted. "No," his voice lowered. "Of course I don't. But the pattern seems to have been set. Someone is grading sins. Mine . . . was not as bad."

"Who do you game with?" Libby pointed at the chairs. "Who fills the chairs? Certainly one of them might be the—the killer. Did you win someone's livelihood, or maybe you simply offended them with your propensity for successful but sinful gambling."

Paul whitened, choked, and then slumped onto a chair. "*Successful* would not be the proper adjective."

"Oh." Libby nodded. Paul Darrow was prone to lose then. "So, who games with you?"

Paul rubbed his hand over his balding head. "Typically, it is me, Dr. Penchan, your father—"

"Mitch?" Libby exclaimed.

286

Paul gave her a look that stated she should not be surprised. "And Harrison Greenwood."

Libby sat in the chair opposite Paul. "Deacon Greenwood gambled here too?"

"Yes." Paul reached for a deck of cards and shuffled them with nervous hands. "We haven't gamed since. It's all been—quite unsettling."

"Dr. Penchan games with you?" Libby was trying to piece the puzzle together. "Because my father wouldn't have targeted you for sinful practices."

Paul's eyebrow quirked over his left eye. "No. Most certainly not." The positioning of his body, resigned and defeated, alerted Libby. She swept the basement with her gaze and then looked to the ceiling rafters as if to see through the floor above into the newspaper. Realization dawned on her.

"Did you sell sixty percent of your paper to Mitch so you would have money to gamble with?" Her voice ended in an accusatory higher pitch.

"Sell?" Paul groused. "Never. Won. Your father *won* it."

"You gambled your paper?" Libby's words bounced off the basement's foundation.

Paul's face sagged. "It's no secret I came into financial difficulty. The only secret was *why*."

Libby was still reeling from the information. "Yes, but most people thought it was due to the paper's popularity falling behind."

"Not at all." Paul scratched the back of his neck. "My paper did—*does*—quite well without your father stirring up stories and trouble."

"So you play in secret? In the basement of the newspaper?"

"I tried to stop." Paul's shoulders slouched.

"So if Harrison Greenwood is dead, my father, quite innocent of it all, that leaves . . . Dr. Penchan?" It made sense really. That the medical examiner who gamed with Paul would know of the illegitimate child and know of Paul's gambling addiction. What didn't make sense was why he'd feel it his duty to cast judgment in a way that stole a life from the earth that he was avowed to save. And how he would know of her own past with Calvin.

Paul removed his spectacles and rubbed his fingers over his eyes. When he looked at Libby, it seemed exhaustion had overtaken his fight. "Dr. Penchan is not behind the deaths of Harrison and Dorothy. He didn't write any of the obituaries."

"How do you know?" Libby noticed Paul shuffling the cards for the tenth time. His hands split the deck with practiced ease and bent the cards only to flip them into each other with skill.

"Because. The night—morning—what-have-you that Harrison hung himself, or was killed, Penchan was here. We'd been gaming through the night into the wee hours. Along with your father."

"But not Deacon Greenwood?"

Paul lifted his eyes. "No, he'd not come that evening, but that wasn't unusual. He wasn't always able to make it due to appeasing his wife, who despised his practices."

Libby didn't respond. Could she blame Elijah's mother? If she knew of the affair, knew her own sister had dabbled with her husband and then bore a son from their indecencies, she certainly was not going to abide his leaving for long periods at night.

"Old Man Whistler sat in that night," Paul finished, interrupting her thought. "He was usually drunk. It was easy to win against him, and frankly . . ." Paul eyed one of the half-full glasses of brandy, as if he wished to gulp it down. "Frankly, I needed to win."

Libby lifted a deck of cards and thumbed through them. The four of spades, the queen of clubs, the two of hearts . . . "I'm still confused why your gambling is so offensive. In truth, it hurt only yourself."

Paul did finally reach for the glass. He swirled the brandy. "Perhaps whoever has decided to make things right for the sake of God doesn't see it that way." He raised the glass to his mouth and stared at Libby over the rim. "Gambling provided a way for Harrison to leave his home. It was an excuse for many years."

"I don't understand," she mumbled, setting down the cards.

Paul tipped his head back and gulped the brandy. "Harrison only came now and then, but he told his wife he was here. This was easier to rectify before her than—"

"Oh my!" Libby's mouth dropped open. "They were still—the dalliance was—" She couldn't say it aloud.

Paul nodded and set the glass down on the table with a thud. "Harrison Greenwood married Elijah's mother two years before her younger sister, Dorothy, returned from boarding school. Once she did, well, this has been going on for years."

Libby paled. "Under everyone's noses?"

Paul shrugged. "Most people didn't know—didn't care to know. Some did."

"And," Libby concluded, "one of those who *cared* realized *you* were enabling it by holding the gambling sessions."

Paul nodded, removing his spectacles and wiping them with the cuff of his sleeve.

"But why relieve *you* of your death sentence?" she asked. Still perplexed. Still bothered by Paul's escape.

He ran a hand over his bald head and put his glasses back on his face. His beady eyes locked on Libby's. "Because I made penance? I'd been going back to church. I'd even gone to two or three of those twins' meetings. And that night you and Elijah and Calvin came to warn me? The obituary—it rang in my ears. I knew what I'd been doing wasn't atonement enough. So I snuck down to the Methodist church. I put all my spare money in an envelope and tucked it in the door. God may not forgive my sin, but I hoped upon hope the killer would."

"So they were watching you." Libby's eyes widened. "They knew you'd paid penance and were repentant."

Paul nodded. "Well, paid penance. They must have assumed repentance was carried with it."

They were silent for a long moment, both of them staring at the cards they'd shuffled and fiddled with, now strewn on the tabletop.

Finally, Paul cleared his throat. "I understand someone finding our sins repulsive. I do. But you? What do you have to do with any of this? And why are you sitting here now? Go make penance somehow so this Grim Reaper moves along!"

Libby paled and lifted her eyes to meet Paul's. "That's my conundrum. I know what I've done, but there is no way, no compensation great enough, to ever pay for my sin."

Paul reached for the last brandy glass, a quarter full. He handed it to her, and she took the glass instinctively before she realized he'd intended it as his way of offering comfort.

"I'm so sorry," he said, his apology empathetic, sad, and very, very final.

CHAPTER 36

Annalise

I'm not quite sure I understand." Doug Larson's words emphasized every footstep as he led Garrett and Annalise down the hallway of the Senior Living Center.

"We have a few questions for your dad," Garrett responded. "Annalise and I have been doing some research on Gossamer Grove. Eugene Hayes. Our families."

Doug shot them a quizzical look over his shoulder. "You're an odd couple to be working together." His glance bounced off Annalise, and an almost triumphant twinkle marred his otherwise blasé tone. He had the mayor in his pocket, the town board on his side, and the wilderness center in his sights. His cooperation now was because of his working relationship with Garrett and the wilderness center. Nothing else.

Annalise stared at Doug's back as he rounded a corner. The floors of the home were shined, a marbled linoleum, but track marks from wheelchairs left dulled spots. Greenery was scattered decoratively, warm wall colors in hues of beige and brown, and landscape paintings meant to give a visual escape from the borders of the home.

"Here we are," Doug said, pushing open the door to his dad's room.

A distinct smell wafted through the air. The remnants from lunch, menthol, old age, and baby powder. A bed sat at the far end of the room, a sterile set of white sheets, a blue bedspread, and a brown throw pillow. In front of the television, a wheelchair was stationed and in it an elderly man. Wispy gray hair on the top of his head, thin shoulders, age spots on the hands that rested in his lap. He looked up, and Annalise was pleasantly surprised to see a full awareness in his eyes. They were sharp, exacting, and wary.

"Whaddya want?" he snapped, glaring at Doug who, for the first time Annalise had ever seen, looked uncomfortable.

"Dad, I've brought some visitors—"

"Really?" His eyebrows shot up in a cranky, sarcastic gesture, and he gave his son a dopey look. "I couldn't see that."

"Dad—"

"Meh!" The elder Mr. Larson waved his hand in dismissal at Doug. "I'm not ancient and I don't have dementia. I broke a hip, for Pete's sake, and I have arthritis. I haven't lost my senses."

"Yes, sir." Doug shifted his stance. "Dad, this is Garrett Greenwood and Annalise Forsythe. They've been doing some—" he paused as if he doubted their story—"research? They wanted to pick your brain about a few things."

"Pick away!" Mr. Larson grabbed the TV remote and snapped the set off. He leveled a handsome and rather remarkably charming smile on Annalise. His eyelid dropped in a wink. "I always had a thing for redheads."

Annalise bit back a smile. Like father, his son was not. Doug emitted a small sigh and backed away. "I'm going to go check in with the doctors."

"You do that!" Mr. Larson raised his voice at his son's back as Doug made a fast exit. "Tell 'em I want outta here in two weeks so I can get back to my apartment!"

Doug disappeared.

Mr. Larson waggled his eyebrows. "Can't help but pick on the boy. Thinks he built Gossamer Grove himself. He's so rich and all." Sarcasm practically dripped from the father's words. He pointed to two straight-backed wooden chairs. "Have a seat. What can I tell you?"

Garrett exchanged glances with Annalise, and they both sat simultaneously. He gave her a quick nod. She smiled. She really, *really* liked Mr. Larson. Maybe because he was one of the few people she'd ever seen put Doug Larson in his place.

"It's a long story," she began.

"Nope. Skip it. Get to the point." Mr. Larson's bark was worse than his bite, but she could tell he wouldn't have a lot of patience.

"All right." Annalise adjusted her weight on the chair and folded her hands as if in prayer. She *should* pray. Maybe it would help. "I'm here about Eugene Hayes. I have questions about his family."

Mr. Larson drew back in his wheelchair. "Eugene! Sure, sure. He was a character. He got me into so much trouble as a kid. Lost touch with him over the years, I guess. But . . . still gonna miss him."

Annalise gave the older man a sympathetic smile. "Did you ever know Eugene's father? Lawrence?"

A shadow fluttered across Mr. Larson's face and his grin dissipated. "Hayes. That's what everyone called him. Just Hayes."

"So, you remember him?" Annalise prompted.

"Sure, I do. Hard to forget a man like that."

"Why?" Garrett interjected.

Mr. Larson scowled at him. "Lawrence Hayes was a dog. Plain and simple." He wagged his index finger at Garrett. "You Greenwoods have a few of them in your history, so don't you go getting on your high horse with me."

Garrett shook his head. "No high horse here."

"Good. What I know about Eugene's dad was that he caroused with more than one woman, probably had more kids than was ever accounted for, and was quick to use the back of his hand on Eugene." Mr. Larson clucked his tongue. "Sorry to say, when his dad passed, Eugene was in Vietnam. But still, he told me when he got word it was like he'd won the war."

Lawrence Hayes, Deacon Harrison Greenwood's illegitimate son with Dorothy, had become quite the character. Annalise reached for her purse and pulled a small notebook out. She needed to keep notes, keep her thoughts and questions in order.

"Did Lawrence ever talk about his father? Or did Eugene know his grandfather?"

Mr. Larson shot a glance at Garrett. Annalise followed his line of sight. Garrett was stiff, uncomfortable, and she was almost certain if he could, he'd escape through the door right after Doug.

Mr. Larson focused again on Annalise. "Has anyone ever told you that sometimes it's better to leave the past in the past?"

"I've lived by that motto," Annalise nodded wryly. She gave Mr. Larson a sardonic look. "It unfortunately has not worked well."

Laughter escaped the older man. He patted his jean-clad knee and then boosted himself up with hands on the arms of the wheelchair to reposition himself. Wincing, he settled in the chair once more. "Hip hurts," he muttered, then ran his hand down his flannel shirt and nodded. "Okay. No one in Gossamer Grove likes to talk about it, least of all, your family." Mr. Larson looked at Garrett.

Garrett squirmed.

Mr. Larson cleared his throat. "One day, Eugene and I were buying candy at the drugstore and a man came in. Oh, we must've been about twelve years old at the time. The man was old. He walked with a cane and wore this old sweater vest that smelled like mothballs. But we knew who he was. Everyone knew who Elijah Greenwood was. The retired town mayor."

"Elijah?" Annalise glanced at Garrett.

"My great-grandfather," Garrett reiterated.

Mr. Larson continued. "Elijah Greenwood looked straight through Eugene as if he were made of mist. But he said hello to me. Later, I asked Eugene why he thought Mayor Greenwood ignored him. Eugene straight out said, ''Cause he's my uncle.' I about fell over dead."

So that confirmed the theory. Lawrence Hayes was in fact the half brother of Elijah Greenwood, and Harrison and Dorothy had been having an affair. Annalise jotted it on her pad of paper. She had to keep this straight if only to draw lines later and connect the dots.

She raised her pencil. "So, Elijah ignored you?"

Mr. Larson shook his head. "No, he ignored *Eugene*. The Greenwoods had washed their hands of anything Hayes. I found out later that when Eugene's grandfather, Harrison Greenwood, died, it all came out and was a huge mess. A scandal."

"Do you know how Harrison Greenwood died?" Annalise held her breath. The obituary written so poetically was almost tattooed on her brain. Insinuation that death was deserved. It didn't line up with a man who'd taken his own life as the town records showed.

"Well, my little redhead, my memory is a bit sketchy since I was just Eugene's friend and sorta came into his family history by accident. But, supposedly, Harrison Greenwood hung himself."

"That's what we heard too." Garrett gave a nod of confirmation.

"Hold up a minute," Mr. Larson said. "I haven't even got to the good part—about that day we ran into Elijah Greenwood at the drugstore."

Annalise waited. She looked at Garrett whose knee bounced.

Mr. Larson coughed into a Kleenex and wiped his mouth. "Well, when I asked Eugene about the old mayor and found out he was Eugene's uncle, then I became curious. What was it about the Greenwoods not wanting to claim Eugene and his daddy? Sure enough, there was an affair."

"Figured that," Garrett grumbled.

"Of course *you* do!" Mr. Larson waved his hand. "Most of Gossamer Grove knows about you Greenwood men. Your own daddy has his own tales to tell."

Garrett stiffened.

"Anyway, Elijah Greenwood supposedly has been one of the few faithful Greenwood men. Never cheated on his wife—so far as the town knows. But your grandpa?" Mr. Larson chuckled. "I can tell you stories about him!"

Garrett shook his head. "I'm not here about anyone other than Eugene and that side of the family."

"Family." Mr. Larson rolled his lips between his teeth. "Good to hear a Greenwood finally say it. Eugene was always haunted by it. Watching your grandpa and your daddy become mayors. Then your sister, of all people. It's like the Greenwoods saturate this town, and here he was, a decorated war vet who no one gave two licks about when he returned home."

"When he returned home . . ." Annalise recalled the picture of her grandma.

Mr. Larson nodded knowingly. "He met your grandma, yep. She had your Aunt Tracy. Of course, no one talked about that either. Eugene and your grandma had some falling-out, she married someone else, life went on, and it was all hush-hush as such things often are."

Annalise felt a knot in her stomach. Her pencil was poised over her notebook. Yes, hush-hush. Even today.

"So then," Mr. Larson went on, blinking rapidly as if to clear his thoughts, "the only other thing I know is that Eugene told me his father swore that his mother and Harrison Greenwood never saw justice for their deaths. Lawrence would rant on nights he drank too much. Go on and on about the past. Seemed the only person he ever remembered with any affection was some woman. Some woman who'd tried hard to prove his parents were murdered."

"Libby Sheffield?" Annalise raised her eyebrows.

Mr. Larson scrunched his face in thought. "Not sure. Could be. Anyway, Lawrence would go on about her, about some obituaries. Strange obituaries that showed up before his mother and his birth father were dead."

Annalise instantly went cold. Obituaries *before* someone was found dead? Could it be that the obituaries with the Edgar Allan

Poe lines were the original obituaries and the newspaper simply rewrote them to be more appropriate after the deaths were confirmed?

She looked down at her notepad. "So . . ."

Mr. Larson shrugged. "So, the newspapers and records say there were investigations, but nothing was ever proven."

"Is there anything else? Anything at all you remember Eugene saying?" Annalise urged Mr. Larson.

He stretched out his hand and she took it. Squeezing her fingers, Mr. Larson spoke, his voice firm and direct. "Eugene said he didn't think his daddy—Lawrence—said anything but the truth when he drank, 'cause when he was sober, it was all lies. The strangest part was when Eugene was overseas, Lawrence got so stone drunk that he passed out on the steps of the Baptist church. When they found him, he was barely alive. But Lawrence started singing, some old revival song, and he kept whispering 'The preacher man was right. All along. The preacher man was right.'"

Chills cascaded up and down Annalise's spine. Mr. Larson gave her hand one last squeeze and let it go.

He heaved a sigh. "Just too bad the Greenwoods put the Hayeses on the outs. It's a darn shame. Especially if they knew what really happened. The story that Gossamer Grove would never tell."

"What story was that?" Garrett finally spoke up.

Mr. Larson raised an eyebrow. "That Elijah Greenwood was more than Lawrence's half brother—he was Lawrence's *whole* brother. Dorothy Hayes and Deacon Harrison Greenwood were having dalliances the entirety of Greenwood's marriage. His wife couldn't have children so she made a deal that she'd say nothing of the affair in exchange for the boy. Elijah."

"Oh my!" Annalise clapped her hand over her mouth. Garrett sagged back in his chair. Dumbfounded.

"Yep." Mr. Larson nodded. "That's what you get when you play around with what God says isn't yours to play with. A whole cellar full of secrets, and people prefer to lock it up and throw away the key. Because, really, who wants to face it? It's better to pretend it never happened. Never happened at all."

Mr. Larson folded his Kleenex absent-mindedly and picked a piece of lint off his pants. "Eugene swore one day he'd figure it all out. He'd put all the pieces together and then he'd make the town come clean. Come clean about what happened way back when, come clean about his daddy, and come clean about his own daughter, your aunt."

It was all so sad. Just sad and meaningless. Annalise exchanged looks with Garrett. "Eugene died before he could do it," she murmured.

Mr. Larson locked eyes with her. "Did he?"

Those two words were filled with purpose and intent. Annalise stiffened, then blinked away tears that sprang to her eyes.

"No," she whispered. "No. He didn't." And she would tell the story that Eugene had uncovered. It was what he wanted. When he willed her his trailer, filled with his searching, his findings, and his story.

CHAPTER 37

Libby

Darkness shrouded the street. The streetlamps had for some reason extinguished, leaving the cobblestone road difficult to traverse. A storm was blowing in. Droplets of rain spit at Libby's face, mocking her travail down the blustery street. Thunder rolled through the sky like a cannon building to its explosion. Her dress whipped around her ankles, and her cloak flapped behind her, twisting inside out as the wind caught it like a kite. Hair plastered across her face.

The revelations from her conversation with Paul made her mind spin. But one thing was certain. With Paul finally being honest, the pieces were falling in place—all of them except her own. She certainly wasn't going to wait for death to visit her. Intent on taking her obituary to the police, Libby had implored Paul to go with her. There was no wisdom, no safety, in going alone. He had started to, but as they walked, Libby realized the man had been imbibing more than the brandy in the basement. The flask he'd lifted to his lips rather frequently was already rendering him useless. She'd left him perched on the steps of the corner drugstore. The remaining seven blocks to the police station was intimidating in the dark, let alone with thunder rumbling in the distance and rain now pelting her face. But the parsonage was on the way. Just knowing the Muellers were nearby gave her some small comfort.

Libby pushed on, her hand wrapped around her obituary held deep in her dress pocket. Her other hand perched over her eyes to shield them from the rain that continued to bluster.

"Libby!"

She froze, spinning around and squinting into the darkness and rain. The outline of a man hurried toward her. No one was out and about but her. No one was venturing to be brave against the oncoming storm.

"Libby, wait!"

Her obituary had been penned, her death prophesied by her killer. She needed to be in the safety of the police station. Turning her back to the figure, she pressed into the wind. The rain fell harder now. She pulled her cape around her like a blanket, shielding her dress from being saturated. Lightning flickered in the sky, illuminating the street. Libby looked over her shoulder. The figure was drawing closer. She could hear their footsteps slapping on the wet walkway.

Run!

Libby surged forward. Her breath came in snatches, stolen away by the downpour. Up ahead, she could make out the outline of the Muellers' porch. She could take refuge there too, if need be. Perhaps Reverend Mueller would be home. Or Calvin. Someone to walk the remaining few blocks with her and keep her safe.

A hand clamped over her shoulder. Libby screamed. Her voice echoed down the empty street and was swallowed by the wind.

"Libby!"

"Reverend Mueller!" she shouted into the wind. "Oh, thank the Lord."

"Libby, you mustn't be out in this weather. You'll catch your death!"

A strange twist of words. Libby shook her head, raising her voice above the wind. "I need to get to the police station."

"No, no. I insist. Come inside first!" Reverend Mueller extended his arm toward their porch. The assaulting rain made it hard to see, and Libby stumbled over a crack in the walk.

"I really need to, Reverend!"

Reverend Mueller's concern was etched into the parts of his face Libby could see. "Come with me. We can use the parsonage telephone to ring the authorities. You should not be out here."

The rain beat on the walk, on the street. They were in front of the parsonage now. The reverend stepped onto the first step. "My housekeeper is home. She can make you tea. Calvin has chased after the Corbin brothers and their ruckus of today. Please! Do come in."

She hurried up the porch stairs and into the humble but tidy entry of the parsonage. Gaslights lit the hallway. Reverend Mueller gave her a smile and shook his head as he removed his hat, water falling onto the wool carpet. "Gracious, child! You're an obstinate one."

Libby pushed back sopping wet hair from her face. She couldn't explain, not to him.

"Let me take your wrap." Reverend Mueller assisted her from her wrap after she unfastened it at her neck. He hung it on a hall tree, drips marring the wood floor beneath it. "Come." He ushered her down the hallway into a small kitchen. Pulling out a chair, he waved her toward it. "Let me go find Mrs. Beaton. She'll make you some tea."

"Thank you." Libby shivered from the cold and dampness.

Reverend Mueller moved to exit the room.

"The telephone?" Libby asked quickly. She had no desire to prolong going to the police. With Paul's admission, the pieces of the puzzle finally making sense, she was certain the police would find her obituary legitimate and concerning. This time there would be no demeaning pat on the shoulder, no "We're looking into it."

Reverend Mueller nodded. "Yes. Let me find Mrs. Beaton so she can put on tea and then we can place the call."

Libby appreciated his attention to decorum. He left her alone, and she heard his footsteps as he disappeared into the recesses of the house. She glanced around the kitchen. It wasn't new to her. She'd spent many hours here with Calvin. Growing up together, they played simple games here in the house, games like marbles.

She eyed the doorway where Reverend Mueller had disappeared through. She needed to tell him. The truth of it hit her hard in the stomach, knotting it and increasing the sense of anxiety that already had increased her rain-soaked shivering. Calvin's story—*her* story—was going to be revealed sooner than later. After all Reverend Mueller had been through, watching his strong teenage son turn into a boy who would never fully grow up, he had been the epitome of a devoted father. With a wife already passed away, Libby had caused the man so much pain, so much grief. Calvin was not the only victim of her selfishness, or cowardice, or whatever the reason had been that she didn't help Calvin that night.

The cast-iron stove with its cream-colored enamel and bread-warming ovens sent off a dull, warm heat that made Libby shiver again. She stood and moved toward it, holding her hands over the stovetop as if it were an open flame. It was late spring, so a piping hot stove would be ridiculous, but even the small amount of warmth would be enough to heat tea.

Libby looked again toward the doorway leading into the hall. It seemed to be taking a long time for Reverend Mueller to find his housekeeper. She rubbed her hands together and shook out her skirts, water droplets landing on the floor. A dull sense of apprehension rose. The feeling that she wasn't safe. Which was very odd. She was safe and in a very familiar place. Yet, something made her heart start pounding. It felt as if she'd walked into a lions' den thinking it empty. But the lions lay in wait, ready to pounce.

She turned from the stove. A book left open on the countertop snagged her attention. The name *E. A. Poe* sent a chill down her spine.

Libby peered down at the book.

"The boundaries which divide Life from Death are at best shadowy and vague. Who shall say where the one ends and where the other begins?"

Though the print was small, the words stood stark on the page, mimicking Libby's obituary. Poe's "The Premature Burial" was typeset at the top of the horror-filled page. She flipped the page to the end. Her eyes skimmed the words.

"There are moments when, even to the sober eye of Reason, the world of our sad Humanity may assume the semblance of a Hell."

Though Poe had penned these words over fifty years prior, Libby knew it was the voice of the obituary writer. He saw today, this existence, a place of doom and their sins—especially illuminated by the flamboyant call to repentance from Jacobus and his brother—something only paid for by the exclamation point of death.

Libby slammed the cover shut. She would never read Poe again—if she survived the night. She spun on her heel and yelped as she almost crashed into Reverend Mueller who'd come up behind her.

"I'm sorry, I—" Libby stopped.

His eyes drifted to the closed book and then back to her face. He shook his head, gray hair and side whiskers still damp from rain. "There are many suppositions as to how Edgar Allan Poe died, you know?"

Libby glanced at the book. She twisted material from her skirt and glanced at the hallway beyond the reverend.

"Did you know?" he insisted.

"No. No, I didn't." Libby's voice quivered. She blinked, trying to comprehend the expression in the reverend's eyes. Apprehension seeped into every ounce of her blood. That knowing of the truth, but the desperate desire to be wrong.

Reverend Mueller reached around her and picked up the book.

His thumb traced the gold embossing of the title. "Some say he had rabies. But others say it was suicide by alcoholism. Still others surmise he may have met his death by the hand of another."

"How sad," Libby murmured. She eyed Reverend Mueller as he opened the book and stroked the pages as if they were the Bible itself. He raised his eyes. They were empty.

"He deserved to die, Poe did. His morbid tales of the grave, of being buried alive, it's like sin. It suffocates one's soul when gone unattended. I believe Poe's went unattended, and many knew not the deeds he'd committed. Perhaps even murder itself."

Libby took a step to the side.

"Where are you going?" Reverend Mueller tossed the book onto the countertop.

"H-home?" Libby hated the way her voice shook. Somehow, her saying *the police* seemed dangerous just now.

"Home?" Reverend Mueller cocked his head and smiled. This time his smile wasn't kind, or gentle, or fatherly at all. "Didn't you know? Didn't you read? Tonight is your time to die."

CHAPTER 38

Annalise

M y brain hurts." Garrett leaned against Annalise's car in the parking lot of the nursing home. Doug Larson had finally returned, ending the conversation with his father. Garrett and Annalise had left the duo to themselves and exited the building.

Annalise knew what Garrett meant. But her hurt was deeper, more vulnerable. Dorothy Hayes was like her in a way, only worse. An affair, two illegitimate children, one of which—Elijah—had been taken from her and given to another woman. Perhaps different pressures, but ultimately the same purpose. To save face. To save reputation. Yet Dorothy had relinquished her son to her sister and continued her affair with Harrison, her sister's husband. *How did one—?* Annalise shook her head. No. She had no right to judge or question. Here she stood next to the man who'd fathered her baby girl, and every time she saw him, her heart beat faster, her eyes skimmed his body—remembering—and most of all, the magnets that had drawn her heart toward him were still powerful. Right or wrong, the pull had increased rather than decreased.

Garrett rubbed his hand over his eyes and dropped it, slapping it against his leg. "Man. My family history is messed up."

Annalise nodded. "Mine too."

Garrett elbowed her. She looked at him, his dark eyes intense and searching. "You do know we're different, don't you?"

"How?" Annalise once again wondered how Garrett could read her thoughts.

"'Cause. We did the right thing, really. Maybe our parents were trying to save face, and we went along, but it was right. We were kids. Raising Gia wouldn't have been smart. I was in a reckless place, and you . . . I'd hurt you. Bad."

Wow. Annalise hadn't expected that from Garrett. That frank admission, taking it all on himself as if he alone were to blame.

"It wasn't just your fault," she replied. "I was a willing party, you know?"

Her question came out breathy. She'd been willing. She'd loved him. Maybe a young, immature love, but she had. In a way, maybe she still did.

Annalise looked away, but Garrett twisted to face her. "God can do pretty stellar things with screwed-up people."

"God don't make no junk." Annalise tried for funny and flopped.

Garrett shook his head. "I mean, we can be stronger."

"Yeah, that'd be nice." Annalise gave him a sad smile. But, Garrett didn't return it. He studied her face. Her breath caught and she bit her bottom lip as he drew closer. His hand rose, and he held her chin with a gentle grip between fingers and thumb.

"I used to think people who talked about God—Jesus—all that was crud. They sin, they forgive, they sin again and God gives them a free pass. But if someone else screwed up, they were judgmental and hypocritical."

"Pretty much," Annalise whispered, noting Garrett drawing just a bit closer.

"But that's not true. Not of real faith. Real faith is knowing forgiveness comes, you change, and then you walk and struggle together. Jam your knees, hit your knuckles, scrapes, bruises, broken legs, whatever. Life is hard and it takes guts, faith, and a massive amount of out-of-this-world grace."

Garrett's words sank into her like the explanation she'd been searching for since he'd left her twelve years ago. She never expected him to be the one to deliver it. To say that forgiveness and moving on could be had without completely abandoning who you were and what had made you into who you were.

"So, to seek grace, it doesn't mean I have to forget Gia?" It was her worst fear really, if she were honest. That to admit her past openly and before God meant to disavow her daughter as a castaway sin that should be forgotten.

"Never forget." Garrett's hand lifted and combed through the side of Annalise's hair. For a moment she thought he might kiss her, might take her in his arms, but he dropped his hand and backed away. It was too soon. It was the wrong time. "Never forget our baby girl."

The tears in his eyes said it all.

—⚹—

She gripped the steering wheel of her car, engine running, but she couldn't shift it out of park. Annalise stared at the dashboard. She missed Gia, missed her original photograph of Gia, missed what was, what could have been, and now she struggled with where she might go. Garrett and Doug Larson had taken off together, headed for Larson's office to go over plans for the center with a promise to meet up again at the newspaper basement. Maybe Tyler had uncovered even more pieces and it would all finally come together.

She reached for the shifter. Garrett had been hesitant to leave her alone, but she assured him she would go straight back to the newspaper. If Tyler was worth his salt, he'd still be combing through the piles of paper work, trying to find out more about Libby Sheffield. Now more than ever, Annalise wanted to know who she was and how she and the Corbin brothers' revival fit into the story.

Annalise startled as the passenger-side door whipped open. "What?" She reached for her door handle, but the electric locks clicked and momentarily stopped her.

"Don't." The one word was laden with intent and made her freeze. Everything in her frantically searched her mental database. She'd planned for this moment. The moment when someone held her at knife point or gun point when they tried to abduct her. Didn't every woman? But confusion and panic slammed into each other. Not to mention, she *knew* him. Not well, but she did.

"What do you want?" She glared at Brian, Nicole's boyfriend. He squeezed his long legs into the passenger seat. He wasn't armed, so Annalise waited. Didn't overreact. Blowing a situation out of proportion into life and death was stupid and would only make things worse.

Nope. There it was.

Brian cradled a pistol against his stomach, aimed at her with the menace of an explosive firearm.

Her hand reached for the door handle.

"Don't," he repeated.

"You'd shoot me?" Annalise tried to hide the tremor in her voice. Online videos had stated there was a higher rate of survival if you ran from an armed gunman than if you agreed to go with them. Dodge and weave. She might get shot, but odds were in her favor she wouldn't die.

Her gut coiled, along with every muscle in her body. Fear began to overtake logic and common sense.

"What do you want?" There it was. The shaking in her voice.

Brian noticed and pointed with the barrel of his pistol at the shifter. "Let's go."

"Where?" Annalise didn't comply.

"Somewhere we can talk."

She grabbed for the door handle, slapping the automatic unlock as she did. The door flew open, and Annalise lunged to escape. Brian shoved across the console and grabbed at her. He snagged her hair and yanked her back inside the vehicle. Annalise cried out, but the nursing home parking lot was empty.

"Get in and shut your door." Brian's cologne filled the car. Suffocating and pungent. Annalise had no choice. His hand still held captive her hair, red strands wrapped around his fingers, the only color in a day that was cloudy and gray.

"Drive," he commanded.

She did. Following his directions, she drove toward the old section of Gossamer Grove.

Brian's jaw muscle twitched as he stared out the window. His silence was more unnerving than if he'd ranted and raged.

"It was you, wasn't it?" Annalise noticed her knuckles were white as she gripped the steering wheel. They passed some run-down Victorian houses from the early days of Gossamer Grove, and the car jostled as it crossed the railroad tracks. The old Greenwood Mill, its abandoned windows staring at them, whipped by on the right side of the car. "You stole Gia's picture, didn't you? You attacked me outside of Eugene Hayes's trailer?"

Brian didn't respond.

He leaned forward, peering through the windshield. The road past the woolen mill had grown rough, the asphalt buckled in places from disuse. Waving his gun toward the right, he barked, "Turn here."

The dirt road was made of hard-packed gravel. The grasses on either side were tall, overgrown, and the trees and shrubbery resembled a Midwestern jungle. Annalise had never been here, and the *No Trespassing* sign indicated she didn't have much hope of someone wandering by. The drive wound into the woods and then came out into a clearing. A pond, maybe an acre in size, met her gaze. Its edges were bordered with slimy, puffy algae, but the middle of the water was blue. A duck spooked and took off from the surface.

A nagging memory sparked in Annalise's mind. The old revival meetings. The Corbin brothers. A tent erected by an old pond—Gossamer Pond.

Ironic.

Gossamer Pond had been forgotten for years, and now here she was, at the very place of the revival meetings—meetings that for some reason Eugene Hayes had thought important in present day.

Brian shifted in his seat and glared at her. "Why did you make me do this, huh? I tried to warn you."

Annalise frowned. "Warn me about what? You put me in the hospital, Brian!"

Brian nodded, giving her such an incredulous look that she almost believed for a moment he was a victim of circumstances. "I didn't want it to come to this!" He looked down at the gun in his hand. "I'm not a killer. I sell cars, for Pete's sake."

Annalise summoned as much calm as she could, keeping her voice low and even. "I don't understand, Brian. Help me understand."

"You and that stupid shelter." Brian raked his free hand through his hair. "It all started with that, and then Eugene."

"Eugene has nothing to do with my shelter," Annalise argued. Maybe by proxy of being destitute, but in no other way.

"He visited Nicole." Brian's eyes flickered with frustration and anger. "Told her he was finding out how the Hayes family and the Greenwood family were linked. Said he looked after you all these years, and if Nicole was going to shut down your cause, he'd shut her down. He'd smear her name and let Gossamer Grove in on how the Greenwoods had a history of not really doing their duty by the community. The unreliability of their ethics." Brian laughed. An ugly laugh that reeked of desperation.

Eugene Hayes was a fighter. He had fought for her! "But—he's dead now. Why steal my baby's picture? Why send it to Tyler? Why out Garrett as the father? Especially since Eugene was already dead."

Brian tilted his head as if she were stupid. He shook his head, his eyes panicked. "It's all out of control! I broke into your house, originally to scare you off. But then I saw your baby's picture. I took it. If you wouldn't stop looking into Eugene, then I needed to discredit you. So people didn't support your cause."

Annalise returned Brian's stare. Was the man unhinged? "Why are you so upset about the shelter? It doesn't have anything to do with you. Is this just because of Eugene's threats to smear the Greenwood reputation and ruin Nicole?"

"No!" Brian stretched his gun arm out and braced the gun against the dashboard as he stared out the window. "Nicole—I never wanted any of it to affect her. But your pantry and its cause, it's been getting to her. She was almost ready to hand the property over to you and turn down Larson! And then when Eugene came, I thought Nicole might give the land to you right then and there. I talked her out of being impulsive."

Annalise still hadn't quite figured him out. She eyed the gun as she moved her hand for the door handle. Slowly. Ever so slowly.

"Why do you care about the land, Brian?"

Brian turned toward her, his brow furrowed. "I invested everything. Everything I own I've put behind Larson's wilderness center. If Nicole and the town board grants the property to your shelter, I've got nothing."

"But you wouldn't lose your investment," Annalise argued.

"No. But I'm so in debt, Annalise. Up to my eyeballs. The car dealership is sinking. I can't be with Nicole, be worthy of her, if I have nothing."

The cold realization of it all swept over Annalise. Eugene's threat, meant to protect her, had in fact helped sway Nicole toward donating the land. Brian had to eliminate what stood in the way of his investment so he could be financially stable.

"Did you . . . *kill* Eugene?"

Brian reared back. "No!" But consternation spread across his face. He rubbed his palm vigorously over his eyes. When he dropped his hand, he stared at her. "I went to talk to him, that's all. Just talk. After he threatened Nicole, she was upset. Do you blame her?"

No. Annalise really couldn't blame her. Regardless of intention, Eugene hadn't handled the sordid family history well at all. Her hand had found the door handle. But Brian's arm dragged from the dashboard, and the gun waved in the air.

"I broke into Eugene's trailer because I figured if I could take the proof he had of all the Greenwood scandal in Gossamer Grove, he'd have nothing to threaten Nicole with. He wouldn't be able to undermine her position with the town, her reputation. The town board would still listen to her and respect the Greenwood name. Garrett's indiscretions aside, it was better than Eugene's entire family tree of unethical Greenwoods. We'd be back on track, and I could convince her to sell the land to Larson. But the old man wasn't away as I'd thought. So I confronted him."

"What happened?" Annalise didn't want to know, and yet she asked anyway. She could only imagine the feisty war veteran facing down the Abercrombie & Fitch car salesman.

Brian sniffed. "The old man got so worked up! Started hollering about how this town has never lived up to its nicey-nice reputation. That they put him on the outs, chased his daughter to another state, made you an exile. Not to mention his father and then his crazy stories about the Greenwoods!"

Brian stopped, his chest heaving for breath as though he'd run a marathon. Annalise was afraid to move. The gun wobbled in his hand, which had been overtaken by tremors. A tear slid down his cheek. Brian's upper lip curled.

"The man didn't care. He said turnabout was fair play, and then he just—he just dropped. He had a heart attack right in front of me, waving your picture and that photo of Nicole's dead great-great-grandfather."

Annalise mentally filled in the gaps. So, Brian had watched Eugene die, thinking the threats, the secrets, would once again be buried. Until Eugene's trailer was found, the pictures, the will stating she owned Eugene's place.

"Why didn't you clean out the trailer? Take the pictures, the evidence, everything? No one would have known."

Brian gave a short laugh. "Because I panicked. I just grabbed a few things, like—like that Darrow obituary, and then I ran. And then the next day Nicole had plans for us. I couldn't get out of it so I didn't say a word. By the time we got back that night, someone had already found him and called it in."

Annalise gagged. She turned to look out her window, trying to keep the nausea at bay. She sensed Brian lean up behind her, his breath hot in her ear.

"I love Nicole. But, I can't ask her to marry me with nothing. *I'm* nothing. I must offer her something. And to do that, I need the wilderness center and that land. I'm sorry, Annalise. I really liked you. I did."

Then a spearing pain shot through her head. The butt of the gun cracked against her skull, and Annalise crumpled against the door.

"Brian . . ." she mumbled as her vision blurred. Annalise sank back against the seat.

Brian leaned over her, his eyes wide and earnest. "I'm sorry, Annalise. I'm so sorry."

The woods, the pond, and Brian faded as darkness swamped her. So, this was it. This was what it felt like to die.

CHAPTER 39

Libby

Reverend Mueller was a disturbed man. Libby eyed him as he paced back and forth in front of the kitchen table. She shivered in her damp dress, sitting obediently in the chair because she had no choice. Her hands were tied behind her, attached to the chair frame with twine that cut into her wrists. He stopped his pacing and stared down at her.

"Why did you do it? Why did you leave Calvin in the fire? None of this would have had to happen. Think of what you did, Libby."

"I do. I have!" Libby sobbed. She wasn't above begging. She had nothing to offer the reverend of any worth. "Please! Don't do this."

"You know," Reverend Mueller said, squatting in front of her, his knees cracking as he did so, "I have always looked on you as a daughter. Always. I have been disgusted by the sin in this community. As a minister of God, it stuns me how unrepentant humanity is. Greenwood, Dorothy Hayes, and even Paul—although he seems to have seen the truth. But you? All this time,

I never imagined, never *fathomed* you would be worse than all of them! You would be guilty of letting my son, my Calvin, be disabled in that fire."

She wanted to ask how he knew. How he'd found out. But it would just make it worse. She would sound unremorseful for her sin, and only sorry she'd been discovered.

Reverend Mueller reached up and pushed hair off her cheek. He answered her unspoken question anyway. "The Corbin brothers have a way of bringing clarity to the need for repentance. They've brought clarity even to Calvin. Jacobus has spent much time with my boy, and Calvin's retained more memories of that night than any of us knew. He was able to finally put them into words, first to the preacher, then to me. A few days ago, my boy told me *everything*."

Libby swallowed hard, blinking as tears blinded her. Tears she couldn't wipe away due to her bindings.

Reverend Mueller stood, stalked over to the doorway, turned and faced her. "Wanton little thing. Calvin remembers you as his girl *and* as Elijah Greenwood's girl."

"No." Libby bit her lip, shaking her head. "It wasn't like that."

"But it's what Calvin remembers."

"Calvin was—*is* my closest friend. But I was enamored with Elijah and—"

"And you played with both of them!" Reverend Mueller hissed. "Toyed with them and played the whore!"

"I didn't!" And she hadn't! "It was nothing more than a kiss — well, a few kisses, and Elijah found us and then the fire started. They were fighting, both of them."

Reverend Mueller marched up to her and glared down on her. "But you left Calvin to die."

"Is that what Calvin said?" She had to know. It might be the awful truth. It might be a truth one could forgive because she was young, or because she'd been so ashamed and frightened. She could hardly stand the idea that Calvin remembered.

"He told me he 'got stuck' and you were fleeing and Elijah saved him. He thinks you ran to get help. To help him, Libby! But we know better, don't we?"

"I was scared," Libby cried. "I—I don't even know why I ran."

"Because you were *guilty*. You still are. And it takes *this*"—Reverend Mueller waved his arm at her bound to the chair—"to get you to confess! If I had known all these years, I'd not have wasted my time on Harrison Greenwood and the rest of the dirty lot."

Reverend Mueller seemed to try to steady himself as his hands shook and his mouth twitched in anger. He lifted a teakettle from the stove. He'd been warming the water for over twenty minutes. Now he pulled a teacup from the cupboard and poured water into it, sloshing over the sides of the cup onto the counter.

Taking a sip, he eyed Libby over the rim of the cup. "As a minister of the Word, I'm privy to much in this community. People pretending to seek confession when they merely want to patch their souls so they can continue in sin. There is no true repentance! This town needs cleansing!"

"Then let God do it!" Libby breathed, wishing instantly she hadn't.

Reverend Mueller slopped tea onto the floor.

"God? He uses His people to enact justice. Think of Samson, of Gideon, the judges of Israel!"

"But—" The idea that Reverend Mueller believed God had accorded him the same position as an Old Testament judge was beyond her. She ventured to speak reason to the reverend. "Yet God spared many. When they confessed," she argued.

"Yes!" Reverend Mueller raised his index finger in the air. "When they *confessed*. But it was sincere confession. Like Paul Darrow. He paid back what he'd taken. Dorothy, Deacon Greenwood, they pretended—but they never paid for what they'd done. Not after Dorothy gave her firstborn Elijah to the deacon's wife, and not after Dorothy bore Lawrence."

Libby froze. Elijah was Dorothy's son? Her stomach turned at the revelation. Elijah was Lawrence's full-blooded brother!

Reverend Mueller set his cup on the table. He rubbed his hands together. "Now. I gave Harrison a chance to truly repent. He refused. Oh, he begged and pleaded, but in the end I couldn't even squeeze a confession from him. Even when I made him write his own suicide note and he could see what I intended. And then there was his lover. Dorothy. I made her stand in her near-nakedness. To make her *feel* the sin of it and she just begged to live. She didn't see her errors." He spat the words like a curse.

"Then why make them look like accidents? And why write their obituaries and drop them at the newspaper before you even killed them? You never intended to let them go."

Reverend Mueller smiled, but it wasn't kind. "I knew they wouldn't confess. They'd had years to and yet they chose to live double lives. Sinful lives. The obituaries were to send a message. A warning to repent. Originally, I thought your news-hungry father would find them and print them. But he didn't. You did. But now I'm glad you found them. Now that I know the truth about my son. The truth of what you did. I will never have my son back—you killed the boy I had."

Spittle dotted her face as the reverend grew angrier. His face reddened. "It's too late now, Libby. It's too late."

"I'm sorry," she whispered. She was. Oh, how she was! "I confess!" It sounded pithy, even to her. The insincerity of a coerced confession. Deacon Greenwood and Dorothy Hayes probably had done the same. Begged for forgiveness, but with Reverend Mueller there was no grace to be found.

The man leaned into her, his fingertip wiping away his spit from her cheek. "I will listen to your pleas, Libby Sheffield, as your last breath seeps from you. But you have come to the gateway of eternity and it is too late. I will bury you alive in your sin. Maybe then, Calvin will be vindicated, and God— God can be at work in this town once again."

317

Annalise

Cold startled Annalise awake. Water soaked her feet and legs. The world was blurry as she opened her eyes, trying to gather where she was, where Brian had disappeared to. She peered out the window.

"Oh, God, help me!" And she meant it. Pond water encased the car. Brian must have pushed the car into Gossamer Pond!

Annalise clawed at the seat, pulling her feet up beneath her, her head hitting the car's ceiling. Water poured through cracks in the doors. The smell of it caught her breath. She coached herself to keep from hyperventilating. Deep breaths. Pushing the car door open would be impossible. She needed to break a window. But, when she did that, she'd lose all oxygen, and the car would flood. At least she could swim.

The water at her knees splashed as she clamored for the glove compartment. The nose of the car shifted down, and through the windshield all she could see was murky water. Annalise looked for something sharp. Something with a point to ram into the driver's window so it would shatter. She didn't think she'd have enough strength to kick it out.

Napkins fell into the pond water on the passenger seat, soaking through, the logo from her coffee shop bleeding off the brown paper. The owner's manual, tire pressure gauge, an old straw. Annalise clawed through the contents of the glove compartment.

A screwdriver! Annalise gripped it tight. She couldn't afford to lose it in the dark, mottled water that was now up to her waist.

In mere minutes she could be face-to-face with God instead of sucking in air and seeing the sky. The ironic thought raced through Annalise's mind. As she repositioned herself on the seat, balancing as the car tilted downward, an odd sense of peace enveloped her. She would be fine. Dead or breathing. Maybe her parents—Garrett's parents—held her life's choices against her, but God didn't.

He never had. She knew that. Deep inside her soul where she never liked to explore. A verse from childhood Sunday school filtered through her brain. More water poured in through the seams in the car. The chill caught her breath as the water hit her chest.

"The wages of sin is death . . ."

Annalise gripped the screwdriver. She probably wouldn't have enough strength to bust through the window.

"But the gift of God . . ."

She aimed the tool like a weapon. Two hands wrapped around each other.

"Is eternal life . . ."

Sucking in a deep breath, she brought her arms down with as much force against the window as she could. The water pushed back against her, but the screwdriver drove into the glass.

"Through Jesus Christ our Lord."

Libby

His fingers were cold. Thumbs pressed into the hollow of her throat. Libby kicked, her legs tangling with Reverend Mueller's. The chair tipped backward and they fell to the floor. Pain surged through Libby's hands, still tied behind her back. Something sharp cut into the side of her hand. The back of the wooden chair had shattered, exposing a nail. Reverend Mueller's grip released in the fall, and for a moment Libby's vision cleared. She coughed, gasping in a deep breath. He repositioned, straddling her body.

"No," he hissed in her face, his hands rising to grip her throat.

Libby pulled her wrists downward against the nail. It bit into the twine and her skin. She did it again and again, flailing her legs and trying to bring her knees up into the reverend's middle to disable him. Her hands broke free, and she pulled her arms out from beneath the weight of the chair and their bodies. She clawed at Reverend Mueller's face.

Pushing her hands into the reverend's nose, she shoved. He grunted and his fingers released her throat. Blood spurted from his nostrils and dripped onto her dress. Libby rolled away and scrambled to her feet. She slipped as she ran, her body slamming into the doorframe of the kitchen. Reverend Mueller was close behind, his hand tearing at her collar as Libby launched herself down the hall toward the front entrance.

Before she could reach for it, the door flew open, rain pelting the darkness in the background, and a silhouette in the doorway.

"Calvin!" Libby screamed. "Please!"

Reverend Mueller had hold of her waist and was pulling her back into the kitchen. He yelled at his son, "Close the door, boy! I will bring justice for you!"

Calvin's eyes widened, and instead of closing the door he spun on his heel and ran back into the storm.

"Calvin!" Libby's scream echoed after him. She twisted in the reverend's grip, scratching his hands at her waist. She drove her elbow into Reverend Mueller's gut, and his breath released in a grunt.

As she fell forward, catching herself against the wall, two men barreled into the room. One grabbed for her, the other slammed into the reverend, tackling him to the floor. She heard a fist smack into the reverend's face, then again and again. Libby buried her face against the chest that held her. She felt the man turn, as if to shield her from the sight, but Libby pulled back and struggled to look around the arms that held her.

Elijah. Elijah held her, shielding her, just as he had since that night. She didn't want to be shielded. Not anymore. Libby squirmed to have him release her.

Another solid fist landed against the reverend's face. A shout. Calvin came rushing through the doorway, two policemen following him. They dragged the second man off Reverend Mueller, who moaned and rolled on the floor, holding his bruised and bloodied face in his hands.

"Get him up!" one of the policeman commanded. The other dragged Reverend Mueller to his feet. Calvin collapsed against the wall, sliding down, sobbing frightened, terrified tears.

"Let me go!" Libby pulled away from Elijah.

Without hesitation, Elijah's hands slid from her, protecting her no longer. She hurried to Calvin, dropping beside him. She cradled her friend—her best friend—against her and held him. A grown man, yet a boy. Reverend Mueller had been right. She had taken Calvin's life, if not his breath, from him.

"I'm so sorry," she cried, her tears mingling with Calvin's. "I never meant for you to get hurt. I was scared. I ran. I'm so sorry," she repeated.

They rocked together, and as they did, Libby looked up at the man whose shadow cast over them. His knuckles were skinned, raw from the force he'd unleashed on Calvin's father. His chest heaved from the exertion, but his eyes were clear. Sure. Strong. It was justice and mercy mingled together.

Jacobus looked less a revivalist and more a lean fighter. His hair was askew, his lip swollen from where Reverend Mueller must have hit him. He gave a small shrug. "Sometimes the soul and the mind aren't enough, Libby Sheffield." It was if he was continuing the conversation from earlier when he'd left her and walked away. Jacobus pressed a handkerchief to his knuckles before casting her a sideways smile. "But I do believe God will also forgive me the sin of a very bad temper."

CHAPTER 40

Annalise

Y ou scared the living tar out of me!" Christen's cry made
Annalise jump, sloshing hot coffee onto a pair of jogging
pants Garrett had brought from his house. She raised an
eyebrow at her friend.

"I was almost shot and almost drowned, and now you're going
to give me third-degree burns." Annalise set her coffee on the hospital table. She drew her legs up to her chest, smelling the scent of
Garrett. He sat on the edge of her hospital bed, wrapping a blanket
over her shoulders and around her hospital gown.

Christen hugged her, burying her face in Annalise's damp hair.
"What happened?"

"I just gave your husband the entire debrief." She leaned back
against Garrett as Christen pulled away. He was strong. For now,
he was safe. When she'd busted the car window, it had only taken
a few kicks to get to the surface of Gossamer Pond. Then she'd
run for what seemed like miles until she found a house. Banging
on the door brought the owners, a cellphone, and in short order
an ambulance and cops. The hospital had been a welcome sight,

the same as it had been a welcome sound to hear Garrett's voice on the end of the line when she'd called him from the ambulance.

Brent had taken her account and left a few minutes before his wife plowed into the hospital room. An APB had been put out for Brian, and apparently a call was made to Mayor Nicole Greenwood.

"This is insane!" Christen plopped into a pleather-covered hospital chair. "Who would've thought it was Brian!"

"It makes sense. Now." Annalise pushed hair behind her ear. Garrett's arm adjusted and she glanced at him. He gave her a small smile.

"I guess." Christen blew a puff of air between her lips, sounding like a mix between a motorboat and a baby blowing bubbles. "All because of Nicole and the land?" Christen's eyes widened. She redirected her gaze at Garrett. "Sorry."

"Don't be." Garrett shook his head. "It's way past time for all this to come out. Every bit of it. Besides, no one has really given this town a chance to forgive people. We keep hiding stuff."

"It's time for Gossamer Grove to show its true grit." Christen nodded in affirmation and conviction. "Show we are a community with a history, but a community of people who can move forward. Together."

Annalise sighed, eyeing the coffee from the hospital and debating calling her coffee shop and having a special delivery made to her hospital room.

"I just want it to be over." A tremor passed through her, and she snuggled deeper against Garrett. "I know it was Brian now. I know he tried to scare me after I started looking into Eugene's findings. Watching me, my slashed tires . . . all of it. But, I still have questions. Libby Sheffield. That revival meeting from 1907. Lawrence and Eugene. What happened to them all? Can you imagine being in their shoes? I mean, they couldn't have imagined years later *we'd* be similar"—she directed her words to Garrett—"or that their descendant would be a mayor with an impeccable legacy to uphold."

Garrett rolled his eyes. "Not exactly *impeccable*."

Christen moved to the edge of her chair. She clapped her hands like a kindergarten teacher, eyes wide behind her blue-framed glasses. "Children, children. Things have developed since you were off designing climbing gyms and plunging beneath the chilly waters of a pond."

"Thanks." Annalise knew her voice was flat and her expression derisive.

Christen smiled, and Annalise loved her for it. "So, I got a babysitter this afternoon and helped Tyler at the paper. We found some stuff."

"Yeah?" Annalise felt Garrett tense behind her.

"Yep. Libby Sheffield? Well, she was quite the woman. Not to mention Paul Darrow."

"Paul wasn't the bad guy?" Garrett asked what Annalise was going to.

Christen looked down her nose at them in full schoolteacher mode. "Paul Darrow was a rascal, like Tyler, because he buried it. All of it. The news stories!"

"I don't get it." Annalise shook her head, perplexed.

Christen leaned forward, resting her arms on her knees. She leveled a serious look on Annalise. "The entire story was written in a series of news articles. Written by Mitch Sheffield, the man who'd been part owner of the paper at the time, and Libby Sheffield's father—per the ancestral website I browsed in."

"Okay?" Annalise reached for the coffee. She needed it. Even if it tasted like mud.

"Tyler and I found a trunk way back under several old crates. It was Paul's, as evidenced by an old monogram and then a label on the inside cover. Inside it was an article written by Mitch Sheffield. And an old obituary for Dorothy Hayes that matches the ones you have for Harrison Greenwood and Paul Darrow! Full of Edgar Allan Poe and really bad original poetry, I might add."

"You read the articles?" Garrett inquired.

Christen shook her head. "No, there's too many. I mean, there are articles about these Corbin brothers who ran the revival. And articles about the trial of the man who killed Harrison Greenwood and Dorothy Hayes."

"Wait. So it *was* proven that they were murdered?" Annalise straightened.

Christen nodded. "Looks like it."

"How come no one remembers it? If it was printed and publicized?" Annalise was incredulous. A century could muddy a lot of history, but that was a very sensational story.

"That's just it. It wasn't printed. The articles were all handwritten and stashed away." Christen laughed. "You should've seen Tyler when we figured that out. Mitch Sheffield pretty much wrote an exposé on how Paul was a proposed victim of the killer—some guy named Reverend Mueller—that Darrow basically aided Greenwood and Dorothy Hayes in their longtime love affair by helping them get time together. He threw poker games in the basement of the paper, and Greenwood used that as a cover to go and be with Dorothy."

"Whoa." Garrett shook his head. "That's seriously messed up."

Annalise shivered as she felt Garrett press a light kiss to her temple.

Christen's eyes flickered when she noticed it. "As best as we can figure, Paul Darrow actually shut down the paper right after things came to a head. It was as if he couldn't stand to be at the paper, or who knows? It didn't reopen until two years later."

"Crazy." Garrett's voice vibrated against Annalise's back.

Annalise took a sip of the coffee. "How did Libby Sheffield fit into this? Please tell me she wasn't murdered."

Christen looked between Garrett and Annalise before leaning back in her chair and crossing her legs. "Libby Sheffield. Funny thing. She's sorta the one who started the whole mess. Who would've known what I'd find when I looked up Reverend Mueller, the man who killed those people and who wrote those creepy old obituaries. There are newspapers from outlying towns that tell all sorts of crazy stuff."

"Like what?" Annalise pressed.

Christen waggled her eyebrows. "How much time do you have?"

Libby's mother wrapped a quilt around her lap. Her eyes were tired as she considered Libby's.

"Your father is going mad with the paper closing. Paul just locked the doors and sent everyone home."

Libby gave her mother a sympathetic look. They were both relieved that Mitch wasn't part of the paper anymore. While Libby had been confronting Paul about her own obituary, Jacobus Corbin was confronting his brother Jedidiah about working alongside Mitch to create a sensation that would boost paper sales and attendance for the revival meetings. Apparently, Jedidiah saw numbers of converted souls as the sign of eternal success. Souls that apparently backslid very fast if Old Man Whistler's drunken altercation in the middle of the town square last night was any indication. And Mitch saw paper sales as success. The fact the two had created a fake death threat and conspired to hang effigies of the brothers to create a mad sensation and potentially inspire more riots had brought Jacobus to the boiling point. He'd outed them to the police after taking his deductions to his brother, confronting him with the suspicions, and gaining perhaps the most honest confession in the entire career of their revivals.

Jacobus had agreed not to press charges against Mitch if he gave up the paper—and gave it back to Paul Darrow.

"I doubt Paul will stay out of the newspaper business forever," Mother continued, breaking into Libby's thoughts. "But we all need time to heal. Including Paul. And your father." Her lips pursed. "Be that as it may, if it can all go away and not be tied to Gossamer Grove, we'll all be better off. There are too many good people here—churchgoing people—and we don't deserve that type of pall hanging over our town because of one man."

"One man?" Libby raised incredulous eyes to her mother. "Good people? We're all broken people. We can't make a secret of these things. For the sake of grace and faith, it will only hurt generations to come. Look at what it's done to me and to Calvin. To Paul and to the Greenwoods."

She thought of Lawrence Hayes, Dorothy's son. Of Elijah, Dorothy's son. It was known now that both boys were the sons of an illegitimate affair. Mrs. Greenwood seemed intent on not speaking of it, insisting the town leave her husband and sister to rest in peace. It seemed that with time, perhaps Gossamer Grove would respect the grieving widow's request. But Elijah? The truth of his birth, of who he was, staggered him. Libby mourned the absence of Elijah in Gossamer Grove. He'd left town shortly after, and whether he ever returned, only time would tell. They'd shared a swift farewell, a strange, longing look that shuttered into a cool nod, and then Elijah had left Libby too.

Her mother reentered the house, leaving Libby alone on the porch. She heard footsteps and raised her eyes to see Calvin coming up the walk. His familiar walk, somewhat hindered as if he had to think about each step before taking them, was accompanied by a smaller form. Lawrence Hayes. The adolescent boy smiled up at Calvin, chattering away as if they were the best of friends. Lawrence's father, Ralph, had been released from jail and seemed to be doing better, although many whispered that in the evenings he hit the bottle rather hard. Everyone knew Ralph had told Lawrence that he wasn't his son, but the man was still going to care for the boy as his own. God help the lad and his future.

"Hello, Lollie." Calvin was more serious, but his smile was genuine. Mrs. Beaton, the Mueller's housekeeper, had been caring for Calvin for the time being. But Libby had seen little of him.

"Hi, Calvin." Libby bit her bottom lip.

"I brought Lawrence. Like you asked." Calvin pushed Lawrence forward.

Libby clasped the item in her hand. Maybe she'd had too many days to think while sitting on the porch recovering from her ordeal.

Maybe she was too sentimental or it had all just gone to her head. But people needed hope. Grace. Something to hold on to in the dark moments, whether by life's doling hand or by one's own choices. She needed to tell Lawrence that too. He was a victim, like Calvin. His mother had been taken, his older brother had abandoned him, and his father might well be on his way to being a drunkard. What hope did Lawrence have?

"Lawrence, I wanted to give you something. Something that, years from now, maybe you'll look at and remember what I tell you."

Lawrence frowned, his young eyes studying hers as if trying to comprehend.

Libby reached for his hand, and he gave it to her. She laid her watch in his palm. It was broken, the hands stopped at the very moment his father had stabbed her shoulder in an attempt to hurt Jacobus.

"Eight thirty-six p.m., Lawrence. It was the moment in my life when time stopped. When I made a choice to do what was right, to turn my back on selfishness." She remembered launching herself in front of Jacobus. He was alive because of that act. She took no pride in it. Her heart ached that she'd not done the same years before when it mattered just as much. Libby glanced at Calvin, who was kicking a stone with his toe.

"I learned that night that the journey to grace is painful but necessary. It's turning your back on yourself in order to give to another. It's beginning the journey toward forgiveness. Remember that. Remember that it can be found, if you look for it. No matter who you become, no matter whose life you hurt, no matter how many regrets you carry with you, there is forgiveness. There is grace. Can you do that? Can you remember that?"

Lawrence gave her a quizzical look, but his fingers closed over the watch. "Sure. I can do that."

Libby knew she would probably always be remembered by him as a strange lady who gave him a broken timepiece. She prayed he wouldn't throw it away. She prayed it would be used one day, to set him or someone else onto a new path of grace.

"Calvin?" She shifted her attention to the man in the overalls.

He lifted soulful eyes and shook his head. "Don't, Lollie."

Her heart sank.

Calvin neared her and took her hand. "My daddy said you ran away and you didn't get help. I know—I know I'm not like Elijah. I'm just a boy."

Lollie bit her lip harder.

Calvin continued. "You may've run then, but you always been here. You didn't run forever, Lollie. You've been my girl forever."

Tears escaped and trailed down her face. Calvin shifted uncomfortably, but Libby couldn't stop. It was overwhelming, the innocence in which Calvin stated his forgiveness. While he didn't comprehend entirely, he remembered enough. He accepted she'd left him. But he also accepted she'd returned, even if it had been too late.

Libby reached out her hand to her old friend. "Yes, Calvin," she nodded. "I'll always be your girl."

Calvin smiled and gave her an eager nod in return. The moment for him was over. He pulled a bag of marbles from his pocket and a piece of chalk and proceeded to draw a circle for the game on the sidewalk. Lawrence trailed beside him, chattering about a cat-eye marble of blue.

Libby wiped the tears from her face. Forgiveness was sometimes a bitter thing. Freeing, but also so undeserved. So very, very undeserved. It made God's grace more precious. And—she watched Calvin flick a marble with his thumb and finger—and Calvin's forgiveness a treasure she would carry with her forever.

CHAPTER 41

Annalise

Annalise stood on a climbing pad, its six-inch depth firm yet able to catch the impact of a falling climber. Granted, Garrett wasn't that high. She craned her neck to look up, her arms extended to "spot" him. He was maybe twelve feet up. There was no catching him if he fell, but she could direct his body onto the crash pad with her arms if needed.

He hung solidly by his fingertips, gripping a small hold on the boulder, his left toe creating leverage against an even smaller ledge on the rock. His muscles rippled through the T-shirt on his back. He made it look effortless.

Garrett reached the top and then dropped onto the pad in full control of his descent. He flopped onto his back and stared up through the trees at the clouds. He cocked an eyebrow and glanced at her. "You gonna stand there and spot nothing?"

Annalise quirked her eyebrow and sat down next to him. She pulled her day pack toward her and dug through it. Finding the item, Annalise pulled it out. She wasn't sure why she'd brought it. A broken watch from her grandmother was an odd item to bring into the wilderness bouldering.

Garrett broke the companionable stillness. "So how do you feel about the land for the shelter?"

"Dumbfounded." Annalise ran her thumb over the face of the watch. "But grateful. I didn't think Nicole would really sway the board to give up the money Larson was offering."

Garrett didn't respond for a moment. Instead, he just stared at the sky. Finally he said, "She's pretty shaken up. I think she wants the town to heal, though. For our community to be stronger."

Annalise closed her fingers around the watch. "Gossamer Grove has good people in it. Needy ones, but strong ones. We can all pull together, and I believe this shelter might serve an even bigger purpose than I'd imagined."

More silence.

Then Annalise ventured, "Is Nicole going to be all right?" Recalling Nicole's veiled warning at the pantry, Annalise understood even then that Nicole was still upset from Eugene's threat and later his death. She'd played no part in anything, but was squeezed between the politics of a small town.

Garrett moved his hands behind his head, his elbows jutting out. "Nic is just lost. Like we've been." He turned thoughtful. "She's trying. All of this is hitting the paper, especially since they arrested Brian. At least Tyler's not being a jerk. His coverage is to the point."

Annalise nodded. "Gossamer Grove is going to take some time to recover. I mean, 'The Biggest-Hearted Small Town in the Midwest' is getting some chinks in its vintage charm."

"Truth." Garrett continued to watch the clouds.

Annalise looked up at the boulder he'd been climbing. Splotches of white chalk marred its face from where his fingers had patterned out a route.

"Brent said you guys talked?" It wasn't really her business, and yet it was. The friends had fallen out when Garrett left and Annalise moved to Connecticut. Brent was lost in the shuffle. Mad at his best friend, stunned for Annalise, and the type of good guy she'd wished for years that Garrett had been.

Garrett nodded. "Yeah. We're good."

He didn't elaborate. Annalise supposed just knowing the two could move forward without any hard feelings was a good thing.

She picked up the watch again. "Christen has really been doing her research about Libby Sheffield."

"Yeah?"

"Yeah." Annalise knew she'd keep the watch forever. Knew she'd forever wonder how it had gotten from being pinned on Libby Sheffield's blouse in the photograph, to Eugene, to Annalise's grandmother. Either way, she wasn't sure it mattered how so much as what the watch represented. A new beginning. A story buried by years and mold and dust brought to light to show her that she could start fresh without forsaking her past.

She recalled Libby Sheffield's family tree that Christen showed her a few days ago. Where Libby had ended up. Where she lived her final days. Her family and generations that came from her who lived in an entirely different part of the United States. And the revival. The pamphlets of the Corbin brothers' revival sort of made sense now too. Piecing together newspapers Tyler found in the basement to Libby's own history and to the revival meetings, it seemed the Corbin brothers had almost been the catapult to cause a local reverend to exact judgment on those who held unconfessed sins.

"What a wicked crazy history this place has," Garrett muttered.

"It does." Annalise slipped the watch back into her pack. She scooted over next to Garrett and looked down at him, laying her hand on his chest. Now that life seemed more under control, she'd spent all night debating this moment. It was here now. She would press forward.

"So, I wanted you to know something." Annalise's stomach flipped when Garrett leveled his dark eyes on hers.

"Okay?"

Boy, this was harder than she'd thought. "I—I'm sorry."

Garrett raised himself up on his elbows. "For what?"

She had to. It was only right. "For blaming you. All these years. We were both a part of what happened. I've been praying I could move on—and with Nicole finding Gia's picture in Brian's stuff, that's helped—but I owe you an apology."

Garrett stared at her for a moment, then accepted it. "Thank you."

"And Gia?"

Garrett heaved a deep sigh, as though he'd contemplated it many times before. "We have to trust her to Him." He looked up at the heavens. "I mean, she's twelve now. It's not fair to her to do anything but pray for her. Maybe one day she'll look us up."

It was what Annalise believed too. But it hurt. Especially now that she and Garrett were—were what?

He sat up and took her hand. "Look at it this way. Gia is the good that came from our bad."

"It wasn't all bad," Annalise whispered. Honest. They had shared happy moments. Good times. Friendship.

"Nah. It wasn't." Garrett grew serious. He trailed a finger down her cheek. "I want to kiss you . . . but I won't."

Annalise was disappointed and relieved at the same time. They had so much history. *So much* history. They needed to move slowly.

"Probably a good idea," she admitted.

"But you know"—Garrett gave her a lazy grin—"maybe later?"

"Maybe later," she laughed. "When we get to know each other better. As people. We never really took enough time to do that when we were in high school."

Garrett reached his hand out and took hers in a handshake. "Hey. I'm Garrett Greenwood."

Annalise smiled, looking down at their hands, at Garrett's casual but solid grip. She laughed again as she responded, "I'm Annalise Forsythe."

"Cool," he said, keeping her hand in his. His grip was warm. It promised her that the past was not a waste. All its mistakes weren't for naught. They could be used to make them more sensitive to the fact that grace was necessary for faith and for each other. Life may not be well-ordered, but it was worth living anyway. The broken moments, and moments like these . . .

Garrett tugged her down. Annalise rested her head on his chest, and together they watched the clouds.

"What time is it?" she whispered.

Garrett glanced at his watch. "Umm, eight thirty-six."

Annalise chuckled. "Figures."

"What do you mean?"

"It seems eight thirty-six is a good time to mark as the beginning of grace."

Annalise smiled toward heaven. Toward the woman she knew little about but who had once worn a dented watch, and who had started Gossamer Grove's long journey to find grace.

Libby

Libby stood at the edge of Gossamer Pond. The grass was flattened where the revival tent had stood. The water rippled in the gentle breeze. The sky was blue overhead, with fluffy clouds. Dandelions danced at her feet. She looked down, smiled, and knelt. Reaching through the grass, she plucked a delicate purple flower, its petals soft in her hand.

"Violets are perhaps the most overlooked of God's flowers."

Jacobus's voice met her ears, and Libby stood, holding the violet carefully in her hand. "Yes. I would agree."

His hands were in his trouser pockets. He didn't wear a coat, and in shirtsleeves he seemed more approachable. The vision of him defending her still replayed in her memory. Heroic and yet at the same time he had empowered her.

Libby gave Jacobus a sideways glance. A nip of sadness tugged her heart. The Corbin brothers were leaving Gossamer Grove. For good. They'd been here for no more than a couple of months, and while it seemed Jedidiah had intended to stay until the entire town was baptized, no one wanted him around anymore. Jacobus had told her earlier that there was no way to be effective in the wake of the damage his brother had done.

"I . . ." Libby began, studying him with hesitation. Jacobus didn't return her look. How did she say she would miss him? They barely knew each other. Circumstances may have thrust them together, but in reality she didn't even know his favorite color.

"Purple," he said.

"Excuse me?"

Jacobus met her incredulous look. He gave her a wan smile. "I like purple. My mother used to wear it all the time. I developed a fondness for it."

"How did you know I was—?" Libby stopped.

He turned to face her. "Because you kept looking at the violet, then at me, then at the violet. It stood to reason I like violets, but did I like their color? What is my favorite color? And we aren't thoroughly familiar with each other, are we? It's a very introductory type of question."

It was probably good Jacobus Corbin was leaving town. He could read not only her soul, but also her mind. That was very dangerous. Libby cleared her throat. "I've a question, before you leave."

"Yes?" Jacobus raised his brows but didn't offer up a suggestion as to what he thought she would ask.

Libby forged ahead. "Calvin. When did he tell you what happened so many years ago?"

Jacobus tilted his head. "I pieced it together. It came out slowly from him over the past few weeks."

"But how did you know to come for me when Reverend Mueller attacked me?"

Jacobus shrugged. "The suspicious deaths—which, by the way,

anyone with half a brain could have figured out weren't acciden-tal—and then Elijah's guilt over Calvin's condition. I had no inten-tion of leaving you completely unprotected, but I had to confront my brother. I was suspicious perhaps even he might be behind the obituary written for you."

"But he wasn't."

"No. Still, there was Elijah."

"You thought he was the obituary writer?" Libby couldn't help the rise in her tone.

Jacobus surprised her by reaching out and fingering one of her curls that blew across her face. "No. But he could help piece it together. The common denominator was Calvin."

"Calvin had nothing to do with Deacon Greenwood or Dorothy Hayes." Libby frowned, partly because Jacobus made no sense and partly because he was still playing with her hair, which was very disconcerting.

"Of course he did. If you observed, Calvin was good friends with everyone in town. He may have trailed behind Jedidiah and me, but he called his own father the Preacher Man. Calvin knows a lot about the goings-on in this town. Far more than people credit him."

"So . . . ?"

Jacobus released the spiral of hair and pushed his hands into his pockets. "So it was just a matter of asking enough questions to conclude that Calvin's father was Deacon Greenwood's reverend, and Dorothy Hayes was indeed Calvin's friend Lawrence's mother. Elijah's too, as it turns out. If anyone had the most knowledge to take it upon themselves to clean the town of its scourge, it was Reverend Mueller."

"And that's when you came to the Muellers' home?" she asked.

"Precisely." He gave a short nod.

"Thank you again." The memory of Jacobus Corbin, the revival-ist with piercing eyes and rather odd face, pummeling a fellow minister of God gave her stomach little swirls of excitement. A feeling she couldn't quite explain.

"Well then," Jacobus said and removed his hands from his pockets. He was hatless, and his hair tossed in the breeze. Libby studied his face, the crags and the angles. He had tiny lines at the corners of his eyes that indicated he might have a wicked sense of humor laced with a hidden passion that matched the force of his unleashed temper.

"This is farewell?" Libby asked. She cursed her breathless whisper.

"Is it?" He cocked an eyebrow.

"Well," she flustered. "I—"

"It needn't be," he stated. His eyes were clear. Direct.

It didn't seem as though he was going to elaborate further, so Libby stuttered, "H-how?"

"I've been invited to a station at a church out east. Come with me. You can disappear from Gossamer Grove forever, and we will bring Calvin with us. Yes? New beginnings for the three of us."

She blinked. Rapidly. Her heart jumped into her throat—even though she knew that really wasn't physically possible—but it felt that way. She hadn't expected this. From a minister, no less.

"That would hardly be appropriate," Libby choked out. Yet for some reason, she dared to hope.

"No? No, it wouldn't be." Jacobus gave a quirk to his mouth as if to dismiss her. "More's the pity." He extended his hand as if to shake hers. "Farewell then, Miss Sheffield."

She refused to take it. This was quite awkward. Libby frantically searched for words, for coherent thoughts. He had her stomach in a muddle, and she was quite—quite—"verklempt!" Libby sputtered.

"Verklempt?" Jacobus echoed.

Blast the man, there was a twinkle in his eye.

Libby drew in a deep breath, very aware of how her chest swelled for a moment, and he fixed his eyes on hers. "I'm quite taken aback, Reverend Corbin."

"Jacobus."

"Jacobus," she attempted his name out loud.

"Very well." He smiled, and this time it was tender. As if he

337

really did know her—very well—somehow. "I suppose I should reiterate. You wouldn't accompany me illicitly. I had set my mind more toward matrimony—after a courtship, of course. You would stay with my aunt for a reasonable period of time. Although I'm afraid grand gestures in proposing defy my personal tastes. I know we may not know each other as well as some might at this point in their . . . acquaintance, yet I find we seem compatible."

"Compatible?" Libby squeaked. These were not the words a woman wished to hear at such a time. There was no romance. Or was there? She saw a glimmer in his eye. Jacobus leaned forward, and suddenly he had pressed his lips against her forehead. Then against her temple. Then, to the detriment of her nerves, right at the opening of her ear.

He whispered, "Come now, Libby, must you fight it? Sometimes a mystery really isn't that mysterious if you open your eyes. As Daniel to King Belshazzar, the writing is on the wall."

Another featherlight kiss sent shivers across Libby's skin.

"Let's leave Gossamer Grove. May our obituaries someday say— preferably after we're dead, of course—that we lived in peace, in love, and mostly in grace."

Libby felt his touch at the hollow of her neck. His fingers tucking something into her top button.

"A promise, of sorts," he whispered.

Libby looked down at the pearl button, the wisp of lace on her blouse, and the fragile petals of the flower he'd gently positioned there.

Life was fragile, grace beautiful. Libby smiled, and words filtered through her lips with the conviction that resided in her soul. "I love violets."

AUTHOR'S NOTE

This novel was born as the brainchild of two people, my associate pastor and me. Oddly we both concocted the idea at separate times, and I'd already submitted my general story line to my editor. But one evening I was researching Billy Sunday and tent revivals, and the idea sprang to mind that a town this opposed to sin needed a catapult to be that tumultuous. Why not an old-fashioned revival? Fast-forward two weeks, I was in Sunday school and Pastor Dan was teaching about the history of our specific community churches. He hearkened back to the early twentieth century and a very unknown but tumultuous revival that spread across our area.

I listened in fascinated awe at this crazy story that sounded so outlandish, I would have almost bet Pastor Dan was reciting fiction. He wasn't. I emailed him, "We have to meet." He emailed back, "I was thinking the same. You *have* to write this into a book someday!"

So we met.

He introduced me to the little known "Morrill Twins." Revivalist brothers who learned under Billy Sunday, rode a tandem bicycle, and created riots wherever they went. Juxtaposed to the riots, they also appeared to have been influential in ushering in true renewals of faith and belief in the gospel message.

The newspaper articles in this novel are altered, but are similar to the actual articles written to the local paper of the time. Old Man Whistler is a purely fictional character, but a defensive letter to the editor was submitted back in the day of the Morrill brothers and was as misspelled and as outraged in the original article as the fictional one in this book. The newspaper also struggled to report the stories surrounding the twins' ministry. Heralding the amazing and profound ministry of the twins with baptisms in bulk, while in the next article refusing to print what they said for fear of being accused of publishing vulgarity.

When Jedidiah, again my fictional revivalist twin, states that the congregates "have no brain in their head," so too did one of the Morrill twins very boldly imply that if they were to defend their own life against the death threats, it would be in vain, for there were no brains in the congregants to be shot through. Effigies of the Morrill twins were also hung in town, along with the teenage boys breaking windows in a local church and throwing in a skunk. Death threats against the twins were made, and the twins were quite public that they would not be intimidated by such antics.

Finally, the Morrill twins' multiple months-long revival ministry in the area ended when a riot erupted at one of their meetings. Cannon crackers, eggs, mobs, and finally the stabbing of a night watchman were the very emphatic exclamation point on the end of the Morrill twins' ministry to the area. The brothers left town shortly thereafter.

Still, the area churches kept with the momentum the revival had started. The local Baptist church—my home church today—had dwindling attendance. But, after the Morrill twins came with impassioned fervor and blunt presentations, the attendance surged and our church has truly never been the same since. We can trace our history back to these bombastic and rather perplexing revivalists and truly see that God was able to do great things in spite of their controversial personalities.

For the record, other than the newspaper articles, I know very little of the Morrill twins' actual personalities. They were younger gentlemen and definitively "angular" in features (at least in my opinion!), but other than that, the Corbin brothers are merely figments of my imagination, concocted in the shadows of two rather oddly inspiring men of history.

One point stands sure. Even though the deliverers of the message of faith are flawed, the story of grace is not. It can come alive and grow, and over a century later, our church stands on foundational seeds left by two intriguing brothers whose testimony was too vulgar to put into public print.

QUESTIONS
FOR DISCUSSION

1. Gossamer Grove is a town filled with behind-closed-doors secrets. Do you ever feel as though your hometown hides behind a happy façade? If we were all more vulnerable, how do you believe that would impact your community? What might be some downsides of everyone being vulnerable?

2. When Garrett returns home, Annalise seems struck with every bad memory she ever had. How do you process bad memories with today's realities? How do you find the grace to forgive others? How is this process different in trying to forgive yourself?

3. The Corbin brothers' revival caused quite a stir in Gossamer Grove. Have you ever attended an "old-time tent revival" in the vein of an evangelical crusade? What was it like? How did it affect you? If you've never been to one, what movie or TV show have you seen that depicted a revival or evangelical crusade? What impression did the production give you of such an event?

4. Annalise is passionate about providing a means for destitute people in her town to find grace and hope. In what ways could you positively affect the lives of those in need in your community? What keeps you from taking action?

5. Society sometimes couples Christianity with judgment and condemnation instead of grace and mercy. In what ways has grace been extended to you by Christians? How have you felt the power of forgiveness in a personal relationship?

ACKNOWLEDGMENTS

In no specific order (because that requires some form of mathematical thinking, which I'm incapable of) I'd like to thank:

> Christen E. Krumm. You really helped poke my brain when it shut down, sent me edits on Voxer (as if I would be able to remember them later), and most of all, walked the streets of Gossamer Grove with me.

> Rachel McMillan. Who fawned over Jacobus Corbin before I ever did, who retracted in an awkward moment when I compared him to my husband, and then returned to swooning when I explained he really wasn't my husband, he was more like Benedict Cumberbatch.

I will pause now in these acknowledgments for you all to swoon. . . . Okay. Moving on.

> Dan Gunderson. Who'da thunk I'd be thanking my childhood buddy who let me play as one of the boys when I was little, christened me as the honorary James West, and fed me historical research for this novel like the pretty cool nerd he is?

Thank you for sharing my passion of history, for giving me the word *bombastic* to use because it's a freakishly cool word, and for always being in my life from the day I was born. A mentor, a friend, and brother.

And to the Sauk County Historical Society, for allowing Dan access to the records of our colorful community.

There are so many I want to thank, but I'm going to resort to a shorter list now or my editor will start including my acknowledgments in the maximum word count.

My agent, Janet Grant. We started with a rush and it hasn't stopped. Thanks for answering my incessant emails, interpreting hoaxes versus actual real people, and being a fabulous woman!

My editor, Raela Schoenherr. Book two! This has been a lot of fun so far. I hope you're not tired of me yet. Though I wouldn't blame you. My emails do tend to ramble on pointlessly.

To the Bethany House team of amazingness. Luke, Amy, Noelle, Jennifer, and all, you make this happen. You really do. I wish you'd let me plaster your names on the book cover too, 'cause you totally deserve to be on it.

Oh gosh. The music is starting to play, isn't it? I'll wrap this up.

My Clutch friends. You are awesome.

My mentors Colleen Coble and Erica Vetsch. You both keep me grounded. Love you both!

Sisters-of-the-Traveling-Us. We seem to miss each other often. Sarah. Alaska, really? And Kara, New Zealand? But regardless, we still find a way to talk EVERY DAY. I would be lost without my Anne Love, Laurie Tomlinson, Kara Isaac, Sarah Varland, and Halee Matthews.

Mom and Dad, and Mom and Dad—I have two complete sets. Not everyone is blessed to be able to claim that. Thank you for modeling marriage, even though at times we all roll our eyes.

Cap'n Hook. Here's to you. My unsentimental, pragmatic man who keeps me grounded and empowers me.

My CoCo and Peter Pan. Let's go for a midnight adventure.

And to Jesus. Need I explain? You gave me grace, You have my soul.

Jaime Jo Wright is the author of the acclaimed novel *The House on Foster Hill*. She's also the *Publishers Weekly* and ECPA bestselling author of two novellas. Jaime works as a human resources director in Wisconsin, where she lives with her husband and two children. To learn more, visit jaimewrightbooks.com.